Canada Grand Trunk Railway Co.

**Season of 1890**

Summer resorts reached by the Grank Trunk railway and its connections including

Niagara Falls, Parry Sound, Georgian Bay, Muskoka Lakes, Lake Simcoe and

Couchiching, MacKinac Island, Midland District Lakes, the Thousand Islands, rapid

Canada Grand Trunk Railway Co.

**Season of 1890**
*Summer resorts reached by the Grank Trunk railway and its connections including Niagara Falls, Parry Sound, Georgian Bay, Muskoka Lakes, Lake Simcoe and Couchiching, MacKinac Island, Midland District Lakes, the Thousand Islands, rapid*

ISBN/EAN: 9783337448837

Printed in Europe, USA, Canada, Australia, Japan

Cover: Foto ©Andreas Hilbeck / pixelio.de

More available books at **www.hansebooks.com**

# SUMMER · RESORTS

REACHED BY THE

# GRAND TRUNK RAILWAY

— AND ITS —

# CONNECTIONS,

— INCLUDING —

*Niagara Falls, Parry Sound, Georgian Bay, Muskoka Lakes, Lakes Simcoe and Couchiching, Mackinac Island, Midland District Lakes, the Thousand Islands, Rapids of the St. Lawrence River, the White Mountains, Montreal, Quebec, the Saguenay River, Rangeley Lakes, and the Sea-Shore.*

## ILLUSTRATED.

*Compliments of Passenger Department.*

# TO · THE · READER.

THIS work is especially designed to aid in the selection of a route for a summer tour, giving such descriptions as will show the avenues of approach, and what is to be seen and enjoyed at the principal pleasure resorts in a journey over the GRAND TRUNK RAILWAY and its connections.

Further information as to TICKETS, SLEEPING-CAR FARES, etc., may be obtained from any agent of the GRAND TRUNK RAILWAY and its connections, or from

**W. C. TALLMAN,**
*New England Passenger Agent,*
280 Washington St., BOSTON, MASS.

**GEO. B. OSWELL,**
*Central Passenger Agent,*
62½ Ford St., OGDENSBURG, N. Y.

**E. P. BEACH,**
*General Agent,*
271 Broadway, NEW YORK, N. Y.

**FRANK P. DWYER,**
*Eastern Passenger Agent C. & G. T. Ry.,*
271 Broadway, NEW YORK, N. Y.

**T. D. SHERIDAN,**
*Northern Passenger Agent,*
177 Washington St., BUFFALO, N. Y.

**W. ROBINSON,**
*Mich. and Southwestern Pass. Agent,*
Cor. Jeff'son and Woodw'd Aves., DETROIT, MICH.

**F. A. PALMER,**
*Asst. Gen'l Pass. Agent Wabash R. R.*
*Representing C., D. & Niag. Falls Short Line.*
201 Clark St., CHICAGO, ILL.

**E. H. HUGHES,**
*Western Passenger Agent,*
*Chicago & Grand Trunk Ry.,*
103 S. Clark St., CHICAGO, ILL.

**R. F. ARMSTRONG,**
*General Agent for Maritime Provinces,*
134 Hollis St., HALIFAX, N. S.

## WM. EDGAR, General Passenger Agent,
### MONTREAL, CANADA.

# SUMMER TRAVEL.

## IN GENERAL.

THE custom of throwing off, for a time, the cares of business, and spending a summer vacation in travel and recreation, has become too well established to need any argument in its favor. The medical fraternity are united in commending the practice as the great panacea for, or preventive of, the injuries inflicted by the restless "work-and-worry" habits of this fast age; while the dictates of fashion and the inclinations of the masses all conspire to perpetuate the institution of summer vacations. The leading question, therefore, raised by the approach of the heated term, is not, "Shall we go?" but, "Where shall we go?" To assist in the answer of this question is the purpose of this little work. The attractions of the various resorts described will not be found overdrawn, the most of them being too well known to require extravagant coloring. It is believed that this work will aid the traveler in deciding upon a tour which will combine comfort, pleasure, recreation or rest, in just such proportions of each as may be most desirable.

## IN PARTICULAR.

Should the readers of these pages be asked to name the most popular pleasure resorts of America, the first, on which there would doubtless be entire unanimity, would be the great Cataract which attracts visitors, not only from all parts of America, but from over the Atlantic, to gaze on the majestic waterfall, the sight of which has inspired the pen of many a poet, and the pencil of multitudes of artists, but to which neither pen nor pencil can do more than faint justice, inspiring though the sight of its mighty waters may be,

Following Niagara, with greater or less accord in giving them precedence, would come the White Mountains, the Thousand Islands, and the rapids of the St. Lawrence, Saratoga, Lake George, the Adirondacks, Portland, the sea-side resorts of the Maine coast, or the beautiful lakes and islands of the Muskoka and Parry Sound districts, which during the past few years have gained a continental reputation. For cities of special interest to summer tourists, those of Canada are deservedly prominent. Toronto, the bustling city by the lake; Ottawa, the Dominion Capital; Montreal, its commercial metropolis; quaint old Quebec, with its mediæval air, its fortified walls and foreign surroundings; these all come to mind, in connection with this subject, as delightful places to visit in a summer tour, either from the salubrity of their climate, the charm of their situation and surroundings, or the associations connected with their history.

In considering this long list of summer resorts, if the reader's attention has not already been called to the subject, he may be surprised to learn that nearly all of them are located on, or reached by,

### THE GRAND TRUNK RAILWAY,

With its numerous divisions and immediate connections. This great highway of travel, reaching from the Atlantic coast to the great lakes, crossing and re-crossing the Canadian border, and serving alike the commercial and business interests of the United States and British America, has justly acquired the title of " The Great International Route." To this appellation it is fast adding, and with equal propriety, that of

### "THE GREAT TOURIST ROUTE OF AMERICA."

The diversified character of the country through which it passes, the many points of interest which it reaches, and the excellent facilities it offers to the traveling public in its superior equipment, through coaches, and sleeping and dining-car service, all conspire to give to this line an enviable reputation, and make it a desirable route for the traveling public in general, and to the summer tourist in particular.

The diversity of scenery, already referred to, is strikingly manifest in considering the topography of the country it traverses. Probably no line of railroad on the American continent embraces in its route so great a variety. From the wave-washed Atlantic coast to the mighty inland seas whose waters swell the volume of the majestic St. Lawrence, a charming panorama of mountain, lake and river scenery passes in pleasing variety before the vision of the tourist, with 'the picture occasionally enlivened by charming villages and flourishing cities, or perchance by a peaceful rural scene, its quiet repose only for the moment awakened as the rapidly moving train quickens its pulse from its usual beat, then leaves it to resume its peaceful stillness.

Another interesting feature of this route is the fact that it lies partly in Canada and partly in the States, thus serving not only to add variety to the scenery, but facilitating an interchange of acquaintance between the citizens of the Union and the Canadian subjects of the Queen, the result of which cannot fail to be mutually beneficial.

The people of the Dominion, while presenting less diversity of nationality than those of the States, are much less cosmopolitan, preserving their national characteristics in a more marked degree. This is especially true of the older and more conservative sections.

For illustration : The visitor from the States will find in the comparatively young City of Toronto much to remind him of bustling Yankeedom. In the older City of Montreal one section is most decidedly English, another thoroughly French, both in people and architecture, while between is a homogenous intermingling of other nationalities similar to that of American cities.

The ancient City of Quebec presents a still stronger contrast, it being thoroughly French to all intents and purposes, while its suburbs, where scarcely a word of English is to be heard, are strongly suggestive of some foreign land.

Going still further from the border, the traveler meets with an Acadian simplicity, absolutely refreshing, and the keen student of human nature will find in this feature alone of his visit to Canada an attraction which no other trip could afford.

Wherever this little work may meet the eye of the prospective summer tourist, whether on the golden coast of California, the broad prairies of the west, the "sunny south," or in the Eastern or Middle States, no better route for a vacation trip can suggest itself than to some of the localities described in the following pages.

In planning your summer journey, be sure that some portion of it is by the Grand Trunk Railway. You may reach it from Boston and other New England points, either at Portland, or by the Central Vermont line at Montreal. From the Middle and South Atlantic States, taking in the Hudson River, Saratoga and Lake George, the Grand Trunk may be reached at Rouse's Point or St. Johns. From the West, Chicago, Detroit or Milwaukee may be the inception of your tour by this line. From the former city a choice of several routes is presented. From the new Dearborn Station, the through trains of the Chicago & Grand Trunk Railway make close connections at Port Huron, with quick service, through coaches, sleeping cars and dining cars, forming a continuous through car line between Chicago and Suspension Bridge, New York and Boston. A magnificent Pullman Vestibuled train, in charge of a special agent, will be run weekly during the season, between Chicago and Portland, Maine, by way of Niagara Falls, Toronto, and Montreal. From the same station, the trains of the "Niagara Falls Short Line" make close connections with the Southern (Great Western) Division at Detroit. The Michigan Central also makes connection at Detroit with the Grand Trunk system.

From Milwaukee a delightful trip may be made across Lake Michigan by the palatial steamer, "City of Milwaukee," to Grand Haven, thence by the Detroit, Grand Haven & Milwaukee Railway to Detroit, or, if preferred, to Durand, there connecting with the

## CHICAGO & GRAND TRUNK RAILWAY.

From Detroit, the tourist has the choice of going via Windsor and the Southern (Great Western) Division, or by the Detroit Division to Port Huron, and there connecting directly with the main line.

It will thus be seen that the Grand Trunk system is not only very extensive in itself, but is accessible from all parts of the country, its direct connections being the most important railway lines of America.

## "THE NIAGARA FALLS ROUTE."

Under this name the Great Western Division (now termed the Southern Division) of the Grand Trunk has an international reputation. Extending from Windsor, opposite Detroit, and from Sarnia, opposite Port Huron, to the world-famous cataract, it forms an important link in the great railway chain across the continent.

A trip through Canada by this line is one of interest and novelty. The long level stretches of country, with easy grades and few curves, permit the making of fast time, and thus add materially to the comfort of the journey. Nor is the scenery devoid of interest. Flourishing towns and villages indicate the prosperity of the inhabitants, while many fine farms add to the attractiveness of the scene. In some sections the views to be obtained from the car windows are absolutely picturesque. This is particularly true of some bits of fine scenery near Dundas, approaching Hamilton. To avoid heavy grades, the railway is built on the side of the mountain, which towers up in grandeur on the one hand, while on the other side, you may gaze upon a charming valley far below, in which nestles the town, the whole forming a picture which becomes a genuine surprise to those who have formed the erroneous opinion that the scenery of this part of Canada is monotonous, from having traveled through it by some other route than the favorite Great Western.

This is also a DINING CAR LINE, and meals are served on the through express trains, east and west, in a style to suit the most fastidious.

During the season of navigation the "Empress of India," a first-class steamer, running between Toronto and Port Dalhousie, makes connection with Grand Trunk trains to and from Niagara Falls.

PORTLAND HARBOR FROM CUSHING'S ISLAND

# THE CITY OF PORTLAND.

PORTLAND, in the State of Maine, the eastern terminal of the Grand Trunk Railway, is beautifully situated on a peninsula in the southwestern extremity of Casco Bay. It was first named Falmouth, was settled by an English colony in 1632, and was three times burnt in the wars with the French and Indians, while, in 1866, a fire destroyed $10,000,000 worth of property. It has a population of some 40,000 inhabitants and possesses broad, shaded streets, and handsome public and private edifices, at the same time forming a centre to the numerous watering-places within reach, where the purest of sea air can be enjoyed. Among these are Old Orchard, Pine Point and Biddeford Pool, all of which are within a few minutes' ride by rail, while Cushing's Island, Peak's Island, Long Island, and Chebeague Island can be reached several times daily by the steamers, which ply in the bay. By those fond of the water, capital boating and yachting can here be enjoyed.

OTTAWA HOUSE, CUSHING'S ISLAND.

## CUSHING'S ISLAND.

CUSHING'S ISLAND, in the beautiful Casco Bay, is two and one half miles from Portland. One of the finest hotels on the coast of Maine is situated on the island, on an eminence of over 100 feet above the sea, commanding, from its broad veranda, unrivaled views of ocean, islands, main-land, harbor and city, with the sublime peaks of the White Mountains in the western horizon. In addition to the hotel, there are also about twenty-five cottages on the Island. The average temperature during the summer months is sixty-six degrees, and because of its altitude and the invigorating sea breezes which continually fan its shores, and the balsamic

VIEW OF WHITE HEAD, CUSHING'S ISLAND.

odors from its fir and spruce groves, the Island has long been famed for its renovating and health-giving powers.

A writer says: "The Island justly claims for itself a combination in exquisite harmony of more conditions which go to make up a truly enjoyable watering place than can be found elsewhere in a month of wanderings along the coast. Where else will you find such restful and recreative qualities and facilities; where, more complete seclusion and isolation from the busy world and its affairs; where, within such limited confines, more natural beauties and attractiveness; where, more refined qualifications for either social or domestic enjoyments; where, more absorbing historical surroundings furnishing a stimulus to healthy mental exertion and research, as its soft yet invigorating atmosphere, with nothing to contaminate its purity, ever tempts to exhilarating bodily exercise?"

One of the most striking features of natural scenery on the Island is White Head, which presents to the sea a precipice of one hundred to one hundred and fifty feet in height. It is composed of a gray, granite rock, split into leaves standing on their edges, fallen into broken fragments, scarred, seamed, jagged, and yet presenting smooth, precipitous walls, painted a warm orange-red by the hardy lichens, whose mission it is to clothe the barren rock with beauty.

The Head projects into the sea in three distinct masses, having between them two deep recesses, or miniature fiords, worn far into the cliff by the waves. Down one of these abysses you may scramble over the fallen rocks, and sit under the projecting cliff, with the foamy sea beating on the barnacled ledges at your feet. Into the other recess there is no descent. Its walls on all three sides fall precipitously into the water, which forms its floor. It is a great ball-room, in which only the waves may dance, while we look on from the galleries above. The south wall of this recess runs out into a point not more than three feet wide at the extremity, and lying flat here one may look straight into the sea, a dizzy depth.

> "The lonely shepherd's love is still
> To bask beneath a shady hill,
>   The herdsman roams the vale:
> With both their fancies I agree,
> But mine the swelling, scooping sea,
>   That is both hill and dale.

> "Oh! who can tell that brave delight
> To see the hissing wave in might,
>   Come rampant like a snake,
> To leap his horrid crest, and feast
> One's eyes upon the briny beast,
>   Left couchant in the wake."

The drives from Portland to Cape Cottage, the Ocean House, the Kirkwood and the Atlantic House cannot be excelled for roads and scenery. Portland is distant about 100 miles from Boston, and 300 miles from Montreal.

POLAND SPRING, WITH HOTEL IN THE DISTANCE.

## POLAND SPRING.

Twenty-five miles from Portland, in a northerly direction, this health and pleasure resort has already acquired a national reputation, both for the curative properties of the spring water, and the attractions offered to guests in the way of scenery, charming drives, and excellent hotel accommodations. From the piazza of the Poland Spring House, the White Mountains, Kearsarge, and several beautiful lakes, are visible, the latter affording plentiful opportunities for boating and fishing. The popularity of this resort is evinced by the fact that its regular visitors include Hon. James G. Blaine, U. S. Senator Frye, and a long list of eminent statesmen, who, with their families, have been more or less frequent guests at the place.

The Springs are reached from Portland by the Grand Trunk Railway, via Danville Junction, where stages will be found in readiness to meet all trains, the hotel being only a few miles distant from the station. Tourists from the West may visit the locality *en route*, by stopping off at Danville Junction, either in going or returning, as may best suit their inclination.

### BAR HARBOR.

A favorite resort, which can easily be reached from Portland by either rail or steamer, is BAR HARBOR, a convenient and pleasantly located harbor on Mount Desert, an Island in Maine, having Frenchman's Bay and five rocky islands called the Porcupines on the east; Mount Desert Rock, twenty miles south in the open sea; the whole island being twelve miles wide and fifteen miles long, and is one mile from the mainland. It is crossed by seven ridges of hills, the highest peak, Mount Adam or Mount Green, rising to an altitude of 1762 feet above the level of the sea; and among the mountains are beautiful lakes of considerable size. It is celebrated for the grandeur and beauty of its scenery, and is much frequented as a summer resort. The island was first discovered by the French in 1608, who named it St. Sauveur, but the settlement was destroyed in 1613 by Samuel Ayall, of Virginia, under the governorship of Sir Thomas Dale. The first house of the future permanent settlement was built by Abraham Soames, in the center of the island, overlooking the head of the sound, in 1761. It has a prosperous community engaged in cod and mackerel fishing, the manufacture of lumber and shipbuilding, and has some twenty excellent hotels. A feature of peculiar attractiveness as compared with many sea-shore resorts, is the combination of mountain and marine scenery.

BAR HARBOR AND MOUNT DESERT.

# THE WHITE MOUNTAINS,

## VIA GORHAM, ON THE G. T. RY.

THE WHITE MOUNTAINS—a mountain chain of New England—commence in Maine and extend nearly across New Hampshire, where they have 20 bold peaks, with deep, narrow gorges, wild valleys, beautiful lakes, lofty cascades and torrents, being aptly designated "The Switzerland of America."

The discovery of these mountains is accredited to Darby Field, 1642. He found many crystals upon them which he mistook for diamonds, and for a long time the chain was called "The Crystal Hills." The Indians bore a great reverence for the mountains, believing them to be the abode of the Great Spirit, and rarely ascended the higher peaks, for it was reported among them that no one who scaled the sacred heights returned alive. The first settlement among the mountains was made in 1792 by a hunter and guide; the first bridle-path to the summit of Mt. Washington was cut in 1819; in the following year a small party of gentlemen slept upon the summit of this mountain and named the different peaks.

Gorham, 90 miles from Portland, and the entrance to the mountains, offers the most striking views. The grandeur and beauty of the mountain scenery, and of the romantic, richly-wooded glens, through which, in an endless variety of silvery cascades and silent pools, run the rivers Androscoggin and Peabody, with their attendant brooks, delight all beholders. The drive by stage from Gorham to the Glen House is exceedingly pleasant, the scenery all around being grand in the extreme. For several years the summit of Mt. Washington has been occupied during the winter as a station of the Meteorological Department of the United States Army. In severe seasons the wind has been known to attain a velocity of 100 miles an hour, and the thermometer has sunk to 59 degrees below zero. The mountains are becoming more and more popular as a summer resort, on account of their delightful temperature and wild and beautiful scenery.

### THE GLEN.

Eight miles from Gorham, between the Presidential Range and the picturesque Carter Range, lies the famous and beautiful Glen. A delightful stage ride of a little over an hour through a country rich in verdure, and offering fine views of the loftiest peaks of the White Mountains, brings the traveler to the Glen House. This hotel was rebuilt in 1885 on the site of the old house, and is furnished with all modern improvements and conveniences. The house accommodates 450 guests. The views of Washington, Jef-

WHITE MOUNTAIN RANGE, AS VIEWED FROM GRAND TRUNK RAILWAY.

ferson, Adams and Madison from this point, are probably the finest to be had of this range. Not only are these peaks remarkably impressive in themselves, but they are rendered doubly grand and beautiful by the singularly striking cloud effects, for it must be remembered that the Glen is 1,650 feet above the sea level, and that the fleece-like clouds often float between it and the mountain tops.

From the hotel veranda is seen the Summit House on Mt. Washington. This is reached by the famous Carriage Road which starts at the Glen, and for eight miles winds its course up the mountain side. The views from the road are varied and remarkable. From no other point can one obtain such impressive and awful views of the great ravines, the Great Gulf and Tuckerman's

GLEN HOUSE, WHITE MOUNTAINS.

Ravine; from no other point can one get so accurate an idea of the extent of the White Mountain region.

There are many points of interest in the Glen, of which the best known are Glen Ellis Falls and Crystal Cascade. The Falls are the finest in this region, and have been rendered famous by artists for whom they have always had an especial attraction. The fall is about seventy feet. Crystal Cascade is a tumbling torrent, eighty feet in height, and in early summer, when the streams are full, is perhaps even more beautiful than the Falls. Tuckerman's Ravine is a stupendous chasm in the side of Washington, and is a favorite objective point for hardy tourists. The walls of the ravine rise abruptly on three sides, and thus shut out the rays of the sun except at about midday. The consequence of this is that the snow, which collects here in immense quantities in the winter, often does

NEAR VIEW OF THE PROFILE.

not disappear until the end of the summer. A huge cavern, commonly called the Snow Arch, is formed by streams running underneath the mass of ice and snow, and is one of the most striking wonders of the White Mountains. An ascent of Washington can be made on foot through Tuckerman's Ravine.

The mountain streams, which, by the way, abound in trout, add great charm and interest to the Glen. In the course of the Ellis River is a beautiful translucent basin, known as Emerald Pool; also the well known cataract, Thompson's Falls, named after the original owner of the Glen House. On the Peabody River is Garnet Pool, also many secluded spots, the favorite haunts of that great trout fisherman, Josh Billings.

On the east side of the Glen rise Wild Cat, Carter Dome, and other picturesque features of the Carter Range. The Imp, a grotesque profile, can be seen from the road above the Glen House. Superb views of the Presidential Range can be had from the top of Wild Cat, which can be climbed in an hour.

Mention should not be omitted of the extensive and thoroughly equipped stage lines connected with the Glen House. The coaches generally used are six-in-hand tally-hos, and are driven by reliable men, who have passed their lives in mountain driving. This is the only region where this delightful means of traveling has continued to be used.

Mount Washington, 6,288 feet, is the highest peak east of the Rockies; a hotel at the top furnishes meals and lodging to tourists who desire to spend the night on the mountain. A newspaper is also published here, and the ride up the mountain with its ever-changing views, as the road winds, is one never to be forgotten. There are in these mountains many waterfalls, some of them of great beauty, the most famous being the falls of Ammonoosuc, descending more than 5,000 feet, in a course of thirty miles.

From the base of Mt. Washington an ordinary railway brings us to Fabyans, from which excursions may be made to Twin Mountain, Bethlehem or Franconia Notch, the latter celebrated as the home of

### THE OLD MAN OF THE MOUNTAIN.

This gigantic profile is seen from a point of observation down the Notch from the Profile House, and is strikingly suggestive in its grimness of the enduring inflexibility of the granite hills of which it forms a part.

In this vicinity are also Eagle Cliff, Echo Lake, Mount Lafayette, and the Flume, in which was formerly suspended the great boulder, since fallen in a spring flood.

The ascent of Mount Lafayette, which is the highest peak of the Franconia Range, may be made on foot, but preferably on horseback, a bridle path extending from near the Profile House to the summit. The view from the crest of the mountain is very fine, second only to that from Mount Washington.

PROFILE HOUSE AND ECHO LAKE, FRANCONIA NOTCH, WHITE MOUNTAIN S. N.H.Y

Of the other attractions, Echo Lake claims a large share of attention. The little valley in which it is situated has remarkable acoustic properties, and as the visitor sails over the surface of the lake, his voice, or the blast of a trumpet, is returned in oft-repeated echoes, growing fainter with each repetition, and finally dying among the more distant cliffs, and with an effect surprisingly beautiful.

" Hark! how the gentle echo from her cell
Talks through the cliffs and murmuring o'er the stream,
Repeats the accents we-shall-part-no-more."

VALLEY OF THE SACO RIVER.

## RANGELEY LAKES.

THE RANGELEY LAKES constitute a series of lakes in northwest Maine, in the great lumber region of Franklin and Oxford Counties, forming a portion of the most picturesque scenery in the American Continent. The chain consists of a number of distinct bodies of water, connected by small streams, and is best reached by the Grand Trunk lines from Portland, Quebec, or Montreal, to Bethel, thence by stage and steamer. The most remote, Oquossuc, or Rangeley Lake, 1511 feet above the level of the sea, is thus connected with Umbagog, partly in New Hampshire, 1,256 feet above the level of the sea, making a distance of nearly fifty miles, comprising a water surface of eighty square miles. The lakes abound in salmon and other delicate fish ; two species of trout, weighing ten pounds, being found in these waters only, and secured with little trouble. This region is unrivaled for hunting and fishing grounds in the size, beauty and abundance of game, of which every variety is represented; while the charming climate and health-giving influences attract thousands of persons annually, who, after a first visit, become devoted, enthusiastic patrons; in fact, there is no more favorite resort for artists, tourists, and sportsmen.

The Androscoggin is a river in Maine and New Hampshire, which rises in Umbagog Lake, running a course of some 160 miles, about half of it in each State. There is some beautiful scenery along this route, which is best reached by the line of the Grand Trunk Railway, via Berlin Falls. A favorite trip is up the Magalloway River to Parmachenee Lake, a perfect paradise for the lover of sport, provided with a romantic, rustic, and comfortable hotel, situated almost in the center of the lake.

From Berlin Falls the best and most varied route is along the Androscoggin River, over a fine stage road, to Chandler's Hotel, the nearest point to several small lakes called Millsfield Ponds. From this point Umbagog Lake is fourteen miles distant, where the steamer may be taken across the lake, and a short drive will land the tourist at Richardson Lake, the first of the Rangeley chain of Lakes.

There are pleasant trips by steamer up the Magalloway River, a point of special interest in that connection being the Aziscohos Falls, surrounded by the grandest of scenery, while old Aziscohos Mountain has no rival, except the famous White Mountain peaks in the New England States. Guides can be obtained at reasonable rates, and the lover of the rod or gun will always be insured the best of sport.

# QUEBEC.

THERE is no city in America more famous in the annals of history than QUEBEC, and few on the continent of Europe more picturesquely situated. Whilst the surrounding scenery reminds one of the unrivaled views of the Bosphorus, the airy site of the citadel and town calls to mind Innspruck and Edinburgh. Quebec has been well termed the "Gibraltar of America," and is the only walled city on the continent. The scenic beauty of

GATE IN THE WALL AT QUEBEC.

Quebec has been the theme of general eulogy. The majestic appearance of Cape Diamond and the fortifications,—the cupolas and minarets, like those of an eastern city, blazing and sparkling in the sun, —the loveliness of the panorama,—the noble basin, like a sheet of purest silver, in which might ride with safety a hundred sail of the line,—the graceful meandering of the river St. Charles,—the numerous village spires on either side of the St. Lawrence,—the fertile fields, dotted with innumerable cottages, the abodes of a rich and moral peasantry,—the distant Falls of Montmorency,—the park-like scenery of Point Levi,—the beauteous Isle of Orleans,—and, more distant still, the frowning Cape Tourmente, and the lofty range of purple mountains of the most picturesque forms which bound the prospect, unite to form a *coup d'œil*, which, without exaggeration, is scarcely to be surpassed in any part of the world. Few cities offer so many striking contrasts as Quebec. A fortress and a commercial city together, built upon the summit of a rock like the nest of an eagle, while her vessels are everywhere wrinkling the face of the ocean; a city of the middle ages by most of its ancient institutions, while it is subject to all the combinations of modern constitutional government; a European city by its civilization and its habits of refinement, and still close by the remnants of the Indian tribes and the barren mountains of the north; a city with about the same latitude as Paris, while successively combining the torrid climate of southern regions with the severities of an hyperborean winter.

Who is there on the American continent that would not wish to see Quebec? The resolute Champlain, the haughty Frontenac, the devoted Laval, and the chivalrous Montcalm, repose here, resting amid the scenes of their labors, after the turmoil of their earnest lives, while a monument on the Plains

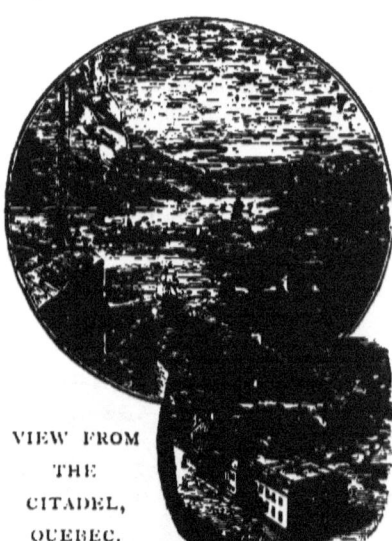

VIEW FROM THE CITADEL, QUEBEC.

of Abraham bears the inscription, as graphic and expressive as any in the English language, "Here died Wolfe, victorious."

WOLFE'S COVE, QUEBEC.

The surrounding district is famed for its beauty, and is filled with objects of interest to the tourist. One of the principal drives is to the FALLS OF MONTMORENCY, eight miles from the city. We cross the St. Charles River—notice in succession the extensive ship building, the curious market wagons and ponies of the French women, who mostly make the garden and market their products, the old cottage where Montcalm had his headquarters, near the scene of the first struggle for the possession of the city—until we reach the Montmorency River, with its "Natural Steps" and the Falls, 50 feet wide and 250 feet high. A solid mass of water falls, like a gossamer veil of beauty, into the stream below and disappears in the St. Lawrence; small streams on each side, parted strands of light, follow the rocky seams, in a delightful tangle, down the chasm. No drive of the same distance, anywhere in the world, affords so much pleasure to the tourist as does this eight-mile drive to the famous Falls of Montmorency. The charming and romantic FALLS OF LORETTE should also be visited. Of them a writer says: "The Lorette cascades would give fame and fortune to any spot in England or France."

The Falls of Montmorency may now be reached by railroad, the Quebec, Montmorency & Charlevoix R'y having recently opened up. This road also extends to St. Anne de Beaupre, an interesting spot for tourists, both on account of its scenic attractions and the fact that many thousand pilgrims visit it every year, attracted by the miraculous cures attributed to "La Bonne St. Anne."

WOLFE'S MONUMENT, QUEBEC.

## THE SAGUENAY.

From Quebec, by the palatial steamers of the Richelieu & Ontario Navigation Co., which run in connection with the Grand Trunk, some most enchanting trips on the lower St. Lawrence may be made.

THE SAGUENAY is unquestionably one of the most remarkable rivers on the continent; it is the outlet of the great Lake St. John, into which eleven rivers fall. The Saguenay is not properly a river. It is a tremendous chasm, like that of the Jordan Valley and the Dead Sea, cleft for sixty miles through the heart of a

TADOUSAC, AT MOUTH OF SAGUENAY RIVER.

mountain wilderness. The bed of the river is 100 fathoms lower than that of the St. Lawrence. The shores were stripped of their forests by a great fire, in 1810, but there are large numbers of hemlock and birch trees in the neighboring glens. The awful maj-

HA-HA BAY, SAGUENAY RIVER.

esty of its unbroken mountain shores, the profound depth of its waters, the absence of life through many leagues of distance, have made the Saguenay unique amongst rivers, and it is yearly visited by thousands of tourists as one of the chief curiosities of the Western World. The Saguenay is 142 miles down the St. Lawrence from Quebec, and in the run down the Island of Orleans is passed, and seventy miles below Quebec are the celebrated FALLS OF ST. ANNE. Five miles below this again is GROSSE ISLE, beautiful, but with sad memories as the resting place of some 6,000 Irish emigrants. Ninety miles down stream is MURRAY BAY, a favorite watering-place of the St. Lawrence River, picturesquely situated amid frowning hills and wild scenery.

RIVIERE DU LOUP passed, a couple of hours conveys the expectant traveler to TADOUSAC, at the mouth of the Saguenay; the scenery of the landward environs is described in the name, which means, in the English language, knobs, or mamelons. The original name of the Saguenay was Chicoutimi, which signifies "deep water," and was so called by the Northern Indians, who here first

CAPES ETERNITY AND TRINITY.

encountered the profound depths of the river; the present name is a corruption of "St. Jean Nez." The water of the river, though crystal in its clearness, appears in many places black as midnight, from the height of the awful cliffs which rise sheer to 1,000 and even 2,000 feet above the water. CAPE ETERNITY, at the entrance to Trinity Bay, springs 2,000 feet upwards, and the river at its feet is more than 600 fathoms deep. The echo in the bay is wonderful, and is usually tested by discharging a gun or blowing a whistle. When the "*Flying Fish*" ascended the river with the Prince of Wales and his suite, one of her heavy 68-pounders was fired off near Cape Trinity. "For the space of half a minute or so

after the discharge there was a dead silence, and then, as if the re-
port and concussion were hurled back upon the decks, the echoes
came down crash upon crash.   It seemed as if the rocks and crags
had all sprung into life under the tremendous din, and as if each
were firing 68-pounders full upon us, in sharp, crashing volleys, till
at last they grew hoarser and hoarser in their anger, and retreated,
bellowing slowly, carrying the tale of invaded solitude from hill to
hill, till all the distant mountains seemed to war and groan at the
intrusion."   Ha! Ha! Bay is an arm of the Saguenay, some seven
miles long; it is ascended between lofty and serrated ridges, bristling
with sturdy and stunted trees.  So broad and stately is this inlet, that
it is said that the early French explorers ascended it in the belief
that it was the main river, and the name originated from their excla-
mations on reaching the end, either of amusement at their mistake,
or of pleasure at the beautiful appearance of the meadows.

Twenty miles further up is CHICOUTIMI, an interesting village
situated at the junction of the Chicoutimi River with the Saguenay.
The Saguenay is navigable for a few miles further up before it is
broken by rapids.   The Chicoutimi River runs a short but violent
course of ten miles from Lake Kenogami, broken by almost continuous rapids and falls.

### THE LAKE ST. JOHN REGION.

Chicoutimi is no longer the most northern point reached by civilization, or frequented by the tourist.   Some sixty miles above
Chicoutimi, the majestic Saguenay flows out of the great LAKE ST.
JOHN, the largest lake in the Province of Quebec, thirty by twenty-
five miles in extent, surrounded by the most fertile lands in lower
Canada, and which have resulted in the construction of the Quebec
& Lake St. John Railway.   Lake St. John is a magnificent sheet
of water abounding in fish, such as the ounaniche (land-locked salmon), pike, dace, and other smaller kinds, which afford the disci-
ples of Izaak Walton excellent sport.   Only on a very fine day can
the other side of the lake be seen ; at all other times it conveys the
impression of an inland sea.   On a calm day its bosom is like a
mirror; but let a stiff north breeze blow for a couple of days, and
white caps will be seen everywhere, while breakers roll on its
shores which would do credit to the Atlantic.   Following up the
west shore of the lake, the scenery is very fine.   A distant blue
point, hardly visible at first, gradually resolves itself into a long
coast-line, dotted with farms, villages and churches, reminding one
of the St. Lawrence below Montreal.   The eye never tires of the
beautiful landscape, so varied and full of interest.   Lake St. John
is distant from Quebec 190 miles, and trains run daily.   This line
opens up a most interesting and unique section of country to the
summer tourist and sportsman, being characterized by great natural beauty, covered with magnificent forests, and penetrated in all

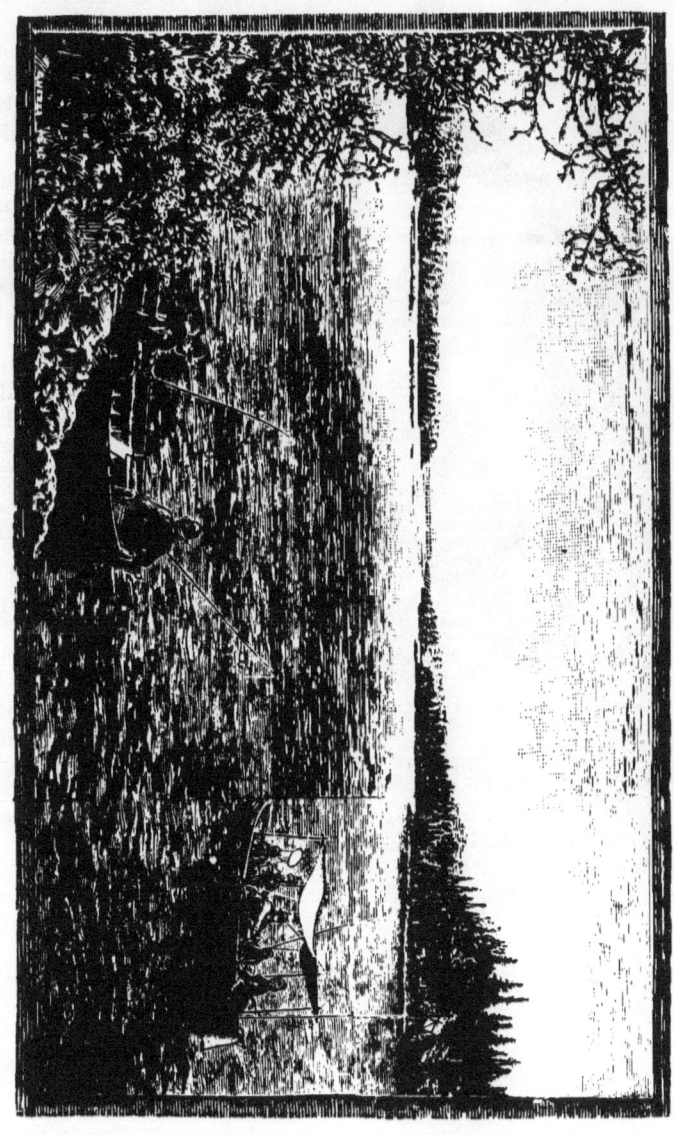

LAKE EDWARD.

directions by many and great rivers.

INDIAN CURIOSITY SELLER.

The Paribouc, which empties itself into Lake St. John, is navigable to canoes nearly three hundred miles, while the Mistassini is traversed for a distance of twenty miles, by a steamboat recently built, capable of carrying three hundred persons. The whole of this northern region abounds with lakes, all of them literally stocked with fish, especially the spotted trout, some of which have been caught weighing from ten to fourteen pounds. The region is remarkably healthy, the air cool, the soil dry and hard, and on many a lake a camp fire has never been lit. In short, the tourist can spend a month in this district with perfect enjoyment. The Adirondacks are not more famous than these woods and waters of the north will soon be.

LAKE EDWARD, about midway between Quebec and Lake St. John, is a lovely lake, twenty-one miles in length, swarming with large trout of a kind peculiar to this lake, having a dark red flesh.

Among other points may be mentioned LAKE ST. JOSEPH, surrounded by mountains, the very base of which is almost touched by the little steamer plying on its waters.

# MONTREAL.

ONTREAL, the commercial capital of the Dominion of Canada, and the "Queen of the St. Lawrence," is one of the most beautiful cities on the continent. It is situated on an Island, at the confluence of the Ottawa and St. Lawrence rivers, containing close on 200 square miles, and which, from its fertility, has been called the "Garden of Canada." Montreal is distant from Quebec 172 miles, from Toronto 333 miles, and from Ottawa 120 miles.

The river front is lined for over a mile with lofty and massive walls, quays and terraces of gray limestone, unequaled elsewhere in the world, except at Liverpool, Paris and St. Petersburg.

Montreal was founded in 1640, on the site of an Indian village, called Hochelaga, which was visited by French Jesuit missionaries in 1542, nearly a hundred years before a permanent settlement was made. Mount Royal, from which the city derives its name, rises 700 feet above the river level, and on the high ground around it are many elegant private residences, and a fashionable drive extends around the mountain, bordered by gardens and ornamental enclosures and affording fine views in all directions. Its ecclesiastical buildings are well worthy of notice. The new Roman Catholic Cathedral of St.

VICTORIA BRIDGE.

Peter, built in imitation of St. Peter's at Rome, is a noble structure, crowned by five domes, one of them 250 feet high. Though smaller than the former Cathedral, the Church of Notre Dame, is one of the finest churches on the continent of America; the view from one of the towers, in which hangs "Gros Bourdon," the great bell, is very extensive and interesting. Christ Church Cathedral is the best representative of English Gothic architecture in America.

By means of the Grand Trunk Railway, Montreal is connected with the Western Provinces, and with Chicago, and the Western States. On the south it connects, at Rouse's Point, with the rail-

MONTREAL, FROM THE MOUNTAIN.

ways for New York City for Ogdensburg, and the whole system of roads in Western and Southern New York. At St. Johns it connects with the roads to Boston and New England; at Quebec it connects with the Intercolonial Railway, and thus with the maritime Provinces; and is in reality, as well as in name, the Grand Trunk Railway of Canada.

THE VICTORIA BRIDGE which crosses the St. Lawrence at Montreal is one of the greatest engineering works of the world. It is the longest tubular bridge ever erected, and was completed in 1859 at a cost of $6,300,000; its length is 9,184 feet; 3,000,000 cubic feet of masonry were used in its construction; 8,250 tons of iron were used in tubes, and the force of men employed was over 3,000.

## ST. ANNE.

St. Anne (Bout de l'Isles), is twenty-one miles from Montreal, and may be reached in an hour by the Grand Trunk Railway. It is much frequented in the summer season, and possesses an ancient church much revered by the Canadian boatmen and voyageurs. The Ottawa is here crossed by a fine railway bridge, and the famous rapids of St. Anne are flanked by a canal. Here Tom Moore wrote his Canadian boat-song, beginning :—

> " Faintly as tolls the evening chime,
>    Our voices keep tune, and our oars keep time.
>  Soon as the woods on the shore look dim
>  We'll sing at St. Anne's our parting hymn.
>    Row, brothers, row; the stream runs fast,
>    The Rapids are near, and the daylight's past.

> " Ottawa's tide! this trembling moon
>  Shall see us float o'er thy surges soon.
>  Saint of this green isle! hear our prayers;
>  O, grant us cool heavens and favoring airs !
>    Blow, breezes blow; the stream runs fast,
>    The Rapids are near, and the daylight's past."

## BELŒIL MOUNTAINS.

One of the most attractive summer resorts in the vicinity of Montreal, and one which is rapidly growing in popularity, is the healthful and elevated plateau known by the above title. It is reached by the trains of the Grand Trunk Railway to St. Hilaire, and the frequent train service on the Portland and Quebec line makes it very accessible, there being five daily trains each way between Montreal and St. Hilaire.

This resort, in addition to the attractions of delightful scenery and a healthful, invigorating atmosphere, affords excellent fishing, boating and bathing, a magnificent lake in the vicinity furnishing abundant opportunities for these recreations. There is a fine hotel,

NEW BONAVENTURE STATION, GRAND TRUNK RAILWAY, MONTREAL.

delightfully located on a high table rock, commanding a beautiful view of the adjacent country. There are also delightful promenades, secluded groves, and, what is of the highest importance at a summer resort, the purest of spring water and perfect drainage.

The summer tourist may conveniently visit this locality by stopping off in the journey between the east and the west, or may make it a side trip from Montreal, as desired.

### *MASSENA SPRINGS.*

This popular summer resort, ninety-six miles distant from Montreal, is reached by a branch of the Grand Trunk Railway. There is excellent hotel accommodation, and, in addition to the Springs, the medicinal qualities of which are well known, lovers of sport find good fishing in the neighborhood.

FRENCH-CANADIAN HOME.

Montreal

Lake Champlain

Lake George

Saratoga

Albany

# MONTREAL TO NEW YORK.

## THE ADIRONDACKS, SARATOGA AND THE CATSKILLS.

THE route to New York City from Montreal lies among some of the most celebrated scenery of America. It embraces Lake Champlain, Fort Ticonderoga, the Adirondacks, Lake George, Saratoga Springs, The Catskills, and the magnificent scenery of the Hudson River. Leaving Montreal by the Grand Trunk Railway, and crossing the St. Lawrence by the famous Victoria Bridge, connection is made at St. Johns with the Central Vermont and at Rouse's Point with the Delaware & Hudson Line. From this point the journey southward may be pursued entirely by rail, or partly by steamer, as desired. If the latter, the tourist may enjoy a delightful trip from Plattsburg to Ticonderoga, over the waters of the beautiful Lake Champlain, among the scenery made memorable by the annals of history.

### ROUSE'S POINT.

Rouse's Point is picturesquely situated on historic Lake Champlain, between the Adirondacks and Green Mountains, whose lofty peaks form a picture of enchanting beauty, as, like majestic sentinels, they stand guard over the placid and cooling waters of beautiful Champlain. Fort Montgomery is located here, on the site of old "Fort Blunder," which name was given from the fact that it was built on Canadian soil, thereby laying the foundation of the famous Ash-Burton treaty.

It was at Rouse's Point, also, that the lake was entered at the time of its discovery, July 4, 1609, by Champlain, after whom it was named.

It is one of the pleasantest and healthiest spots in Northern New York, and added to the beautiful location, the cool nights and balmy days, and honored historical waters, there are health and life-giving waters, and also a valuable sulphur spring. Excellent fishing is to be obtained here, black bass, pike, pickerel, mascalonge and yellow being abundant; while the hotel accommodation is everything that could be desired.

### THE ADIRONDACKS.

The mountain region of Northwestern New York, known as the Adirondacks, presents many attractions to the summer tourist. Surrounded on all sides by civilization, the traveler has only to pursue his journey a few miles to find himself in a veritable wilderness. Once fairly beyond the haunts of men he reaches the forest fastness, and is alone with Nature and her children. The atmosphere is charged with the balsamic odor of the pine and spruce, and the clear waters of mountain streams lend their health-giving properties

LONG GALLERY, AUSABLE CHASM.

to make the region a delightful retreat for the invalid or the toil-worn seeker for recreation and variety.

The celebrated Au Sable Chasm is reached by the Delaware & Hudson Road from Platts-burg, or by rail or stage from Port Kent, and is well worthy of a visit.

KATTERSKILL FALLS.

Lake George is a long, narrow body of water, dot-ted with beautiful islands, and surrounded by attract-ive mountain scenery. It is one of the most fashion-able summer resorts of America, its proximity to Saratoga bringing the two into natural association by pleasure-seekers. The sum-mer houses of wealthy New Yorkers are numerous on its shores, and elegant hotels and superior board-ing-houses are found at Caldwell,. the fashionable center for this locality.

Mount Mar-cy, 5,337 feet in height, is exceeded in this part of the country only by Mount Washington. The peaks of the Adiron-dacks are con-ical, the slopes abrupt, and the scenery is wild and grand. The rivers Saranac and Au Sable flow from them north-east, and the Hudson, Cedar and Boreas to the south. In the tract are many ponds and lakes; Racquette Lake, very irregular in outline, being the largest. The Adirondack region once abounded in caribou, moose, deer, bear, panther, beaver, otter and smaller game; it is still a favorite hunting country, and is famous for salmon, trout, pike and other game fish. It is now one of the most popular summer resorts for those who desire life in camp, or wild scenery.

## SARATOGA SPRINGS.

Lying in the direct highway of pleasure travel, and with an established reputation, the SARATOGA SPRINGS may well be included as a stopping place, between Montreal and New York.

These famous springs, twenty-eight in number, are situated on a plateau ten miles west of the Hudson, and thirty-two miles from Albany.

There are annually from 40,000 to 50,000 visitors, while the hotels, which are of great magnitude, can accommodate some 20,000 people. Four miles from the village is Saratoga Lake, reached by the Boulevard, a drive 100 feet wide, and lined with trees. Six of the springs of Saratoga are spouting springs; and all are charged with carbonic acid gas, and variously impregnated with magnesia, sulphur and iron; some are chalybeate.

The mineral springs of Saratoga were greatly used by the Indians. The first frame house was built there by General Philip Schuyler in 1784; the large hotels have been built since 1815; and here the English under Peter Schuyler defeated the French under De Manteth in 1693.

## THE CATSKILLS.

As immortalized by Washington Irving in his charming legends of the Hudson, the region of the Catskill Mountains has been made memorable to all readers of American fiction. The tide of summer travel has made them scarcely less conspicuous in modern lore, so delightful are they to the visitor, not only for their intrinsic attractions, but from the legends associated with the various localities, where, according to Irving, Rip Van Winkle, with dog and gun, wandered in search of game, and slept his memorable long nap.

An immense number of summer boarders are accommodated through this region, not only in hotels, which are excellently appointed, but also in countless farm houses and village homes. The views from the various peaks are wonderfully varied and beautiful, reaching from the Green Mountains in Vermont to the Highlands at West Point, and taking in nearly 100 miles of the Hudson River and valley. The highest point is the top of Overlook, 3,800 feet; other prominent elevations are Hunter Mountain, High Peak and Round Top. One of the sights of the region is "The Clove," or ravine, and the falls therein. This ravine is about five miles long; at its head two rivulets unite and flow rapidly to a point where the mountain divides and forms a deep hollow, into which the brook rushes over a cascade of 180 feet.

# OTTAWA.

OTTAWA, the political capital of the Dominion of Canada, is most picturesquely situated at the junction of the Rideau River with the Ottawa. Next to Quebec, the scenery around Ottawa is the most beautiful in the Dominion. The range of mountains which closes in the horizon to the north and east is the last of the picturesque chain of the Laurentides; from the summer house on Parliament Hill the view is one not easily forgotten. The broad river below the hills glowing in the sunset, the Chaudiere white with spray, and the magnificent pile of public buildings, all contribute to form a most striking landscape. THE CHAUDIERE FALLS, a pleasant drive from Ottawa, are considered

RAFTS IN THE RAPIDS.

by many to rank next in importance, beauty and grandeur to those of Niagara, and the cataract is remarkable enough to have impressed even the stolidity of the Indians; for in old days they always threw a little tobacco into the Chaudiere (the name signifying a caldron) before commencing the *portage* to the quiet above. Close at hand are the "timber slides," by which the lumber from the upper river passes down without damage to the navigable water below. To go down these slides upon a crib or timber is a unique experience a visitor should endeavor to make; for while it is unattended with danger, the novelty and excitement are most absorbing. Close to the city are also the RIDEAU FALLS, and the

RIDEAU CANAL, connecting the Ottawa and St. Lawrence Rivers, exca-
vated at the base of a ravine 150 feet below the roadway. The great
sight at Ottawa is, however, her magnificent pile of government
buildings. They cover an area of four acres, and occupy a very
commanding site on the river bank; they are built in the Italian-
gothic style and were erected at a cost of $3,000,000   The library
is the most architecturally beautiful building for the purpose in
America. It is polygonal in shape, with a buttress at each of its
sixteen angles, upon which are flying buttresses, which support
the dome. The library contains over 100,000 volumes. RIDEAU
HALL, the residence of the Governor-General, is during the session
of Parliament the scene of much gaiety and hospitality.

PARLIAMENT BUILDINGS, OTTAWA.

### KINGSTON.

Kingston is a city which has played an important *role* in Canadian history, and was first settled in 1673 by the Count de Frontenac. It is one of the pleasantest of Canada's towns, and enjoys
a cool summer temperature, from its neighborhood to the lake and
river. Its old importance, both as a military post and as a political center—for it was once a capital—has now passed away; but
the country around is so pleasant that it will always be a favorite
residence. Picturesque martello towers rise from the water, and
are posted along the environs of the town to where Fort Henry, on
the hill to the southward, dominates the landscape. The traces of
the old French fort built by Frontenac are still visible,

# THE THOUSAND ISLANDS.

IN descending the St. Lawrence from Kingston by the RICHE-LIEU & ONTARIO NAVIGATION STEAMERS the far-famed THOUSAND ISLANDS are reached. There are in reality some 1800 of them, packed in a river stretch of 40 miles, and there is no more favored summer resort in America than

> "Amid the thousand Isles that seem
> The joy and glory of the stream."

The width of the river is here about seven miles, the rocky wood-clad group of islets separating the deep, strong-running channels.

Imagine a vast English park with its massive trees, its hills and slopes, and its laps of verdure. Replace its green turf with water, blue, transparent and crystaline. Over an area twelve leagues

THE THOUSAND ISLANDS.

long and two or three wide, on which ever side you turn your eyes you see nothing but islands of every kind and form—some raising their pyramidal heads boldly above the water, others lying just above the level of the river as if bowed to receive its blessing as it passed. Some are bristling with firs and pines, others lie open and level like a field awaiting the husbandman's care. Some are but an arid rock, as wild and picturesque as those seen among the Faroe Islands; others have a group of trees or a solitary pine, and others bear a crown of flowers or a little hillock of verdure like a dome of malachite, among which the river slowly glides, embracing with equal fondness the great and the small, now receding afar and now retracing its course, like the good patriarch visiting his domains, or like the god Proteus counting his snowy flocks. In the old Indian days this beautiful extent of the river was called Manatoana, or Garden of the Great Spirit, and well might the islands, when covered with thick forests, the deer swimming from wooded isle to wooded isle, and each little lily-padded bay nestling in among the hills and bluffs of the island, and teeming with water fowl, seem to the Indian in his half-poetic mood like some beautiful region dedicated to his Supreme Deity.   In the bays and by the sides of the islands is excellent fishing, bass and pickerel being the principal fish, but the famous maskalonge is sufficiently numerous to warrant the fisherman in expecting an electric bite from him at any moment which will test both his strength and skill.

The Thousand Islands may be also reached from Gananoque, a thriving and enterprising town on the St. Lawrence, by steamer, while the finely equipped vessels of the Richelieu & Ontario Navigation Company pass here in daylight from Toronto to points East, and also make the exciting passage of the Lachine Rapids.

### THOUSAND ISLAND PARK.

More widely known, perhaps, than any of the other St. Lawrence resorts, is the great camp-meeting park of the Methodist denomination bearing the above title.   It is located at the upper end of Wells Island, and has rapidly grown to large proportions, combining, as it does, the religious, social and pleasure-seeking elements, often united in the same individuals.   It has a large village of permanent cottages, which is greatly increased in the summer by the "cotton houses" of those who come for a brief stay, either in attendance upon the religious services or for a short respite from business in camp life.   It has a postoffice, public buildings, stores, and the conveniences of town life, together with boat-houses, landings, dock room, etc., and being in the main channel of the river, it is readily accessible to visitors, as the boats make it one of their important landings.

Westminster Park is on the lower portion of Wells Island, and is also under the control of a religious association, being owned by a regularly chartered society called the Westminster Park Association.   The Park comprises about five hundred acres, occupying an irregular neck of upland, rising in some places to a commanding height, overlooking the scene for miles in extent.   Tasteful cottages occupy the building lots into which a large portion of the Park has been divided.   Directly opposite from this park, on the New York shore, is

### ALEXANDRIA BAY,

Sometimes called the "Saratoga of the St. Lawrence."   As a summer resort, it is fairly entitled to the name, being one of the most popular watering-places in America.   Its summer hotels are among the most commodious and attractive to be found anywhere, while private cottages and villas have sprung up on every available site, both on the shore, and on all the islands near.   The facilities for fishing and boating, combined with the pure and invigorating atmosphere, and the beautiful scenery, attract to the place a tide of summer visitors, ever increasing in volume with each succeeding year. The approach, by boat, is charming, as the pretty cottages come in view all along the shore, succeeded by the imposing hotel fronts as the harbor is neared. Among the handsome villas, that of the late Dr. J. G. Holland, "Bonnie Castle," is a conspicuous object, occupying a promontory which projects just below the landing.

The last of the Thousand Islands are called the Three Sisters, from their resemblance and proximity to each other. They are nearly opposite Brockville on the Canada shore, and Morristown on the New York side, the two towns being directly opposite each other.

BROCKVILLE, named in honor of General Brock, is called the "Thousand Island City," and from its situation well merits the title. Its glittering towers and church spires give an appearance of splendor, which the tourist will observe is a peculiarity of the Canadian cities to be seen in his trip, the metal with which they are covered retaining its brightness in a remarkable degree, owing to the purity and dryness of the atmosphere.

OGDENSBURG AND PRESCOTT.—These two cities, like those last mentioned, are opposite each other, and are both important points. The former lies on both sides of Oswegatchie River, at its junction with the St. Lawrence. On account of its beautiful foliage, it has been appropriately entitled Maple City. Its extensive river front, with its railroad facilities, gives it a decided advantage as a grain port. Large elevators and warehouses, for the transhipment of grain and other freight from the lake steamers, are among the important enterprises of the place.

PRESCOTT, on the Canadian shore, has in its vicinity several places of historical interest, among them being "Windmill Point" and "Chimney Island." Here, also, the tourist may resume the journey by rail, if satiated with steamboating; but those who have never made the trip through the rapids will desire to remain on the boat to the finish at Montreal. Between Prescott and Montreal there are a number of rapids, among them being the Long Sault, Cedars and Cascades; but the most famous of all, are of course the

## LACHINE RAPIDS.

LACHINE is nine miles from Montreal, and is a deservedly favorite summer resort; it was so named by Champlain in 1613, because he believed that beyond the rapids the river led to China (La Chine). The passage of these rapids, the most interesting on the St. Lawrence, is thus graphically described: "Suddenly a scene of wild grandeur burst upon the eye. Waves are lashed into spray and into breakers of a thousand forms by the submerged rocks, which they are dashed against in the headlong impetuosity of the river. Whirlpools, a storm-lashed sea, the chasm below Niagara, all mingle their sublimity in a single rapid. Now passing with lightning speed within a few yards of rocks, which, did your vessel but touch them, would reduce her to an utter wreck before the crash could sound upon the ear; did she even diverge in the least from her course,—if her head were not kept straight with the course of the rapid,—she would be instantly submerged and rolled over and over. Before us is an absolute precipice of waters; on every side of it breakers, like dense avalanches, are thrown high into the air. Ere we can take a glance at the scene, the boat descends

the wall of waves and foam like a bird, and in a second afterwards you are floating on the calm, unruffled bosom of 'below the rapids.'" An experienced Indian pilot, who knows each rock and eddy, has guided the steamers which make the "shoot" for years, and no accident of any consequence has ever happened, nor has a single life been lost.

### TORONTO—THE "QUEEN CITY."

The town which Governor Simcoe founded in 1794, he called York, and it was not till 1834, when the city was incorporated, that the musical Iroquois word—TORONTO—was adopted. At that time it had a population of 9,254 which has now grown to over 120,000. Unlike Montreal and Quebec, Toronto owes little, except the security of its harbors, and the excellent sanitary results from its graded terrace of site, to nature. It has been made what it is by the enterprise and energy of its inhabitants. Much of the prosperity of the city has been caused by the enterprise which at an early date centered a complete railway system here. Owing to the influence of Lake Ontario, which bounds it on the South, the climate is remarkably pleasant and salubrious. It is highly favored in parks and squares, and its public buildings are handsome, massive structures, which add greatly to the architectural beauty of the "Queen City." Toronto has sometimes been called the "City of Churches" and the number and beauty of its sacred edifices would any where attract attention. St. Andrew's Presbyterian Church is the finest Norman piece of architecture in America. Toronto is the political, commercial, legal, religious, literary and educational center of Ontario. Large numbers of Americans visit this city annually, and the best hotel accommodation can be secured at most reasonable rates. In the summer season the bay is alive with ferry boats and small craft of all kinds, plying between the city and Hanlan's Island, and there are daily pleasant excursions by water in all directions.

# NIAGARA FALLS.

THE Falls of Niagara, the grandest specimen of Nature's handiwork in the whole world, are equally magnificent at all seasons and under all circumstances; whether viewed by moonlight or sunlight, or the dazzling glare of the electric light, winter or summer, their wonderful proportions are always sublime.

The whirling floods, the unvarying thunderous roar, the vast sheets of spray and mist that are caught in their liquid depths by

sunbeams and formed into radiant rainbows—all seem as if homage were paid by the skies to creation's greatest contract—a temple not made by hands.

The Niagara Falls received their name from the Indians, in whose language the word Niagara means the "thunder of water." The Niagara River receives the waters of all the upper lakes—the Erie, St. Clair, Huron, Michigan, Superior and a number of smaller ones, and neither the snows of winter nor the evaporation of summer, neither rains nor drought, materially affect it. Its waters flow on full and clear, perpetually the same, with the exception that about once every seven years they have a gradual rise and fall, which is attributed to some undiscovered disturbance that effects Lake Erie.

SUSPENSION BRIDGE.

The great maelstrom, called the Whirlpool, some distance below the Falls, excites much interest. Its depths are unknown; a 1,000-foot cord was found too short to reach its bottom. There are three distinct cataracts; the Horseshoe Fall, so called from its crescent shape, is by far the largest, being 2,600 feet wide and 154 feet high; the American Fall is 660 feet wide, and the Central Falls, 243 feet, each having a fall of 163 feet. The two latter are separated from each other and the former by Goat Island. The aggregate width

FATHER HENNEPIN'S SKETCH OF THE FALLS.

is thus 2,900 feet and the water discharged is computed to be 1,000,000 tons per hour. Thanks to the energies of Lord Dufferin, then Governor-General of Canada, and Governor Robinson of New York, parks on either side have been opened up free to the public. The Suspension Bridge which is crossed by the Southern (Great Western) Division of the Grand Trunk is one of the engineering triumphs of the age. It has a span of 1,230 feet from tower to tower, and the floor is 256 feet above the water level. This bridge was opened January 1, 1869; it is a two-storied structure, the upper story being used for the purposes of the Grand Trunk Railway, and the bottom story for foot and passenger traffic.

There is no more graphic description of Niagara Falls than that of Mr. Charles Dickens, who thus in his own characteristic style says: "We were at the foot of the American Falls; I could see an immense torrent of water tearing headlong down from some immense height, but had no idea of shape or situation, or anything but vague immensity. When we were seated in the little ferry-boat and were crossing the swollen river, immediately before both cataracts, I began to feel what it was; but I was in a measure stunned and unable to comprehend the vastness of the scene. It was not until I came on Table Rock and looked—Great Heaven! on what a fall of bright green water!—that it came upon me in its full might and majesty. Then, when I felt how near to my Creator I was standing, the first effect, and the enduring one—instant and lasting—of the tremendous spectacle, was peace. Peace, of mind, tranquility, calm recollections of the dead, great thoughts of eternal rest and happiness; nothing of gloom and terror. Niagara

GOAT ISLAND BRIDGE.

was at once stamped upon my heart, an image of beauty, to remain there, changeless and indelible, until its pulses cease to beat forever." In short, the whole line of the Grand Trunk opens up a fruitful field to those who are open to the sweet influences of nature, and who with the poet can—

"Tread this wondrous world:
See all its store of inland waters hurled
In one vast volume down Niagara's steep,
Or calm behold them, in transparent sleep,
Where the blue hills of old Toronto shed
Their evening shadows o'er Ontario's bed;
Should trace the grand Catarqui, and glide
Down the white rapids of his lordly tide.
Through mossy woods, 'mid islets flowering fair,
And blooming glades, where the first sinful pair
For consolation might have weeping trod,
When banished from the garden of their God."

# THE MIDLAND LAKES.

HE Midland Division of the Grand Trunk Railway takes the tourist through some of the most picturesque and varied scenery—a pleasant and ever-changing panorama, while, at the same time, it is a perfect sportsman's paradise.

The Midland has four terminal stations, TORONTO, WHITBY, PORT HOPE, and BELLEVILLE, and from all these the chief points of interest are easily and speedily reached. Toronto has already been amply described; Whitby, once a Seneca village, and early settled by the French, is thirty miles east, bordering on Lake Ontario; Port Hope, formerly the Ganeraske of the Indians, is one of the pleasantest of the lake-side towns. It boasts of a capital harbor, and during the season of navigation the large steamer "Norseman" plies regularly between this place and Rochester, many sportsmen choosing this route to reach the famous hunting grounds of Midland, Ontario; reduced fares being made for fishermen and shooters. Belleville is an incorporated city, beautifully situated on the Bay of Quinte. The River Moira passes through the city, and furnishes water-power for the numerous manufacturing industries of the place. In the summer time steamers leave daily for different ports along the bay and River St. Lawrence. Massassauga Point on this bay is quite a resort, and excellent fishing is to be had here. Among the winding and romantic shores of this bay the more destructive form of enterprise has happily stayed its hand, so that much of the primitive beauty survives. Then, too, the charm of this famous bay is in no slight measure due to cloud effects and the changeful humor of the sun, while the inlets and wooded headlands, and the waving barley fields beyond—for the barley of the Bay of Quinte is far-famed—all add to the beauty of the surrounding scenery.

One of the first things to be visited in this district is the charming TRENT RIVER, which may be reached from either Trenton or Campbellford. It is navigable for canoes, with one or two short portages, some picturesque falls are met with, and its waters teem with maskalonge and black bass. In the summer of 1883, the American Canoe Association met here, and so charmed were they with the delightful scenery and the places they visited, that in the following year their visit was renewed. As numerous tourists now seek a summer outing in a canoe, it may not be uninteresting to follow the members of the Association in their trip, who, with their friends and families, number some four hundred. Passing up the Trent River, RICE LAKE was reached, one of the prettiest of the inland waters, and which is specially reserved by Government for fishing purposes, a permit being granted to applicants at a nominal cost. This lake was most appropriately named, for as the early pilgrims approached this water they found it deeply fringed with wild rice, over which hovered clouds of wild fowl—beautiful wood-duck, with summer glistening in their plumage; also fall and winter duck just returned from the north. Throughout this lake are scattered conical islets, wooded with maples, whose bright leaves at times fall on the water like flakes of fire. A township on the lower edge of Rice Lake has been aptly named Asphodel—no unfit designation for well-watered meadows, where the shades of Indian heroes may still linger!

> " My footsteps press where centuries ago
>   The Red Men fought and conquered; lost and won.
>   Whole tribes and races, gone like last year's snow,
>   Have found the Eternal Hunting grounds and run
>   The fiery gauntlet of their active days,
>   Until few are left to tell the mournful tale;
>   And these inspire us with such wild amaze,
>   They seem like spectres passing down a vale
>   Steeped in uncertain moonlight, on their way
>   Towards some bourne where darkness blinds the day,
>   And night is wrapped in mystery profound.
>   We cannot lift the mantle of the past;
>   We seem to wander over hallowed ground;
>   We scan the trail of thought, but all is overcast."

On Rice Lake the chief Indian settlement is Hiawatha—named after the hero of Ojibbeway mythology, whom Longfellow has immortalized in his melodious trochaics. Here you may still find, in the ordinary language of the Ojibbeway, fragments of fine imagery and picture-talk, often in the very words which the American poet has so happily woven together, while the scenery of this Trent Valley reproduces that of the Vale of Tawasentha. Here are "the wild rice of the river," and "the Indian village," and "the groves of singing pine trees, ever sighing, ever singing." At Fenelon Falls we have "Minnehaha"—"Laughing Water,"—and not far below is Sturgeon Lake, the realm of the "Kingly Fishes." Sturgeon of portentous size are yet met with, though falling somewhat short of the comprehensive fish sung by Longfellow, which swallowed Hiawatha, canoe and all.

Still *revenons a nos moutons*, and pursuing the course of our canoes, the Otonabee—"Mouthwater"—River was next entered, and the journey continued to Lakefield, a station of the Midland Division of the Grand Trunk system. The Otonabee here expands into Lake Ketchewanook, the "Lake of the Rapids;" thence, between bold and rocky banks, it races, rather than flows, to Peterboro, the channel descending 150 feet in nine miles. Clear Lake, where the overflow of the whole lake chain is gathered into a crystal funnel, is next entered, and junction made with Stony Lake, which owes its wild beauty to the Laurentian formation, which often abruptly closes the vista with beetling crags of red or gray gneiss, and which here formed the islands, which, in the years

above alluded to, were whitened by the tents of the Canoe Association. Birdie Falls, Love-Sick Lake, Fairy Lake, are all a continu-
ation of this water system, and offer the canoeist an uninterrupted
course of some 500 miles through a variety of scenery, which the
world can nowhere excel for natural and picturesque beauty.

If you seek to know how the time of the members of this Association was passed, Emerson can well answer:—

> " Ask you, how went the hours?
> All day we swept the lake, searched every cove,
> North from Camp Maple, south to Osprey Bay,
> Watching when the loud dogs should drive in deer;

WATCHING FOR DEER.

> Or whipping its rough surface for a trout;
> Or bathers, diving from the rock at noon;
> Challenging echo by our guns and cries;
> Or listening to the laughter of the loon;
> Or in the evening twilight's latest red,
> Beholding the procession of the pines;
> Or, later yet, beneath a lighted jack,
> In the boat's bows, a silent night-hunter,
> Stealing with paddle to the feeding grounds
> Of the red deer, to aim at a square mist.
> Hark to that muffled roar! A tree in the woods
> Is fallen; but hush! it has not scared the buck,
> Who stands astonished at the meteor light,
> Then turns to bound away,—is it too late?"

By the Trent Valley Canal the charming and romantic village of
Bobcaygeon is reached. The steamer "Beaubocage," which plies
between Lindsay and Bobcaygeon, would evidently associate the

name with the French explorers, and to their outspoken admiration of the "lovely woodlands" on these waters. Without doubt, the fishing in this neighborhood is the very finest to be had in the country. The village is surrounded by water on all sides, and the ripples of the falls can be plainly heard. There is excellent hunting to be had in these parts; deer abound, and guides are readily procured, the season lasting from October 15th to December 15th. Bobcaygeon was founded by the ancestors of Mr. Mossum Boyd, a gentleman resident here, whose generous hospitality has been freely granted to many a seeker of sport in his locality. From this place a pleasant excursion by means of the Trent Valley Navigation Co.'s

PORT PERRY.

Steamers may be made to Sturgeon Point, where is located one of the best summer hotels in Canada, with capital fishing near by; thence through Sturgeon Lake and Scugog River to Lindsay.

LINDSAY, charmingly situated on the Scugog River, is one of the pleasantest of the inland towns of Canada. It has a population of upwards of 5,000 inhabitants; is the county seat of Victoria County, contains the county buildings, and several fine churches and schools, while its river facilities offer many pleasant excursions by water.

North of Lindsay are FENELON FALLS, named after the early French missionary of Canada, who was a brother of the great archbishop. These falls enlist the admiration of all who see them. They are picturesquely situated where Lake Cameron empties itself into the Fenelon River; and the government has erected locks here to complete this chain of inland communication. Progressing in a northerly direction HALIBURTON is reached, by a branch of the Grand Trunk, formerly known as the Victoria Railway. Here are to be found the great lumber regions of the English Colonization Company, where are numerous lakes and streams; where lovers of the gentle art can meet with the best of sport, while there is no section of country where deer are more plentiful. There are important stone quarries here, while Mount Snowden may be regarded as a solid mountain of iron. South of Lindsay is Port Perry, a prettily situated town of some 3,000 inhabitants, on the Scugog, possessing many attractions to the tourist.

Thirty miles north of Port Hope, and ninety miles northeast of Toronto, is the thriving town of PETERBORO, which is now entering

PETERBORO.

the dignity of a city, and whose growth and development have been rapid and well assured. No part of Canada owes more to its pioneers than this charming and most healthful lake-land. Some of the finest towns were, two generations ago, jungles reeking with malaria, and infested by wolves, black flies, black snakes and black bears. Now all is transformed. The history of Peterboro dates back to 1825, when Peter Robinson led thither his first band of Irish emigrants. The town has now a population of some 10,000 inhabitants, and is joined to the Village of Ashburnham, opposite, by a handsome bridge. There is good hotel acccommodation, excellent fishing in the river, and no one making a tour in Midland Ontario should neglect a visit to this place.

Further east, and a terminal point of the line, is Madoc, which can also be reached from Belleville, a distance of some thirty miles.

To the miner and metallurgist Madoc Township became in the fall of 1866 an object of the keenest interest, from the discovery of gold on the upper course of the Moira.

Iron mining in this district has long been associated with the township of Marmora. This region affords some splendid scenery; there is capital hunting and good hotels, while Lake Moira, named after an early governor, the Earl of Moira, is without doubt one of the prettiest lakes in the world.

A two hours' trip from Toronto lands the tourist in the beautiful village of Sutton, chiefly populated by old English settlers, and which abounds in points of interest and picturesque scenery. At Jackson's Point, one mile from the village, has been erected, under the auspices of the citizens of Toronto and the residents of Sutton, one of the finest summer hotels in Canada, while capital fishing is to be had here, and from this point steamers ply across Lake Simcoe to Big Bay Point, thence to Barrie, to Orillia and to Lake Couchiching, all of which interesting places are described further on. Lake Simcoe is one of the most beautiful and favored lakes of Canada, and to those desiring a pleasant and cheap stay on its shores, Jackson's Point is strongly commended as a most charming summer resort.

Lake Simcoe is not wanting in historic interest, for in its neighborhood were enacted the dreadful tragedies of the Huron-Iroquois war. Here, were there space, could be narrated deeds of the loftiest heroism and of the most fiendish cruelty. In this corner of Ontario a nation was saved from utter extermination only by the intervention of the white strangers. Had the French arrived fifty years later the Huron nation would have disappeared as utterly as did the Mound-builders. Later on it became the scene of five great battles, in which the Mississaugas, an Ojibbeway tribe, overcame the Iroquois and drove them out of the country.

### TORONTO TO BALSAM LAKE.

There are so many pleasant trips to be taken in connection with this Midland route, that only a personal visit can succinctly portray the beauties and infinite varieties of this region.

A very popular trip is that to BALSAM LAKE, which may be easily reached from Coboconk, a terminal point of the Midland Division. This lake has many attractions for the tourist, the surrounding scenery must please all, while for fishing and hunting this district is unsurpassed by any. A charming residence in this neighborhood is that of Mr. George Laidlaw, whose hospitality has always been so freely and openly extended to visitors to this neighborhood. A very pleasant steamboat excursion may be made from Coboconk, through Balsam Lake and some small heavily-wooded streams, to Fenelon Falls, and thence by rail or steamer to Lindsay. In short, throughout this region there is no more ubiquitous system of railroads than this Midland Division of the Grand Trunk. It is no surprise that railroads are the wonder of the world. Nothing during the last half century has created so marvelous a change as the great iron revolution of science. Beneath it the features of old Christendom have been changed, and its wealth and physical grandeur augmented. Other revolutions have scattered luminous influences over the world, but it remained for the new generation of railways to bring about one of the mightiest moral and social revolutions that ever hallowed the annals of any age. Omnipresence is one of the principles of their progress. Content with no limits, they have thrown a girdle round the world itself. Far-off India wooes them over its waters. China listens to the voice of the charmer. The Atlantic and Pacific seaboards are connected. The ruined hills and broken altars of ancient Greece re-echo the whistle of the locomotive, and are converted to shrines open to commerce, by the power of these magnificent agencies, by which rivers are spanned, territories traversed, commerce enfranchised, confederacies consolidated, and man assumes a lordship over time and space.

Another place interesting to the tourist is Chemong Lake, which may be reached from any of the frontier termini, via Peterboro, and a branch of the Grand Trunk Railway. From Chemong, the terminus of the branch, steamers may be taken to Bobcaygeon, etc. Tourists may also make a pleasant trip to Stony and Clear Lakes, and thence to Bobcaygeon, Sturgeon Lake and Lindsay.

### MIDLAND.

The northern terminus of this division of the Grand Trunk is at Midland, a thriving and enterprising town, pleasantly situated on the Georgian Bay, and which possesses historical. associations of interest. There is an old fort here, the traces of which are yet to be seen, and old muskets and bayonets are often dug up. Strange as it may seem to any one studying the map of Canada, by Midland was the early route from East to West, prior to any knowledge of Lake Ontario, the path taken being by the Ottawa River, and thus to the Georgian Bay, from which a Government road led to Lake Simcoe, then by canoes to Beaverton, and by the Yonge-street road to Toronto.

From Midland, by the Muskoka & Georgian Bay Navigation Company, a daily service is given to Parry Sound, and a semi-weekly service to Byng Inlet. One of the greatest attractions afforded by this line are the facilities granted to camping expeditions. Annually several thousand families are carried to the various islands which dot the Georgian Bay, and which in number and variety surpass the Thousand Isles, and here establish a summer camp, while the steamers which ply this route make a daily call at all inhabited islands, for the purpose of furnishing necessaries, delivering or receiving mails and other requirements.

At Honey Harbour on this route, are established apiaries, under the charge of the Rev. Dr. Clark, in connection with the American and Canadian Bee Association. There are four or five distinct apiaries, located in various islands, where different breeds are cultivated, but sufficiently far apart to prevent intermingling.

This is a capital sporting center, while an immense amount of grain is received here from Chicago, and duly forwarded to the markets of the East. Midland harbor is without exception the finest in the Upper Lakes of America; vessels drawing sixteen feet can come along-side the wharves and esplanade without pilots or steam tugs. This harbor was jointly made by the Grand Trunk Railway and the Government of Canada. There is here one of the largest grain elevators in the Dominion with a capacity of 300,000 bushels; while the town is the center of a large lumber business, being second only to that of Ottawa; there being some thirty lumber mills, with an annual output of 150,000,000 feet.

In short, in this neighborhood will be found the most attractive of Canada's forest shrines, encircled—

" By the laughing tides that lave *
Those Edens of the Northern wave."

# THE NORTHERN LAKES.

B Y their recent acquirement of the Northern and Northwestern Railways, the Grand Trunk have added an important connection to their already extended system. There is no portion of Canada which offers so inviting a field to the summer tourist as the varied scenery to be found in the Muskoka district and along the shores of the Georgian Bay, all of which points are reached by the Northern & Northwestern division of the Grand Trunk. The Muskoka region, with its many hundreds of lakes and streams, is undoubtedly the best place on the continent for fishing, shooting or camping. The fishing, consisting of brook and salmon

VIEW ON LAKE COUCHICHING.

trout, black bass, maskalonge and pickerel, is unequaled; partridge abound and deer are plentiful. As a health resort it cannot be surpassed. The many lakes here to be found are among the highest on the continent, being 750 feet above Lake Ontario, 415 feet above Lake Huron, and 390 feet above Lake Superior.

At Lefroy is seen the first view of Lake Simcoe, the first of the various chains of inland lakes which are now met with in succession. A ferry steamer keeps up constant connection with Roach's Point, a pretty village which is much frequented by tourists in summer on account of its excellent boating and fishing. Barrie, on this lake, is a delightful summer resort, with an excellent fleet of boats and yachts, and with good fishing streams in the neighborhood.

Ten miles from Barrie, on the shores of Lake Simcoe and Kempenfeldt Bay, is Peninsular Park—Big Bay Point—with its summer hotels.   This is an excellent and popular resort.   Steamers ply regularly between Barrie and this point, making connection with trains from and to Hamilton and Toronto.

At the foot of Lake Couchiching, which is joined to Lake Simcoe by a channel known as the "Narrows," is Orillia, a favorite center of summer travel, and a town which is fast rising in importance. The Indian nomenclature of Couchiching is especially appropriate and descriptive; here the varying breezes, welcome adjuncts of a summer resort, that fan the surface of the lake, have given the Indian name for "Lake of Many Winds." A pleasant place is Couchiching Park, situated on the point of a narrow promontory projecting a mile and a half northward into the lake, and surrounded on three sides by water; thus, come from whatever quarter it may, every breeze has play, while the lake on the one side or the other, being protected by the point from wind and wave, pleasure boating is safe, and calm waters can at all times be enjoyed.

Strawberry Island, ten miles from Orillia, on Lake Simcoe, is well deserving of a visit.   There is here a capital hotel and fine summer cottages.   This resort is owned by Capt. Chas. McInnes, who has a first-class steamer, by means of which connection is kept up daily between the Island and Orillia.   At Rama, on this lake, is the "reservation" of the last remnants of the Ojibbeways.   Splendid brook

LAKE COUCHICHING HOTEL (BEFORE IT WAS DESTROYED BY FIRE).

trout are caught in the streams in the neighborhood, and the finest black bass fishing in America is in these surrounding lakes.

First among the sporting districts of the northern lakes is the Severn River, which, after a short run, leads to Sparrow Lake, which has long been celebrated for the excellence of its fishing, but particularly for the deer, duck and ruffled grouse shooting, obtaina-ble in their proper seasons.

W. J. WELCH. S? L.ROLAND.

GRANITE NOTCH.

After passing the Severn nothing but granite meets the eye; massive in form, deep red in color, and with a micaceous sheen shining through it. Winding through the "divide" the granite rocks raise high their lofty sides, bluff cliffs overhang the railway as it curves around their bases, in some places the front portion of the train is lost to sight from the rear, but finally the "Granite Notch" is reached, and the railway slips through a natural gap, fortunately left for its passage by nature.

The Muskoka district—known as the "Highlands of Ontario"—has some eight hundred lakes of all sizes, from thirty miles in length to mere ponds, which, with their river connections, occupy no less than one-tenth of the surface. By means of the Muskoka & Georgian Bay Navigation Company a fine line of steamers make connection with this interesting chain of lakes. Boats leave Muskoka Wharf for Bala, Bracebridge, Beaumaris, Port Carling, Windermere,

HIGH FALLS.

Rosseau and intermediate places. There is a tri-weekly service to Bala and Rosseau Falls; daily to Clevelands, Gregory, Port Sandfield, Redwood, Craigielea, Port Cockburn, and semi-weekly to Juddhaven, all of which are places well worthy of a visit from the tourist, and where excellent sport can always be obtained.

At Gravenhurst and Bracebridge railway connections are made with trains of the Northern & Northwestern division of the Grand

Trunk to Burk's Falls and other points, thence per steamer "Wenonah" on the upper Maganetawan waters, and from Midland and Penetanguishene to Parry Sound, Byng Inlet, and French River. To facilitate travel, for business-men and others, arrangements have been made for an interchange of tickets between Bracebridge and Gravenhurst, and parties purchasing return tickets between these points have the choice of routes, either rail or water.

GREAT SOUTH FALLS, MUSKOKA RIVER.

Lake Muskoka is one of the largest of the lakes comprised under the generic term of the "Lakes of Muskoka," being twenty-two miles long and nine miles wide, while it is studded with some 350 islands, and affords splendid fishing.

Bracebridge, the chief town of the Muskoka district, and a station of the Northern & Northwestern division of the Grand Trunk, is agreeably situated on the cliffs of the river Muskoka, and the neighborhood merits a sojourn from the tourist to visit its interesting surroundings. Near by are the High Falls, and the Great South Falls, the most commanding natural feature in Muskoka. Beaumaris, the southermost of these summer resorts, and which boasts of a large and excellent hotel, is situated on Tondern Island. Here is capital bathing and a sandy beach. Immediately opposite, and on the route which the steamer takes when crossing to the western side of the lake is a cluster of small islands, known

SOUTH FALLS, MUSKOKA RIVER.

as the "Kettles," where the very best bass fishing and splendid trolling for salmon trout may be found.

Port Carling is the most central of all the villages on the lakes, being the converging point for all the steamers running to and fro on the three lakes, thus access to all parts can most conveniently be obtained from this center. At this point locks connect Lakes Muskoka and Rosseau.

Lake Rosseau is fourteen miles long in its extremest points, and is one of the most interesting and charming of lakes in this region. The scenery is much varied, and at one point there is a most remarkable echo. The southern portion of this lake is fairly gemmed with islets, and as they were early selected for their beauty and admirable situation, more island population has been accumulated in this part than in any other. The lower part of Lake Rosseau is

THE BRIDAL VEIL FALLS.

called "Venetia," and it is aptly designated, for not in Venice itself are boats more used or needed.

The Shadow River, one of the most wonderful natural curiosities of the Muskoka region, empties its waters into the bay on the shores of which Port Rosseau stands. In front and behind, the river winds like a silver creek, hemmed in on either side by forest trees, and losing itself in the distant curves. The surface is as motionless as glass, and everything is duplicated in marvelous detail, each leaf and branch having its reflected counterpart, even more distinct than it appears itself.

> " The fair trees look over, side by side,
>   And see themselves below."

On a small tributary of the Shadow River are the Bridal Veil Falls, which make silver music in the forest grove, and a visit per-

EAGLE'S NEST, LAKE ROSSEAU.

chance may give some hesitating, anxious swain an opportunity of freeing from his halting tongue the words which cleave so closely to his heart.   The lofty headland of Eagle's Nest is a conspicuous and interesting spot on this lake.

Lake Joseph, the third of the series of the Lakes of Muskoka, was for a long time a *mare incognitum*, except to venturous spirits, though those who have viewed the charms of this lake claim for it a beauty surpassing that of all others. Its islands rise more abruptly, and to higher elevations, and more rugged cliffs line its shores, than do those of the other lakes. All who have visited these charming regions will agree with the enconiums paid to these three lakes—Muskoka, Rosseau, and Joseph. It is hard to say which of the three is the most beautiful; but no more enchanting summer tour is offered on this continent, while most comfortable and home-like hotels are everywhere to be found.

The extension of this Northern & Northwestern division of the Grand Trunk to Lake Nipissing has opened up a new and most inviting field to the tourist and sportsman.

Twenty-four miles by train from Gravenhurst, Utterson, a station of this line is reached, where within easy access is Mary Lake, one of the gems of Muskoka. Its surface is studded with many islands, where berries of various kinds are plentiful in the season, and where delightful spots may be chosen for picnics and camps. At the foot of the lake, upon a gentle elevation overlooking its length, is Port Sydney. A good supply of boats is kept here, and most pleasant trips may be made upon these romantic little lakes.

Progressing further to the north, Huntsville, a rapidly-growing commercial center, and an important tourist point, is reached. Connection is here made with a new chain of lakes, whose waters may be followed, either west to their source, or east and south, until they are drained by the Muskoka River.

From Huntsville, a most seductive trip may be made up the lakes, either by steamer or canoe. Throughout these upper waters, and in the tributary streams, there is excellent trout fishing.

Katrine is an important railway point, and is the center of a splendid lake country; and here connection may be made with the Maganetawan River Chain. The railway continues following the banks for four miles, during which the river is crossed four times, and Burk's Falls is reached. This station again opens up another and entirely new region in steamboat navigation to tourist and sportsman, who can now reach with comparatively little trouble a district which has hitherto been accessible only to those with ample means and time. This chain of lakes and the Maganetawan River are just equidistant between the Muskoka and Nipissing chain of waters, and drain a surface of about 4,000 square miles.

A writer in *Forest and Farm* thus speaks of the Maganetawan: "Now a word about the region. If a man can stand out-door life, and live on venison, trout, bass, partridges, ducks, pork, tea and crackers, there is no better place to go to in America that is as accessible. A man can go there in July, August, September, or October with comfort, if he will go in the right way, and shoot deer and catch trout to his heart's content. June to August for trout, after that for deer. Remember the Maganetawan is as large as the Schuylkill at Philadelphia, or considerably wider and deeper than the Harlem at High Bridge, and that the trout have an unlimited range, and are seldom disturbed, so that they have a chance to grow. Deer can be bagged in great numbers if you choose to do so; with a couple of good hounds magnificent sport could be had in the fall. I have shot partridges with my rifle from the canoe while traveling, as they were strutting on the shore, and their 'drumming' was one of the pleasantest, every-day sounds. Do not try to go without some guide. There are men who know the country, and they should be secured, for if you get in there alone, you will have little sport and much trouble. I have no possible interest in noticing this region except that I believe it to be unsurpassed in many ways."

From Burk's Falls a steamer of the Muskoka & Georgian Bay Navigation Company may be taken. For fifteen miles the river is followed, winding to and fro, as all Muskoka rivers seem to do.

After passing through the locks the steamer continues for three miles more in the river, and then enters the lovely Lake Ah-Mic. This is another of the gems of Muskoka; most quaint in form, its arms and elongations form a very maze of interlacings, so their constant vistas of projecting heights with glimpses of distant waters and high ridges with closely-wooded forests of hard wood trees, give soft rounded outlines to the distant scenery.

In summer this combination of the rich greens of the maple, oak, and birch, is most beautiful; but when in autumn the bright red tints show forth their resplendent colors, it is simply indescribable.

At Callander, 108 miles from Gravenhurst, near which the Canadian Pacific Railway is tapped, the first glimpse is obtained of Lake Nipissing, and here the steamers touch for various parts of this interesting lake. This lake is about forty-five miles in length, and its greatest breadth is twenty-eight miles. Its waters are mostly received from the north by the Sturgeon River, which connects it with a chain of smaller lakes; the only outlet is French River, by which the lake discharges into Georgian Bay.

This lake is named after an Indian tribe—known as the Nipissings who lived in this district, and who were regarded by Cartier, and other French adventurers, as a peculiarly superstitious race.

In short the whole of the Muskoka district may be deemed a very sportsman's paradise. The waters of the lakes and streams abound in fish, while the forests afford excellent shooting. The hunter and fisherman is certain to find almost unlimited sport, the game embracing a large variety, from partridge, duck, geese, etc., up to deer, moose and bear; while the waters yield to the angler their treasures of bass, pickerel, brook trout, salmon trout and mascalonge. Steamers ply upon the lakes, which are connected by rivers and streams, large and small. on some of which are pretty cascades and waterfalls.

Penetanguishene, one of the termini of the Northern & North-western Division of the Grand Trunk, is pleasantly situated on a land-locked bay at the foot of Georgian Bay. It is one of the historic spots of Canada. It was once the naval depot, on the upper lakes of the British Navy, and under the waters of its harbor lie the remains of four gun-boats. In the year 1634 the Jesuit Fathers first settled in Ontario, at Ihonatiria—now Penetang—in commemoration of which the Jesuits have built a very beautiful church, one of the grandest ecclesiastical structures in America.

The channels which dot the entrance to the harbor are excellent for pickerel, mascalonge and bass fishing. The steamer Maxwell runs daily, on arrival of trains from Toronto and Hamilton, between Penetang, Midland and Parry Sound, and from thence semi-weekly to Byng Inlet and French River. The scenery from Penetang to Parry Sound is amongst the most varied and picturesque anywhere to be found, the steamer winding in and out a continuous series of islands of every description, which cannot but enchant the tourist.

From Collingwood, which may be almost termed the terminal point of the Northern & Northwestern Division of the Grand Trunk, a line of steamers, the property of the Great Northern Transit Company, which run in connection with the Grand Trunk, make frequent trips through what must rightly be called the most enchanting water scenery of this continent. Every Monday and Thursday, during the season of navigation, the "Northern Belle," on the arrival of trains from Toronto and Hamilton, makes trips to Parry Sound, which place is reached after a few hours' sail through some of the most romantic of scenery, passing through a succession of the most beautiful and varied islands, which in their number and variety far surpass the famed Thousand Islands, as it is computed that there are over 20,000 islands in the Georgian Bay, of all sizes, from mere dots to hundreds of acres, with high towering cliff-like centers.   Resting a night at Parry Sound, the steamer the next morning proceeds to Byng Inlet, a famous fishing resort, and thence to French River, another famous resort for lovers of the rod.   This is the terminal point of this line of route, the return journey being made twice a week to Collingwood.

Collingwood is a charming, cleanly town, and presents attrac-tions in itself, which awaken a general desire for a further acquaintance, and a few days may be spent here very pleasantly.

Meaford, twenty miles away, is delightfully situated under the shelter of Cape Rich, a bold headland, stretching ten miles out into the bay.   The "Big Head" and "Beaver Rivers" near by are celebrated for their brook trout.

## MACKINAC AND NORTH SHORE ROUTE.

Possibly the most charming and popular water trip offered on the continent of America, is that from Collingwood, along the North Shore Route to the far-famed Island of Mackinac.   The boats leave every Tuesday, Thursday and Saturday, on arrival of morning trains from Toronto and Hamilton, and, calling at Meaford and Wiarton, sail up the Georgian Bay through a succes-sion of varied and picturesque islands to Killarney on the North Shore.   Steaming down the North Channel, calling alternately at places of interest on Manitoulin Island and the mainland, the most enchanting scenery is met with at every turn and winding, caused by the numerous islands and rocks; each moment opens up new vistas, and brings into view fresh scenes of beauty.   Many of the islands are clothed with rich verdure down to the water's edge; lofty pines tower from the cliffs, or the light, delicate-looking birches dis-play their fresh, graceful foliage, interspersed with tamaracks and balsams.   Others are sterile and barren patches of rock, save where, perhaps, some few stunted trees cling, with gnarled and contorted roots, to the fissures and clefts in the stony mass.   Thus, hour after hour, islands succeed islands in an unbroken continuity as we glide on; islands of every conceivable size and shape—islands barren, wooded, sandy, rocky, columnar gracefully rounded, precipitous and gently sloping, wind-swept and storm-polished, large, diminutive and infinitesimal, illustrating the truth of the old refrain that—

" Bigger fleas have little fleas
Upon their backs to bite 'em ;
And little fleas have lesser fleas
And so *ad infinitum.*"

For one hundred and seventy miles we steam through this panorama of inland scenery.   Gore Bay, on Manitoulin Island, is a lovely spot, with excellent hotel accommodations, while Spanish River, on the North Shore, merits the attention of the tourist.

Hilton on St. Joseph Island, has a very fine Government dock, recently finished.· Connection is made both here and at Sault Ste. Marie with the N. W. T. Company's Line of Steamers, which run to all points on Lake Superior, Duluth and Port Arthur.

Garden River, at the head of Lake George, is an Indian reserve, and here one must visit an old Jesuit Church, one of the early landmarks of the settlement of the French in Canada.

Sault Ste. Marie, or in the language of the country, "The Soo," is a place which is rapidly growing in importance, and a most enthusiastic "boom" is now progressing; buildings and hotels are rapidly springing up, and capital is being freely invested here.

The Falls of St. Mary have rendered canals necessary, by which communication is kept up between Lakes Huron and Superior. "The Soo" was an important place in old days, when grand councils of Indian Nations were convened here, and voyageurs held their revels on their return from the Far West. At this point connection is made with the Duluth, South Shore & Atlantic Railway, and with all the American lines of steamers for Lake Michigan and the upper lakes, which lead away to the West to that land to which

> . . . departed Hiawatha,
> Hiawatha the Beloved,
> In the glory of the sunset,
> In the purple mists of evening,
> To the regions of the homewind,
> Of the Northwest wind Keewaydin,
> To the islands of the Blessed,
> To the kingdom of Ponemah,
> To the land of the Hereafter.

## MACKINAC ISLAND.

Mackinac Island is the next point made for when leaving Sault Ste. Marie, and all who have ever visited this favored spot of nature are ceaseless in its praise. It is among the grandest and most romantic of islands, and every section of the country sends visitors annually. It is noted as a sanitarium for those suffering from hay-fever and bronchial affections. Great numbers visit this region to escape from or get relief of these maladies, while the surrounding country offers endless attractions to the tourist and sportsman. It is the central point of the three great lakes; it knows no land breeze, hence, the winds are always cool and refreshing. They no sooner cease blowing from Lake Michigan than they come from Lake Huron, and Lake Superior is never behind. The island comprises 2,221 acres, of which the National Park contains 821, and the military reservation 103 acres. The scenery is unsurpassed, for nature seems to have exhausted herself in the manifold objects of interest which meet the eye in every direction, while an additional romance is added to this spot as having been the birthplace of Hiawatha, whom Longfellow has immortalized in verse. Mackinac may well be termed the Parnassus of America, and the Goddess Hygeia might well place her temple here, for it is one of the purest, clearest and most health-giving of atmospheres. This atmosphere is never sultry or malarious; living streams of pure water, cooled down to the temperature of forty-four degrees, gush from the lime rock precipices. Its cool air and pure water are just what are needed to bring back the glow of health to the faded cheek, and send the warm currents of life dancing through the system with youthful vigor.

The very best of hotel accommodation can be had here, the "Grand" being a most palatial house.

From Mackinac the return journey is commenced, the whole round trip occupying just seven days. This service is done by three superbly-equipped steamers, the "Pacific," the "Atlantic," and the "Baltic," which rank as A 1, and have accommodation for 150 to 250 passengers.

### THE CITY OF HAMILTON.

Hamilton, the "Ambitious City," forty miles from Toronto, is reached by the Southern Division of the Grand Trunk Railway. The city is built upon one of the steps or terraces which surround the lake, and which would appear at one time to have formed the immediate shore. Looking down from the elevation of the "Mountain," its streets slope away towards the lake and diminish in the distant perspective. The form of the harbor, closed in from the open water by the Burlington Beach, is clearly limned, and away to the left stretches the pretty valley in the midst of which can be seen the spires and chimneys of the little town of Dundas.

Hamilton is the very center of a remarkable grain-producing country; and the rapid increase of its population is remarkable. In 1841 the population was but 3,500, twenty years later it was under 20,000; while at the present time it exceeds 40,000. To-day this city produces one-thirty-fourth in value of all the manufactures in the Dominion of Canada, and consumes one-fourteenth of all the coal used in the province of Ontario. Dundurn Park, on the heights towards the edge of the bay, is a favorite resort, and there are many pleasant drives in the neighborhood.

### BURLINGTON BEACH.

Opposite to Hamilton, across the bay, is the famous Burlington Beach, with which constant communication is kept up by the company's suburban train service during the summer season.

The sweeping action of the easterly storms has in long centuries formed a narrow, continuous bank, or bar of sand, stretching from shore to shore, and varying from 600 to 1,000 feet in width. On the east the rollers of Lake Ontario toss their surge; to the west, protected by it, lie the placid waters of Burlington Bay, the harbor of Hamilton. Composed of clear, shingly pebbles and pure sharp sand, its five miles length of level beach resembles the sea-shore in its extent, and the distant blue horizon of the great lake, where the sails of passing vessels fade away and disappear beneath its edge, adds to the illusion. The railway runs along the crown of the bank between the separated waters; and near the swing-bridge over the canal, which has been cut through the bank to join the lake and harbor, is the pretty Burlington Beach Station. The un-rivaled situation and fresh and airy surroundings of this locality make it a very favorite resort, at which numerous visitors annually spend weeks in the summer. There is excellent fishing in the neighborhood. A fleet of row boats on the bay side gives plenty of scope for amusement; and to anyone fond of yachting, there is no more favorable place on the inland lakes.

## ANCASTER MINERAL SPRING.

On the Hamilton Mountain Range, nine miles from the City of Hamilton, and three and-a-half miles from the town of Dundas, are the Ancaster Mineral Spring and Mansion, a popular summer resort and sanitarium. The spring is situated in one of the most charming locations to be found in the whole Province of Ontario. Its altitude is over 600 feet above the level of Lake Ontario, and from the plateau on which the Mansion stands the view embraces a vast stretch of undulating country—hill and dale, mountain and valley, lake and stream—a panorama of nature's handiwork, that for picturesque beauty it would be difficult to equal. Those suffer-ing from rheumatism, malaria, asthma and lung troubles, will find immediate relief from the dryness and purity of such an elevated atmosphere, added to the magical qualities of the water. The Mansion is replete with every convenience; it is supplied from the home-farm, the gardens of which abound in fruit and vegetables. The ornamental grounds surrounding it, in the shape of spacious lawns, woodland avenues and.groves, are over thirty acres in ex-tent, and offer a quiet, pleasant and invigorating retreat to those in search of health. The drives in the neighborhood are of the most picturesque character, and comfortable conveyances with reliable drivers are at all times to be had.

## THE CITY OF ST. CATHARINES.

Thirty-three miles to the south of Toronto, and twelve miles from Niagara Falls, is the thriving city of St. Catharines, pleas-antly located on the Welland Canal. The surrounding country is very picturesque. The well-known mineral well of St. Catharines, whose water is of great value as a remedial agent, supplies on an average 130,000 gallons a day. Of these waters, a large quantity, partially evaporated, is sent out through the country. A second well similar to the first is also in use. St. Catharines has well been called the Saratoga of British North America; and its hotels are equal to any in the Province.

## PRESTON MINERAL BATHS.

Preston is one of the prettiest little towns in Western Canada, with its beautiful, cool, shady walks and drives, its lovely valleys, with the charming little River Speed flowing through it, until it reaches the Grand River. It has long been noted for its mineral springs. The remarkable curative qualities of the water, combined with its acknowledged recuperative powers, are amply testified to by numerous visitors from all parts of the American continent.

Preston is situated on the line of the Wellington, Grey & Bruce branch of the Grand Trunk. The grounds attached to the spring are tastefully laid out, and at the bathing-house baths can be had at any temperature, at any hour. This resort must commend itself to invalids in preference to any other in the country, from the fact of its being free from the excitement and noise so usual at such places in large towns and cities.

## WESTERN ONTARIO.

Progressing further West, the City of London is reached on this line, so called after its great namesake, and those who sigh for the original will find a lovely river called the Thames, a Hyde Park, a St. Paul's Church, and, if low spirits supervene on seeing that these are not quite so dingy as at home, they may cure their spleen by a conscientious course of White Sulphur baths, which the metropolis of Great Britain has not. These baths attract many invalids from a distance, and are very highly spoken of. London is a progressive, go-a-head city of some 30,000 to 40,000 inhabitants.

Other points of interest, all termini of various sections of the Grand Trunk system are Goderich, Kincardine and Southampton, all pleasantly situated on Lake Huron, and from which charming trips may be made—

> " Within the wilderness
> Of Huron, clasping those transparent bays,
> Those deeps of unimagined crystal where
> The bark canoe seems hung in middle air."

From Sarnia, which is separated from Port Huron by the River St. Clair, the Northwest Transportation Company's line of boats run to Sault Ste. Marie, and the upper lakes, calling at Port Arthur and Duluth. Connection is also made with these Steamers at Goderich and Kincardine, thriving towns on the lake shore.

Port Dover, a terminal point of a branch of the Grand Trunk, on Lake Erie, annually attracts large numbers on account of its excellent boating facilities and pleasant surroundings. Some of the best duck shooting to be had in the world may be enjoyed in this locality. There is one long promontory, twenty miles in length, which juts out into Lake Erie and is called Long Point. This ground has been taken by a club, who have a charter from the Ontario Government, enabling them to preserve the game. The headquarters of the club are situated several miles from the further end of the curious ridge of land and marsh which forms the territory which is the property of the members.  It is reached by steamer from Port Dover, and the voyager sees as he starts nothing but the blue horizon of the lake before him.  By and by dots are seen on the surface of the water, and on nearing them they are seen to be trees standing on the highest ground of Long Point. Far as the eye can see on either hand are great beds of high reeds; among these stands a little village, consisting of the sportsmen's huts, placed like the houses of the old lake-dwellers, on platforms supported on piles driven into the shallow water.  The platforms are connected by wooden causeways.

Further west is St. Thomas, dignified as a "City," and the growth of which in the last few years has been of a highly phe-nomenal character, indicative of that spirit of western enterprise so observable on the whole of this continent.

A pleasant place to spend the summer is Kingsville, Ont., on the shore of Lake Erie, which is reached by the Lake Erie, Essex & Detroit River R'y from Walkerville (a suburb of Windsor, just opposite Detroit), a distance of about 30 miles from Detroit.  A new summer hotel has lately been opened where tourists can obtain every comfort.

### THE CITY OF DETROIT.

Detroit, the chief city of Michigan, the oldest city by far in the west of the United States, and older than either Baltimore or Phil-adelphia, on the sea-board, was founded by the French of Canada, in 1670, as an outpost for the prosecution of the fur trade, on the bank of the river of its own name.  Its river-side location, its miles of well-shaded avenues, its perfectly paved streets, its level but raised site, and its many modern improvements, are not sur-passed by any city on the American Continent, and it is aptly named the "City of the Straits."  As late as 1830 the place con-tained only 2,222 inhabitants; but in 1840, the population had risen to 9,102; in 1850, it was 21,019; in 1870, 79,577, while at the present time it numbers upwards of 150,000.

The view of Detroit from the tower of the City Hall is of such beauty that it will well repay the trouble of climbing to that coin of vantage.  Stretching away in the distance, as far as the eye can reach, the various avenues which converge to the hall present the appearance of a vista of trees, interspersed with elegant and costly edifices.  The surrounding parks, the river scenery, the opposite shore of Canada, the many sails of the lake craft, the swift rush-ing hither and thither of a steam flotilla, all these and many other sights combine to form a vivid picture of American enterprise and progress.  Fort Wayne, a picturesque military post in the neigh-borhood is worthy of a visit, but the greatest charm of all lies in the beauties of Michigan Straits, "the like of which in all the States cannot be found."  Belle Isle Park is perfect in its way, and further up the river is Lake St. Clair, "one of the most beautiful bodies of water in the great chain of inland seas." Romantic bits of woodland, pretty villages and handsome villas dot its shores.

St. Clair Flats is a noted duck-shooting locality, at the mouth of the St. Clair river, twenty-seven miles from Detroit. It is an immense sheet of shallow water entirely overgrown with rice grass, through which the cool current of the water is constantly rushing. It is a splendid rendezvous for fish, which remain hard and firm through-out the warm weather. Perch and black bass abound, and pike, pickerel and mascalonge are numerous. The rice grass is also a natural feeding ground for ducks, as well as reed birds and snipe, and after September first the shooting is superb.

Star Island is a favorite resort for fishermen. The village of St. Clair, with its mineral springs, Port Huron, standing sentinel at the mouth of Lake Huron, with Sarnia opposite, on the Canadian shore, are all places of interest.

Within two or three hours' ride of Detroit are Orion Orchard and Walled Lake, both charming little inland resorts. The churches of Detroit are numerous, handsome and representative, beautiful edifices having been erected in every style of architecture and devoted to each form of worship.

## MOUNT CLEMENS MINERAL SPRINGS.

Within easy access of Detroit, and on the line of the Grand Trunk Railway, are the far-famed Mount Clemens Mineral Springs and Baths. These waters have been so thoroughly tested that no doubt remains as to their true value in the treatment of disease. The most remarkable cures, some even bordering on the miraculous, have been effected by bathing in these waters. Thousands of in-valids have found relief when every other known remedy had failed. These springs are of a saline-sulphur nature, but hold in solution numerous other ingredients of great medicinal value.

## BUFFALO,

The Queen City of the Lakes, situated at the foot of Lake Erie, and the head of the Niagara River and Erie Canal, and distant from Niagara Falls 22 miles, is a charming city of upwards of 250,000 inhabitants.

The lower portion of the city, near the railway depots, is devoted principally to extensive manufacturing establishments, coal docks, etc., but Buffalo's attraction for tourists is in the handsome avenues, lined with elegant residences with well-kept lawns, fine public build-ings and hotels, and grand system of parks. There are over 70 miles of Buffalo streets paved with asphalt. There are many pleasure resorts along the beautiful Niagara River. Buffalo's com-merce is immense; over 118,000,000 bushels of grain were received in 1889. It is the largest coal distributing point in the world, and, with Tonawanda, the greatest lumber center. The second largest cattle market and largest sheep market. It has 43 elevators, 2,500 manufacturing establishments, and in *unparalelled* possession of more than *660 miles* of railroad tracks within the city limits. There are a dozen or more trains daily to Niagara Falls, and the run is made in 50 minutes.

## CHICAGO.

Chicago, the western terminus of the Grand Trunk system, is the most remarkable city in the world for its rapid growth. The name is of Indian origin, signifying "wild onion," and the place was first settled in 1831, prior to which it was a mere frontier post; in 1832 it contained about a dozen families, besides the officers and soldiers in Fort Dearborn. The town was organized by the election of a board of trustees, August 10, 1833. The population in 1833 was 3,265; in 1840 it was 4,470; in 1850 it was 29,963; in 1860 it was 109,260; in 1870 it was 298,977; in 1880 it was 503,185; while now it is computed at between 1,100,000 and 1,200,000. The city is built on a plain on the western shore of Lake Michigan, at the mouth of the Chicago river, which latter with its two branches divides the city into three parts, called the north, south and west divisions. The city is regularly laid out, the principal avenues running parallel with the lake shore ; the streets are wide and regularly built, and are generally well paved. Few cities boast of finer private residences, and since the fire of October, 1871, which destroyed property to the value of over $200,000,000, splendid buildings have been erected for business purposes. Chicago is supplied with an abundance of pure water from Lake Michigan by a process which is one of the wonders of modern engineering skill. Two cylindrical brick tunnels, the one six feet and the other seven feet in diameter, starting from the shore at different points, extend a distance of two miles under the lake, and meet in an immense crib, inclosing a grated cylinder, through which the water descends into them in a stream as unfailing as the lake itself. These tunnels cost over $1,500,000, while the water-works altogether have cost more than $5,000,000.

Chicago is one of the largest grain markets in the world, and is the center of speculation in that commodity, as well as in hogs and live-stock.

Thus on paper we have traversed the chief points of interest reached by the Grand Trunk System, but the reality and enjoyment of these varied scenes paralyze the pen of description, and in order to be fully realized must be personally visited, while the refrain of each and all will be, —

"I've really had a pleasant visit here,
And mean to come again, another year."

# GENERAL INFORMATION.

THE Tourist Fares shown on the following pages cover only the principal resorts reached by the lines of this Company and its connections. If trips from or to other points, or additional routes are required, fares will be furnished on application at any ticket office of the Company.

The Tourist Tickets by routes given herein are on sale at the City Ticket Offices of the Grand Trunk Railway Company at the following places:—

| | | | |
|---|---|---|---|
| Detroit, Mich. | | Peterboro, - Ont. | |
| London, - Ont. | | Belleville, " | |
| St. Thomas, " | | Kingston, " | |
| Woodstock, " | | Brockville, " | |
| Stratford, " | | Prescott, " | |
| Brantford, " | | Ottawa, " | |
| Guelph, " | | Ogdensburg, N. Y. | |
| Hamilton, " | | Montreal, Que. | |
| Buffalo, N. Y. | | " (Balmoral Hotel.) | |
| Niagara Falls, " | | " (Windsor Hotel.) | |
| Niagara Falls, Ont. | | Sherbrooke, Que. | |
| New York, - N. Y. | | Quebec, " | |
| Toronto, - Ont. | | Boston, Mass. | |
| St. Catharines, " | | Halifax, N. S. | |

Only routes marked ‡ are on sale at principal station ticket offices of the Company, but any of the tickets can be obtained by giving the station ticket agent (or the city ticket agent at places not named above) a few days notice.

Where the letters "R. W." appear against Round Trip Tours, going one way and returning the other, it is to be understood that they can be reversed at the time of purchase, if more convenient to the Tourist.

Tourist tickets are on sale from June 1st to September 30th, and, unless otherwise specified, are available for travel until November 1st of the year in which issued. * Stop-over privileges will be allowed as follows :—

**Adirondack Railway.**
> (See D. & H. C. Co.'s R. R.)

**Bennington & Rutland R. R.**
> Stop-over checks good for thirty days issued upon application to conductor.

**Boston & Albany R. R.**
> Stop-over allowed for ten days on notice to conductor.

**Boston & Maine R. R.**
> Stop-over for ten days allowed at any station (except between Salem or Reading and Boston) on notice to conductor.

**Canada Atlantic Railway.**
> Stop-over allowed on notice to conductor.

* NOTE—It should be understood that the stop-over privileges extended by the several lines (as noted above) require passenger to take such trains or boats as make stops regularly at the desired stopping-place. These stop-over privileges do not apply on tickets limited to continuous passage.

**Canadian Pacific Railway.**
Stop-over allowed on notice to conductor.

**Central Vermont R. R.**
Stop-over allowed at any station on notice to conductor.

**Champlain Transportation Co. (Str. on Lake Champlain).**
Stop-over allowed on notice to purser.

**Chateaugay R. R.**
Stop-over allowed on notice to conductor.

**Cheshire R. R.**
Stop-over checks good for thirty days issued on notice to conductor.

**Concord & Montreal R. R.**
Stop-over allowed at any station on notice to conductor.

**Connecticut River R. R.**
Stop-over allowed at any station on notice to conductor.

**Day Line Steamers (on Hudson River).**
Stop-over allowed on notice to purser.

**Delaware & Hudson Canal Co.'s R. R.**
Stop-over allowed at any station on notice to conductor.

**Detroit & Cleveland Steam Nav. Co.**
Stop-over allowed at Oakland Hotel, Alpena and Mackinac on notice to purser.

**Empress of India Steamer.**
No intermediate stops.

**Fall River Line (Old Colony S. B. Line).**
Stop-over allowed at Newport, R. I., in either direction, on notice to purser.

**Fitchburg R. R.**
Stop-over allowed on notice to conductor.

**Grand Trunk Railway.**
Stop-over allowed at any station on notice to conductor.

**Great Northern Transit Co.'s Steamers.**
Stop-over of fifteen days allowed on notice to purser

**Hudson River Day Line.**
Stop-over allowed on notice to purser.

**Intercolonial Railway.**
Stop-over allowed at any station on notice to conductor

**International Steamship Line.**
Stop-over allowed at any landing.

**Lake George Steamboat Co.**
Stop-over allowed on notice to purser.

**Lake Michigan & Lake Superior Transportation Co.**
Stop-over allowed at all points except Milwaukee.

**Lake Superior Transit Co.**
Stop-over of fifteen days allowed at any intermediate point.

**Maine Central R. R.**
Stop-over allowed at any station on notice to conductor, except on excursion tickets which are limited to continuous passage in each direction.

**Michigan Central R. R.**
Stop-over allowed.

**Montpelier & Wells River R. R.**
Stop-over allowed at any station on notice to conductor.

**Mt. Washington Railway.**
No intermediate stops.

**Muskoka & Georgian Bay Navigation Co.**
Stop-over allowed.

**New Brunswick Railway.**
Stop-over allowed at principal points.

**New London Northern R. R.**
No stop-over privileges allowed.

**New York Central & Hudson River R. R.**
Stop-over allowed at any station on notice to conductor.

**New York, Lake Erie & Western R. R.**
Stop-over allowed on notice to conductor.

**New York & New England R. R.**
Stop-over allowed on notice to conductor.

**New York, New Haven & Hartford R. R.**
Stop-over allowed on notice to conductor.

**Niagara Navigation Co.**
Stop-over allowed on notice to purser.

**Northern Adirondack R. R.**
Stop-over allowed at any station on notice to conductor.

**Northern (N. H.) R. R.**
Stop-over allowed on notice to conductor.

**North-West Transportation Co.'s Steamers.**
Stop-over allowed on notice to purser.

**Norwich Line (Norwich & N. Y. Transportation Line).**
Steamers make no intermediate landings.

**Old Colony R. R.**
One stop-over allowed at any station on notice to conductor.

**Old Colony Steamboat Line (Fall River Line).**
Stop-over allowed at Newport R. I., in either direction, on notice to purser.

**Ottawa River Navigation Co.**
Stop-over allowed at Carillon, Grenville and Caledonia Springs—at other points on notice to purser.

**People's (Night) Line Steamers (on Hudson River).**
Steamers make no intermediate landing.

**Portland, Mt. Desert & Machias Steamboat Line.**
Stop-over allowed at any landing on notice to purser.

**Portland Steam Packet Line.**
Steamers make no intermediate landings.

**Profile & Franconia Notch R. R.**
Stop-over allowed at any station on notice to conductor.

**Providence Line.**
Steamers make no intermediate landing.

**Providence & Worcester R. R.**
No stop-over privileges.

**Quebec & Lake St. John Railway.**
Stop-over allowed on notice to conductor.

**Richelieu & Ontario Navigation Co.**
Stop-over allowed on notice to purser.

**St. Johnsbury & Lake Champlain R. R.**
Stop-over allowed on notice to conductor.

**Stonington Line (Providence & Stonington S. S. Line).**
Steamers make no intermediate landing.

**Vermont Valley R. R.**
Stop-over allowed at any station on notice to conductor.

**Whitefield & Jefferson R. R.**
Stop-over allowed at any station on notice to conductor.

**York Harbor & Beach R. R.**
(See Boston & Maine.)

Transfers between stations are not included in these Tourist Ticket unless specially noted. There are not many points where transfers are required and they are mostly places at which passengers would wish to stop over.

Tickets which read optional by boat or rail must be used to destination of coupon on the rail if journey is commenced on rail, or on the boat if journey is commenced on boat. Passengers can change from boat to rail, or *vice versa* only at points from or to which coupons read.

Many of the steamer lines, and some of the railroads in the White Mountain District, cease running or make irregular trips prior to the close of the Tourist season, Nov. 1st, and passengers should consult the advertisements of each Company and be guided accordingly.

When it is desired to make one or more of the side trips shown herein tickets covering the transportation should be purchased at starting point, as in some cases the cost of trip will be higher when ticket is purchased at junction point.

Meals and berths are extra on all steamer lines, unless especially noted to the contrary.

Children between five and twelve years of age will be charged half fare; over twelve years, full fare.

Tickets are not transferable, and if unused in whole or part, application should be made to the General Passenger Agent for refund of value.

---

## CHOICE OF ROUTES TO TORONTO.

Purchasers of tickets to Kingston, and points east, optional rail or steamer from Toronto or Kingston to Montreal, have the choice of the following routes to Toronto:—

From DETROIT—                                          FOR

1. Grand Trunk Railway to Toronto........... ................T 5
2. { Grand Trunk Railway to Suspension Bridge (Niagara Falls)..T 5
   { Grand Trunk Railway to Toronto...............................T 6
3. { Grand Trunk Railway to Suspension Bridge (Niagara Falls)..T 5
   { Grand Trunk Railway to Port Dalhousie................... ..T
   { Steamer "Empress of India" to Toronto .....................T
4. { Grand Trunk Railway to Suspension Bridge (Niagara Falls)..T 5
   { New York Central & Hudson River R.R. to Lewiston..........T12
   { Niagara Navigation Co.'s steamers to Toronto ................T 1
5. { Grand Trunk Railway to Suspension Bridge (Niagara Falls)..T 5
   { Michigan Central R.R. to Niagara........................ ......T10
   { Niagara Navigation Co.'s steamers to Toronto................T 5

From PORT HURON—

1. Grand Trunk Railway to Toronto........................T 7
2. { Grand Trunk Railway to Suspension Bridge (Niagara Falls)..T 7
   { Grand Trunk Railway to Toronto...............................T 6
3. { Grand Trunk Railway to Suspension Bridge (Niagara Falls)..T 7
   { Grand Trunk Railway to Port Dalhousie .....................T
   { Steamer "Empress of India" to Toronto.....................T
4. { Grand Trunk Railway to Suspension Bridge (Niagara Falls)..T 7
   { New York Central & Hudson River R.R. to Lewiston........T12
   { Niagara Navigation Co.'s steamers to Toronto................T11
5. { Grand Trunk Railway to Suspension Bridge (Niagara Falls)..T 7
   { Michigan Central R.R. to Niagara .................... .....T10
   { Niagara Navigation Co.'s steamers to Toronto ................T 5

Purchasers of tickets from Detroit or Port Huron to Montreal, ALL RAIL must take the Grand Trunk Railway direct to Toronto.

From LONDON—                                        FORM.

    1.  Grand Trunk Railway to Toronto..... ...... ........ T 76

From NIAGARA FALLS, N. Y.—

    1. { New York, Lake Erie & Western R.R. to Niagara Falls, Ont....T   1
        { Grand Trunk Railway to Toronto ...................... .........T 60

    2. { New York Central & Hudson River R.R. to Suspens'n Bridge..T   2
        { Grand Trunk Railway to Toronto......................... .........T 60

    3. { New York, Lake Erie & Western R.R. to Niagara Falls, Ont...T   1
        { Grand Trunk Railway to Port Dalhousie...................... T   3
        { Steamer " Empress of India " to Toronto. .... ...... .........T   4

    4. { New York Central & Hudson River R.R. to Suspens'n Bridge.T   2
        { Grand Trunk Railway to Port Dalhousie..................... T   3
        { Steamer "Empress of India" to Toronto............. ......T   4

    5. { New York Central & Hudson River R.R. to Suspens'n Bridge.T   2
        { Michigan Central R.R. to Niagara....................T102
        { Niagara Navigation Co.'s steamers to Toronto.............. T 59

    6. { New York, Lake Erie & Western R.R. to Niagara Falls, Ont...T   1
        { Michigan Central R. R. to Niagara............. ...........T102
        { Niagara Navigation Co.'s steamers to Toronto..... ..........T 59

---

# CHOICE OF ROUTES TO MONTREAL.

From **Detroit and Port Huron**:—On tickets sold at all-rail fares passengers will require to use Grand Trunk Railway direct to Montreal. On tickets sold at optional fares, passengers have choice of routes to Toronto as above.

From **London**:—Passengers wishing to make side trip from Hamilton to Suspension Bridge (Niagara Falls) and back will require to pay $2.35 for the privilege, in addition to the fares given in this book. except that they will not be charged more than the fares from Port Huron for optional tickets to same destination.

From **Niagara Falls**:—Passengers have the choice of routes to Toronto as above.

Routes from **Toronto** to **Montreal** are as follows:—           FORM.

    1.  Grand Trunk Railway to Montreal ........................T 32

        { Grand Trunk Railway to Kingston............................T 76
    2. { Grand Trunk R'y or Rich. & Ont. Nav. Co.'s Str. to Prescott...T 55
        { Grand Trunk R'y or Rich. & Ont. Nav. Co.'s Str. to Montreal..T 56

        { Grand Trunk R'y or Rich. & Ont. Nav. Co.'s Str. to Kingston..T   5
    3. { Grand Trunk R'y or Rich. & Ont. Nav. Co.'s Str. to Prescott...T 55
        { Grand Trunk R'y or Rich. & Ont. Nav. Co.'s Str. to Montreal..T 56

According to fare paid.

# ROUTES AND FARES.

*One-Way Trips.—Eastbound.*

## To ALEXANDRIA BAY, N. Y.

Route S 1--

Choice of routes to Toronto (see pages 84 and 85).

|  | FORM. |
|---|---|
| Grand Trunk Railway to Gananoque Junction | T 76 |
| Thousand Islands Railway to Gananoque | T 7 |
| Deseronto Navigation Co.'s steamer to Alexandria Bay | T 8 |

Fares:—

| | | | |
|---|---|---|---|
| Detroit | $12.45 | Niagara Falls | $6.85 |
| Port Huron | 10.95 | Buffalo | 7.35 |
| London | 9.15 | Toronto | 5.85 |
| Hamilton | 6.85 | Kingston | 1.00 |

Route S 2—

Choice of routes to Toronto (see pages 84 and 85).

| | |
|---|---|
| Grand Trunk Railway or R. & O. N. Co.'s steamer to Kingston | T 5 |
| Richelieu & Ontario Navigation Co.'s steamer to Alexandria Bay | T 6 |

Fares:—

| | | | |
|---|---|---|---|
| Detroit | $12.45 | Hamilton | $6.85 |
| Port Huron | 10.95 | Niagara Falls | 6.85 |
| London | 9.15 | Buffalo | 7.35 |

## To BANGOR, Me.

Route S 3—

Choice of routes to Montreal (see page 85).

| | |
|---|---|
| Grand Trunk Railway to Portland | T 32 |
| Maine Central Railroad to Bangor | T 52 |

Fares.—

| | | | |
|---|---|---|---|
| Detroit | *$23.50 | Toronto | $21.50 |
| Port Huron | * 23.50 | Kingston | 16.75 |
| London | * 23.50 | Brockville | 15.25 |
| Hamilton | 22.70 | Ottawa | 15.00 |
| Niagara Falls | 23.00 | Montreal | 11.50 |
| Buffalo | 23.50 | Quebec | † 12.50 |

## To BAR HARBOR, Me.

Route S 4—

Same as Route S 3 to Portland.

| | |
|---|---|
| Maine Central Railroad to Bar Harbor | T 52 |

Fares:—

| | | | | |
|---|---|---|---|---|
| Detroit | *$25.50 | Toronto | $23.50 | ¶$22.50 |
| Port Huron | * 25.50 | Kingston | 18.75 | ¶ 17.75 |
| London | * 25.50 | Brockville | 17.25 | ¶ 16.25 |
| Hamilton | 24.70 | ¶$23.70 | Ottawa | 17.00 ¶ 16.00 |
| Niagara Falls | 25.00 | ¶ 24.00 | Montreal | 13.50 ¶ 12.50 |
| Buffalo | 25.50 | ¶ 24.50 | Quebec | †14.50 ¶ 13.50 |

*All rail to Montreal. For tickets optional rail or steamer, Kingston to Prescott and Prescott to Montreal, add 75c. from Detroit, and for tickets optional rail or steamer, Toronto to Kingston, Kingston to Prescott and Prescott to Montreal, add $1.60 from Detroit, 20c. from Port Huron and 10c. from London.

†Via Grand Trunk direct, not coming into Montreal.

¶Limited continuous passage east of Portland.

## To BAR HARBOR, Me.—*Continued.*

Route S 5—

    Same as Route S 3 to Portland.

    Portland, Mt. Desert & Machias Steamboat Co. to Bar Harbor . . . . . . . . . . . . . . .T107 FORM.

    Fares :—

| | | | |
|---|---|---|---|
| Detroit | *$25.50 | Toronto | $20.75 |
| Port Huron | * 25.50 | Kingston | 16.00 |
| London | * 24.05 | Brockville | 14.50 |
| Hamilton | 21.95 | Ottawa | 14.25 |
| Niagara Falls | 22.50 | Montreal | 10.75 |
| Buffalo | 23.00 | Quebec | † 11.75 |

## To BOSTON, Mass.

· Route S 6—

    Choice of routes to Montreal (see page 85).

    Grand Trunk Railway to Portland and Gorham . . . . . . . . . . . . . . . . . . . . . . } X 15

    Boston & Maine Railroad to Boston . . . . . . . . . . . . . . . . . . . . . . . . . . }

    Fares :—

| | | | |
|---|---|---|---|
| Detroit | *$23.00 | Toronto | $18.00 |
| Port Huron | * 22.90 | Kingston | 13.90 |
| London | * 21.30 | Brockville | 12.35 |
| Hamilton | 19.20 | Ottawa | 12.00 |
| Niagara Falls | 19.50 | Montreal | 10.50 |
| Buffalo | 20.00 | Quebec | † 11.00 |

‡ Route S 7—

    Choice of routes to Montreal (see page 85).

    Grand Trunk Railway or R. & O. N. Co.'s Steamer to Quebec . . . . . . . . . }

    Grand Trunk Railway to Gorham and Portland . . . . . . . . . . . . . . . . . . } X 11

    Boston & Maine Railroad to Boston . . . . . . . . . . . . . . . . . . . . . . }

    Fares :—

| | | | |
|---|---|---|---|
| Detroit | *$26.50 | Toronto | $21.50 |
| Port Huron | * 26.40 | Kingston | 16.75 |
| London | * 24.80 | Brockville | 15.25 |
| Hamilton | 22.70 | Ottawa | 14.00 |
| Niagara Falls | 23.00 | Montreal | 11.50 |
| Buffalo | 23.50 | | |

‡ Route S 8—

    Choice of routes to Montreal (see page 85).

    Grand Trunk Railway to St. Johns . . . . . . . . . . . . . . . . . . . . . . }

    Central Vermont Railroad to St. Albans and White River Junction . . }

    Boston & Maine Railroad to Concord . . . . . . . . . . . . . . . . . . . . } X 16

    Concord & Montreal Railroad to Nashua . . . . . . . . . . . . . . . . . . }

    Boston & Maine Railroad to Boston . . . . . . . . . . . . . . . . . . }

    Fares :—

| | | | |
|---|---|---|---|
| Detroit | *$23.00 | Toronto | $18.00 |
| Port Huron | * 22.90 | Kingston | 13.90 |
| London | * 21.30 | Brockville | 12.40 |
| Hamilton | 19.20 | Ottawa | 12.00 |
| Niagara Falls | 19.50 | Montreal | 9.00 |
| Buffalo | 20.00 | Quebec | 11.00 |

Route S 9—

    Choice of routes to Montreal (see page 85).

    Grand Trunk Railway to St. Johns . . . . . . . . . . . . . . . . . . . . . . . . . . . . . . . . .T 11

    Central Vermont Railroad to St. Albans, Burlington and Windsor . . . . . .T 12

    Vermont Valley Railroad to Bellows Falls . . . . . . . . . . . . . . . . . . . . . . .T 13

    Cheshire Railroad to Fitchburg . . . . . . . . . . . . . . . . . . . . . . . . . . . . . .T 14

    Fitchburg Railroad to Boston . . . . . . . . . . . . . . . . . . . . . . . . . . . . . . . . .T 15

    Fares :—Same as Route S 8.

    *All rail to Montreal. For tickets optional rail or steamer, Kingston to Prescott and Prescott to Montreal, add 75c. from Detroit; and for tickets optional rail or steamer, Toronto to Kingston, Kingston to Prescott, and Prescott to Montreal, add $1.60 from Detroit, 20c. from Port Huron, and 10c. from London.

    †Via Grand Trunk direct, not coming into Montreal.

# To BOSTON.—*Continued.*

Route S 10

| | | FORM. |
|---|---|---|
| Choice of routes to Montreal (see page 85). | | |
| Grand Trunk Railway to Rouse's Point....... ........ ...........T | | 16 |
| Delaware & Hudson Railroad to Plattsburg.............. ...........T | | 17 |
| Champlain Transportation Company's Steamer to Burlington..........T | | 18 |
| Central Vermont Railroad to Windsor............. ...............T | | 12 |
| Vermont Valley Railroad to Bellows Falls .............................T | | 13 |
| Cheshire Railroad to Fitchburg...................................T | | 14 |
| Fitchburg Railroad to Boston ...................................T | | 15 |

Fares :—

| Detroit ..............*$24.25 | Toronto ...... ......$19.25 |
|---|---|
| Port Huron ...........* 24.15 | Kingston .............. 13.90 |
| London .......... * 22.55 | Brockville ........... 12.40 |
| Hamilton .... ...... 20.45 | Ottawa .............. 12.00 |
| Niagara Falls ....... 20.75 | Montreal............ 9.25 |
| Buffalo............... 21.25 | Quebec ............. 11.75 |

Route S 11—

| Choice of routes to Montreal (see page 85). | | |
|---|---|---|
| Grand Trunk Railway to Rouse's Point...................... ........T | | 16 |
| Delaware & Hudson Railroad to Plattsburg......................T | | 17 |
| Champ. Trans. Co.'s Str. or D. & H. Railroad to Fort Ticonderoga .......T | | 19 |
| Delaware & Hudson Railroad to Saratoga....................T | | 20 |
| Delaware & Hudson Railroad to Rutland.....................T | | 21 |
| Central Vermont Railroad to Bellows' Falls ......................T | | 12 |
| Cheshire Railroad to Fitchburg ..............................T | | 14 |
| Fitchburg Railroad to Boston ................................T | | 15 |

Fares :—

| Detroit ... .......*$26.65 | Toronto...............$ 21.65 |
|---|---|
| Port Huron...........* 26.55 | Kingston ............. 16.90 |
| London........ ....* 24.95 | Brockville ........... 15.40 |
| Hamilton ............ 22.85 | Ottawa .. ........... 14.15 |
| Niagara Falls ........ 23.15 | Montreal............. 11.65 |
| Buffalo............... 23.65 | Quebec.............. 13.65 |

Route S 12—

| Choice of routes to Montreal (see page 85). | | |
|---|---|---|
| Grand Trunk Railway to Rouse's Point.......................T | | 16 |
| Delaware & Hudson Railroad to Plattsburg......................T | | 17 |
| Champlain Trans. Co.'s Str. or D. & H. Railroad to Fort Ticonderoga...T | | 19 |
| Delaware & Hudson Railroad to Baldwin....................T | | 20 |
| Lake George Steamer to Caldwell.............................T | | 22 |
| Delaware & Hudson Railroad to Saratoga.....................T | | 21 |
| Same as Route S 11 to Boston. | | |

Fares :—

| Detroit..... .......*$28.65 | Toronto .............$ 23.65 |
|---|---|
| Port Huron ....... .* 28.55 | Kingston............. 18.90 |
| London......... * 26.95 | Brockville ........... 17.40 |
| Hamilton............ 24.85 | Ottawa .............. 16.15 |
| Niagara Falls........ 25.15 | Montreal............. 13.65 |
| Buffalo ........... ... 25.65 | Quebec ........... .. 15.65 |

Route S 13—

| Same as Route S 12 to Caldwell. | | |
|---|---|---|
| Delaware & Hudson Railroad to Saratoga, Troy.......................T | | 21 |
| Fitchburg Railroad to Boston ..................................T | | 15 |

Fares same as Route S 12.

Route S 14—

| Same as Route S 11 to Fort Ticonderoga. | | |
|---|---|---|
| Delaware & Hudson Railroad to Saratoga, Albany......................T | | 20 |
| Boston & Albany Railroad to Boston................................T | | 23 |

Fares same as Route S 11.

*All rail to Montreal  For tickets optional rail or steamer, Kingston to Prescott and Prescott to Montreal, add 75c. from Detroit, and for tickets optional rail or steamer, Toronto to Kingston, Kingston to Prescott and Prescott to Montreal, add $1.60 from Detroit, 20c. from Port Huron, and 10c. from London.

# To BOSTON.—*Continued.*

**Route S 15—**

    Choice of routes to Montreal (see page 85).

    FORM.

    Grand Trunk Railway to St. Johns.......................... T 11
    Central Vermont Railroad to St. Albans, Burlington. ................. T 12
    Champlain Transportation Co. to Fort Ticonderoga ............. T 18
    Delaware & Hudson Railroad to Baldwin...................... T 20
    Lake George Steamer to Caldwell ........................... T 22
    Delaware & Hudson Railroad to Saratoga, Troy................ T 21
    Fitchburg Railroad to Boston .............................. T 15

    **Fares same as Route S 12.**

**Route S 16—**

    Same as Route S 12 to Caldwell.
    Delaware & Hudson Railroad to Saratoga, Albany.............. T 21
    Boston & Albany Railroad to Boston......................... T 23

    **Fares same as Route S 12.**

**Route S 17—**

    Choice of routes to Montreal (see page 85).
    Grand Trunk Railway to Rouse's Point ...................... T 16
    Delaware & Hudson Railroad to Plattsburg.................. T 17
    Champ. Trans. Co.'s Steamer or D. & H. Railroad to Ft. Ticonderoga.... T 19
    Delaware & Hudson Railroad to Baldwin .................... T 20
    Lake George Steamer to Caldwell .......................... T 22
    Delaware & Hudson Railroad to Saratoga, Albany............. T 21
    People's Line Steamers to New York........................ T 71
    Sound Line Steamer to Boston ............................. T126

    **Fares:—**

| Detroit | *$29.95 | Toronto | $ 24.95 |
|---|---|---|---|
| Port Huron | * 29.85 | Kingston | 20.20 |
| London | * 28.25 | Brockville | 18.70 |
| Hamilton | 26.15 | Ottawa | 17.45 |
| Niagara Falls | 26.45 | Montreal | 14.95 |
| Buffalo | 26.95 | Quebec | 16.95 |

**Route S 18—**

    Choice of routes to Montreal (see page 85).
    Grand Trunk Railway to St. Johns............................ T 11
    Central Vermont Railroad to St. Albans, Burlington............... T 12
    Champ. Trans. Co.'s Steamer to Fort Ticonderoga............. T 18
    Delaware and Hudson Railroad to Baldwin ................... T 20
    Lake George Steamer to Caldwell .......................... T 22
    Delaware & Hudson Railroad to Saratoga, Albany............. T 21
    Day Line Steamer to New York............................. T 72
    Sound Line Steamer to Boston ............................. T126

    **Fares:—**

| Detroit | *$30.60 | Toronto | $ 25.60 |
|---|---|---|---|
| Port Huron | * 30.50 | Kingston | 20.85 |
| London | * 28.90 | Brockville | 19.35 |
| Hamilton | 26.80 | Ottawa | 18.10 |
| Niagara Falls | 27.10 | Montreal | 15.60 |
| Buffalo | 27.60 | Quebec | 17.60 |

**;Route S 19—**

    Choice of routes to Montreal (see page 85).
    Grand Trunk Railway to St. Johns ......
    Central Vermont Railroad to St. Albans, Montpelier
    Montpelier & Wells River Railroad to Wells River
    Concord & Montreal Railroad to Bethlehem Jct.
    Profile & Franconia Notch Railroad to Profile House
    Profile & Franconia Notch Railroad to Bethlehem Jct............ } X 227
    Concord & Montreal Railroad to Fabyans
    Maine Central Railroad to Crawford House
    Maine Central Railroad to Fabyans.........
    Concord & Montreal Railroad to Nashua....
    Boston & Maine Railroad to Boston....................

*All rail to Montreal. For tickets optional rail or steamer, Kingston to Prescott and Prescott to Montreal, add 75c. from Detroit; and for tickets optional rail or steamer, Toronto to Kingston, Kingston to Prescott, and Prescott to Montreal, add $1.60 from Detroit, 20c. from Port Huron, and 10c. from London.

# To BOSTON.—*Continued.*

Fares :- -

| | | | |
|---|---|---|---|
| Detroit | *$29.10 | Toronto | $ 24.10 |
| Port Huron | * 29.00 | Kingston | 19.35 |
| London | * 27.40 | Brockville | 17.85 |
| Hamilton | 25.30 | Ottawa | 16.60 |
| Niagara Falls | 25.60 | Montreal | 14.10 |
| Buffalo | 26.10 | Quebec | 16.60 |

‡Route S 20—

Choice of routes to Montreal (see page 85).                          **FORM.**
Grand Trunk Railway to St. Johns ......................................
Central Vermont Railroad to St. Albans, Montpelier .................
Montpelier & Wells River Railroad to Wells River. ..............⎫
Concord & Montreal Railroad to Fabyans ........................⎬ X 280
Maine Central Railroad to North Conway ........................
Boston & Maine Railroad to Boston ...........................⎭

Fares :—

| | | | |
|---|---|---|---|
| Detroit | *$25.50 | Toronto | $20.50 |
| Port Huron | * 25.40 | Kingston | 15.75 |
| London | * 23.80 | Brockville | 14.25 |
| Hamilton | 21.70 | Ottawa | 13.00 |
| Niagara Falls | 22.00 | Montreal | 10.50 |
| Buffalo | 22.50 | Quebec | 13.00 |

Route S 21—

Choice of routes to Montreal (see page 85).
Grand Trunk Railway to St. Johns........................................T 11
Central Vermont Railroad to St. Albans, Montpelier ........T 12
Montpelier & Wells River Railroad to Wells River ...........T 24
Concord & Montreal Railroad to Bethlehem Jct...............T 25
Profile & Franconia Notch Railroad to Profile House.........T 26
Profile & Franconia Notch Railroad to Bethlehem Jct........T 26
Concord & Montreal Railroad to Fabyans and Base........ T 25
Mount Washington Railway to Summit......................T 41
Milliken's Stage to Glen House......................T 40
Milliken's Stage to Gorham ....................T 79
Grand Trunk Railway to Portland ...........................T 74
Boston & Maine Railroad to Boston................................T 50

Fares :—

| | | | |
|---|---|---|---|
| Detroit | *$37.75 | Toronto | $32.75 |
| Port Huron | * 37.65 | Kingston | 28.00 |
| London | * 36.05 | Brockville | 26.50 |
| Hamilton | 33.95 | Ottawa | 25.25 |
| Niagara Falls | 34.25 | Montreal | 22.75 |
| Buffalo | 34.75 | Quebec | 25.25 |

Route S 22—

Choice of routes to Montreal (see page 85).
Grand Trunk Railway to Sherbrooke ........................T 32
Boston & Maine Railroad to Newport and White River Jct .......T 33
Boston & Maine Railroad to Concord.......... T 35
Concord & Montreal Railroad to Nashua ..................T 34
Boston & Maine Railroad to Boston.............................. T 29

Fares same as Route S 8.

Route S 23—

Choice of routes to Montreal (see page 85).
Grand Trunk Railway to Sherbrooke ..........................T 32
Boston & Maine Railroad to Newport and Wells River............T 33
Concord & Montreal Railroad to Nashua ........................T 25
Boston & Maine Railroad to Boston.............................T 29

Fares same as Route S 8.

*All rail to Montreal. For tickets optional rail or steamer, Kingston to Prescott and Prescott to Montreal, add 75c. from Detroit, and for tickets optional rail or steamer, Toronto to Kingston, Kingston to Prescott and Prescott to Montreal, add $1.60 from Detroit, 20c. from Port Huron, and 10c. from London.

# To BOSTON.—*Continued.*

**Route S 24—**

Choice of routes to Montreal (see page 85).       FORM.
Grand Trunk Railway or R. & O. N. Co.'s Steamer to Quebec . ..........T 36
Ferry to Levis.................... ......... .............. ..............T 37
Grand Trunk Railway to Sherbrooke. ...... ... .................. .......T 27
Boston & Maine Railroad to Newport, Wells River and White River Jct.T 33
Boston & Maine Railroad to Concord ... .......................... .....T 35
Concord & Montreal Railroad to Nashua .... .... ......... ...........T 34
Boston & Maine Railroad to Boston.... ......... ................. .....T 29

**Fares same as Route S 7.**

**Route S 25—**

Same as S 24 to Sherbrooke.
Boston & Maine Railroad to Newport and Wells River ...............T 33
Concord & Montreal Railroad to Nashua..... .......................T 25
Boston & Maine Railroad to Boston........ .........................T 29

**Fares same as Route S 7.**

**Route S 26—**

Choice of routes to Montreal (see page 85).
Grand Trunk Railway or R. & O. N. Co.'s Steamer to Quebec .........T 36
Ferry to Levis.................................................. .......T 37
Grand Trunk Railway to Sherbrooke.........................T 27
Boston & Maine Railroad to St. Johnsbury .......................T 33
St. Johnsbury & Lake Champlain Railroad to Lunenburg .............T 38
Maine Central Railroad to Bethlehem Jct........................T 28
Profile & Franconia Notch Railroad to Profile House ............T 26
Profile & Franconia Notch Railroad to Bethlehem Jct.............T 26
Maine Central Railroad to Crawford House.......................T 28
Maine Central Railroad to Fabyans ....  .......................T 28
Concord & Montreal Railroad to Base............................T 25
Mount Washington Railway to Summit .....  .....................T 41
Milliken's Stage to Glen House........  ........ ...............T 40
Milliken's Stage to Gorham. ...  ..............................T 79
Grand Trunk Railway to Portland... ...  .......................T 74
Boston & Maine Railroad to Boston..............................T 50

**Fares :—**

| | | | |
|---|---|---|---|
| Detroit...... .........*$41.85 | Toronto..............$ 36.85 |
| Port Huron . ........* 41.75 | Kingston ............ 32.10 |
| London ...........* 40.15 | Brockville .......... 30.60 |
| Hamilton ............ 38.05 | Ottawa ............ 29.35 |
| Niagara Falls........ 38.35 | Montreal ........... 26.85 |
| Buffalo ... ........... 38.85 | Quebec ...... ........† 24.35 |

**Route S 27—**

Choice of routes to Montreal (see page 85).
Grand Trunk Railway or R. & O. N. Co.'s Steamer to Quebec ......... T 36
Ferry to Levis......................................................T 37
Grand Trunk Railway to Sherbrooke.................................T 27
Boston & Maine Railroad to Newport, St. Johnsbury....................T 33
St. Johnsbury & Lake Champlain Railroad to Lunenburg .............T 38
Maine Central Railroad to North Conway............................T 28
Boston & Maine Railroad to Boston.................................T 30

**Fares :—**

| | | | |
|---|---|---|---|
| Detroit..............*$29.00 | Toronto..............$ 24.00 |
| Port Huron ... ......* 28.90 | Kingston ............ 19.25 |
| London ...............* 27.30 | Brockville .......... 17.75 |
| Hamilton............. 25.20 | Ottawa ............ 16.50 |
| Niagara Falls........ 25.50 | Montreal......... .... 14.00 |
| Buffalo ............... 26.00 | Quebec.............† 11.50 |

*All rail to Montreal. For tickets optional rail or steamer, Kingston to Prescott and Prescott to Montreal, add 75c. from Detroit; and for tickets optional rail or steamer, Toronto to Kingston, Kingston to Prescott, and Prescott to Montreal, add $1.60 from Detroit, 20c. from Port Huron, and 10c. from London.
†Via Sherbrooke direct, not coming into Montreal.

## To BOSTON.—*Continued.*

Route S 28—
    Choice of routes to Montreal (see page 85).         FORM.

| | |
|---|---|
| Grand Trunk Railway to Groveton Jct | T 32 |
| Concord & Montreal Railroad to Nashua | T 25 |
| Boston & Maine Railroad to Boston | T 29 |

   Fares same as Route S 8.

Route S 29—
    Choice of routes to Montreal (see page 85).

| | |
|---|---|
| Grand Trunk Railway or R. & O. N. Co.'s Steamer to Quebec | T 36 |
| Ferry to Levis | T 37 |
| Grand Trunk Railway to Groveton Jct | T 27 |
| Concord & Montreal Railroad to Nashua | T 25 |
| Boston & Maine Railroad to Boston | T 29 |

   Fares same as Route S 7.

Route S 30—
    Choice of routes to Montreal (see page 85).

| | |
|---|---|
| Grand Trunk Railway to Groveton Jct | T 32 |
| Concord & Montreal Railroad to Fabyans | T 25 |
| Concord & Montreal Railroad to Bethlehem Jct | T 25 |
| Profile & Franconia Notch Railroad to Profile House | T 26 |
| Profile & Franconia Notch Railroad to Bethlehem Jct | T 26 |
| Concord & Montreal Railroad to Nashua | T 25 |
| Boston & Maine Railroad to Boston | T 29 |

   Fares :—

| | | | |
|---|---|---|---|
| Detroit | *$28.50 | Toronto | $ 23.50 |
| Port Huron | * 28.40 | Kingston | 18.75 |
| London | * 26.80 | Brockville | 17.25 |
| Hamilton | 24.70 | Ottawa | 16.00 |
| Niagara Falls | 25.00 | Montreal | 13.50 |
| Buffalo | 25.50 | Quebec | † 14.50 |

Route S 31—
    Choice of routes to Montreal (see page 85).

| | |
|---|---|
| Grand Trunk Railway to Gorham | T 32 |
| Milliken's Stage to Glen House | T 79 |
| Milliken's Stage to Summit | T 39 |
| Mount Washington Railway to Base | T 41 |
| Concord & Montreal Railroad to Fabyans and Bethlehem Jct | T 25 |
| Profile & Franconia Notch Railroad to Profile House | T 26 |
| Stage to North Woodstock | T 79 |
| Concord & Montreal Railroad to Nashua | T 25 |
| Boston & Maine Railroad to Boston | T 29 |

   Fares :—

| | | | |
|---|---|---|---|
| Detroit | *$39.65 | Toronto | $ 34.65 |
| Port Huron | * 39.55 | Kingston | 29.90 |
| London | * 37.95 | Brockville | 28.40 |
| Hamilton | 35.85 | Ottawa | 27.15 |
| Niagara Falls | 36.15 | Montreal | 24.65 |
| Buffalo | 36.65 | Quebec | † 25.65 |

Route S 32—
    Choice of routes to Montreal (see page 85).

| | |
|---|---|
| Grand Trunk Railway or R. & O. N. Co.'s Steamer to Quebec | T 36 |
| Ferry to Levis | T 37 |
| Intercolonial Railway to Halifax | T 42 |
| Intercolonial Railway to St. Johns | T 46 |
| International Steamship Co. to Portland | T 49 |
| Boston & Maine Railroad to Boston | T 50 |

   Fares :—

| | | | |
|---|---|---|---|
| Detroit | *$38.00 | Toronto | $33.00 |
| Port Huron | ° 37.90 | Kingston | 28.25 |
| London | * 36.30 | Brockville | 26.75 |
| Hamilton | 34.20 | Ottawa | 25.50 |
| Niagara Falls | 34.50 | Montreal | 23.00 |
| Buffalo | 35.00 | | |

*All rail to Montreal. For tickets optional rail or steamer, Kingston to Prescott and Prescott to Montreal, add 75c. from Detroit, and for tickets optional rail or steamer, Toronto to Kingston, Kingston to Prescott and Prescott to Montreal, add $1.60 from Detroit, 20c. from Port Huron, and 10c. from London.

†Via Grand Trunk direct, not coming into Montreal. Form T 27 to be used from Levis to Gorham.

# To BOSTON.—*Continued.*

**Route S 33—**

| | FORM. |
|---|---|
| Choice of routes to Montreal (see page 85). | |
| Grand Trunk Railway or R. & O. N. Co.'s Steamer to Quebec ... ....... T | 36 |
| Ferry to Levis .... ... .. .. ............. .............. T | 37 |
| Intercolonial Railway to Halifax .... ............. ............ T | 42 |
| Windsor & Annapolis Railway to Annapolis ........ ............ T | 47 |
| Bay of Fundy Steamship Co to St. John ................. ............. T | 48 |
| International Steamship Co. to Portland ............. ..• ......... T | 49 |
| Boston & Maine Railroad to Boston.. ................. ............. T | 50 |

**Fares same as Route S 32.**

**Route S 34—**

| | FORM. |
|---|---|
| Same as Route S 32 or 33 to St. John. | |
| New Brunswick Railway to Vanceboro'... .......... .. ......... T | 51 |
| Maine Central Railroad to Portland....... ............ ............. T | 52 |
| Boston & Maine Railroad to Boston............. .... . ... .......... T | 50 |

**Fares :—**

| | | | |
|---|---|---|---|
| Detroit ...............*$42.00 | Toronto ........ ....$37.00 |
| Port Huron ....... ....* 41.90 | Kingston............. 32.25 |
| London ............... * 40.30 | Brockville ....... .... 30.75 |
| Hamilton ............... 38.20 | Ottawa................. 29.50 |
| Niagara Falls...... . 38.50 | Montreal.............. 27 00 |
| Buffalo .... .......... 39.00 | |

**Route S 35—**

| | FORM. |
|---|---|
| Choice of routes to Montreal (see page 85). | |
| Grand Trunk Railway or R. & O. N. Co.'s Steamer to Quebec.......... T | 36 |
| Ferry to Levis ...... ...... .. ..... ............. .......... T | 37 |
| Intercolonial Railway to Pointe du Chene . ............. ........ T | 42 |
| Prince Edward Island S. N. Co. to Summerside............... ...... T | 43 |
| Prince Edward Island Railway to Charlottetown ..... .............. T | 44 |
| Steamer to Pictou................. ................... ............. T | 45 |
| Intercolonial Railway to Halifax............. ........... ........ T | 46 |
| Windsor & Annapolis Railway to Annapolis.... ............... T | 47 |
| Bay of Fundy Steamship Co.'s Steamer to St. John..., ,.......... T | 48 |
| International Steamship Co.'s Steamer to Portland ... ............ T | 49 |
| Boston & Maine Railroad to Boston.................T | 50 |

**Fares :—**

| | | | |
|---|---|---|---|
| Detroit ...............*$43.60 | Toronto ..............$38.60 |
| Port Huron .. ........* 43.50 | Kingston............. 33.85 |
| London ........ ....* 41.90 | Brockville ............ 32.35 |
| Hamilton ............. 39.80 | Ottawa........ ..... 31.10 |
| Niagara Falls. ....... 40.10 | Montreal.............. 28.60 |
| Buffalo . ............. 40.60 | |

**Route S 36—**

| | FORM. |
|---|---|
| Same as Route S 35 to St. John. | |
| New Brunswick Railway to Vanceboro'................... ...... T | 51 |
| Maine Central Railroad to Portland ................ ............. . ....T | 52 |
| Boston & Maine Railroad to Boston................. ............. T | 50 |

**Fares :—**

| | | | |
|---|---|---|---|
| Detroit ...............*$47.60 | Toronto ...........$42.60 |
| Port Huron...........* 47.50 | Kingston. ... ........ 37.85 |
| London ........ ....* 45.90 | Brockville ............ 36.35 |
| Hamilton ............. 43.80 | Ottawa.... ...... 35.10 |
| Niagara Falls......... 44.10 | Montreal.............. 32.60 |
| Buffalo ................ 44.60 | |

**Route S 37—**

| | FORM. |
|---|---|
| Choice of routes to Montreal (see page 85). | |
| Grand Trunk Railway or R. & O. N. Co.'s Steamer to Quebec........... T | 36 |
| Quebec Steamship Co. (on alternate Tuesdays only) to Pictou..........T | 53 |
| Intercolonial Railway to Halifax................. ........... ........ T | 46 |
| Intercolonial Railway to St. John ..................... ........... T | 46 |
| International Steamship Co. to Portland . ....................... T | 49 |
| Boston & Maine Railroad to Boston ... .................. ......... T | 50 |

*All rail to Montreal. For tickets optional rail or steamer, Kingston to Prescott and Prescott to Montreal, add 75c. from Detroit, and for tickets optional rail or steamer, Toronto to Kingston, Kingston to Prescott and Prescott to Montreal, add $1.60 from Detroit, 20c. from Port Huron and 10c. from London.

# To BOSTON.—*Continued.*

Fares :—

| | | | |
|---|---|---|---|
| Detroit | *$39.00 | Toronto | $34.00 |
| Port Huron | * 38.90 | Kingston | 29.25 |
| London | * 37.30 | Brockville | 27.75 |
| Hamilton | 35.20 | Ottawa | 26.50 |
| Niagara Falls | 35.50 | Montreal | 24.00 |
| Buffalo | 36.00 | | |

Route S 38—

|  |  | FORM. |
|---|---|---|
| Same as Route S 37 to Halifax. | | |
| Windsor & Annapolis Railway to Annapolis | | T 47 |
| Bay of Fundy Steamship Co. to St. John | | T 48 |
| International Steamship Co. to Portland | | T 49 |
| Boston & Maine Railroad to Boston | | T 50 |

Fares same as Route S 37.

Route S 39—

|  |  | FORM. |
|---|---|---|
| Choice of routes to Montreal (see page 85). | | |
| Grand Trunk Railway to Gorham and Portland | | T 32 |
| Portland Steam Packet Co. to Boston | | T 81 |

Fares :—

| | | | |
|---|---|---|---|
| Detroit | *$23.00 | Toronto | $18.00 |
| Port Huron | * 22.90 | Kingston | 13.75 |
| London | * 21.30 | Brockville | 12.25 |
| Hamilton | 19.20 | Ottawa | 12 00 |
| Niagara Falls | 19.50 | Montreal | 8.50 |
| Buffalo | 20.00 | | |

Route S 40—

|  |  | FORM. |
|---|---|---|
| Choice of routes to Montreal (see page 85). | | |
| Grand Trunk Railway or R. & O. N. Co.'s Steamer to Quebec | | T 36 |
| Ferry to Levis | | T 37 |
| Grand Trunk Railway to Gorham and Portland | | T 27 |
| Portland Steam Packet Co. to Boston | | T 81 |

Fares :—

| | | | |
|---|---|---|---|
| Detroit | *$26.50 | Toronto | $ 21.50 |
| Port Huron | * 26.40 | Kingston | 16.75 |
| London | * 24.80 | Brockville | 15.25 |
| Hamilton | 22.70 | Ottawa | 14.00 |
| Niagara Falls | 23.00 | Montreal | 11.50 |
| Buffalo | 23.50 | Quebec | † 9.50 |

# To CLAYTON, N. Y.

Route S 41—

|  |  | FORM. |
|---|---|---|
| Choice of routes to Toronto (see pages 84 and 85). | | |
| Grand Trunk Railway to Gananoque Jct. | | T 76 |
| Thousand Islands Railway to Gananoque | | T 7 |
| Deseronto Nav. Co.'s Steamer to Clayton | | T 8 |

Fares :—

| | | | |
|---|---|---|---|
| Detroit | $12.45 | Niagara Falls | $ 6.35 |
| Port Huron | 10.95 | Buffalo | 6.85 |
| London | 8.65 | Toronto | 5.85 |
| Hamilton | 6.35 | Kingston | 1.00 |

Route S 42—

|  |  | FORM. |
|---|---|---|
| Choice of routes to Toronto (see pages 84 and 85). | | |
| Grand Trunk Railway or R. & O. N. Co.'s Steamer to Kingston | | T 76 |
| Richelieu & Ontario Navigation Co.'s Steamer to Clayton | | T 6 |

Fares :—

| | | | |
|---|---|---|---|
| Detroit | $12.45 | Hamilton | $ 6.35 |
| Port Huron | 10.95 | Niagara Falls | 6.35 |
| London | 8.65 | Buffalo | 6.85 |

*All rail to Montreal. For tickets optional rail or steamer, Kingston to Prescott and Prescott to Montreal, add 75c. from Detroit, and for tickets optional rail or steamer, Toronto to Kingston, Kingston to Prescott and Prescott to Montreal, add $1.00 from Detroit, 20c. from Port Huron, and 10c. from London.
†Via Grand Trunk direct, not coming into Montreal. Form T 27 to be used from Levis.

## To CRAWFORD HOUSE, N. H.

Route S 43—

Choice of routes to Montreal (see page 85).

|  |  | FORM |
|---|---|---|
| Grand Trunk Railway to Groveton Jct. | | T 32 |
| Concord & Montreal Railroad to Scott's | | T 25 |
| Maine Central Railroad to Crawford House | | T 28 |

Fares :—

| | | | |
|---|---|---|---|
| Detroit | *$21.30 | Toronto | $ 16.30 |
| Port Huron | * 21.20 | Kingston | 11.55 |
| London | * 19.60 | Brockville | 10.05 |
| Hamilton | 17.50 | Ottawa | 9.80 |
| Niagara Falls | 17.80 | Montreal | 6.30 |
| Buffalo | 18.30 | Quebec | † 7.30 |

Route S 44—

Choice of routes to Montreal (see page 85).

| | |
|---|---|
| Grand Trunk Railway to St. Johns | T 11 |
| Central Vermont Railroad to Montpelier | T 12 |
| Montpelier & Wells River Railroad to Wells River | T 24 |
| Concord & Montreal Railroad to Fabyans | T 25 |
| Maine Central Railroad to Crawford House | T 28 |

Fares :—

| | | | |
|---|---|---|---|
| Detroit | *$21.30 | Toronto | $16.30 |
| Port Huron | * 21.20 | Kingston | 11.55 |
| London | * 19.60 | Brockville | 10.05 |
| Hamilton | 17.50 | Ottawa | 9.80 |
| Niagara Falls | 17.80 | Montreal | 6.30 |
| Buffalo | 18.30 | Quebec | 8.80 |

## To FABYANS, N. H.

Route S 45—

Choice of routes to Montreal (see page 85).

| | |
|---|---|
| Grand Trunk Railway to Groveton Jct. | T 32 |
| Concord & Montreal Railroad to Fabyans | T 25 |

Fares :—

| | | | |
|---|---|---|---|
| Detroit | *$21.00 | Toronto | $ 16.00 |
| Port Huron | * 20.90 | Kingston | 11.25 |
| London | * 19.30 | Brockville | 9.75 |
| Hamilton | 17.20 | Ottawa | 9.50 |
| Niagara Falls | 17.50 | Montreal | 6.00 |
| Buffalo | 18.00 | Quebec | † 7.00 |

Route S 46—

Choice of routes to Montreal (see page 85).

| | |
|---|---|
| Grand Trunk Railway to Sherbrooke | T 32 |
| Boston & Maine Railroad to Newport and St. Johnsbury | T 33 |
| St. Johnsbury & Lake Champlain Railroad to Lunenburg | T 38 |
| Maine Central Railroad to Fabyans | T 28 |

Fares same as Route S 45.

Route S 47—

Choice of routes to Montreal (see page 85).

| | |
|---|---|
| Grand Trunk Railway to St. Johns | T 11 |
| Central Vermont Railway to Montpelier | T 12 |
| Montpelier & Wells River Railroad to Wells River | T 24 |
| Concord & Montreal Railroad to Fabyans | T 25 |

Fares :—

| | | | |
|---|---|---|---|
| Detroit | *$21.00 | Toronto | $16.00 |
| Port Huron | * 20.90 | Kingston | 11.25 |
| London | * 19.30 | Brockville | 9.75 |
| Hamilton | 17.20 | Ottawa | 9.50 |
| Niagara Falls | 17.50 | Montreal | 6.00 |
| Buffalo | 18.00 | Quebec | 8.50 |

*All rail to Montreal. For tickets optional rail or steamer, Kingston to Prescott and Prescott to Montreal, add 75c. from Detroit, and for tickets optional rail or steamer, Toronto to Kingston, Kingston to Prescott and Prescott to Montreal, add $1.60 from Detroit, 20c. from Port Huron and 10c. from London.
†Via Grand Trunk direct, not coming into Montreal. Form T 27 to be used from Levis to Gorham.

## To FABYANS, N. H.—*Continued.*

Route S 48—

| | FORM. |
|---|---|
| Choice of routes to Montreal (see page 85). | |
| Grand Trunk Railway to St. Johns | T 11 |
| Central Vermont Railroad to Montpelier | T 12 |
| Montpelier & Wells River Railroad to Wells River | T 24 |
| Concord & Montreal Railroad to Bethlehem Jct. | T 25 |
| Profile & Franconia Notch Railroad to Profile House | T 26 |
| Profile & Franconia Notch Railroad to Bethlehem Jct | T 26 |
| Concord & Montreal Railroad to Fabyans | T 25 |

Fares:—

| | | | |
|---|---|---|---|
| Detroit | *$24.00 | Toronto | $19.00 |
| Port Huron | * 23.90 | Kingston | 14.25 |
| London | * 22.30 | Brockville | 12.75 |
| Hamilton | 20.20 | Ottawa | 12.50 |
| Niagara Falls | 20.50 | Montreal | 9.00 |
| Buffalo | 21.00 | Quebec | 11.50 |

## To GORHAM, N. H.

‡Route S 49—

| | |
|---|---|
| Choice of routes to Montreal (see page 85). | |
| Grand Trunk Railway to Gorham | X 13 |

Fares:—

| | | | |
|---|---|---|---|
| Detroit | *$21.00 | Toronto | $ 16.00 |
| Port Huron | * 20.90 | Kingston | 11.25 |
| London | * 19.30 | Brockville | 9.75 |
| Hamilton | 17.20 | Ottawa | 9.50 |
| Niagara Falls | 17.50 | Montreal | 6.00 |
| Buffalo | 18.00 | Quebec | † 7.00 |

## To HALIFAX, N. S.

Route S 50—

| | |
|---|---|
| Choice of routes to Montreal (see page 85). | |
| Grand Trunk Railway or R. & O. N. Co.'s Steamer to Quebec | T 36 |
| Ferry to Levis | T 37 |
| Intercolonial Railway to Halifax | T 42 |

Fares:—

| | | | |
|---|---|---|---|
| Detroit | *$27.50 | Toronto | $22.50 |
| Port Huron | * 27.40 | Kingston | 21.75 |
| London | * 25.80 | Brockville | 20.25 |
| Hamilton | 23.70 | Ottawa | 20.00 |
| Niagara Falls | 24.00 | Montreal | 16.50 |
| Buffalo | 24.50 | | |

Route S 51—

| | |
|---|---|
| Choice of routes to Montreal (see page 85). | |
| Grand Trunk Railway or R. O. N. Co.'s Steamer to Quebec | T 36 |
| Quebec Steamship Co. (on alternate Tuesdays only) to Pictou | T 53 |
| Intercolonial Railway to Halifax | T 46 |

Fares:—

| | | | |
|---|---|---|---|
| Detroit | *$28.50 | Toronto | $23.50 |
| Port Huron | * 28.40 | Kingston | 19.75 |
| London | * 26.80 | Brockville | 18.25 |
| Hamilton | 24.70 | Ottawa | 18.00 |
| Niagara Falls | 25.00 | Montreal | 14.50 |
| Buffalo | 25.50 | | |

*All rail to Montreal. For tickets optional rail or steamer, Kingston to Prescott and Prescott to Montreal, add 75c. from Detroit, and for tickets optional rail or steamer, Toronto to Kingston, Kingston to Prescott and Prescott to Montreal, add $1.60 from Detroit, 20c. from Port Huron, and 10c. from London.
†Via Grand Trunk direct, not coming into Montreal. Form T 27 to be used from Levis.

# To KINGSTON, Ont.

Route S 52—
    Choice of routes to Toronto (see pages 84 and 85).
                                                               FORM.
    Grand Trunk Railway or R. & O. N. Co.'s Steamer to Kingston.........T   5

Fares :—

| | | | |
|---|---|---|---|
| Detroit ...............$11.45 | Hamilton ...... ......$ 6.05 |
| Port Huron........... 9.95 | Niagara Falls......... 6.35 |
| London ........... .... 8.25 | Buffalo............... 6.85 |

# To LANCASTER, N. H.

Route S 53—
    Choice of routes to Montreal (see page 85).
    Grand Trunk Railway to Groveton Jct.............................. ...T  32
    Concord & Montreal Railroad to Lancaster........... .................T  25

Fares :—

| | | | |
|---|---|---|---|
| Detroit.................*$21.00 | Toronto.............$16.00 |
| Port Huron...........* 20.90 | Kingston............. 11.25 |
| London ...............* 19.30 | Brockville ......... 9.75 |
| Hamilton ............. 17.20 | Ottawa.......... 9.50 |
| Niagara Falls ........ 17.50 | Montreal..... ..... 6.00 |
| Buffalo ............... 18.00 | |

Route S 54—
    Choice of routes to Montreal (see page 85).
    Grand Trunk Railway or R. & O. N. Co.'s Steamer to Quebec............T  36
    Ferry to Levis............. ............................................ ......T  37
    Grand Trunk Railway to Groveton Jct.............................. ......T  27
    Concord & Montreal Railroad to Lancaster....................T  25

Fares :—

| | | | |
|---|---|---|---|
| Detroit.................*$24.50 | Toronto .............$ 19.50 |
| Port Huron...........* 24.40 | Kingston . ........ 14.75 |
| London ...............* 22.80 | Brockville ........... 13.25 |
| Hamilton ............. 20.70 | Ottawa............... 13.00 |
| Niagara Falls......... 21.00 | Montreal ........ .... 9.50 |
| Buffalo ............... 21.50 | Quebec .............† 7.00 |

# To MONTREAL, Que.

Route S 55—
    Grand Trunk Railway to Montreal.

Fares :—

| | | | |
|---|---|---|---|
| Detroit.................$15.00 | Buffalo.................$12.00 |
| Port Huron........... 14.90 | Toronto............... 10.00 |
| London ............... 13.30 | Kingston ............. 5.25 |
| Hamilton ............. 11.20 | Brockville ..... ...... 3.75 |
| Niagara Falls.......... 11.50 | Quebec................ 3.50 |

Route S 56—
    Choice of routes to Toronto (see pages 84 and 85).
    Grand Trunk Railway to Kingston....... ............................T  76
    Grand Trunk Railway or R. & O. N. Co.'s Steamer to Prescott...........T  55
    Grand Trunk Railway or R. & O. N. Co.'s Steamer to Montreal..........T  56

Fares :—

| | | | |
|---|---|---|---|
| Detroit.................$15.75 | Niagara Falls.........$11.50 |
| Port Huron........... 15.10 | Buffalo ............ .... 12.00 |
| London ............... 13.40 | Toronto............... 10.00 |
| Hamilton ........... .. 11.20 | |

    *All rail to Montreal. For tickets optional rail or steamer, Kingston to Prescott and Prescott to Montreal, add 75c. from Detroit, and for tickets optional rail or steamer, Toronto to Kingston, Kingston to Prescott and Prescott to Montreal, add $1.60 from Detroit. 20c. from Port Huron, and 10c. from London.
    †Via Grand Trunk Railway direct.

# To MONTREAL, Que.—*Continued.*

Route S 57—

FORM.
Choice of routes to Toronto (see pages 84 and 85).
Grand Trunk Railway to Gananoque Jct ................................. T 76
Thousand Islands Railway to Gananoque ......................... T 7
Deseronto Navigation Co.'s Steamer to Clayton, Round Island, Thousand
    Island Park, Alexandria Bay ............................................. T 8
§Richelieu & Ontario Navigation Co.'s Steamer to Montreal............T 6

Fares same as Route S 56.

Route S 58—

Choice of routes to Toronto (see pages 84 and 85).
Grand Trunk Railway or R. & O. N. Co.'s Steamer to Kingston......... T 5
Grand Trunk Railway or R. & O. N. Co.'s Steamer to Prescott.... ...... T 55
Grand Trunk Railway or R. & O. N. Co.'s Steamer to Montreal .........T 56

Fares :—

| | | | |
|---|---|---|---|
| Detroit | $16.60 | Hamilton | $11.20 |
| Port Huron | 15.10 | Niagara Falls | 11.50 |
| London | 13.40 | Buffalo | 12.00 |

# To NEW YORK.

‡Route S 59—

Choice of routes to Montreal (see page 85).
Grand Trunk Railway to Rouse's Point ......................................
Delaware & Hudson Railroad to Plattsburg....
D. & H. Railroad or Champ. Trans. Co.'s Steamer to Fort Ticonderoga ⟩ X 21
Delaware & Hudson Railroad to Saratoga, Troy.....................
New York Central & Hudson River Railroad to New York ...........

Fares :—

| | | | |
|---|---|---|---|
| Detroit | *$25.00 | Toronto | $20.00 |
| Port Huron | * 24.90 | Kingston | 15.25 |
| London | * 23.30 | Brockville | 13.75 |
| Hamilton | 21.20 | Ottawa | 12.50 |
| Niagara Falls | 21.50 | Montreal | 10.00 |
| Buffalo | 22.00 | Quebec | 12.00 |

‡Route S 60—

Choice of routes to Montreal (see page 85).
Grand Trunk Railway to St. Johns...................................
Central Vermont Railroad to Rutland .................................
Bennington & Rutland Railroad to White Creek..................... ⟩2752
Fitchburg Railroad to Troy..........................................
New York Central & Hudson River Railroad to New York............

Fares same as Route S 59.

‡Route S 61—

Choice of routes to Montreal (see page 85).
Grand Trunk Railway to Rouse's Point...........................
Delaware & Hudson Railroad to Plattsburg ......................
D. & H. Railroad or Champ. Trans. Co. to Fort Ticonderoga ......... ⟩X290
Delaware & Hudson Railroad to Saratoga, Albany,....................
West Shore Railroad to New York .....................................

Fares same as Route S 59.

‡Route S 62—

Choice of routes to Montreal (see page 85).
Grand Trunk Railway to St. Johns......................................
Central Vermont Railroad to St. Albans, Burlington, Bellows Falls....
Vermont Valley Railroad to Brattleboro............................... ⟩ X 46
Central Vermont Railroad to South Vernon .........................
Connecticut River Railroad to Springfield .........................
New York, New Haven & Hartford Railroad to Hartford, New York..

Fares same as Route S 59.

*All rail to Montreal. For tickets optional rail or steamer, Kingston to Prescott and Prescott to Montreal, add 75c. from Detroit; and for tickets optional rail or steamer, Toronto to Kingston, Kingston to Prescott, and Prescott to Montreal, add $1.60 from Detroit, 20c. from Port Huron, and 10c. from London.
§ Passengers can, if they desire it, change this for ticket back to Gananoque and thence to Montreal by rail, on application to the captain of Deseronto Navigation Co.'s Steamer.

# To NEW YORK.—*Continued.*

**Route S 63—**

Choice of routes to Montreal (see page 85).         FORM.
Grand Trunk Railway to St. Johns.. ...................................T 11
Central Vermont Railroad to St. Albans, White River Jct., Windsor.....T 12
Vermont Valley Railroad to Brattleboro ..........................T 13
Central Vermont Railroad to South Vernon..........................T 12
Connecticut River Railroad to Springfield .........................T 68
New York, New Haven & Hartford Railroad to New Haven ............T 69
New York, New Haven & Hartford Railroad to New York .....T 70

Fares same as Route S 59.

**‡Route S 64—**

Choice of routes to Montreal (see page 85).
Grand Trunk Railway to Rouse's Point........... ... ..........⎫
Delaware & Hudson Railroad to Plattsburg... ... .........⎪
D. & H. Railroad or Champ. Trans. Co. to Fort Ticonderoga. ......⎬ X 22
Delaware & Hudson Railroad to Saratoga, Albany . .. ...........⎪
People's Line Steamers to New York.................. ...⎭

Fares :—

| | | | |
|---|---|---|---|
| Detroit.... | *$23.95 | Toronto.... | $18.95 |
| Port Huron.......... | * 23.85 | Kingston.......... | 14.20 |
| London.............. | * 22.25 | Brockville .......... | 12.70 |
| Hamilton........ | 20.15 | Ottawa .... | 11.45 |
| Niagara Falls... ..... | 20.45 | Montreal ... ........ | 8.95 |
| Buffalo .............. | 20.95 | Quebec.............. | 10.95 |

**‡Route S 65—**

Same as Route S 64 to Albany.... ...... .. .........⎫ X 27
Day Line Steamers to New York.. ...... ..............⎭

Fares :—

| | | | |
|---|---|---|---|
| Detroit......... | *$24.60 | Toronto.............. | $19.60 |
| Port Huron.......... | * 24.50 | Kingston........ | 14.85 |
| London..... ...... | * 22.90 | Brockville .. ... ..... | 13.35 |
| Hamilton.......... | 20.80 | Ottawa.... .... | 12.10 |
| Niagara Falls........ | 21.10 | Montreal............ | 9.60 |
| Buffalo.............. | 21.60 | Quebec ... ....... | 11.60 |

**‡Route S 66—**

Choice of routes to Montreal (see page 85)
Grand Trunk Railway to Rouse's Point .................⎫
Delaware & Hudson Railroad to Plattsburg.......... ......⎪
D. & H. Railroad or Champ. Trans. Co. to Fort Ticonderoga ..........⎪
Delaware & Hudson Railroad to Baldwin ...........................⎬ X 19
Lake George Steamer to Caldwell ...... ... ...........⎪
Delaware & Hudson Railroad to Saratoga, Troy ...... ... .........⎪
New York Central & Hudson River Railroad to New York .... ....⎭

Fares :—

| | | | |
|---|---|---|---|
| Detroit................. | *$27.00 | Toronto.......... .....$22.00 | |
| Port Huron........... | * 26.90 | Kingston.......... | 17.25 |
| London..... ........ | * 25.30 | Brockville .......... . | 15.75 |
| Hamilton........ | 23.20 | Ottawa.............. | 14.50 |
| Niagara Falls........ | 23.50 | Montreal............ | 12.00 |
| Buffalo ..... ...... | 24.00 | Quebec ........... ... | 14.00 |

**‡Route S 67—**

Same as Route S 66 to Caldwell.
Delaware & Hudson Railroad to Saratoga, Albany........... ...... ....⎫X291
West Shore Railroad to New York ...... ......... ...... . ............⎭

Fares same as Route S 66.

**‡Route S 68—**

Same as Route S 67 to Albany.
People's Line Steamers to New York. .. ....... ..................... X 20

*All rail to Montreal. For tickets optional rail or steamer, Kingston to Prescott and Prescott to Montreal, add 75c. from Detroit; and for tickets optional rail or steamer, Toronto to Kingston, Kingston to Prescott, and Prescott to Montreal, add $1.60 from Detroit, 20c. from Port Huron, and 10c. from London.

# To NEW YORK.—*Continued.*

Fares :—

| | | | |
|---|---|---|---|
| Detroit | *$25.95 | Toronto | $20.95 |
| Port Huron | * 25.85 | Kingston | 16.20 |
| London | * 24.25 | Brockville | 14.70 |
| Hamilton | 22.15 | Ottawa | 13.45 |
| Niagara Falls | 22.45 | Montreal | 10.95 |
| Buffalo | 22.95 | Quebec | 12.95 |

‡Route S 69—

Same as Route S 67 to Albany.

FORM.

Day Line Steamers to New York ....................................X 26

Fares :—

| | | | |
|---|---|---|---|
| Detroit | *$26.60 | Toronto | $21.60 |
| Port Huron | * 26.50 | Kingston | 16.85 |
| London | * 24.90 | Brockville | 15.35 |
| Hamilton | 22.80 | Ottawa | 14.10 |
| Niagara Falls | 23.10 | Montreal | 11.60 |
| Buffalo | 23.60 | Quebec | 13.60 |

Route S 70—

Choice of routes to Montreal (see page 85).

| | |
|---|---|
| Grand Trunk Railway to Rouse's Point | T 16 |
| Delaware & Hudson Railroad to Plattsburg | T 17 |
| Champ. Trans. Co.'s Steamer to Burlington | T 18 |
| Central Vermont Railroad to Montpelier | T 12 |
| Montpelier & Wells River Railroad to Wells River | T 24 |
| Concord & Montreal Railroad to Base | T 25 |
| Mount Washington Railway to Summit | T 41 |
| Mount Washington Railway to Base | T 41 |
| Concord & Montreal Railroad to Fabyans | T 25 |
| Maine Central Railroad to North Conway | T 28 |
| Boston & Maine Railroad to Boston | T 30 |
| Choice of Sound Steamer Lines to New York | T 73 |

Fares :—

| | | | |
|---|---|---|---|
| Detroit | *$37.35 | Toronto | $32.35 |
| Port Huron | * 37.25 | Kingston | 27.60 |
| London | * 35.65 | Brockville | 26.10 |
| Hamilton | 33.55 | Ottawa | 24.85 |
| Niagara Falls | 33.85 | Montreal | 22.35 |
| Buffalo | 34.35 | Quebec | 24.85 |

Route S 71—

Choice of routes to Montreal (see page 85).

| | |
|---|---|
| Grand Trunk Railway to St. Johns | T 11 |
| Central Vermont Railroad to St. Albans, Burlington, Rutland | T 61 |
| Bennington & Rutland Railroad to White Creek | T 62 |
| Fitchburg Railroad to Troy | T 63 |
| New York Central & Hudson River Railroad to Albany | T127 |
| People's Line Steamers to New York | T 71 |

Fares same as Route S 64.

Route S 72—

Same as Route S 71 to Albany.

Day Line Steamer to New York....................................T 72

Fares same as Route S 65.

‡Route S 73—

Choice of routes to Montreal (see page 85).

| | |
|---|---|
| Grand Trunk Railway to St. Johns | ⎫ |
| Central Vermont Railroad to St. Albans, Burlington | ⎪ |
| Champlain Transportation Co.'s Steamer to Fort Ticonderoga | ⎬ X 42 |
| Delaware & Hudson Railroad to Saratoga, Albany | ⎪ |
| Day Line Steamer to New York | ⎭ |

Fares same as Route S 65.

*All rail to Montreal. For tickets optional rail or steamer, Kingston to Prescott and Prescott to Montreal, add 75c. from Detroit, and for tickets optional rail or steamer, Toronto to Kingston, Kingston to Prescott and Prescott to Montreal, add $1.60 from Detroit, 20c. from Port Huron and 10c. from London.

# To NEW YORK.—*Continued.*

‡Route S 74—
    Choice of routes to Montreal (see page 85).                FORM.
    Grand Trunk Railway to St. Johns.......................
    Central Vermont Railroad to St. Albans, Burlington...........
    Champlain Transportation Co.'s Steamer to Fort Ticonderoga........
    Delaware & Hudson Railroad to Baldwin..........................} X 43
    Lake George Steamer to Caldwell ............................
    Delaware & Hudson Railroad to Saratoga, Albany................
    Day Line Steamer to New York .......... .................

    **Fares same as Route S 69.**

Route S 75—
    Choice of routes to Ogdensburg (see page 107).
    Central Vermont Railroad to Rouse's Point ................... T 12
    Central Vermont Railroad to St. Albans, Burlington............ T 12
    Champlain Transportation Co.'s Steamer to Fort Ticonderoga.... T 18
    Delaware & Hudson Railroad to Saratoga, Albany............... T 20
    Day Line Steamer to New York............................... T 72

    Fares :—

| | | | |
|---|---|---|---|
| Detroit | $24.95 | Hamilton | $19.80 |
| Port Huron | 23.45 | Niagara Falls | 19.80 |
| London | 22.00 | Buffalo | 20.30 |

Route S 76—
    Same as Route S 72 to Fort Ticonderoga.
    Delaware & Hudson Railroad to Baldwin..................... T 20
    Lake George Steamer to Caldwell ......................... T 22
    Delaware & Hudson Railroad to Saratoga, Albany........... T 21
    Day Line Steamer to New York............................. T 72

    Fares :—

| | | | |
|---|---|---|---|
| Detroit | $26.95 | Hamilton | $21.80 |
| Port Huron | 25.45 | Niagara Falls | 21.80 |
| London | 24.00 | Buffalo | 22.30 |

Route S 77—
    Choice of routes to Montreal (see page 85).
    Grand Trunk Railway to St. Johns......................... T 11
    Central Vermont Railroad to St. Albans, Burlington......... T 12
    Champlain Transportation Co.'s Steamer to Fort Ticonderoga..... T 18
    Delaware & Hudson Railroad to Baldwin.................... T 20
    Lake George Steamer to Caldwell ......................... T 22
    Delaware & Hudson Railroad to Saratoga, Albany ......... T 21
    New York Central & Hudson River Railroad to New York ......... T 65

    **Fares same as Route S 66.**

Route S 78—
    Choice of routes to Montreal (see page 85).
    Grand Trunk Railway to St. Johns........................ T 11
    Central Vermont Railroad to St. Albans, Montpelier ............ T 12
    Montpelier & Wells River Railroad to Wells River............. T 24
    Concord & Montreal Railroad to Bethlehem Jct.................. T 25
    Profile & Franconia Notch Railroad to Profile House .......... T 26
    Profile & Franconia Notch Railroad to Bethlehem Jct ......... T 26
    Concord & Montreal Railroad to Fabyans...................... T 25
    Maine Central Railroad to Portland ......................... T 52
    Boston & Maine Railroad to Boston.......................... T 50
    Choice of Sound Steamer Lines to New York ............... T 73

    Fares :—

| | | | |
|---|---|---|---|
| Detroit | *$32.00 | Toronto | $27.00 |
| Port Huron | *31.90 | Kingston | 22.25 |
| London | *30.30 | Brockville | 20.75 |
| Hamilton | 28.20 | Ottawa | 19.50 |
| Niagara Falls | 28.50 | Montreal | 17.00 |
| Buffalo | 29.00 | Quebec | 19.50 |

\*All rail to Montreal. For tickets optional rail or steamer, Kingston to Prescott and Prescott to Montreal, add 75c. from Detroit; and for tickets optional rail or steamer, Toronto to Kingston, Kingston to Prescott, and Prescott to Montreal, add $1.60 from Detroit, 20c. from Port Huron, and 10c. from London.

¶All rail to Prescott. For tickets optional, Toronto to Kingston and Kingston to Prescott, add 10c. from Detroit, 20c. from Port Huron, and 10c. from London.

# To NEW YORK.—*Continued.*

Route S 79—

                                                                   FORM.

Same as Route S 78 to Fabyans.

Maine Central Railroad to Crawford House, North Conway ............T 28

Boston & Maine Railroad to Boston........ ....................T 30

Choice of Sound Steamer Lines to New York ........ ...............T 73

    **Fares same as Route S 78.**

Route S 80—

Choice of routes to Montreal (see page 85).

Grand Trunk Railway to Sherbrooke........ .................T 32

Boston & Maine Railroad to Newport, Wells River, White River Jct....T 33

Central Vermont Railroad to Windsor .. ............................T 12

Vermont Valley Railroad to Brattleboro ....................... .....T 13

Central Vermont Railroad to South Vernon .......................T 12

Connecticut River Railroad to Springfield........ ...............T 68

New York, New Haven & Hartford Railroad to New Haven ... .........T 69

New York, New Haven & Hartford Railroad to New York............T 70

    **Fares †same as Route S 59.**

Route S 81—

Choice of routes to Montreal (see page 85).

Grand Trunk Railway or Rich. & Ont. Nav. Co.'s Steamer to Quebec....T 36

Ferry to Levis................... ............................T 37

Grand Trunk Railway to Sherbrooke .... ......................T 27

Same as Route S 80 to New York.

    Fares :—

| | | | |
|---|---|---|---|
| Detroit ...............*$28.50 | | Toronto ........... .$ 23.50 |
| Port Huron...........* 28.40 | | Kingston .......... 19.75 |
| London .............* 26.80 | | Brockville .......... 18.25 |
| Hamilton ............ 24.70 | | Ottawa............. 17.00 |
| Niagara Falls........ 25.00 | | Montreal........ .... 14.50 |
| Buffalo ............. 25.50 | | Quebec ........ ......† 12.00 |

Route S 82—

Choice of routes to Montreal (see page 85).

Grand Trunk Railway to Sherbrooke........ .................T 32

Boston & Maine Railroad to Newport, Wells River, White River Jct....T 33

Boston & Maine Railroad to Concord ...........................T 35

Concord & Montreal Railroad to Nashua ... .....................T 34

Boston & Maine Railroad to Boston...........................T 29

Choice of Sound Steamer Lines to New York .....................T 73

    Fares :—

| | | | |
|---|---|---|---|
| Detroit ...............*$27.00 | | Toronto ..............$22.00 |
| Port Huron...........* 26.90 | | Kingston ......... 17.25 |
| London .... ........* 25.30 | | Brockville ......... 15.75 |
| Hamilton ........... 23.20 | | Ottawa ... .......... 14.50 |
| Niagara Falls........ 23.50 | | Montreal............. 12.00 |
| Buffalo ............... 24.00 | | |

Route S 83—

Choice of routes to Montreal (see page 85).

Grand Trunk Railway to Sherbrooke........ .................T 32

Boston & Maine Railroad to Newport, Wells River .................T 33

Concord & Montreal Railroad to Nashua.........................T 25

Boston & Maine Railroad to Boston...........................T 29

Choice of Sound Steamer Lines to New York .....................T 73

    **Fares same as Route S 82.**

Route S 84—

Choice of routes to Montreal (see page 85).

Grand Trunk Railway or R. & O. N. Co.'s Steamer to Quebec............T 36

Ferry to Levis.............. .............................T 37

Grand Trunk Railway to Sherbrooke.......................... ......T 27

Same as Route S 82 to New York.

    *All rail to Montreal. For tickets optional rail or steamer, Kingston to Prescott and Prescott to Montreal, add 75c. from Detroit, and for tickets optional rail or steamer, Toronto to Kingston, Kingston to Prescott and Prescott to Montreal, add $1.60 from Detroit, 20c. from Port Huron, and 10c. from London.

    †From Quebec via Grand Trunk direct, not coming into Montreal. Use Form T 27, Levis to Sherbrooke.

# To NEW YORK.—*Continued.*

Fares:—

| | | | |
|---|---|---|---|
| Detroit | *$30.50 | Toronto | $25.50 |
| Port Huron | * 30.40 | Kingston | 20.75 |
| London | * 28.80 | Brockville | 19.25 |
| Hamilton | 26.70 | Ottawa | 18.00 |
| Niagara Falls | 27.00 | Montreal | 15.50 |
| Buffalo | 27.50 | Quebec | 13.00 |

**Route S 85—**

| | FORM. |
|---|---|
| Choice of routes to Montreal (see page 85). | |
| Grand Trunk Railway or R. & O. N. Co.'s Steamer to Quebec | T 36 |
| Ferry to Levis | T 37 |
| Grand Trunk Railway to Sherbrooke | T 27 |
| Same as Route S 83 to New York. | |

**Fares same as Route S 84.**

**Route S 86—**

| | |
|---|---|
| Choice of routes to Montreal (see page 85). | |
| Grand Trunk Railway or R. & O. N. Co.'s Steamer to Quebec | T 36 |
| Ferry to Levis | T 37 |
| Grand Trunk Railway to Gorham | T 27 |
| Milliken's Stage to Glen House | T 79 |
| Milliken's Stage to Summit | T 39 |
| Mount Washington Railway to Base | T 41 |
| Concord & Montreal Railroad to Fabyans | T 25 |
| Maine Central Railroad to Crawford House | T 28 |
| Maine Central Railroad to Fabyans | T 28 |
| Concord & Montreal Railroad to Bethlehem Jct. | T 25 |
| Profile & Franconia Notch Railroad to Profile House | T 26 |
| Profile & Franconia Notch Railroad to Bethlehem Jct. | T 26 |
| Concord & Montreal Railroad to Nashua | T 25 |
| Boston & Maine Railroad to Boston | T 29 |
| Choice of Sound Steamer Lines to New York | T 73 |

Fares :—

| | | | |
|---|---|---|---|
| Detroit | *$46.60 | Toronto | $ 41.60 |
| Port Huron | * 46.50 | Kingston | 36.85 |
| London | * 44.90 | Brockville | 35.35 |
| Hamilton | 42.80 | Ottawa | 34.10 |
| Niagara Falls | 43.10 | Montreal | 31.60 |
| Buffalo | 43.60 | Quebec | † 29.10 |

**Route S 87—**

| | |
|---|---|
| Choice of routes to Montreal (see page 85). | |
| Grand Trunk Railway to St. Johns | T 11 |
| Central Vermont Railroad to St. Albans, Montpelier | T 12 |
| Montpelier & Wells River Railroad to Wells River | T 24 |
| Concord & Montreal Railroad to Bethlehem Jct. | T 25 |
| Profile & Franconia Notch Railroad to Profile House | T 26 |
| Profile & Franconia Notch Railroad to Bethlehem Jct. | T 26 |
| Concord & Montreal Railroad to Base | T 25 |
| Mount Washington Railway to Summit | T 41 |
| Milliken's Stage to Glen House | T 40 |
| Milliken's Stage to Gorham | T 79 |
| Grand Trunk Railway to Portland | T 74 |
| Boston & Maine Railroad to Boston | T 50 |
| Choice of Sound Steamer Lines to New York | T 73 |

Fares :—

| | | | |
|---|---|---|---|
| Detroit | *$41.25 | Toronto | $ 36.25 |
| Port Huron | * 41.15 | Kingston | 31.50 |
| London | * 39.55 | Brockville | 30.00 |
| Hamilton | 37.45 | Ottawa | 28.75 |
| Niagara Falls | 37.75 | Montreal | 26.25 |
| Buffalo | 38.25 | Quebec | † 27.25 |

*All rail to Montreal. For tickets optional rail or steamer, Kingston to Prescott and Prescott to Montreal, add 75c. from Detroit; and for tickets optional rail or steamer, Toronto to Kingston, Kingston to Prescott, and Prescott to Montreal, add $1.60 from Detroit, 20c. from Port Huron, and 10c. from London.

†Via Grand Trunk direct, not coming into Montreal.

# To NEW YORK.—*Continued.*

**Route S 88—**

Choice of routes to Montreal (see page 85).

| | FORM. |
|---|---|
| Grand Trunk Railway or R. & O. N. Co.'s Steamer to Quebec | T 36 |
| Ferry to Levis | T 37 |
| Grand Trunk Railway to Sherbrooke | T 27 |
| Boston & Maine Railroad to St. Johnsbury | T 33 |
| St. Johnsbury & Lake Champlain Railroad to Lunenburg | T 38 |
| Maine Central Railroad to Bethlehem Jct. | T 28 |
| Profile & Franconia Notch Railroad to Profile House | T 26 |
| Profile & Franconia Notch Railroad to Bethlehem Jct. | T 26 |
| Concord & Montreal Railroad to Base | T 25 |

Same as Route S 87 to New York.

**Fares :—**

| | | | |
|---|---|---|---|
| Detroit | *$44.75 | Toronto | $ 39.75 |
| Port Huron | * 44.65 | Kingston | 35.00 |
| London | * 43.05 | Brockville | 33.50 |
| Hamilton | 40.95 | Ottawa | 32.25 |
| Niagara Falls | 41.25 | Montreal | 29.75 |
| Buffalo | 41.75 | Quebec | † 27.25 |

**Route S 89—**

Same as Route S 88 to Base, Mount Washington.

| | |
|---|---|
| Mount Washington Railway to Summit | T 41 |
| Mount Washington Railway to Base | T 41 |
| Concord & Montreal Railroad to Fabyans | T 25 |
| Maine Central Railroad to North Conway | T 28 |
| Boston & Maine Railroad to Wolfboro | T 31 |
| Steamer to Weirs | T 78 |
| Concord & Montreal Railroad to Nashua | T 25 |
| Boston & Maine Railroad to Boston | T 29 |
| Choice of Sound Steamer Lines to New York | T 73 |

**Fares :—**

| | | | |
|---|---|---|---|
| Detroit | *$44.25 | Toronto | $ 39.25 |
| Port Huron | * 44.15 | Kingston | 34.50 |
| London | * 42.55 | Brockville | 33.00 |
| Hamilton | 40.45 | Ottawa | 31.75 |
| Niagara Falls | 40.75 | Montreal | 29.25 |
| Buffalo | 41.25 | Quebec | † 26.75 |

**‡Route S 90—**

Choice of routes to Montreal (see page 85).

| | |
|---|---|
| Grand Trunk Railway or R. & O. N. Co.'s Steamer to Quebec | ⎫ |
| Grand Trunk Railway to Sherbrooke | ⎪ |
| Boston & Maine Railroad to Newport, St. Johnsbury | ⎪ |
| St. Johnsbury & Lake Champlain Railroad to Lunenburg | ⎪ |
| Maine Central Railroad to Bethlehem Jct. | ⎪ |
| Profile & Franconia Notch Railroad to Profile House | ⎬ 3063 |
| Profile & Franconia Notch Railroad to Bethlehem Jct. | ⎪ |
| Maine Central Railroad to Fabyans, Crawford House, North Conway, Portland | ⎪ |
| Boston & Maine Railroad to Boston | ⎪ |
| Choice of Sound Steamer Lines to New York | ⎭ |

**Fares '—**

| | | | |
|---|---|---|---|
| Detroit | *$35.50 | Toronto | $ 30.50 |
| Port Huron | * 35.40 | Kingston | 25.75 |
| London | * 33.80 | Brockville | 24.25 |
| Hamilton | 31.70 | Ottawa | 23.00 |
| Niagara Falls | 32.00 | Montreal | 20.50 |
| Buffalo | 32.50 | Quebec | † 18.00 |

*All rail to Montreal. For tickets optional rail or steamer, Kingston to Prescott and Prescott to Montreal, add 75c. from Detroit, and for tickets optional rail or steamer, Toronto to Kingston, Kingston to Prescott and Prescott to Montreal, add $1.00 from Detroit, 20c. from Port Huron and 10c. from London.
†Via Grand Trunk direct, not coming into Montreal.

# To NEW YORK.—*Continued.*

### Route S 91—

Choice of routes to Montreal (see page 85).

|  | FORM. |
|---|---|
| Grand Trunk Railway to Groveton Jct. | T 32 |
| Concord & Montreal Railroad to Base. | T 25 |
| Mount Washington Railway to Summit. | T 41 |
| Milliken's Stage to Glen House. | T 40 |
| Stage to Glen Station. | T 79 |
| Maine Central Railroad to North Conway. | T 28 |
| Boston & Maine Railroad to Boston. | T 30 |
| Choice of Sound Steamer Lines to New York. | T 73 |

Fares :—

| | | | |
|---|---|---|---|
| Detroit | *$38.25 | Toronto | $ 33.25 |
| Port Huron | * 38.15 | Kingston | 28.50 |
| London | * 36.55 | Brockville | 27.00 |
| Hamilton | 34.45 | Ottawa | 25.75 |
| Niagara Falls | 34.75 | Montreal | 23.25 |
| Buffalo | 35.25 | Quebec | † 24.25 |

### ‡Route S 92—

Choice of routes to Montreal (see page 85).

| | |
|---|---|
| Grand Trunk Railway to Gorham, Portland | |
| Boston & Maine Railroad to Boston | X 24 |
| Choice of Sound Steamer Lines to Boston | |

**Fares same as Route S 82.**

### ‡Route S 93—

Choice of routes to Montreal (see page 85).

| | |
|---|---|
| Grand Trunk Railway or R. & O. N. Co.'s Steamer to Quebec | |
| Ferry to Levis | X 25 |
| Grand Trunk Railway to Gorham, Portland | |

Same as Route S 92 to New York.

**Fares same as Route S 84.**

### Route S 94—

Choice of routes to Montreal (see page 85).

| | |
|---|---|
| Grand Trunk Railway to Gorham | T 32 |
| Milliken's Stage to Glen House | T 79 |
| Milliken's Stage to Summit | T 39 |
| Mount Washington Railway to Base | T 41 |
| Concord & Montreal Railroad to Bethlehem Jct. | T 25 |
| Profile & Franconia Notch Railroad to Profile House | T 26 |
| Profile & Franconia Notch Railroad to Bethlehem Jct. | T 26 |
| Concord & Montreal Railroad to Nashua | T 25 |
| Boston & Maine Railroad to Boston | T 29 |
| Choice of Sound Steamer Lines to New York | T 73 |

Fares :—

| | | | |
|---|---|---|---|
| Detroit | *$42.50 | Toronto | $ 37.50 |
| Port Huron | * 42.40 | Kingston | 32.75 |
| London | * 40.80 | Brockville | 31.25 |
| Hamilton | 38.70 | Ottawa | 30.00 |
| Niagara Falls | 39.00 | Montreal | 27.50 |
| Buffalo | 39.50 | Quebec | † 28.50 |

### Route S 95—

Same as Route S 94 to Profile House.

| | |
|---|---|
| Stage to North Woodstock | T 79 |
| Concord & Montreal Railroad to Nashua | T 25 |
| Boston & Maine Railroad to Boston | T 29 |
| Choice of Sound Steamer Lines to New York | T 73 |

**Fares same as Route S 94.**

*All rail to Montreal. For tickets optional rail or steamer, Kingston to Prescott and Prescott to Montreal, add 75c. from Detroit, and for tickets optional rail or steamer, Toronto to Kingston, Kingston to Prescott and Prescott to Montreal, add $1.60 from Detroit, 20c. from Port Huron, and 10c. from London.

†Via Grand Trunk direct, not coming into Montreal.

# To NEW YORK.—*Continued.*

**Route S 96—**

| | | FORM. |
|---|---|---|
| Choice of routes to Montreal (see page 85). | | |
| Grand Trunk Railway or R. & O. N. Co.'s Steamer to Quebec | | T 36 |
| Ferry to Levis | | T 37 |
| Grand Trunk Railway to Gorham | | T 27 |
| Milliken's Stage to Glen House | | T 79 |
| Milliken's Stage to Summit | | T 39 |
| Mount Washington Railway to Base | | T 41 |
| Concord & Montreal Railroad to Fabyans | | T 25 |
| Maine Central Railroad to Portland | | T 52 |
| Boston & Maine Railroad to Boston | | T 50 |
| Choice of Sound Steamer Lines to New York | | T 73 |

**Fares:—**

| | | | |
|---|---|---|---|
| Detroit | *$43.00 | Toronto | $38.00 |
| Port Huron | * 42.90 | Kingston | 33.25 |
| London | * 41.30 | Brockville | 31.75 |
| Hamilton | 39.20 | Ottawa | 30.50 |
| Niagara Falls | 39.50 | Montreal | 28.00 |
| Buffalo | 40.00 | Quebec | † 25.50 |

**Route S 97—**

| | |
|---|---|
| Same as Route S 96 to Summit. | |
| Milliken's Stage to Glen House | T 40 |
| Stage to Glen Station | T 79 |
| Maine Central Railroad to Fabyans | T 28 |
| Concord & Montreal Railroad to Wells River | T 25 |
| Boston & Maine Railroad to White River Jct. | T 31 |
| Central Vermont Railroad to Windsor | T 12 |
| Vermont Valley Railroad to Brattleboro' | T 13 |
| Central Vermont Railroad to South Vernon | T 12 |
| Connecticut River Railroad to Springfield | T 68 |
| New York, New Haven & Hartford Railroad to New Haven | T 69 |
| New York, New Haven & Hartford Railroad to New York | T 70 |

**Fares:—**

| | | | |
|---|---|---|---|
| Detroit | *$43.95 | Toronto | $ 38.95 |
| Port Huron | * 43.85 | Kingston | 34.20 |
| London | * 42.25 | Brockville | 32.70 |
| Hamilton | 40.15 | Ottawa | 31.45 |
| Niagara Falls | 40.45 | Montreal | 28.95 |
| Buffalo | 40.95 | Quebec | † 26.45 |

**Route S 98—**

| | |
|---|---|
| Same as Route S 96 to Summit. | |
| Mount Washington Railway to Base | T 41 |
| Concord & Montreal Railroad to Fabyans | T 25 |
| Maine Central Railroad to Crawford House | T 28 |
| Maine Central Railroad to Fabyans | T 28 |
| Concord & Montreal Railroad to Bethlehem Jct. | T 25 |
| Profile & Franconia Notch Railroad to Profile House | T 26 |
| Profile & Franconia Notch Railroad to Bethlehem Jct. | T 26 |
| Concord & Montreal Railroad to Wells River | T 25 |
| Montpelier & Wells River Railroad to Montpelier | T 24 |
| Central Vermont Railroad to Burlington | T 12 |
| Champlain Trans. Co.'s Steamer to Fort Ticonderoga | T 18 |
| Delaware & Hudson Railroad to Baldwin | T 20 |
| Lake George Steamer to Caldwell | T 22 |
| Delaware & Hudson Railroad to Saratoga, Albany | T 21 |
| Day Line Steamer to New York | T 72 |

**Fares:—**

| | | | |
|---|---|---|---|
| Detroit | *$51.00 | Toronto | $ 46.00 |
| Port Huron | * 50.90 | Kingston | 41.25 |
| London | * 49.30 | Brockville | 39.75 |
| Hamilton | 47.20 | Ottawa | 38.50 |
| Niagara Falls | 47.50 | Montreal | 36.00 |
| Buffalo | 48.00 | Quebec | † 33.50 |

*All rail to Montreal. For tickets optional rail or steamer, Kingston to Prescott and Prescott to Montreal, add 75c. from Detroit; and for tickets optional rail or steamer, Toronto to Kingston, Kingston to Prescott, and Prescott to Montreal, add $1.00 from Detroit, 20c. from Port Huron, and 10c. from London.

†Via Grand Trunk direct, not coming into Montreal.

# To NEW YORK.--*Continued.*

**Route S 99—**
Choice of routes to Montreal (see page 85).                                    FORM.
Grand Trunk Railway or R. & O. N. Co.'s Steamer to Quebec .......... T  36
Ferry to Levis ........................................................ T  37
Intercolonial Railway to Halifax............................. T  42
Intercolonial Railway to St. John............................. T  46
International Steamship Co. to Portland....................... T  49
Boston & Maine Railroad to Boston ...................... T  50
Choice of Steamer Lines to New York ..................... T  73

**Fares:—**

| | | | |
|---|---|---|---|
| Detroit | *$42.00 | Toronto | $37.00 |
| Port Huron | * 41.90 | Kingston | 32.25 |
| London | * 40.30 | Brockville | 30.75 |
| Hamilton | 38.20 | Ottawa | 29.50 |
| Niagara Falls | 38.50 | Montreal | 27.00 |
| Buffalo | 39.00 | | |

**Route S 100—**
Same as Route S 99 to Halifax.
Windsor & Annapolis Railway to Annapolis..................... T  47
Bay of Fundy Steamship Co. to St. John...................... T  48
International Steamship Co. to Portland...................... T  49
Boston & Maine Railroad to Boston .......................... T  50
Choice of Sound Steamer Lines to New York .............. T  73

**Fares same as Route S 99.**

**Route S 101—**
Choice of routes to Montreal (see page 85).
Grand Trunk Railway or R. & O. N. Co.'s Steamer to Quebec .......... T  36
Ferry to Levis ........................................... T  37
Grand Trunk Railway to Sherbrooke ....................... T  27
Boston & Maine Railroad to St. Johnsbury ................ T  33
St. Johnsbury & Lake Champlain Railroad to Lunenburg ...... T  38
Maine Central Railroad to Bethlehem Jct.................. T  28
Profile & Franconia Notch Railroad to Profile House...... T  26
Profile & Franconia Notch Railroad to Bethlehem Jct...... T  26
Maine Central Railroad to Crawford House................. T  28
Maine Central Railroad to Fabyans........................ T  28
Concord & Montreal Railroad to Base...................... T  25
Mount Washington Railway to Summit....................... T  41
Milliken's Stage to Glen House........................... T  40
Milliken's Stage to Gorham .............................. T  79
Grand Trunk Railway to Portland ......................... T  74
Boston & Maine Railroad to Boston ....................... T  50
Choice of Sound Steamer Lines to New York ............... T  73

**Fares:—**

| | | | |
|---|---|---|---|
| Detroit | *$45.35 | Toronto | $ 40.35 |
| Port Huron | * 45.25 | Kingston | 35.60 |
| London | * 43.65 | Brockville | 34.10 |
| Hamilton | 41.55 | Ottawa | 32.85 |
| Niagara Falls | 41.85 | Montreal | 30.35 |
| Buffalo | 42.35 | Quebec | † 27.85 |

# To OGDENSBURG, N. Y.

**Route S 102—**
Choice of routes to Toronto (see pages 84 and 85).
Grand Trunk Railway to Prescott......................... T  76
Omnibus Transfer to Wharf............................... T  80
Ferry to Ogdensburg .................................... T  75

**Fares:—**

| | | | |
|---|---|---|---|
| Detroit | $ 13.15 | Niagara Falls | $ 8.10 |
| Port Huron | 11.65 | Buffalo | 8.60 |
| London | 10.20 | Toronto | 6.90 |
| Hamilton | 8.10 | | |

*All rail to Montreal. For tickets optional rail or steamer, Kingston to Prescott and Prescott to Montreal, add 75c. from Detroit; and for tickets optional rail or steamer, Toronto to Kingston, Kingston to Prescott, and Prescott to Montreal, add $1.60 from Detroit, 20c. from Port Huron, and 10c. from London
†Via Grand Trunk direct to Portland, not coming into Montreal. Use Form T 27 from Levis.

## To OGDENSBURG, N. Y.—*Continued.*

Route S 103—

Choice of routes to Toronto (see pages 84 and 85).         FORM.
Grand Trunk Railway or R. & O. N. Co.'s Steamer to Kingston.........T   5
Grand Trunk Railway or R. & O. N. Co.'s Steamer to Prescott.........T  55
Ferry to Ogdensburg ...................................................T  75

Fares:—

| | | | |
|---|---|---|---|
| Detroit | $ 13.25 | Hamilton | $ 8.10 |
| Port Huron | 11.75 | Niagara Falls | 8.10 |
| London | 10.40 | Buffalo | 8.60 |

## To PORTLAND, Me.

‡Route S 104—

Choice of routes to Montreal (see page 85).
Grand Trunk Railway to Gorham, Portland ...........................X  14

Fares:—

| | | | |
|---|---|---|---|
| Detroit | *$22.50 | Toronto | $17.50 |
| Port Huron | * 22.40 | Kingston | 12.75 |
| London | * 20.80 | Brockville | 11.25 |
| Hamilton | 18.70 | Ottawa | 11.00 |
| Niagara Falls | 19.00 | Montreal | 7.50 |
| Buffalo | 19.50 | | |

‡Route S 105—

Choice of routes to Montreal (see page 85).
Grand Trunk Railway or R. & O. N. Co.'s Steamer to Quebec .........
Ferry to Levis .......................................................} X 10
Grand Trunk Railway to Gorham, Portland ........................

Fares:—

| | | | |
|---|---|---|---|
| Detroit | *$26.00 | Toronto | $ 21.00 |
| Port Huron | * 25.90 | Kingston | 16.25 |
| London | * 24.30 | Brockville | 14.75 |
| Hamilton | 22.20 | Ottawa | 13.50 |
| Niagara Falls | 22.50 | Montreal | 11.00 |
| Buffalo | 23.00 | Quebec | † 8.50 |

## To PRESCOTT, Ont.

Route S 106—

Choice of routes to Toronto (see pages 84 and 85).
Grand Trunk Railway to Prescott ....................................T  76

Fares:—

| | | | |
|---|---|---|---|
| Detroit | $ 13.15 | Niagara Falls | $ 8.10 |
| Port Huron | 11.65 | Buffalo | 8.60 |
| London | 9.95 | Toronto | 6.65 |
| Hamilton | 7.85 | | |

Route S 107—

Choice of routes to Toronto (see pages 84 and 85).
Grand Trunk Railway or R. & O. N. Co.'s Steamer to Kingston.........T   5
Grand Trunk Railway or R. & O. N. Co.'s Steamer to Prescott. .........T  55

Fares:—

| | | | |
|---|---|---|---|
| Detroit | $ 13.25 | Hamilton | $ 7.95 |
| Port Huron | 11.75 | Niagara Falls | 8.10 |
| London | 10.15 | Buffalo | 8.60 |

*All rail to Montreal. For tickets optional rail or steamer, Kingston to Prescott and Prescott to Montreal, add 75c. from Detroit, and for tickets optional rail or steamer, Toronto to Kingston, Kingston to Prescott and Prescott to Montreal, add $1.60 from Detroit, 20c. from Port Huron and 10c. from London.
†Via Grand Trunk direct to Portland, not coming into Montreal. Use Form T 27 from Levis.

# To PROFILE HOUSE, N. H.

Route S 108—

Choice of routes to Montreal (see page 85).             FORM.
Grand Trunk Railway to St. Johns......................................... T 11
Central Vermont Railroad to Montpelier................................. T 12
Montpelier & Wells River Railroad to Wells River................. T 24
Concord & Montreal Railroad to Bethlehem Jct...................... T 25
Profile & Franconia Notch Railroad to Profile House.............. T 26

Fares:—

| | | | |
|---|---|---|---|
| Detroit............... | *$22.50 | Toronto............... | $17.50 |
| Port Huron........... | * 22.40 | Kingston............. | 12.75 |
| London............... | 20.80 | Brockville.......... | 11.25 |
| Hamilton............. | 18.70 | Ottawa.............. | 11.00 |
| Niagara Falls...... | 19.00 | Montreal............ | 7.50 |
| Buffalo.............. | 19.50 | Quebec.............. | 10.00 |

Route S 109—

Choice of routes to Montreal (see page 85).
Grand Trunk Railway to Groveton Jct.................................. T 32
Concord & Montreal Railroad to Bethlehem Jct...................... T 25
Profile & Franconia Notch Railroad to Profile House.............. T 26

Fares same as Route S 108—

Route S 110—

Choice of routes to Montreal (see page 85).
Grand Trunk Railway or R. & O. N. Co.'s Steamer to Quebec........... T 36
Ferry to Levis.............................................................. T 37
Grand Trunk Railway to Sherbrooke.................................... T 27
Boston & Maine Railroad to St. Johnsbury........................... T 33
St. Johnsbury & Lake Champlain Railroad to Lunenburg.......... T 38
Maine Central Railroad to Bethlehem Jct............................. T 28
Profile & Franconia Notch Railroad to Profile House.............. T 26

Fares:—

| | | | |
|---|---|---|---|
| Detroit............... | *$26.00 | Toronto............... | $21.00 |
| Port Huron........... | * 25.90 | Kingston............. | 16.25 |
| London............... | * 24.30 | Brockville.......... | 14.75 |
| Hamilton............. | 22.20 | Ottawa.............. | 13.50 |
| Niagara Falls....... | 22.50 | Montreal............ | 11.00 |
| Buffalo.............. | 23.00 | Quebec.............. | † 8.50 |

Route S 111—

Same as Route S 110 to Levis.
Grand Trunk Railway to Groveton Jct.................................. T 27
Concord & Montreal Railroad to Bethlehem Jct...................... T 25
Profile & Franconia Notch Railroad to Profile House.............. T 26

Fares same as Route S 110.

# To QUEBEC, Que.

‡Route S 112—

Choice of routes to Montreal (see page 85).
Grand Trunk Railway or R. & O. N. Co.'s Steamer to Quebec........... X 7

Fares:—

| | | | |
|---|---|---|---|
| Detroit............... | *$17.50 | Toronto............... | $ 13.50 |
| Port Huron........... | * 17.40 | Kingston............. | 8.75 |
| Niagara Falls....... | * 14.00 | Brockville.......... | 7.25 |
| Buffalo.............. | 14.50 | Ottawa.............. | 7.00 |

*All rail to Montreal. For tickets optional rail or steamer, Kingston to Prescott and Prescott to Montreal, add 75c. from Detroit, and for tickets optional rail or steamer, Toronto to Kingston, Kingston to Prescott and Prescott to Montreal, add $1.60 from Detroit, 20c. from Port Huron, and 10c. from London.
†Via Grand Trunk direct to Portland, not coming into Montreal. Use Form T 27 from Levis.

# To ROUND ISLAND, N. Y.

Route S 113—
Choice of routes to Toronto (see pages 84 and 85).          FORM.
Grand Trunk Railway to Gananoque Junction ..................... ....T 76
Thousand Islands Railway to Gananoque........................T 7
Deseronto Navigation Co.'s Steamer to Round Island ..................T 8

Fares :—

| | | | |
|---|---|---|---|
| Detroit .............. | $ 12.45 | Niagara Falls. . ...$ | 6.60 |
| Port Huron . .. .. | 10.95 | Buffalo... ... ...... | 7.10 |
| London ... .. ... | 8.90 | Toronto . . ......... | 5.85 |
| Hamilton .......... | 6.60 | Kingston ........... | 1.00 |

Route S 114—
Choice of routes to Toronto (see pages 84 and 85).
Grand Trunk Railway or R. & O. N. Co.'s Steamer to Kingston..........T 5
Richelieu & Ontario Navigation Co.'s steamer to Round Island ........T 6

Fares :—

| | | | |
|---|---|---|---|
| Detroit .............. | $ 12.45 | Hamilton ... ......$ | 6.60 |
| Port Huron... ..... | 10.95 | Niagara Falls....... | 6.60 |
| London ............. | 8.90 | Buffalo............. | 7.10 |

# To ST. ANDREWS, N. B.

Route S 115—
Choice of routes to Montreal (see page 85).
Grand Trunk Railway to Portland . ........................................T 32
Maine Central Railroad to Vanceboro' ....................................T 52
New Brunswick Railway to St. Andrews.............................T 51

Fares :—

| | | | | | |
|---|---|---|---|---|---|
| Detroit ......*$23.50 | ........ | Toronto ..... $$$21.50 | ¶$20.05 | | |
| Port Huron .* 23.50 | ........ | Kingston.... 18.75 | ........ | | |
| London.....* 23.50 | ¶$22.35 | Brockville .. 17.25 | ........ | | |
| Hamilton....§ 22.70 | ¶ 20.05 | Ottawa...... 17.00 | ........ | | |
| Niagara Falls§ 23.00 | ¶ 20.05 | Montreal ... 13.50 | ........ | | |
| Buffalo ......§ 23.50 | ¶ 20.55 | Quebec .....† 15.00 | ........ | | |

Route S 116—
Same as Route S 115 to Portland.
International Steamship Co. to St. Andrews ........................ ......T 49

Fares :—

| | | | |
|---|---|---|---|
| Detroit......*$23.50 | ........ | Toronto ..... $21.50 | ¶$20.05 |
| Port Huron..* 23.50 | ........ | Kingston..... 16.75 | ....... |
| London ...* 23.50 | ¶$22.35 | Brockville ... 15.25 | ....... |
| Hamilton.... 22.70 | ¶ 20.05 | Ottawa ...... 15.00 | ....... |
| Niagara Falls 23.00 | ¶ 20.05 | Montreal .... 11.50 | ... ... |
| Buffalo ....... 24.00 | ¶ 20.55 | Quebec ...... 12.50 | ....... |

# To ST. JOHN, N. B.

Route S 117—
Choice of routes to Montreal (see page 85).
Grand Trunk Railway or R. & O. N. Co.'s Steamer to Quebec...........T 36
Ferry to Levis .................... ..... .............. .............T 37
Intercolonial Railway to St. John ......... ....................... ......T 42

*All rail to Montreal. For tickets optional rail or steamer, Kingston to
Prescott and Prescott to Montreal, add 75c. from Detroit; and for tickets
optional rail or steamer, Toronto to Kingston, Kingston to Prescott, and Prescott to
Montreal, add $1.00 from Detroit, 20c. from Port Huron, and 10c. from London.
§Limited to continuous passage east of Montreal.
¶All rail, and limited to continuous passage entire journey. For St. John
Form T 32 to be issued, reading Montreal to Levis.

# To ST. JOHN, N. B.—*Continued.*

Fares :—

| | | | | |
|---|---|---|---|---|
| Detroit | *$23.50 | ........ | Toronto ......$21.50 | ¶$20.05 |
| Port Huron..* | 23.50 | ........ | Kingston..... 18.75 | ........ |
| London .....* | 23.50 | ⸿$22.35 | Brockville ... 17.25 | ........ |
| Hamilton .... | 22.70 | ¶ 20.05 | Ottawa....... 17.00 | ........ |
| Niagara Falls | 23.00 | ¶ 20.05 | Montreal .... 13.50 | ........ |
| Buffalo ....... | 23.50 | ¶ 20.55 | | |

**Route S 118—**

Choice of routes to Montreal (see page 85).  FORM.

Grand Trunk Railway or R. & O. N. Co.'s Steamer to Quebec ....... ....T  36

Quebec Steamship Co. (on alternate Tuesdays only) to Pointe du Chene.T  53

Intercolonial Railway to St. John.........................................T  46

Fares :—

| | | | |
|---|---|---|---|
| Detroit | .............*$30.40 | Toronto | .............$25.40 |
| Port Huron | ..........* 30.30 | Kingston | ............. 20.65 |
| London | ................* 28.70 | Brockville | ... ...... 19.15 |
| Hamilton | .......... 26.60 | Ottawa | ............. 17.90 |
| Niagara Falls | ........ 26.90 | Montreal | ......... 15.40 |
| Buffalo | ............... 27.40 | | |

**Route S 119—**

Choice of routes to Montreal (see page 85).

Grand Trunk Railway to Portland .....................................T  32

Maine Central Railroad to Vanceboro.......... ...............T  52

New Brunswick Railway to St. John..............................T  51

Fares :—

| | | | | |
|---|---|---|---|---|
| Detroit | .......*$23.50 | ........ | Toronto .....§§$21.50 | ¶$20.05 |
| Port Huron..* | 23.50 | | Kingston..... 18.75 | ........ |
| London ......* | 23.50 | ⸿$22.35 | Brockville ... 17.25 | ........ |
| Hamilton ....§ | 22.70 | ⸿ 20.05 | Ottawa...... 17.00 | ........ |
| Niagara Falls§ | 23.00 | ⸿ 20.05 | Montreal.... 13.50 | ........ |
| Buffalo.......§ | 23.50 | ¶ 20.60 | | |

# To SARATOGA, N. Y.

**‡Route S 120—**

Choice of routes to Montreal (see page 85).

Grand Trunk Railway to Rouse's Point.....................................⎫

Delaware & Hudson Railroad to Plattsburg ...............................⎪ X  23

Champ. Trans. Co.'s Str. or D. & H. Railroad to Fort Ticonderoga .....⎬

Delaware & Hudson Railroad to Saratoga.................................⎭

Fares :—

| | | | |
|---|---|---|---|
| Detroit | ....*$21.50 | Toronto | .............$ 16.50 |
| Port Huron | ..........* 21.40 | Kingston | ............ 11.75 |
| London | ................* 19.80 | Brockville | ......... 10.25 |
| Hamilton | .......... 17.70 | Ottawa | .............. 10.00 |
| Niagara Falls | ........ 18.00 | Montreal. | ......... 6.50 |
| Buffalo | .... ........... 18.50 | Quebec | .... ...... 8.50 |

**‡Route S 121—**

Same as Route S 120 to Fort Ticonderoga.

Delaware & Hudson Railroad to Baldwin............................⎫

Lake George Steamer to Caldwell...................................⎬ X  18

Delaware & Hudson Railroad to Saratoga............................⎭

Fares :—

| | | | |
|---|---|---|---|
| Detroit | .............*$23.50 | Toronto | .............$ 18.50 |
| Port Huron | ..........* 23.40 | Kingston | ............. 13.75 |
| London | ................* 21.80 | Brockville | ........... 12.25 |
| Hamilton | .......... 19.70 | Ottawa | ............. 12.00 |
| Niagara Falls | ........ 20.00 | Montreal | ..... ..... 8.50 |
| Buffalo | ............... 20.50 | Quebec | ............... 10.50 |

*All rail to Montreal. For tickets optional rail or steamer, Kingston to Prescott and Prescott to Montreal, add 75c. from Detroit; and for tickets optional rail or steamer, Toronto to Kingston, Kingston to Prescott, and Prescott to Montreal, add $1.60 from Detroit, 20c. from Port Huron, and 10c. from London.

§Limited to continuous passage east of Montreal.

¶All rail, and limited to continuous passage entire journey. For St. John Form T 32 to be issued, reading Montreal to Levis.

# To SARATOGA, N. Y.--*Continued.*

‡Route S 122—

    Choice of routes to Montreal (see page 85).
    Grand Trunk Railway to St. Johns...................................... ⎫ FORM.
    Central Vermont Railroad to St. Albans, Burlington.................. ⎬ X 52
    Champ. Trans. Co.'s Steamer to Fort Ticonderoga................... ⎪
    Delaware and Hudson Railroad to Saratoga . ....................... ⎭

    **Fares same as Route S 120.**

‡Route S 123—

    Same as Route S 122 to Fort Ticonderoga.
    Delaware & Hudson Railroad to Baldwin.......................... ⎫
    Lake George Steamer to Caldwell ..... .......................... ⎬ X 53
    Delaware & Hudson Railroad to Saratoga.......................... ⎭

    **Fares same as Route S 121.**

Route S 124—

    Choice of routes to Montreal (see page 85).
    Grand Trunk Railway to St. Johns..................................T 11
    Central Vermont Railroad to St. Albans, Burlington, Rutland..........T 61
    Delaware & Hudson Railroad to Whitehall, Saratoga................T 21

    **Fares same as Route S 120.**

Route S 125—

    Choice of routes to Montreal (see page 85).
    Grand Trunk Railway to Gorham... ...............................T 32
    Milliken's Stage to Glen House.....................................T 79
    Milliken's Stage to Summit.........................................T 39
    Mount Washington Railway to Base ................................T 41
    Concord & Montreal Railroad to Fabyans...........................T 25
    Maine Central Railroad to Crawford House .........................T 28
    Maine Central Railroad to Fabyans.................................T 28
    Concord & Montreal Railroad to Bethlehem Jct.....................T 25
    Profile & Franconia Notch Railroad to Profile House................T 26
    Profile & Franconia Notch Railroad to Bethlehem Jct...............T 26
    Concord & Montreal Railroad to Wells River .......................T 25
    Montpelier & Wells River Railroad to Montpelier . .................T 24
    Central Vermont Railroad to Burlington.............................T 12
    Champlain Transportation Co.'s Steamer to Fort Ticonderoga ........T 18
    Delaware & Hudson Railroad to Baldwin...........................T 20
    Lake George Steamer to Caldwell .................................T 22
    Delaware & Hudson Railroad to Saratoga..........................T 21

    Fares :—

| | | | |
|---|---|---|---|
| Detroit | *$45.90 | Toronto .. ......... | $ 40.90 |
| Port Huron | * 45.80 | Kingston ........... | 36.15 |
| London | * 44.20 | Brockville ......... | 34.65 |
| Hamilton | 42.10 | Ottawa ........... | 33.40 |
| Niagara Falls | 42.40 | Montreal . ........ | 30.90 |
| Buffalo | 42.90 | Quebec ............ | † 31.90 |

Route S 126—

    Same as Route S 125 to Profile House.
    Stage to North Woodstock ........................................T 79
    Concord & Montreal Railroad to Wells River .......................T 25
    Same as Route S 125 to Saratoga.

    Fares :—

| | | | |
|---|---|---|---|
| Detroit | *$47.10 | Toronto............ | $ 42.10 |
| Port Huron | * 47.00 | Kingston ........ | 37.35 |
| London | * 45.40 | Brockville ...... ... | 35.85 |
| Hamilton | 43.30 | Ottawa..... ...... | 34.60 |
| Niagara Falls | 43.60 | Montreal............ | 32.10 |
| Buffalo | 44.10 | Quebec .............. | † 33.10 |

    *All rail to Montreal. For tickets optional rail or steamer, Kingston to Prescott and Prescott to Montreal, add 75c. from Detroit, and for tickets optional rail or steamer, Toronto to Kingston, Kingston to Prescott and Prescott to Montreal, add $1.60 from Detroit, 20c. from Port Huron and 10c. from London.
    †Via Grand Trunk direct, not coming into Montreal. Use Form T 27 from Levis.

## To THOUSAND ISLAND PARK, N. Y.

Route S 127—

Choice of routes to Toronto (see pages 84 and 85). FORM.
Grand Trunk Railway to Gananoque Jct.............................T 76
Thousand Islands Railway to Gananoque..........................T 7
Deseronto Navigation Co. to Thousand Island Park.............T 8

Fares :—

| | | | |
|---|---|---|---|
| Detroit | $12.45 | Niagara Falls | $ 6.70 |
| Port Huron | 10.95 | Buffalo | 7.20 |
| London | 9.00 | Toronto | 5.85 |
| Hamilton | 6.70 | Kingston | 1.00 |

Route S 128—

Choice of routes to Toronto (see pages 84 and 85).
Grand Trunk Railway or R. & O. N. Co.'s Steamer to Kingston........ T 5
R. & O. N. Co.'s Steamer to Thousand Island Park....................T 6

Fares :—

| | | | |
|---|---|---|---|
| Detroit | $12.45 | Hamilton | $ 6.70 |
| Port Huron | 10.95 | Niagara Falls | 6.70 |
| London | 9.00 | Buffalo | 7.20 |

# Round-Trip Tours

TO POINTS IN

## Muskoka, Thousand Islands, Rangeley Lake District, Adirondacks, White Mountains, and Sea-Bathing Resorts on Atlantic Sea Coast and St. Lawrence River.

ALSO TO

## *MONTREAL, NIAGARA FALLS AND TORONTO.*

### To Alexandria Bay, N. Y., and Return.

Route R T 1—

Choice of routes to Toronto (see pages 84 and 85). FORM.
Grand Trunk Railway to Gananoque Jct...........................T 76
Thousand Islands Railway to Gananoque.........................T 7
Deseronto Nav. Co.'s Steamer to Alexandria Bay...............T 8
Returning same route to Gananoque Jct.........................
Grand Trunk Railway to starting point..........................T 76

Fares :—

| | | | |
|---|---|---|---|
| Detroit | $21.10 | Toronto | †$10.10 |
| Port Huron | 18.60 | Kingston, limited 1 month † | 2.30 |
| London | 15.60 | Brockville, " " † | 3.15 |
| Hamilton | 12.10 | Montreal | † 9.50 |
| Niagara Falls | 12.50 | Quebec | † 14.50 |
| Buffalo | 13.50 | | |

Route R T 2—

Choice of routes to Toronto (see pages 84 and 85).
Grand Trunk Railway or R. & O. N. Co.'s Steamer to Kingston..........T 5
Richelieu & Ontario Navigation Co.'s Steamer to Alexandria Bay......T 6
Richelieu & Ontario Navigation Co.'s Steamer to Kingston............T 6
Grand Trunk Railway to starting point.................................T 76

†Direct to Gananoque Jct.

## To Alexandria Bay, N. Y., and Return.—*Continued.*

Fares :—

| | | | |
|---|---|---|---|
| Detroit | $21.10 | Niagara Falls | $12.50 |
| Port Huron | 18.60 | Buffalo | 13.50 |
| London | 16.35 | Toronto | 10.50 |
| Hamilton | 12.50 | | |

Route R T 3—

| | FORM. |
|---|---|
| Grand Trunk Railway to Gananoque Jct. | T 76 |
| Thousand Islands Railway to Gananoque | T 7 |
| Deseronto Navigation Co.'s Steamers to Alexandria Bay | T 8 |
| Rich. & Ont. Nav. Co.'s Steamer to Brockville or Montreal | T 6 |

Fares :—

| | | | |
|---|---|---|---|
| Brockville | $ 2.75 | Quebec | ¶ $14.50 |
| Montreal | 9.50 | | |

Route R T 4—

| | |
|---|---|
| Grand Trunk Railway to Kingston City | T 76 |
| Richelieu & Ontario Navigation Co.'s Steamer to Alexandria Bay | T 6 |
| Richelieu & Ontario Navigation Co.'s Steamer to Brockville or Montreal | T 6 |

Fares :—

| | | | |
|---|---|---|---|
| Brockville | $ 3.40 | Quebec | ¶ $14.50 |
| Montreal | 9.50 | | |

## All Round Muskoka Lakes and Return.

‡Route R T 5—

Grand Trunk Railway to Gravenhurst via Toronto, Muskoka & Georgian Bay Navigation Co.'s Steamer All Round the Lakes and Return. Grand Trunk Railway to starting point. } 5062 R or X382

Fares :—

| | | | |
|---|---|---|---|
| Detroit | $14.60 | Toronto | $ 7.00 |
| Port Huron | 12.70 | Kingston | 13.50 |
| London | 10.10 | Brockville | 15.35 |
| Hamilton | 7.00 | Ottawa | 17.40 |
| Niagara Falls | 8.90 | Montreal | 19.25 |
| Buffalo | 9.90 | Quebec | 24.25 |

## To Andover, Me., and Return.

Route R T 6—

Choice of routes to Montreal (see page 85.)

| | |
|---|---|
| Grand Trunk Railway to Bryant's Pond | T 32 |
| Stage to Andover | T 79 |
| Stage to Bryant's Pond | T 79 |
| Grand Trunk Railway to starting point | T 76 |

Fares :—

| | | | |
|---|---|---|---|
| Detroit | *$35.00 | Toronto | *$27.50 |
| Port Huron | * 34.85 | Kingston | * 20.40 |
| London | * 32.60 | Brockville | * 18.10 |
| Hamilton | * 29.30 | Ottawa | 17.50 |
| Niagara Falls | * 29.75 | Montreal | 12.50 |
| Buffalo | * 30.75 | Quebec | § 14.50 |

## To Bala (Muskoka Lakes) and Return.

‡Route R T 7—

Grand Trunk Railway to Gravenhurst via Toronto. Muskoka & Georgian Bay Nav. Co.'s Steamers to Bala. Return same route. } 5062 R

*All rail to Montreal. For tickets optional rail or steamer, Kingston to Prescott and Prescott to Montreal, on eastbound journey, add 75c. from Detroit and $1.60 from Kingston, and for tickets optional rail or steamer, Toronto to Kingston, Kingston to Prescott, and Prescott to Montreal, on eastbound journey add $1.60 from Detroit, 20c. from Port Huron, $2.45 from London (not exceeding Port Huron), $2.20 from Hamilton, $1.75 from Niagara Falls, $1.75 from Buffalo, and $3.00 from Toronto.

¶Optional rail or steamer, Montreal to Quebec. Use form T 36.

§Via Grand Trunk direct, not coming into Montreal. Use form T 27 from Levis.

# To Bala (Muskoka Lakes) and Return.—*Continued.*

Fares :—

| | | | |
|---|---|---|---|
| Detroit | $13.10 | Toronto | $ 5.50 |
| Port Huron | 11.20 | Kingston | 12.00 |
| London | 8.60 | Brockville | 13.85 |
| Hamilton | 5.50 | Ottawa | 15.90 |
| Niagara Falls | 7.40 | Montreal | 17.75 |
| Buffalo | 8.40 | Quebec | 22.75 |

## To Bar Harbor, Me., and Return.

Route R T 8—

Choice of routes to Montreal (see page 85).                                    FORM.
Grand Trunk Railway to Portland ............................................. T  32
Maine Central Railroad to Bar Harbor ...................................... T  52
Maine Central Railroad to Portland. ......................................... T  52
Grand Trunk Railway to starting point ...................................... T  74

Fares :—

| | | | | |
|---|---|---|---|---|
| Detroit | *$41.50 | Toronto | .*$36.50 | *¶$34.00 |
| Pt. Huron* | 41.35 | Kingston.* | 29.40 | *¶ 26.90 |
| London ...* | 41.35 | *¶$39.10 | Bro'kville* | 27.10 | *¶ 24.60 |
| Hamilton..* | 38.30 | *¶ 35.80 | Ottawa.... | 26.50 | ¶ 24.00 |
| Niag'ra Fls* | 38 75 | *¶ 36.25 | Montreal.. | 21.50 | ¶ 19.00 |
| Buffalo ....* | 39.75 | *¶ 37.25 | Quebec...† | 23.50 | †¶ 21.00 |

Route R T 9—

Same as Route R T 8 to Portland.
Portland, Mt. Desert & Machias S. B. Co.'s Steamer to Bar Harbor ..... T  107
Portland, Mt. Desert & Machias S. B. Co.'s Steamer to Portland... .... T  107
Grand Trunk Railway to starting point ..................................... T   74

Fares :—

| | | | |
|---|---|---|---|
| Detroit | *$39.00 | Toronto | .*$31.50 |
| Port Huron | * 38.85 | Kingston | * 24.40 |
| London | * 36.60 | Brockville | * 22.10 |
| Hamilton | * 33.30 | Ottawa | 21.50 |
| Niagara Falls | * 33.75 | Montreal | 16.50 |
| Buffalo | * 34.75 | Quebec | 18.50 |

## To Beaumaris (Muskoka Lakes) and Return.

‡Route R T 10—

Grand Trunk Railway to Gravenhurst, via Toronto.  Muskoka &  ⎫
    Georgian Bay Navigation Co.'s Steamer to Beaumaris.  Re- ⎬5062 R
    turn same route ................................................................ ⎭

Fares :—

| | | | |
|---|---|---|---|
| Detroit | $12.90 | Toronto | $ 5.30 |
| Port Huron | 11.00 | Kingston | 11.80 |
| London | 8.40 | Brockville | 13.65 |
| Hamilton | 5.30 | Ottawa | 15.70 |
| Niagara Falls | 7.20 | Montreal | 17.50 |
| Buffalo | 8.20 | Quebec | 22.50 |

## To Berlin Falls, N. H., Bethel, Me., or Bryant's Pond, Me., and Return.

(Gateways for Androscoggin or Rangeley Lake country).

Route R T 11—

Choice of routes to Montreal (see page 85)
Grand Trunk Railway to Berlin Falls, Bethel, or Bryant's Pond ....... T   32
Grand Trunk Railway to starting point ...................................... T   76

*See first foot note on page 114.
†Via Grand Trunk Railway direct, not coming into Montreal.  Use form T
27 from Levis.
¶Limited to continuous passage each way between Portland and Bar Harbor.
Tickets to be endorsed accordingly.

## To Berlin Falls, N. H., Etc.—*Continued.*

Fares:—

| | | | |
|---|---|---|---|
| Detroit | *$32.00 | Toronto | *$24.50 |
| Port Huron | * 31.85 | Kingston | * 17.40 |
| London | * 29.60 | Brockville | * 15.10 |
| Hamilton | * 26.30 | Ottawa | 14.50 |
| Niagara Falls | * 26.75 | Montreal | 9.50 |
| Buffalo | * 27.75 | Quebec | † 11.50 |

## To Bethlehem, N. H., and Return.

Route R T 12—
Choice of routes to Montreal (see page 85).

| | | FORM. |
|---|---|---|
| Grand Trunk Railway to Groveton Jct | T | 32 |
| Concord & Montreal Railroad to Bethlehem Jct | T | 25 |
| Profile & Franconia Railroad to Bethlehem | T | 26 |
| Return same route to Groveton Jct. | | |
| Grand Trunk Railway to starting point | T | 76 |

Fares:—

| | | | |
|---|---|---|---|
| Detroit | *$33.00 | Toronto | *$25.50 |
| Port Huron | * 32.85 | Kingston | * 18.40 |
| London | * 30.60 | Brockville | * 16.10 |
| Hamilton | * 27.30 | Ottawa | 15.50 |
| Niagara Falls | * 27.75 | Montreal | 10.50 |
| Buffalo | * 28.75 | Quebec | † 12.50 |

## To Bluff Point (Hotel Champlain), N. Y., and Return.

Route R T 13—
Choice of routes to Montreal (see page 85).

| | | |
|---|---|---|
| Grand Trunk Railway to Rouse's Point | T | 16 |
| Delaware & Hudson Railroad to Bluff Point | T | 21 |
| Delaware & Hudson Railroad to Rouse's Point | T | 21 |
| Grand Trunk Railway to starting point | T | 76 |

Fares:—

| | | | |
|---|---|---|---|
| Detroit | *$27.05 | Toronto | *$19.55 |
| Port Huron | * 26.90 | Kingston | * 12.45 |
| London | * 24.65 | Brockville | * 10.15 |
| Hamilton | * 21.35 | Ottawa | 9.55 |
| Niagara Falls | * 21.80 | Montreal | 4.55 |
| Buffalo | * 22.80 | Quebec | 9.55 |

## To Boston, Mass., and Return.

Route R T 14—
Choice of routes to Montreal (see page 85).

| | | |
|---|---|---|
| Grand Trunk Railway to St. Johns | T | 11 |
| Central Vermont Railroad to White River Jct | T | 84 |
| Boston & Maine Railroad to Concord | T | 35 |
| Concord & Montreal Railroad to Nashua | T | 34 |
| Boston & Maine Railroad to Boston | T | 29 |
| Return same route to St. Johns. | | |
| Grand Trunk Railway to starting point | T | 76 |

Fares:—

| | | | |
|---|---|---|---|
| Detroit | §$38.50 | Toronto | §$28.50 |
| Port Huron | § 36.15 | Kingston | § 22.45 |
| London | § 33.60 | Brockville | 19.95 |
| Hamilton | § 30.30 | Ottawa | 18.00 |
| Niagara Falls | § 30.75 | Montreal | 16.00 |
| Buffalo | § 31.75 | Quebec | 18.00 |

*See first foot note on page 114.

§All rail to Montreal. For tickets optional rail or steamer, Kingston to Prescott and Prescott to Montreal on eastbound journey, add 75c. from Detroit; $3.05 from Kingston, and for tickets optional rail or steamer, Toronto to Kingston, Kingston to Prescott, and Prescott to Montreal on eastbound journey, add $1.60 from Detroit. $2.40 from Port Huron, $4.95 from London, $4.70 from Hamilton, $4.25 from Niagara Falls, $4.25 from Buffalo, and $5.50 from Toronto.

†Via Grand Trunk Railway direct, not coming into Montreal. Use Form T 27 from Levis.

# To Boston, Mass., and Return.--*Continued.*

**Route R T 15—**

Choice of routes to Montreal (see page 85).
| | | FORM. |
|---|---|---|
| Grand Trunk Railway to Portland........................ | T | 32 |
| Boston & Maine Railroad to Boston ..................... | T | 50 |
| Boston & Maine Railroad to Portland : ................. | T | 50 |
| Grand Trunk Railway to starting point................. | T | 74 |

Fares :—

| Detroit .....§§$38.50 *¶$37.50 | Toronto....§§$28.50 |
|---|---|
| Port Huron § 36.15 | Kingston .§ 22.45 |
| London.....§ 33.60 | Brockville 19.95 |
| Hamilton...§ 30.30 | Ottawa .. 18.00 |
| Niag'a Falls§ 30.75 | Montreal .. 16.00 ¶$15.00 |
| Buffalo......§ 31.75 | Quebec.... 18.00 ¶ 17.00 |

**Route R T 16—**

Choice of routes to Montreal (see page 85).
| | | |
|---|---|---|
| Grand Trunk Railway to Portland........................ | T | 32 |
| Portland Steam Packet Co. to Boston ................... | T | 81 |
| Portland Steam Packet Co. to Portland... ............. | T | 81 |
| Grand Trunk Railway to starting point................. | T | 47 |

Fares :—

| Detroit ................*$35.00 | Toronto ............*$27.50 |
|---|---|
| Port Huron...........* 34.85 | Kingston ...........* 20.40 |
| London ............* 32.60 | Brockville ........* 18.10 |
| Hamilton.... ...* 29.30 | Ottawa............ 17.50 |
| Niagara Falls.........* 29.75 | Montreal............ 12.50 |
| Buffalo ...............* 30.75 | Quebec............. 14.50 |

**Route R T 17—**

Choice of routes to Montreal (see page 85).
| | | |
|---|---|---|
| Grand Trunk Railway to Portland........................ | T | 32 |
| Boston & Maine Railroad to Boston.. .................. | T | 50 |
| Boston & Maine Railroad to Nashua..................... | T | 29 |
| Concord & Montreal Railroad to Concord............... | T | 34 |
| Boston & Maine Railroad to White River Jct........... | T | 35 |
| Central Vermont Railroad to St. Johns ................ | T | 84 |
| Grand Trunk Railway to starting point................. | T | 76 |

*(margin: R.W.)*

Fares same as Route R T 14.

**‡Route R T 18—**

Choice of routes to Montreal (see page 85).
| | | |
|---|---|---|
| Grand Trunk Railway to Portland...................... | T | 32 |
| Portland Steam Packet Co.'s Steamer to Boston......... | T | 81 |
| Same as Route R T 17 to starting point. | | |

*(margin: R.W.)*

Fares same as Route R T 14.

**Route R T 19—**

Choice of routes to Montreal (see page 85).
| | | |
|---|---|---|
| Grand Trunk Railway to Groveton Jct...... | T | 32 |
| Concord & Montreal Railroad to Scotts ......... ...... | T | 25 |
| Maine Central Railroad to North Conway. ............. | T | 28 |
| Boston & Maine Railroad to Boston ................... | T | 30 |
| Returning to Montreal same as Route R T 14. | | |

*(margin: R.W.)*

Fares :—

| Detroit.. ............*$41.00 | Toronto ...........*$33.50 |
|---|---|
| Port Huron ........* 40.85 | Kingston ...........* 26.40 |
| London .......... ....* 38.60 | Brockville ..........* 24.10 |
| Hamilton......... * 35.30 | Ottawa ............ 23.50 |
| Niagara Falls.........* 35.75 | Montreal ............ 18.50 |
| Buffalo ...............* 36.75 | Quebec .............† 20.50 |

*See first foot note on page 114.

§All rail to Montreal. For tickets optional rail or steamer, Kingston to Prescott and Prescott to Montreal on eastbound journey, add 75c. from Detroit; $3.05 from Kingston, and for tickets optional rail or steamer, Toronto to Kingston, Kingston to Prescott, and Prescott to Montreal on eastbound journey, add $1.60 from Detroit, $2.40 from Port Huron, $4.95 from London, $4.70 from Hamilton, $4.25 from Niagara Falls, $4. 25 from Buffalo. and $5.50 from Toronto.

†Via Grand Trunk Railway direct, not coming into Montreal. Use Form T 27 from Levis.

¶Limited to continuous passage.

## To Boston, Mass., and Return.—*Continued.*

**Route R T 20—**

R.W.

| | FORM. |
|---|---|
| Choice of routes to Montreal (see page 85) | |
| Grand Trunk Railway to St. Johns | T 11 |
| Central Vermont Railroad to Montpelier | T 12 |
| Montpelier & Wells River Railroad to Wells River | T 24 |
| Concord & Montreal Railroad to Fabyans | T 25 |
| Maine Central Railroad to North Conway | T 28 |
| Boston & Maine Railroad to Boston | T 30 |
| Returning to Montreal same as Route R. T. 14. | |

Fares same as Route R T 19 (except Quebec. $22.00).

**Route R T 21—**

| | FORM. |
|---|---|
| Choice of routes to Montreal (see page 85). | |
| Grand Trunk Railway to St. Johns | T 11 |
| Central Vermont Railroad to White River Jct | T 84 |
| Boston & Maine Railroad to Concord | T 35 |
| Concord & Montreal Railroad to Nashua | T 34 |
| Boston & Maine Railroad to Boston | T 29 |
| Fitchburg Railroad to Rotterdam | T 15 |
| West Shore Railroad to Suspension Bridge | T 66 |
| Grand Trunk Railway to starting point. | |

Fares :—

| | | | |
|---|---|---|---|
| Detroit | $37.00 | Niagara Falls | $27.50 |
| Port Huron | 34.60 | Buffalo | 28.00 |
| London | 31.35 | Toronto | 27.50 |
| Hamilton | 27.50 | Kingston | 27.50 |

**Route R T 22—**

| | FORM. |
|---|---|
| Choice of routes to Montreal (see page 85). | |
| Grand Trunk Railway to Portland | T 32 |
| Boston & Maine Railroad to Boston | T 50 |
| Returning same as Route R T 21. | |

Fares same as Route R T 21.

**Route R T 23—**

| | FORM. |
|---|---|
| Choice of routes to Montreal (see page 85). | |
| Grand Trunk Railway to Portland | T 32 |
| Portland Steam Packet Co. to Boston | T 81 |
| Returning same as Route R T 21. | |

Fares same as Route R T 21.

## To Bracebridge (Muskoka) and Return.

**Route R T 24—**

| | |
|---|---|
| Grand Trunk Railway to Gravenhurst via Toronto | |
| G. T. R. or Muskoka & Georgian Bay Nav. Co.'s Str. to Bracebridge | 5062 R |
| Returning same route. | |

Fares .—

| | | | |
|---|---|---|---|
| Detroit | $ 12.60 | Toronto | $ 5.00 |
| Port Huron | 10.55 | Kingston | 11.50 |
| London | 8.10 | Brockville | 13.35 |
| Hamilton | 5.00 | Ottawa | 15.40 |
| Niagara Falls | 6.90 | Montreal | 17.35 |
| Buffalo | 7.90 | Quebec | 22.35 |

## To Brockville, Ont., and Return.

**Route R T 25—**

| | FORM. |
|---|---|
| Choice of routes to Toronto (see pages 84 and 85). | |
| Grand Trunk Railway or R. & O. N. Co.'s Steamer to Kingston | T 5 |
| Grand Trunk Railway or R. & O. N. Co.'s Steamer to Brockville | T 57 |
| Grand Trunk Railway to starting point | T 76 |

¶All rail Toronto to Montreal. For tickets optional rail or steamer, Toronto to Kingston, Kingston to Prescott and Prescott to Montreal, add $1.50 to fares shown.

# To Brockville, Ont., and Return.--*Continued.*

Fares :—

| | | | |
|---|---|---|---|
| Detroit | $ 21.60 | Niagara Falls | $13.25 |
| Port Huron | 19.10 | Buffalo | 14.25 |
| London ..limited 1 month. | 16.70 | Toronto...limited 1 month | 11.00 |
| Hamilton " " | 13.00 | | |

‡Route R T 26—

Grand Trunk Railway to Brockville ............................... } FORM.
Grand Trunk Railway or R. & O. N. Co.'s Steamer to Montreal ...... } 2888

Fares :—

| | | |
|---|---|---|
| Montreal . limited 5 days. ¶$ 6.25 | Quebec . limited 5 days. ¶$11.25 | |

# To Burk's Falls (Muskoka) and Return.

‡Route R T 27—

Grand Trunk Railway to Burk's Falls via Toronto and return..........2900

Fares :—

| | | | |
|---|---|---|---|
| Detroit | $ 14.55 | Toronto | $ 6.95 |
| Port Huron | 12.50 | Kingston | 13.45 |
| London | 10.05 | Brockville | 15.30 |
| Hamilton | 6.95 | Ottawa | 16.75 |
| Niagara Falls | 8.80 | Montreal | 16.75 |
| Buffalo | 9.80 | Quebec | 21.75 |

# To Cacouna, Que., and Return.

‡Route R T 28—

Grand Trunk Railway to Levis.................................. }
Intercolonial Railway to Cacouna .............................. } 2852
Return same route.

Fares :—

| | | | |
|---|---|---|---|
| Detroit | *$30.50 | Toronto | *$23.00 |
| Port Huron | * 30.35 | Kingston | * 15.90 |
| London | * 28.10 | Brockville | * 13.60 |
| Hamilton | * 24.80 | Ottawa | 13.00 |
| Niagara Falls | * 25.25 | Montreal | 8.00 |
| Buffalo | * 26.25 | | |

# To Charlottetown, P. E. I., and Return.

‡Route R T 29—

Grand Trunk Railway to Levis.................... ... ......... }
Intercolonial Railway to Pointe du Chene ....................... }
Prince Edward Island Steam Nav. Co. to Summerside .............. } 2763
Prince Edward Island Railway to Charlottetown................... }
Return same route.

Fares :—

| | | | |
|---|---|---|---|
| Detroit | *$46.85 | Toronto | *$39.35 |
| Port Huron | * 46.70 | Kingston | * 32.25 |
| London | ¶ 43.70 | Brockville | 29.95 |
| Hamilton | ¶ 39.85 | Ottawa | 29.35 |
| Niagara Falls | ¶ 39.85 | Montreal | 24.35 |
| Buffalo | ¶ 40.85 | | |

‡Route R T 30—

Grand Trunk Railway to Levis .................................. } 467 R
Quebec S. S. Co. (on alternate Tuesdays only) to Charlottetown..... }
Return same route.

Fares :—

| | | | |
|---|---|---|---|
| Detroit | *$43.25 | Toronto | *$35.75 |
| Port Huron | * 43.10 | Kingston | * 28.65 |
| London | * 40.85 | Brockville | * 26.35 |
| Hamilton | * 37.55 | Ottawa | 25.75 |
| Niagara Falls | * 38.00 | Montreal | 20.75 |
| Buffalo | * 39.00 | | |

*See first foot note on page 114.
¶All rail to Montreal. For tickets optional rail or steamer, Toronto to Kingston, Kingston to Prescott, and Prescott to Montreal, add $1.75 from London Hamilton, Niagara Falls and Buffalo.

# To Chautauqua, N. Y., and Return.

‡Route R T 31—                                                    FORM.
Grand Trunk Railway to Suspension Bridge .................... .....⎫ 4424R
N. Y. C. & H. R. R. R. (1142) or N. Y. L. E. & W. R. R. (1143) to Buffalo ⎪ 1142R
Western New York & Pennsylvania Railroad to Chautauqua......... ⎬ or
Returning same route. .............................................⎭ 1143R

Fares :—

| | | | | |
|---|---|---|---|---|
| Detroit, ....limited 1 month | $14.75 | Kingston | ............ | $14.10 |
| Port Huron | " " 13.00 | Brockville | ...... ..... | 16.45 |
| London, .... | " " 8.95 | Ottawa | ............. | 19.00 |
| Hamilton, | " " 6.10 | Montreal | ............ | 22.75 |
| Toronto, | " " 8.10 | Quebec | ............ | 27.75 |

## To Chicoutimi and Ha! Ha! Bay (Saguenay River) and Return.

‡Route R T 32—
Choice of routes to Montreal (see page 85).
Grand Trunk Railway to Quebec.........................................⎫ 2900
R. & O. N. Co.'s Steamer to Chicoutimi or Ha! Ha! Bay...............⎬ and
Returning same route. ...... ............. .....................⎭ x351

Fares :—

| | | | | |
|---|---|---|---|---|
| Detroit | *$34.50 | Toronto | ............ | *$27.00 |
| Port Huron | * 34.35 | Kingston | ............ | * 19.90 |
| London | * 32.10 | Brockville | ............ | * 17.60 |
| Hamilton | * 28.80 | Ottawa | ............. | 17.00 |
| Niagara Falls | * 29.25 | Montreal | ............ | 12.00 |
| Buffalo | * 30.25 | | | |

## To Clayton, N. Y., and Return.

Route R T 33—
Choice of routes to Toronto (see pages 84 and 85).
Grand Trunk Railway to Gananoque Jct............................T 76
Thousand Islands Railway to Gananoque ..........................T 7
Deseronto Navigation Co.'s Steamer to Clayton....................T 8
Returning same route to Gananoque Jct.
Grand Trunk Railway to starting point ...........................T 76

Fares :—

| | | | | |
|---|---|---|---|---|
| Detroit | $21.10 | Toronto | ...... | $10.10 |
| Port Huron | 18.60 | Kingston, limited 1 month | † | 1.80 |
| London | 15.60 | Brockville. " " | † | 2.90 |
| Hamilton | 11.75 | Montreal | † | 9.50 |
| Niagara Falls | 11.75 | Quebec | † | 14.50 |
| Buffalo | 12.75 | | | |

Route R T 34—
Choice of routes to Toronto (see pages 84 and 85).
Grand Trunk Railway or R. & O. N. Co.'s Steamer to Kingston.........T 5
Richelieu & Ontario Navigation Co.'s Steamer to Clayton...... .......T 6
Richelieu & Ontario Navigation Co.'s Steamer to Kingston...... ......T 6
Grand Trunk Railway to starting point. ..................T 76

Fares :—

| | | | |
|---|---|---|---|
| Detroit | $21.10 | Niagara Falls | $11.75 |
| Port Huron | 18.60 | Buffalo | 12.75 |
| London | 15.60 | Toronto | 10.50 |
| Hamilton | 11.75 | | |

Route R T 35—
Grand Trunk Railway to Gananoque Jct...... ..................T 76
Thousand Islands Railway to Gananoque ..........................T 7
Deseronto Navigation Co.'s Steamer to Clayton, Alexandria Bay.......T 8
Richelieu & Ontario Nav. Co.'s Steamer to Brockville or Montreal.....T 6

Fares :—

| | | | |
|---|---|---|---|
| Brockville | $ 2.75 | Quebec | † $14.50 |
| Montreal | 9.50 | | |

*See first foot note on page 114.
†Direct to Gananoque Jct.

## To Clayton, N. Y., and Return.—*Continued.*

Route R T 36—
    Grand Trunk Railway to Kingston City............................T   76
    Richelieu & Ontario Navigation Co.'s Steamer to Clayton ...........T   6
    Richelieu & Ontario Nav. Co.'s Steamer to Brockville or Montreal.....T   6
    Fares :—

| | | | |
|---|---|---|---|
| Brockville | $ 3.40 | Quebec | §$ 14.50 |
| Montreal | 9.50 | | |

## To Colebrook, N. H., and Return.

Route R T 37—
    Choice of routes to Montreal (see page 85).
    Grand Trunk Railway to North Stratford.......................T   32
    Upper Coos Railway to Colebrook............................T   83
    Upper Coos Railway to North Stratford......................T   83
    Grand Trunk Railway to starting point.......................T   76

Fares :—

| | | | |
|---|---|---|---|
| Detroit | *$33.05 | Toronto | *$25.55 |
| Port Huron | * 32.90 | Kingston | * 18.45 |
| London | * 30.65 | Brockville | * 16.15 |
| Hamilton | * 27.35 | Ottawa | 15.55 |
| Niagara Falls | * 27.80 | Montreal | 10.55 |
| Buffalo | * 28.80 | Quebec | † 12.55 |

## To Dalhousie, N. B., and Return.

;Route R T 38—
    Grand Trunk Railway to Levis.................................⎫
    Intercolonial Railway to Dalhousie...........................⎬2852
    Returning same route.........................................⎭

Fares :—

| | | | |
|---|---|---|---|
| Detroit | *$37.25 | Toronto | *$29.75 |
| Port Huron | * 37.10 | Kingston | * 22.65 |
| London | * 34.85 | Brockville | 20.35 |
| Hamilton | * 31.55 | Ottawa | 19.75 |
| Niagara Falls | * 32.00 | Montreal | 14.75 |
| Buffalo | * 33.00 | | |

## To Errol, N. H. (Rangeley Lakes), and Return.

Route R T 39—
    Choice of routes to Montreal (see page 85).
    Grand Trunk Railway to Berlin Falls .........................T   32
    Stage to Errol (Umbagog House)..............................T   79
    Stage to Berlin Falls .......................................T   79
    Grand Trunk Railway to starting point.......................T   76

Fares :—

| | | | |
|---|---|---|---|
| Detroit | *$35.00 | Toronto | *$27.50 |
| Port Huron | * 34.85 | Kingston | * 20.40 |
| London | * 32.60 | Brockville | 18.10 |
| Hamilton | * 29.30 | Ottawa | 17.50 |
| Niagara Falls | * 29.75 | Montreal | 12.50 |
| Buffalo | * 30.75 | Quebec | † 14.50 |

## To Fabyans, N. H. and Return.

Route R T 40—
    Choice of routes to Montreal (see page 85).
    Grand Trunk Railway to Groveton Jct.........................T   32
    Concord & Montreal Railroad to Fabyans......................T   25
    Concord & Montreal Railroad to Groveton Jct .................T   25
    Grand Trunk Railway to starting point .......................T   76

*See first foot note on page 114.
†Via Grand Trunk Railway direct, not coming into Montreal.
§Direct to Gananoque Jct.

## To Fabyans, N. H., and Return.—*Continued.*

Fares :—

| | | | |
|---|---|---|---|
| Detroit | *$32.00 | Toronto | *$24.50 |
| Port Huron | * 31.85 | Kingston | * 17.40 |
| London | * 29.60 | Brockville | 15.10 |
| Hamilton | * 26.30 | Ottawa | 14.50 |
| Niagara Falls | * 26.75 | Montreal | 9.50 |
| Buffalo | * 27.75 | Quebec | † 11.50 |

Route R T 41—

| | FORM. |
|---|---|
| Same as Route R T 40 to Groveton Jct. | |
| Concord & Montreal Railroad to Scott's | T 25 |
| Maine Central Railroad to Fabyans | T 28 |
| Maine Central Railroad to Scott's | T 28 |
| Concord & Montreal Railroad to Groveton Jct. | T 25 |
| Grand Trunk Railway to starting point | T 76 |

Fares same as Route R T 40.

Route R T 42—

| | |
|---|---|
| Choice of routes to Montreal (see page 85). | |
| Grand Trunk Railway to St. Johns | T 11 |
| Central Vermont Railroad to Montpelier | T 12 |
| Montpelier & Wells River Railroad to Wells River | T 24 |
| Concord & Montreal Railroad to Fabyans | T 25 |
| Return same route to St. Johns | |
| Grand Trunk Railway to starting point | T 76 |

Fares same as Route R T 40 (except Quebec, $13.50).

## To Gaspe, Que., and Return.

‡Route R T 43—

| | |
|---|---|
| Grand Trunk Railway to Levis | |
| Intercolonial Railway to Dalhousie | }  2932 |
| Steamer "Admiral" to Gaspé | |
| Return same route | |

Fares :—

| | | | |
|---|---|---|---|
| Detroit | *$43.25 | Toronto | *$35.75 |
| Port Huron | * 43.10 | Kingston | * 28.65 |
| London | * 40.85 | Brockville | 26.35 |
| Hamilton | * 37.55 | Ottawa | 25.75 |
| Niagara Falls | * 38.00 | Montreal | 20.75 |
| Buffalo | * 39.00 | | |

‡Route R T 44—

| | |
|---|---|
| Grand Trunk Railway to Quebec | |
| Quebec Steamship Co. (on alternate Tuesdays only) to Gaspé | }467R |
| Return same route | |

Fares :—

| | | | |
|---|---|---|---|
| Detroit | *$39.50 | Toronto | *$32.00 |
| Port Huron | * 39.35 | Kingston | * 24.90 |
| London | * 37.10 | Brockville | 22.60 |
| Hamilton | * 33.80 | Ottawa | 22.00 |
| Niagara Falls | * 34.25 | Montreal | 17.00 |
| Buffalo | * 35.25 | | |

## To Gorham, N. H., and Return.

(WHITE MOUNTAINS.)

‡Route R T 45—

| | |
|---|---|
| Choice of routes to Montreal (see page 85). | |
| Grand Trunk Railway to Gorham | }2900 |
| Grand Trunk Railway to starting point | |

Fares :—

| | | | |
|---|---|---|---|
| Detroit | *$32.00 | Toronto | *$24.50 |
| Port Huron | * 31.85 | Kingston | * 17.40 |
| London | * 29.60 | Brockville | 15.10 |
| Hamilton | * 26.30 | Ottawa | 14.50 |
| Niagara Falls | * 26.75 | Montreal | 9.50 |
| Buffalo | * 27.75 | Quebec | † 11.50 |

*See first foot note on page 114.

†Via Grand Trunk Railway direct, not coming into Montreal.

# To Gravenhurst (Muskoka) and Return.

:Route R T 46—
Grand Trunk Railway to Gravenhurst via Toronto.............. ....... } 2900
Return same route.... .........................................................

Fares:—

| | | | |
|---|---|---|---|
| Detroit................. | $12.15 | Toronto........... | $ 4.55 |
| Port Huron........... | 10.10 | Kingston........... | 11.05 |
| London........ ........ | 7.65 | Brockville............ | 12.90 |
| Hamilton............... | 4.55 | Ottawa............... | 14.95 |
| Niagara Falls......... | 6.40 | Montreal.......... | 16.75 |
| Buffalo...... ......... | 7.40 | Quebec......... ... | 21.75 |

# To Ha! Ha! Bay (Saguenay River), Que., and Return.

### SEE CHICOUTIMI.

# To Halifax, N. S., and Return.

:Route R T 47—
Grand Trunk Railway to Levis...............................................
Intercolonial Railway to Halifax........................................ } 2852
Returning same route.... ..........................................

Fares :—

| | | | |
|---|---|---|---|
| Detroit.............. | *$47.50 | Toronto............. | *$40.00 |
| Port Huron......... | * 47.35 | Kingston............ | * 32.90 |
| London............... | 45.10 | Brockville........... | 30.60 |
| Hamilton.......... .. | § 41.80 | Ottawa........... .... | 30.00 |
| Niagara Falls......... | * 42.00 | Montreal............ | 25.00 |
| Buffalo................ | * 43.00 | | |

:Route R T 48—
Grand Trunk Railway to Levis....................................
Quebec S. S. Co.'s Steamer (on alternate Tuesdays only) to Pictou.... } 467R
Intercolonial Railway to Halifax........ ......................
Return same route.

Fares :—

| | | | |
|---|---|---|---|
| Detroit.............. | *$44.60 | Toronto............. | *$37.10 |
| Port Huron.......... | * 44.45 | Kingston......... ... | * 30.00 |
| London.............. | * 42.20 | Brockville... ...... | 27.70 |
| Hamilton............. | * 38.80 | Ottawa............. | 27.10 |
| Niagara Falls.... ... | * 39.35 | Montreal............ | 22.10 |
| Buffalo.............. | * 40.35 | | |

Route R T 49—
Choice of routes to Montreal (see page 85).
Grand Trunk Railway or R. & O. N. Co.'s Steamer to Quebec...........T 36
Ferry to Levis.................................................................T 37
Intercolonial Railway to Halifax .........................................T 42
Quebec S. S. Co.'s Steamer (fortnightly only) to Quebec............ ....T 53
Ferry to Levis.................................................................T 37
Grand Trunk Railway to starting point ..................................T 27

*R.W.*

Fares :—

| | | | |
|---|---|---|---|
| Detroit............. | *$48.50 | Toronto ............. | *$41.00 |
| Port Huron........... | * 48.35 | Kingston............ | * 33.90 |
| London............... | * 46.10 | Brockville........... | 31.60 |
| Hamilton............ | * 42.80 | Ottawa............... | 31.00 |
| Niagara Falls......... | * 43.25 | Montreal............ | 26.00 |
| Buffalo................ | * 44.25 | | |

*See first foot note on page 114.
§All rail to Montreal. For tickets optional rail or steamer, Toronto to Kingston, Kingston to Prescott, and Prescott to Montreal, on eastbound journey, add $1.95 from Hamilton.

## To Halifax, N. S., and Return.—*Continued.*

Route R T 50—

Choice of routes to Montreal (see page 85).                                    FORM.

Grand Trunk Railway or R. & O. N. Co.'s Steamer to Quebec........ ..T  36
Ferry to Levis .................................................................T  37
Intercolonial Railway to Halifax...........................................T  42
Intercolonial Railway to St. John..........................................T  46
International S. S. Co.'s Steamer to Portland...............................T  49
Boston & Maine Railroad to Boston .........................................T  50
Boston & Maine Railroad to Nashua ........................................T  29
Concord & Montreal Railroad to Concord ...................................T  34
Boston & Maine Railroad to White River Jct.............................. ..T  35
Central Vermont Railroad to St. Johns.....................................T  84
Grand Trunk Railway to starting point .... .................T  76

Fares :—

| | | | |
|---|---|---|---|
| Detroit | *$53.50 | Toronto | *$46.00 |
| Port Huron | * 53.35 | Kingston | * 38.90 |
| London | * 51.10 | Brockville | 36.60 |
| Hamilton | * 47.80 | Ottawa | 36.00 |
| Niagara Falls | * 48.25 | Montreal | 31.00 |
| Buffalo | * 49.25 | | |

Route R T 51—

Going same as Route R T 50.
Canada Atlantic Steamship Co. to Boston.............................T  78
Returning same as Route R T 50.

Fares :—

| | | | |
|---|---|---|---|
| Detroit | *$48.00 | Toronto | *$40.50 |
| Port Huron | * 47.85 | Kingston | * 33.40 |
| London | * 45.60 | Brockville | 31.10 |
| Hamilton | * 42.30 | Ottawa | 30.50 |
| Niagara Falls | * 42.75 | Montreal | 25.50 |
| Buffalo | * 43.75 | | |

Route R T 52—

Going same as Route R T 50.
Intercolonial Railway to St. John ......................................T  46
International Steamship Co.'s Steamer to Portland.....................T  49
Boston & Maine Railroad to Boston.....................................T  50
Fitchburg Railroad to Rotterdam.......................................T  15
West Shore Railroad to Suspension Bridge..............................T  66
Grand Trunk Railway to starting point ................................T  60

Fares :—

| | | | |
|---|---|---|---|
| Detroit | ¶$52.00 | Niagara Falls | ¶$42.50 |
| Port Huron | ¶ 49.60 | Buffalo | ¶ 43.00 |
| London | ¶ 46.35 | Toronto | ¶ 42.50 |
| Hamilton | ¶ 42.50 | Kingston | ¶ 42.50 |

Route R T 53—

Going same as Route R T 50.
Canada Atlantic Steamship Co.'s Steamer to Boston.....................T  78
Returning same as Route R T 52.

Fares :—

| | | | |
|---|---|---|---|
| Detroit | ¶$46.65 | Niagara Falls | ¶$37.15 |
| Port Huron | ¶ 44.25 | Buffalo | ¶ 37.65 |
| London | ¶ 41.00 | Toronto | ¶ 37.15 |
| Hamilton | ¶ 37.15 | Kingston | ¶ 37.15 |

## To Huntsville (Muskoka) and Return.

‡Route R T 54—

Grand Trunk Railway to Huntsville via Toronto...................} 2900
Return same route ...........................................}

Fares :—

| | | | |
|---|---|---|---|
| Detroit | $ 13.55 | Toronto | $ 5.95 |
| Port Huron | 11.50 | Kingston | 12.45 |
| London | 9.05 | Brockville | 14.30 |
| Hamilton | 5.95 | Ottawa | 16.35 |
| Niagara Falls | 7.80 | Montreal | 16.75 |
| Buffalo | 8.80 | Quebec | 21.75 |

*See first foot note on page 114.
¶ All rail. For tickets optional rail or steamer, Toronto to Montreal, on eastbound journey, Kingston, add $1.50 to fares shown.

# To Lakeside (Cambridge) N. H., and Return.

### (RANGELEY LAKES.)

Route R T 55—
Choice of routes to Montreal (see page 85).
Grand Trunk Railway to Bethel......................................T  32
Stage to Lakeside.......................................... ... .......T  79
Stage to Bethel .............................................. .......T  79
Grand Trunk Railway to starting point .............. ..... T  76

Fares :—

| | | | |
|---|---|---|---|
| Detroit...............| *$37.00 | Toronto ...........| *$29.50 |
| Port Huron...........| * 36.85 | Kingston ..... ....| * 22.40 |
| London ..............| * 34.60 | Brockville .........| 20.10 |
| Hamilton ...........| * 31.30 | Ottawa.............| 19.50 |
| Niagara Falls........| * 31.75 | Montreal...........| 14.50 |
| Buffalo ... .........| * 32.75 | Quebec ............| † 16.50 |

# To Lancaster, N. H., and Return.

Route R T 56—
Choice of routes to Montreal (see page 85).
Grand Trunk Railway to Groveton Jct .....................................T  32
Concord & Montreal Railroad to Lancaster ...........................T  25
Concord & Montreal Railroad to Groveton Jct.......................T  25
Grand Trunk Railway to starting point.................................T  76

Fares:—

| | | | |
|---|---|---|---|
| Detroit...............| *$31.25 | Toronto ...........| *$23.75 |
| Port Huron ..........| * 31.10 | Kingston ...... ....| * 16.65 |
| London .............| * 28.85 | Brockville .........| 14.35 |
| Hamilton ...........| * 25.55 | Ottawa ............| 13.75 |
| Niagara Falls........| * 26.00 | Montreal...........| 8.75 |
| Buffalo..............| * 27.00 | Quebec ..........| † 10.75 |

# To Little Metis, Que., and Return.

‡Route R T 57—
Grand Trunk Railway to Levis.... ... ......................⎫
Intercolonial Railway to Little Metis......................⎬ 2852
Returning same route ..............................................⎭

Fares:—

| | | | |
|---|---|---|---|
| Detroit...............| *$34.60 | Toronto ...........| *$27.10 |
| Port Huron ..........| * 34.45 | Kingston .....| * 20.00 |
| London ..............| * 32.20 | Brockville.........| 17.70 |
| Hamilton.............| * 28.90 | Ottawa ..........| 17.10 |
| Niagara Falls........| * 29.35 | Montreal .........| 12.10 |
| Buffalo........ ....| .* 30.35 | | |

# To Montreal, Que., and Return.

‡Route R T 58—
Choice of routes to Toronto (see pages 84 and 85).
Grand Trunk Railway to Kingston..........................⎫
Grand Trunk Railway or R. & O. N. Co.'s Steamer to Prescott........⎬ X 71
Grand Trunk Railway or R. & O. N. Co.'s Steamer to Montreal........⎭
Grand Trunk Railway to starting point.

Fares :—

| | | | |
|---|---|---|---|
| Detroit...............| $25.75 | Niaagra Falls ......| $19.00 |
| Port Huron...........| 25.05 | Buffalo .........| 20.00 |
| London ..............| 22.85 | Toronto.............| 18.00 |
| Hamilton .............| 19.00 | Kingston ...........| 9.50 |

‡Route R T 59—
Choice of routes to Toronto (see pages 84 and 85).
Grand Trunk Railway or R. & O. N. Co.'s Steamer to Kingston......⎫
Grand Trunk Railway or R. & O. N. Co.'s Steamer to Prescott.......⎬ 4309 R
Grand Trunk Railway or R. & O. N. Co.'s Steamer to Montreal......⎭
Grand Trunk Railway to starting point.

*See first foot note on page 114.
†Via Grand Trunk Railway direct, not coming into Montreal.

## To Montreal, Que., and Return.—*Continued.*

Fares:—

| | | | |
|---|---|---|---|
| Detroit | $26.60 | Niagara Falls | $19.00 |
| Port Huron | 25.05 | Buffalo | 20.00 |
| London | 22.85 | Toronto | 18.00 |
| Hamilton | 19.00 | | |

## To Mt. Washington (Summit) and Return.

### SEE SUMMIT MT. WASHINGTON.

## To Murray Bay, Que., and Return.

Route R T 60—

Grand Trunk Railway to Quebec..................................... } 2900
Richelieu & Ontario Navigation Co.'s Steamer to Murray Bay......... } and
Returning same route.............................................. } X351

Fares:—

| | | | |
|---|---|---|---|
| Detroit | *$30.50 | Toronto | *$ 23.00 |
| Port Huron | * 30.35 | Kingston | * 15.90 |
| London | * 28.10 | Brockville | 13.60 |
| Hamilton | * 24.80 | Ottawa | 13.00 |
| Niagara Falls | * 25.25 | Montreal | 8.00 |
| Buffalo | * 26.25 | | |

## To New York, N. Y., and Return.

Route R T 61—

Choice of routes to Montreal (see page 85).
Grand Trunk Railway to Rouse's Point...............................T 16
Delaware & Hudson Railroad to Albany...............................T 67
New York Central & Hudson River Railroad to New York.... .......T 65
Returning same route to Rouse's Point...............................
Grand Trunk Railway to starting point..............................T 76

Fares:—

| | | | |
|---|---|---|---|
| Detroit | *$40.75 | Toronto | *$ 33.25 |
| Port Huron | * 40.60 | Kingston | * 26.15 |
| London | * 38.35 | Brockville | 23.85 |
| Hamilton | * 35.05 | Ottawa | 23.25 |
| Niagara Falls | * 35.50 | Montreal | 18.25 |
| Buffalo | * 36.50 | Quebec | 23.25 |

Route R T 62—

Choice of routes to Montreal (see page 85).
Grand Trunk Railway to St. Johns...................................T 11
Central Vermont Railroad to Rutland................................T 61
Bennington & Rutland Railroad to White Creek.......................T 62
Fitchburg Railroad to Troy.........................................T 63
New York Central & Hudson River Railroad to New York.... ...T 64
Returning same route to St. Johns..................................T
Grand Trunk Railway to starting point.............. .............T 76

Fares same as Route R T 61.

Route R T 63—

Choice of routes to Montreal (see page 85).
Grand Trunk Railway to St. Johns...................................T 11
Central Vermont Railroad to Windsor................................T 12
Vermont Valley Railroad to Brattleboro.............................T 13
Central Vermont Railroad to South Vernon...........................T 12
Connecticut River Railroad to Springfield..........................T 68
New York, New Haven & Hartford Railroad to New Haven...............T 69
New York, New Haven & Hartford Railroad to New York................T 70
Returning same route to St. Johns..................................
Grand Trunk Railway to starting point..............................T 76

Fares same as Route R T 61.

*See first foot note on page 114.

## To New York, N. Y., and Return.—*Continued.*

**Route R T 64—**

Same as Route R T 63 to New York.                                                    FORM.
New York Central & Hudson River Railroad to Troy ............ .... ....T 64
Fitchburg Railroad to White Creek ..................... ..... ....T 63
Bennington & Rutland Railroad to Rutland ...................T 62
Central Vermont Railroad to St. Johns.......................T 61
Grand Trunk Railway to starting point .....................T 76

**Fares same as Route R T 61.**

**Route R T 65—**

Choice of routes to Montreal (see page 85).
Grand Trunk Railway to Rouse's Point .....................T 16
Delaware & Hudson Railroad to Plattsburg..................T 19
Champlain Trans. Co.'s Str. or Del. & Hudson R.R.to Fort Ticonderoga T 17
Delaware & Hudson Railroad to Baldwin.....................T 20
Lake George Steamer to Caldwell ..........................T 22
Delaware & Hudson Railroad to Albany.....................T 21
Day Line Steamer to New York.............................T 72
New York Central & Hudson River Railroad to Albany.........T 65
Delaware & Hudson Railroad to Rouse's Point ...............T 67
Grand Trunk Railway to starting point ....................T 76

Fares :—

| | | | |
|---|---|---|---|
| Detroit ............. | *$43.30 | Toronto .......... | *$35.80 |
| Port Huron.......... | * 43.15 | Kingston............. | * 28.70 |
| London ............. | * 40.90 | Brockville .......... | 26.40 |
| Hamilton ........... | * 37.60 | Ottawa........... | 25.80 |
| Niagara Falls........ | * 38.05 | Montreal........... | 20.80 |
| Buffalo ...... ..... | * 39.05 | Quebec ... ...... | 25.80 |

**Route R T 66—**

Choice of routes to Montreal (see page 85).
Grand Trunk Railway to Portland...................... ....T 32
Boston & Maine Railroad to Boston........................T 50
Choice of Sound Steamer Lines to New York ...... ... ......T 73
Returning to Montreal same as Route R T 65 or Route R T 64.

Fares:—

| | | | |
|---|---|---|---|
| Detroit............... | *$44.50 | Toronto........... | *$37.00 |
| Port Huron.......... | * 44.35 | Kingston ............ | * 29.90 |
| London ............. | * 42.10 | Brockville ........ | * 27.60 |
| Hamilton ........... | * 38.80 | Ottawa........... | 27.00 |
| Niagara Falls........ | * 39.25 | Montreal........ ... | 22.00 |
| Buffalo ............. | * 40.25 | Quebec ........ .....† | 25.00 |

**Route R T 67—**

Choice of Routes R T 61, R T 62 and R T 63 going.
Choice of any direct line to Suspension Bridge...................T
Grand Trunk Railway to starting point ....................T

Fares :—

| | | | |
|---|---|---|---|
| Detroit .............¶ | $ 37.75 | Niagara Falls .......¶ | $28.25 |
| Port Huron .........¶ | 35.35 | Buffalo.............¶ | 28.75 |
| London .............¶ | 32.10 | Toronto ............¶ | 28.25 |
| Hamilton ...........¶ | 28.25 | Kingston ............¶ | 28.25 |

## To Niagara Falls and Return.

**‡Route R T 68—**

Grand Trunk Railway to Niagara Falls......... ...................} 2900
Return same route ....................................................

Fares :—

| | | | |
|---|---|---|---|
| Detroit...limited 1 month..$12.00 | | Brockville ...........$12.70 | |
| Port Huron, " .. 9.45 | | Ottawa............... 15.25 | |
| Toronto, " .. 4.35 | | Montreal............. 19.00 | |
| Kingston.......... .... 10.35 | | Quebec .............. 24.00 | |

*See first foot note on page 114.
†Going via Grand Trunk Railway direct, not via Montreal.
¶All rail to Montreal. For tickets optional rail or steamer, Toronto to Montreal, on eastbound journey, add $1,50 to fares shown.

# To Niagara Falls and Return.—*Continued.*

‡Route R T 69—

Grand Trunk Railway to Toronto ......................... } FORM.
Steamer "Empress of India" to Port Dalhousie..................... } 4404R
Grand Trunk Railway to Niagara Falls............................. }
Returning same route ........................................... }

Fares :—

| | | | |
|---|---|---|---|
| Kingston.............. | $ 10.35 | Montreal............. | $ 19.00 |
| Brockville ............ | 12.70 | Quebec.............. | 24.00 |
| Ottawa................ | 15.25 | | |

Route R T 70—

Grand Trunk Railway to Toronto............ ...........T 76
Steamer "Empress of India" to Port Dalhousie.....................T 4
Grand Trunk Railway to Niagara Falls.............................T 3
Returning same route to Toronto
Grand Trunk Railway or R. & O. N. Co.'s Steamer to Kingston (T 5),
    Brockville (T 57), Prescott (T 55), Montreal (T 56), or Quebec (T 36).

Fares :—

| | | | |
|---|---|---|---|
| Kingston ........ ....$ 10.35 | | Montreal............$ 19.00 | |
| Brockville ............ 13.25 | | Quebec.............. 24.00 | |
| Ottawa............ .. 15.25 | | | |

Route R T 71—

Grand Trunk Railway to Niagara Falls (Suspension Bridge)............T 60
Grand Trunk Railway to Port Dalhousie......... .............T 3
Steamer "Empress of India" to Toronto.......................... T 4
Grand Trunk Railway or R. & O. N. Co.'s Steamer to Kingston (T 5),
    Brockville (T 57), Prescott (T 55), Montreal (T 56), or Quebec (T 36).

Fares same as Route R T 70.

‡Route R T 72—

Grand Trunk Railway to Toronto................................... }
Niagara Nav. Co.'s Steamer to Lewiston .......................... } 166R
New York Central & Hudson River Railroad to Niagara Falls......... }
Returning same route .. ........................................ }

Fares same as Route R T 69.

‡Route R T 73—

Grand Trunk Railway to Toronto ...................................T 76
Niagara Nav. Co.'s Steamer to Lewiston ..........................T 10
New York Central & Hudson River Railroad to Niagara Falls .. ........T 9
Returning same route to Toronto ................
Grand Trunk Railway or R. & O. N. Co.'s Steamer to Kingston (T 5),
    Brockville (T 57), Prescott (T 55), Montreal (T 56), or Quebec (T 36).

Fares same as Route R T 70.

‡Route R T 74.

Grand Trunk Railway to Niagara Falls (Suspension Bridge) ....T 60 } or X
New York Central & Hudson River Railroad to Lewiston... ....T 9 } 
Niagara Nav. Co.'s Steamer to Toronto..........................T 10 } 273.
Grand Trunk Railway or R. & O. N. Co.'s Steamer to Kingston (T 5),
    Brockville (T 57), Prescott (T 55), Montreal (T 56), or Quebec (T 36).

Fares same as Route R T 70.

# To Old Orchard Beach and Return.

‡Route R T 75—

Grand Trunk Railway to Portland ............................ }
Boston & Maine Railroad to Old Orchard Beach ............. } 2519
Returning same route............. ......... .. ............. }

Fares :—

| | | | |
|---|---|---|---|
| Detroit..............*$33.50 | | Toronto..............*$26.00 | |
| Port Huron ..........* 33.35 | | Kingston............* 18.90 | |
| London .............* 31.10 | | Brockville ........... 16 60 | |
| Hamilton ...........* 27.80 | | Ottawa...... ...... 16.00 | |
| Niagara Falls.......* 28.25 | | Montreal ... .. 11.00 | |
| Buffalo ........ ....* 29.25 | | Quebec ............. 13.00 | |

*See first foot note on page 114.

# To Parry Sound, Ont., and Return.

‡Route R T 76—                                                FORM.

Grand Trunk Railway to Penetang or Midland ............ } 5060 R (Penetang)
Muskoka & Georgian Bay Nav. Co. to Parry Sound ........ }4415 R (Midland)
Return same route ...... ................................. }

Fares:—

| | | | |
|---|---|---|---|
| Detroit..... ........ | $ 15.10 | Toronto........... | $ 7.50 |
| Port Huron  .......... | 13.20 | Kingston............. | 14.00 |
| London ............... | 10.60 | Brockville ........ | 15.85 |
| Hamilton ............. | 7.50 | Ottawa.............. | 17.90 |
| Niagara Falls......... | 9.40 | Montreal............ | 20.35 |
| Buffalo ............... | 10.40 | Quebec ............. | 25.35 |

⸭Route R T 77—

Grand Trunk Railway to Midland via Toronto ..................... }
North Shore Navigation Co.'s Steamer to Parry Sound ............. }5516 R
Return same route ......... ...... ... ........................ }

Fares same as Route R T 76.

‡Route R T 78—

Grand Trunk Railway to Collingwood via Toronto.............. ··· }4808 R
Great Northern Transit Co.'s Steamer to Party Sound...... .......... }
Return same route ...... ...................................... }

Fares same as Route R T 76.

‡Route R T 79—

Grand Trunk Railway to Gravenhurst (Muskoka Wharf) via Toronto... ] 5098 R
Muskoka & Georgian Bay Nav. Co.'s Steamer to Rosseau............ ] or
**R. W.** Stage to Parry Sound ............................................... ] 5100 R
Muskoka & Georgian Bay N. Co.'s Steamer to Midland or Penetang. ] (R. W.)
Grand Trunk Railway to starting point............................ ]

Fares :—

| | | | |
|---|---|---|---|
| Detroit .................$ 15.60 | | Toronto ............$ 8.00 |
| Port Huron........... 13.70 | | Kingston............ 14.50 |
| London ..... ...... 11.10 | | Brockville ........... 16.35 |
| Hamilton............. 8.00 | | Ottawa.............. 18.40 |
| Niagara Falls......... 9.90 | | Montreal............ 20.35 |
| Buffalo ............... 10.90 | | Quebec ............. 25.35 |

# To Paul Smith's, N. Y., and Return.

### (ADIRONDACKS).

Route R T 81—

Choice of routes to Toronto (see pages 84 and 85).
Grand Trunk Railway or R. & O. N. Co.'s Steamer to Kingston........T      5
Grand Trunk Railway or R. & O. N. Co.'s Steamer to Prescott. ........T    55
Omnibus Transfer to wharf............................................T    80
Ferry to Ogdensburg ....................................... ..T    75
Central Vermont Railroad to Moira ......................................T    12
Northern Adirondack Railroad to Paul Smith's Station ..............T   109
Stage to Paul Smith's.......... ......................................T    79
Returning same route to Prescott........................................
Grand Trunk Railway to starting point.... ...........................T    76

Fares :—

| | | | |
|---|---|---|---|
| Detroit .......... .....$ 29.85 | | Toronto.......... ...$ 19.80 |
| Port Huron...... ..... 27.35 | | Niagara Falls........ 21.15 |
| London................ 25.00 | | Buffalo .............. 22.15 |
| Hamilton.............. 21.15 | | |

Route R T 82—

Choice of routes to Montreal (see page 85).
Grand Trunk Railway to Rouse's Point .............................T    16
Delaware & Hudson River Railroad to Plattsburg....................T    17
Chateaugay Railway to Bloomingdale...............................T   113
Stage to Paul Smith's .............................................T    79
Return same route to Rouse's Point ... ...........................
Grand Trunk Railway to starting point..............................T    76

## To Paul Smith's, N. Y., and Return.—*Continued.*

Fares:—

| | | | |
|---|---|---|---|
| Detroit | *$34.50 | Toronto | *$27.00 |
| Port Huron | * 34.35 | Kingston | * 19.90 |
| London | * 32.10 | Brockville | 17.60 |
| Hamilton | * 28.80 | Ottawa | 17.00 |
| Niagara Falls | * 29.25 | Montreal | 12.00 |
| Buffalo | * 30.25 | Quebec | 17.00 |

## To Pictou, N. S., and Return.

‡Route R T 83—

Grand Trunk Railway to Levis ..................................... } FORM.
Intercolonial Railway to Pictou ................................... } 2852
Return same route ................................................ )

Fares:—

| | | | |
|---|---|---|---|
| Detroit | *$47.50 | Toronto | *$40.00 |
| Port Huron | * 47.35 | Kingston | * 32.90 |
| London | * 45.10 | Brockville | 30.60 |
| Hamilton | ¶ 41.80 | Ottawa | 30.00 |
| Niagara Falls | * 42.00 | Montreal | 25.00 |
| Buffalo | * 43.00 | | |

‡Route R T 84—

Grand Trunk Railway to Quebec ................................... } 467R
Quebec S. S. Co.'s Steamer (on alternate Tuesdays only) to Pictou ... }
Return same route ................................................ )

Fares:—

| | | | |
|---|---|---|---|
| Detroit | *$43.25 | Toronto | *$35.75 |
| Port Huron | * 43.10 | Kingston | * 28.65 |
| London | * 40.85 | Brockville | 26.35 |
| Hamilton | * 37.55 | Ottawa | 25.75 |
| Niagara Falls | * 38.00 | Montreal | 20.75 |
| Buffalo | * 39.00 | | |

## To Port Carling (Muskoka) and Return.

‡Route R T 85—

Grand Trunk Railway to Gravenhurst ............................... }
Muskoka & Georgian Bay Nav. Co.'s Steamer to Port Carling ....... } 5062R
Return same route ................................................ )

Fares:—

| | | | |
|---|---|---|---|
| Detroit | $ 13.15 | Toronto | $ 5.55 |
| Port Huron | 11.25 | Kingston | 12.05 |
| London | 8.65 | Brockville | 13.90 |
| Hamilton | 5.55 | Ottawa | 15.95 |
| Niagara Falls | 7.45 | Montreal | 17.75 |
| Buffalo | 8.45 | Quebec | 22.75 |

## To Port Cockburn (Muskoka) and Return.

‡Route R T 86—

Grand Trunk Railway to Gravenhurst ............................... }
Muskoka & Georgian Bay Co.'s Steamer to Port Cockburn .......... } 5062R
Return same route ................................................ )

Fares:—

| | | | |
|---|---|---|---|
| Detroit | $ 14.10 | Toronto | $ 6.50 |
| Port Huron | 12.20 | Kingston | 13.00 |
| London | 9.60 | Brockville | 14.85 |
| Hamilton | 6.50 | Ottawa | 16.90 |
| Niagara Falls | 8.40 | Montreal | 18.75 |
| Buffalo | 9.40 | Quebec | 23.75 |

*See first foot note on page 114.
* All rail to Montreal. Add $1.95 for tickets optional rail or steamer, **Toronto** to Montreal, eastbound.

## To Portland, Me., and Return.

‡Route R T 87—                                                                FORM.
    Grand Trunk Railway to Portland..................................... } 2900
    Return same route.....................................................

Fares:—

| | | | |
|---|---|---|---|
| Detroit | *$33.00 | Toronto | *$25.50 |
| Port Huron | * 32·85 | Kingston | * 18.40 |
| London | * 30.60 | Brockville | 16.10 |
| Hamilton | * 27.30 | Ottawa | 15.50 |
| Niagara Falls | * 27.75 | Montreal | 10.50 |
| Buffalo | * 28.75 | Quebec | 12.50 |

Route R T 88—

R.W.
    Grand Trunk Railway to St. Johns.................................T  11
    Central Vermont Railroad to Montpelier..........................T  12
    Montpelier & Wells River Railroad to Wells River................T  24
    Concord & Montreal Railroad to Fabyans.........................T  25
    Maine Central Railroad to Portland.............................T  52
    Grand Trunk Railway to starting point..........................T  74

Fares:—

| | | | |
|---|---|---|---|
| Detroit | *$35.00 | Toronto | *$27.50 |
| Port Huron | * 34.85 | Kingston | * 20.40 |
| London | * 32.60 | Brockville | 18.10 |
| Hamilton | * 29.30 | Ottawa | 17.50 |
| Niagara Falls | * 29.75 | Montreal | 12.50 |
| Buffalo | * 30.75 | Quebec | 16.00 |

Route R T 89—

R.W.
    Grand Trunk Railway to Groveton Jct............................T  32
    Concord & Montreal Railroad to Fabyans.........................T  25
    Maine Central Railway to Portland..............................T  52
    Grand Trunk Railway to starting point..........................T  74

Fares:—

| | | | |
|---|---|---|---|
| Detroit | *$35.00 | Toronto | *$27.50 |
| Port Huron | * 34.85 | Kingston | * 20.40 |
| London | * 32.60 | Brockville | 18 10 |
| Hamilton | * 29.30 | Ottawa | 17.50 |
| Niagara Falls | * 29.75 | Montreal | 12.50 |
| Buffalo | * 30.75 | Quebec | † 14.50 |

Route R T 90—

R.W.
    Grand Trunk Railway to Groveton Jct............................T  32
    Concord & Montreal Railroad to Scotts..........................T  25
    Maine Central Railroad to Portland.............................T  52
    Grand Trunk Railway to starting point..........................T  74
Fares same as Route R T 89.

## To Port Sandfield (Muskoka) and Return.

‡Route R T 91—
    Grand Trunk Railway to Gravenhurst......................
    Muskoka & Georgian Bay Nav. Co.'s Steamer to Port Sandfield ..... } 5062R
    Return same route....................................
Fares:—

| | | | |
|---|---|---|---|
| Detroit | $ 13.40 | Toronto | $ 5.80 |
| Port Huron | 11.50 | Kingston | 12.30 |
| London | 8.90 | Brockville | 14.15 |
| Hamilton | 5.80 | Ottawa | 16.20 |
| Niagara Falls | 7.70 | Montreal | 18.00 |
| Buffalo | 8.70 | Quebec | 23.00 |

## To Prescott, Ont., and Return.

Route R T 92—
    Choice of routes to Toronto (see pages 84 and 85).
    Grand Trunk Railway or R. & O. N. Co.'s Steamer to Kingston .........T  5
    Grand Trunk Railway or R. & O. N. Co.'s Steamer to Prescott .........T  55
    Grand Trunk Railway to starting point ................. ...............T  76

    *See first foot note on page 114.
    †Via Grand Trunk direct, not coming into Montreal.

## To Prescott, Ont., and Return.—*Continued.*

Fares :—

| | | | |
|---|---|---|---|
| Detroit | $ 22.05 | Niagara Falls | $ 13.35 |
| Port Huron | 19.55 | Buffalo | 14.35 |
| London ..limited 1 month | 17.20 | Toronto..limited 1 month | 11.50 |
| Hamilton " " | 13.35 | | |

‡Route R T 93.

Grand Trunk Railway to Prescott ............................... } FORM.
G. T. R. or R. & O. N. Co.'s Steamer to Montreal or Quebec... . } 2502
from Montreal.

Fares :—

Montreal ...limited 5 days.. $5.60          Quebec ...limited 5 days..$10.60

## To Profile House, N. H., and Return.

Route R T 94—

Choice of routes to Montreal (see page 85).
Grand Trunk Railway to Groveton Jct........... ................T 32
Concord & Montreal Railroad to Bethlehem Jct.................... T 25
Profile & Franconia Notch Railroad to Profile House....................T 26
Return same route to Groveton Jct....................................
Grand Trunk Railway to starting point .........................T 76

Fares :—

| | | | |
|---|---|---|---|
| Detroit | *$35.00 | Toronto | *$27.50 |
| Port Huron | * 34.85 | Kingston | * 20.40 |
| London | * 32.60 | Brockville | 18.10 |
| Hamilton | * 29.30 | Ottawa | 17.50 |
| Niagara Falls | * 29.75 | Montreal | 12.50 |
| Buffalo | * 30.75 | Quebec | † 14.50 |

Route R T 95—

Choice of routes to Montreal (see page 85).
Grand Trunk Railway to St. Johns ......................T 11
Central Vermont Railroad to Montpelier.................................T 12
Montpelier & Wells River Railroad to Wells River ......................T 24
Concord & Montreal Railroad to Bethlehem Jct....................T 25
Profile & Franconia Notch Railroad to Profile House....................T 26
Return same route to St. Johns........................ .............
Grand Trunk Railway to starting point .........................T 76

Fares same as Route R T 94 (except Quebec, $16.50).

## To Quebec, Que., and Return.

‡Route R T 96—

Grand Trunk Railway to Quebec ....................................... }
Return same route ...... ........ ..... .................... } 2900

Fares :—

| | | | |
|---|---|---|---|
| Detroit | *$27.50 | Toronto | *$ 20.00 |
| Port Huron | * 27.35 | Kingston | * 12.90 |
| London | * 25.10 | Brockville | * 10.60 |
| Hamilton | * 21.80 | Ottawa | * 10.00 |
| Niagara Falls | * 22.25 | Montreal | ✓ 5.85 |
| Buffalo | * 23.25 | | |

## To Quebec and Back to Montreal.

Route R T 97—

Choice of routes to Montreal (see page 85).
Grand Trunk Railway or R. & O. N. Co.'s Steamer to Quebec ..... ... .T 36
Grand Trunk Railway or R. & O. N. Co.'s Steamer to Montreal .... ....T 36

Fares :—

| | | | |
|---|---|---|---|
| Detroit | *$20.00 | Niagara Falls | *$16.50 |
| Port Huron | * 19.90 | Buffalo | * 17.00 |

*See first foot note on page 114. Quebec tickets optional rail or steamer, Kingston or Toronto to Montreal, may also be made optional rail or steamer between Montreal and Quebec in either or both directions.
†Via Grand Trunk direct, not coming into Montreal.
‡May be made optional rail or steamer on either going or returning journey.

# To Richibucto, N. B., and Return.

:Route R T 98—

FORM.

Grand Trunk Railway to Levis...................................... ⎞ 2852
Intercolonial Railway to Kent Jct................................. ⎬ and
Kent Northern Railway to Richibucto............................... ⎠ X397 R
Returning same route.

Fares:—

| | | | |
|---|---|---|---|
| Detroit | *$43.00 | Toronto | ˙$35.50 |
| Port Huron | * 42.85 | Kingston | * 28.40 |
| London | † 39.85 | Brockville | 26.10 |
| Hamilton | † 36.00 | Ottawa | 25.50 |
| Niagara Falls | † 36.00 | Montreal | 20.50 |
| Buffalo | † 37.00 | | |

# To Rosseau (Muskoka) and Return.

:Route R T 99—

Grand Trunk Railway to Gravenhurst................................ ⎞
Muskoka & Georgian Bay Nav. Co.'s Steamer to Rosseau.............. ⎬5062R
Returning same route.............................................. ⎠

Fares:—

| | | | |
|---|---|---|---|
| Detroit | $ 13.85 | Toronto | $ 6 25 |
| Port Huron | 11.95 | Kingston | 12.75 |
| London | 9.35 | Brockville | 14.60 |
| Hamilton | 6.25 | Ottawa | 16.65 |
| Niagara Falls | 8.15 | Montreal | 18.50 |
| Buffalo | 9.15 | Quebec | 23.50 |

# To Round Island Park and Thousand Island Park, N. Y., and Return.

Route R T 100—

Choice of routes to Toronto (see pages 84 and 85).
Grand Trunk Railway to Gananoque Jct.............................. T 76
Thousand Islands Railway to Gananoque............................. T 7
Deseronto Nav. Co.'s Steamer to Alexandria Bay ................... T 8
Returning same route to Gananoque Jct.............................
Grand Trunk Railway to starting point ............................ T 76

Fares:—

| | | | |
|---|---|---|---|
| Detroit | $ 21.10 | Toronto | $ 10.10 |
| Port Huron | 18.60 | Kingston | 1.80 |
| London | 15.60 | Brockville | 2.90 |
| Hamilton | 12.10 | Montreal | 9.50 |
| Niagara Falls | 12.25 | Quebec | 14.50 |
| Buffalo | 13.25 | | |

Route R T 101—

Choice of routes to Toronto (see pages 84 and 85).
Grand Trunk Railway or R. & O. N. Co.'s Steamer to Kingston ...... T 5
R. & O. N. Co.'s Steamer to Round Island (or Thousand Island Park).... T 6
R & O N Co.'s Steamer to Kingston ............................... T 6
Grand Trunk Railway to starting point ........................... T 76

Fares:—

| | | | |
|---|---|---|---|
| Detroit | $ 21.10 | Niagara Falls | $ 12.25 |
| Port Huron | 18.60 | Buffalo | 13.25 |
| London | 16.10 | Toronto | 10.50 |
| Hamilton | 12.25 | | |

Route R T 102—

Grand Trunk Railway to Gananoque Jct............................. T 76
Thousand Islands Railway to Gananoque ........................... T 7
Deseronto Nav. Co.'s Steamer to Round Island (or Thousand Island Park)..... T 8
R. & O. N. Co.'s Steamer to Brockville or Montreal .............. T 6

*See first foot note on page 114.
¶All rail. For tickets optional rail or steamer, Toronto to Montreal, add $2.25 from Toronto.
†All rail. For tickets optional rail or steamer, Toronto to Montreal, add $1.75 from London, Hamilton, Niagara Falls or Buffalo.

## To Round Island Park and Thousand Island Park, N. Y., and Return.—*Continued.*

Fares:—

| | | | |
|---|---|---|---|
| Brockville | $ 2.75 | Quebec | $ 14.50 |
| Montreal | 9.50 | | |

Route R T 103— FORM.

Grand Trunk Railway to Kingston City .................................................T 76
R. & O. N. Co.'s St'r to Round Island (or Thousand Island Park, Alexandria Bay)....T 6
R. & O. N. Co.'s Steamer to Brockville or Montreal ................. ......T 6

Fares:—

| | | | |
|---|---|---|---|
| Brockville | $ 3.40 | Quebec | $ 14.50 |
| Montreal | 9.50 | | |

## To St. Andrews, N. B., and Return.

Route R T 104—

Grand Trunk Railway to Portland ........................................T 74
Maine Central Railway to Vanceboro ......................................T 52
New Brunswick Railway to St. Andrews......................... ... ....T 51
Returning same route.

Fares:—

| | | | | |
|---|---|---|---|---|
| Detroit | $ 37.50 | | Toronto | $ 34.00 ¶$32.25 |
| Port Hur'n | 37.35 | | Kingston. | 26.90 |
| London | 37.35 | ¶$36.10 | Bro'kville | 24.60 |
| Hamilton | § 34.00 | ¶ 32.25 | Ottawa | 24.00 |
| Niag'ra F's | § 34.00 | ¶ 32.25 | Montreal. | 19.00 |
| Buffalo | § 35.00 | ¶ 33.25 | Quebec | 21.00 |

Route R T 105—

Choice of routes to Toronto (see pages 84 and 85).
Grand Trunk Railway or R. & O. N. Co.'s Steamer to Kingston.........T 5
Grand Trunk Railway or R. & O. N. Co.'s Steamer to Prescott..........T 55
Grand Trunk Railway or R. & O. N. Co.'s Steamer to Montreal .........T 56
Same as Route R T 104 to St. Andrews and return to starting point.

Fares:—

| | | | |
|---|---|---|---|
| Detroit | $39.10 | Niagara Falls | §$34.00 |
| Port Huron | 37.55 | Buffalo | § 35.00 |
| London | 37.55 | Toronto | § 34.00 |
| Hamilton | § 34.00 | | |

Route R T 106—

Choice of routes to Montreal (see page 85).
Grand Trunk Railway to Portland ......................................T 74
International Steamship Co.'s Steamer to St. Andrews.................T 49
International Steamship Co.'s Steamer to Portland ................. ...T 49
Grand Trunk Railway to starting point .................................T 74

Fares:—

| | | | |
|---|---|---|---|
| Detroit | *$37.50 | Toronto | *$30.00 |
| Port Huron | * 37.35 | Kingston | * 22.90 |
| London | * 35.10 | Brockville | 20.60 |
| Hamilton | * 31.80 | Ottawa | 20.00 |
| Niagara Falls | * 32.25 | Montreal | 15.00 |
| Buffalo | * 33.25 | | |

## To St. John, N. B., and Return.

‡Route R T 107—

Grand Trunk Railway to Levis...........................................⎫
Intercolonial Railway to St. John ........ ............ ............⎬2852
Returning same route ....................................... . . ⎭

*See first foot note on page 114.
¶ Limited continuous passage each way.
§Limited east of Montreal.

# To St. John, N. B., and Return.—*Continued.*

Fares :—

| | | | | |
|---|---|---|---|---|
| Detroit | *$41.50 | Toronto | *$34.00 |
| Port Huron | * 41.35 | Kingston | * 26.90 |
| London | † 38.35 | Brockville | 24.60 |
| Hamilton | † 34.50 | Ottawa | 24.00 |
| Niagara Falls | * 34.50 | Montreal | 19.00 |
| Buffalo | * 35.50 | | |

Route R T 108—

| | FORM. |
|---|---|
| Grand Trunk Railway to Portland | T 74 |
| Maine Central Railroad to Vanceboro | T 52 |
| New Brunswick Railway to St. John | T 51 |
| Returning same route | |

Fares :—

| | | | |
|---|---|---|---|
| Detroit | *$41.50 | Toronto | *$34.00 |
| Port Huron | * 41.35 | Kingston | * 26.90 |
| London | § 38.35 | Brockville | 24.60 |
| Hamilton | § 34.50 | Ottawa | 24.00 |
| Niagara Falls | § 34.50 | Montreal | 19.00 |
| Buffalo | § 35.50 | Quebec | 21.00 |

Route R T 109—

Choice of routes to Toronto (see pages 84 and 85).

| | FORM. |
|---|---|
| Grand Trunk Railway or R. & O. N. Co.'s Steamer to Kingston | T 5 |
| Grand Trunk Railway or R. & O. N. Co.'s Steamer to Prescott | T 55 |
| Grand Trunk Railway or R. & O. N. Co.'s Steamer to Montreal | T 56 |

Same as Route R T 108 to St. John and return to starting point.

Fares :—

| | | | |
|---|---|---|---|
| London | ¶$40.10 | Buffalo | ¶$37.25 |
| Hamilton | ¶ 36.25 | Toronto | ¶ 36.25 |
| Niagara Falls | ¶ 36.25 | | |

Route R T 110—

Choice of routes to Montreal (see page 85).

| | FORM. |
|---|---|
| Grand Trunk Railway to Portland | T 32 |
| International Steamship Co.'s Steamer to St. John | T 49 |
| International Steamship Co.'s Steamer to Portland | T 49 |
| Grand Trunk Railway to starting point | T 74 |

Fares :—

| | | | |
|---|---|---|---|
| Detroit | *$40.00 | Toronto | *$32.50 |
| Port Huron | * 39.85 | Kingston | * 25.40 |
| London | * 37.60 | Brockville | 23.10 |
| Hamilton | * 34.30 | Ottawa | 22.50 |
| Niagara Falls | * 34.50 | Montreal | 17.50 |
| Buffalo | * 35.50 | Quebec | 19.50 |

# To St. John's, Newfoundland, and Return.

Route R T 111—

Grand Trunk Railway to Montreal ....................................⎫
Black Diamond Steamship Co.'s Steamer (every week or ten days)  ⎬ 4440R
   to St. John's, Newfoundland............................⎭
Returning same route ......

Fares :—

| | | | |
|---|---|---|---|
| Detroit | *$72.50 | Buffalo | *$68.25 |
| Port Huron | * 72.35 | Toronto | * 65.00 |
| London | * 70.10 | Kingston | 57.90 |
| Hamilton | * 66.80 | Brockville | 55.60 |
| Niagara Falls | * 67.25 | Ottawa | 55.00 |

*See first foot note on page 114.
§All rail. Limited continuous passage each way.
†All rail to Montreal. For tickets optional rail or steamer, Toronto to Montreal, add $1.75 from London, and Hamilton.
¶Limited continuous passage east of Montreal.

# To Saratoga, N. Y., and Return.

‡Route R T 112—

Grand Trunk Railway to Rouse's Point...................... } FORM. X357

Delaware & Hudson Railroad to Saratoga .............. ....... } (from Montreal)

Returning same route.

Fares:—

| | | | |
|---|---|---|---|
| Detroit | *$34.25 | Toronto | *$26.75 |
| Port Huron | * 34.10 | Kingston | * 19.65 |
| London | * 31.85 | Brockville | 17.35 |
| Hamilton | * 28.55 | Ottawa | 16.75 |
| Niagara Falls | * 29.00 | Montreal | 11.75 |
| Buffalo | * 30.00 | Quebec | 16.75 |

‡Route R T 113—

Choice of routes to Montreal (see page 85).

Grand Trunk Railway to Rouse's Point...................... ⎤

Delaware & Hudson Railroad to Baldwin .............. ⎥ X358

Lake George Steamer to Caldwell.... ..................... ⎬

Delaware & Hudson Railroad to Saratoga...................... ⎥ (from Montreal)

Delaware & Hudson Railroad to Rouse's Point ...... ......... ⎦

Grand Trunk Railway to starting point.

Fares:—

| | | | |
|---|---|---|---|
| Detroit | *$36.25 | Toronto | *$28.75 |
| Port Huron | * 36.10 | Kingston | * 21.65 |
| London | * 33.85 | Brockville | 19.35 |
| Hamilton | * 30.55 | Ottawa | 18.75 |
| Niagara Falls | * 31.00 | Montreal | 13.75 |
| Buffalo | * 32.00 | Quebec | 18.75 |

# To Severn, Ont., and Return.

‡Route R T 114—

Grand Trunk Railway to Severn, via Toronto, and return............. 2900

Fares:—

| | | | |
|---|---|---|---|
| Detroit | $ 11.70 | Toronto | $ 4.10 |
| Port Huron | 9.60 | Kingston | 10.60 |
| London | 7.20 | Brockville | 12.45 |
| Hamilton | 4.10 | Ottawa | 14.50 |
| Niagara Falls | 5.95 | Montreal | 16.75 |
| Buffalo | 6.95 | Quebec | 21.75 |

# To Shelburne, N. H., and Return.

‡Route R T 115—

Grand Trunk Railway to Shelburne and return........................ 2900

Fares:—

| | | | |
|---|---|---|---|
| Detroit | *$32.00 | Toronto | *$24.50 |
| Port Huron | * 31.85 | Kingston | * 17.40 |
| London | * 29.60 | Brockville | 15.10 |
| Hamilton | * 26.30 | Ottawa | 14.50 |
| Niagara Falls | * 26.75 | Montreal | 9.50 |
| Buffalo | * 27.75 | Quebec | † 11.50 |

# To South River, Ont., and Return.

‡Route R T 116—

Grand Trunk Railway to South River, via Toronto, and return........ 2900

Fares:—

| | | | |
|---|---|---|---|
| Detroit | $ 15.30 | Toronto | $ 7.70 |
| Port Huron | 13.20 | Kingston | 14.20 |
| London | 10.80 | Brockville | 16.05 |
| Hamilton | 7.70 | Ottawa | 16.75 |
| Niagara Falls | 9.55 | Montreal | 16.75 |
| Buffalo | 10.55 | Quebec | 21.75 |

*See first foot note on page 114.

†Via Grand Trunk direct, not coming into Montreal on going journey.

# To Summit Mt. Washington, N. H., and Return.

Route R T 117—

| | | FORM. |
|---|---|---|
| Choice of routes to Montreal (see page 85). | | |
| Grand Trunk Railway to Gorham... ................... | T | 32 |
| Milliken's Stage to Glen House ................ | T | 79 |
| Milliken's Stage to Summit ................... | T | 39 |
| Mt. Washington Railway to Base ................... | T | 41 |
| Concord & Montreal Railroad to Fabyans, Wells River........... | T | 25 |
| Montpelier & Wells River Railroad to Montpelier........ | T | 24 |
| Central Vermont Railroad to St. Johns............ ...... | T | 12 |
| Grand Trunk Railway to starting point........ .............. | T | 76 |

Fares:—

| | | | |
|---|---|---|---|
| Detroit............... | *$45.00 | Toronto.... ... | *$37.50 |
| Port Huron.... ....... | * 44.85 | Kingston............. | * 30.40 |
| London............. | * 42.60 | Brockville.... .... | 28.10 |
| Hamilton......... | * 39.30 | Ottawa............. | 27.50 |
| Niagara Falls.... .... | * 39.75 | Montreal............. | 22.50 |
| Buffalo............... | * 40.75 | Quebec.............. | § 26.00 |

Route R T 118—

| | | |
|---|---|---|
| Choice of routes to Montreal (see page 85). | | |
| Grand Trunk Railway to St. Johns............... | T | 11 |
| Central Vermont Railroad to Montpelier........... | T | 12 |
| Montpelier & Wells River Railroad to Wells River ............ | T | 24 |
| Concord & Montreal Railroad to Fabyans, Base............. | T | 25 |
| Mount Washington Railway to Summit............... | T | 41 |
| Milliken's Stage to Glen House............ | T | 40 |
| Milliken's Stage to Gorham............. | T | 79 |
| Grand Trunk Railway to starting point ................. | T | 76 |

Fares:—

| | | | |
|---|---|---|---|
| Detroit............. | *$43.00 | Toronto ............. | *$35.50 |
| Port Huron........... | * 42.85 | Kingston......... | * 28.40 |
| London............. | * 40.60 | Brockville ......... | 26.10 |
| Hamilton ............ | * 37.30 | Ottawa .... ... | 25.50 |
| Niagara Falls........ | * 37.75 | Montreal........ | 20.50 |
| Buffalo............. | *· 38.75 | Quebec ........ | 24.00 |

Route R T 119—

| | | |
|---|---|---|
| Choice of routes to Montreal (see page 85). | | |
| Grand Trunk Railway to Gorham............. ............ | T | 32 |
| Milliken's Stage to Glen House................... | T | 79 |
| Milliken's Stage to Summit................... | T | 39 |
| Milliken's Stage to Glen House............ | T | 40 |
| Milliken's Stage to Gorham.............. | T | 79 |
| Grand Trunk Railway to starting point ................. | T | 76 |

Fares:—

| | | | |
|---|---|---|---|
| Detroit............... | *$40.00 | Toronto......... | *$32.50 |
| Port Huron........... | * 39.85 | Kingston............ | * 25.40 |
| London............. | * 37.60 | Brockville .......... | 23.10 |
| Hamilton ........... | * 34.30 | Ottawa ............ | 22.50 |
| Niagara Falls........ | * 34.75 | Montreal............. | 17.50 |
| Buffalo ............. | * 35.75 | Quebec ............. | † 19.50 |

## To Sundridge, Ont., and Return.

:Route R T 120—

| | |
|---|---|
| Grand Trunk Railway to Sundridge via Toronto..... .. .......... } | 2900 |
| Returning same route........................................ | |

Fares:—

| | | | |
|---|---|---|---|
| Detroit............... | $ 15.10 | Toronto......... ..... | $ 7.50 |
| Port Huron........... | 13.00 | Kingston ............ | 14.00 |
| London .............. | 10.60 | Brockville ......... | 15.85 |
| Hamilton ............ | 7.50 | Ottawa............. | 16.95 |
| Niagara Falls........ | 9.35 | Montreal............. | 16.75 |
| Buffalo .............. | 10.35 | Quebec ..... ........ | 21.75 |

*See first foot note on page 114.
†Via Grand Trunk direct, not coming into Montreal.
§Via Grand Trunk direct, not coming into Montreal on going journey.

# To Sydney, Cape Breton, and Return.

†Route R T 121—
   Choice of routes to Montreal (see page 85).
   Black Diamond Steamship Co.'s Steamer (every week or ten days) }
     to Sydney ...................................................... } 4440 R
   Returning same route................................................. }

FORM.

Fares:—

| | | | |
|---|---|---|---|
| Detroit | *$52.50 | Buffalo | *$48.25 |
| Port Huron | * 52.35 | Toronto | * 45.00 |
| London | * 50.10 | Kingston | * 37.90 |
| Hamilton | * 46.80 | Brockville | 35.60 |
| Niagara Falls | * 47.25 | Ottawa | 35.00 |

# To Tadousac, Que., and Return.

### (SAGUENAY RIVER.)

‡Route R T 122—
   Grand Trunk Railway to Quebec....................................... } 2900
   R. & O. N. Co.'s Steamer to Tadousac................................. } and
   Returning same route................................................ } X351

Fares:—

| | | | |
|---|---|---|---|
| Detroit | *$31.50 | Toronto | *$24.00 |
| Port Huron | * 31.35 | Kingston | * 16.90 |
| London | * 29.10 | Brockville | 14.60 |
| Hamilton | * 25.80 | Ottawa | 14.00 |
| Niagara Falls | * 26.25 | Montreal | 9.00 |
| Buffalo | * 27.25 | | |

# To Thousand Island Park and Return.

### SEE ROUND ISLAND PARK.

# To Toronto, Ont., and Return.

Route R T 123—
   Grand Trunk Railway to Toronto .........................................T 76
   Grand Trunk Railway or R. & O. N. Co.'s Steamer to Kingston .........T 5
   Grand Trunk Railway or R. & O. N. Co.'s Steamer to Prescott .........T 55
   Grand Trunk Railway or R. & O. N. Co.'s Steamer to Montreal .........T 56
   Grand Trunk Railway or R. & O. N. Co.'s St'r to Quebec (for Quebec only) ...T 36

Fares:—
   Montreal ...............$ 18.00     Quebec... .........$ 23.00

# To Twin Mountain House, N. H., and Return.

Route R T 124—
   Choice of routes to Montreal (see page 85).
   Grand Trunk Railway to Groveton Jct ................................T 32
   Concord & Montreal Railroad to Twin Mountain House.................T 25
   Concord & Montreal Railroad to Groveton Jct ...... ...T 25
   Grand Trunk Railway to starting point ..............................T 76

Fares:—

| | | | |
|---|---|---|---|
| Detroit | *$32.00 | Toronto | *$24.50 |
| Port Huron | * 31.85 | Kingston | * 17.40 |
| London | * 29.60 | Brockville | 15.10 |
| Hamilton | * 26.30 | Ottawa | 14.50 |
| Niagara Falls | * 26.75 | Montreal | 9.50 |
| Buffalo | * 27.75 | Quebec | † 11.50 |

Route R T 125—
   Choice of routes to Montreal (see page 85.)
   Grand Trunk Railway to St Johns ......................................T 11
   Central Vermont Railroad to Montpelier...............................T 12
   Montpelier & Wells River Railroad to Wells River....................T 24
   Concord & Montreal Railroad to Twin Mountain House............ ......T 25
   Return same route to St. Johns.........................................
   Grand Trunk Railway to starting point ...............................T 76
Fares same as Route R T 124 (except Quebec, $13.50).

   *See first foot note on page 114.
   †Via Grand Trunk direct, not coming into Montreal.

# Tourist or Excursion Tickets

## *TO THE GREAT LAKES, MICHIGAN POINTS, Etc.*

On sale till September 30th and good till October 31st, by rail, or until the close of Navigation by steamer, unless otherwise indicated.

---

Fares are shown from principal stations only, but fares can be made from other stations by adding ordinary return or tourist return fare (if any) to the fare shown from whichever of the principal stations will make the lowest through fare, not exceeding the fare shown from a point beyond in the opposite direction.

Agents not having coupon tickets must issue exchange orders on nearest exchange office or on station at lake port (if by lake steamer), being carful to specify the form or route number and fare paid.

## To Ashland, Wis., and Return.

‡Route R T 126—          FORM.
    Grand Trunk Railway to Port Huron..................................... } 773R
    *Lake Superior Transit Co.'s Steamer to Ashland.......................
    Returning same route.
    Fares:—

| | | | |
|---|---|---|---|
| London | $37.10 | Kingston | $45.30 |
| St. Thomas | 37.85 | Brockville | 47.40 |
| Hamilton | 38.00 | Ottawa | 49.70 |
| Niagara Falls | 40.25 | Montreal | 53.00 |
| Buffalo | 41.25 | Quebec | 58.00 |
| Toronto | 38.00 | Sherbrooke | 57.00 |

Route R T 127—
    Grand Trunk Railway to Port Huron...................................T 76
    *Lake Superior Transit Co.'s Steamer to Ashland..........................T 88
    Choice of lines to Chicago as follows :—
        Wisconsin Central Line to Chicago.....................................T 89
        Chicago & North Western Railway to Chicago........................T 93
  OR, { Milwaukee, Lake Shore & Western Railway to Milwaukee .........T 92
        { Chicago & North Western Railway to Chicago.......................T 93
    Transfer to Chicago & Grand Trunk Depot.............................T 80
    Chicago & Grand Trunk Railway to Port Huron ......................T 90
    Grand Trunk Railway to starting point................................T 76
    Fares:—

| | | | |
|---|---|---|---|
| London | $38.80 | Kingston | $49.05 |
| St. Thomas | 39.10 | Brockville | 51.15 |
| Hamilton | 40.75 | Ottawa | 53.45 |
| Niagara Falls | 43.10 | Montreal | 56.75 |
| Buffalo | 44.10 | Quebec | 61.75 |
| Toronto | 41.75 | Sherbrooke | 60.75 |

Route R T 128—
    Same as route R T 127 to Ashland and return to Chicago.
    Transfer to Wabash Depot.............................................T 80
    Wabash Railroad to Detroit........ ..................................T 91
    Grand Trunk Railway to starting point...............................T 58
  Fares same as route R T 127.

## To Banff Hot Springs and Return.

‡Route R T 129—
    Grand Trunk Railway to Port Huron.....................................]
    Chicago & Grand Trunk Railway to Chicago  ......................
    Any line to St. Paul.................................................. } Ex74
    Great Northern Railway to Gretna....................................
    Canadian Pacific Railway to Banff Hot Springs.......................]
    Return same route.
    *Meals and Berths included.

# To Banff Hot Springs and Return.—*Continued*.

Fares :—

| | | | |
|---|---|---|---|
| London | $ 96.75 | Kingston | $110.00 |
| St. Thomas | 97.50 | Brockville | 110.00 |
| Hamilton | 100.90 | Ottawa | 111.00 |
| Niagara Falls | 103.50 | Montreal | 113.00 |
| Buffalo | 103.50 | Quebec | 118.00 |
| Toronto | 103.50 | Sherbrooke | 117.00 |

‡Route R T 130—                                                                 FORM.

Grand Trunk Railway to Detroit ..................................... ⎫
Wabash Railroad to Chicago.................................. ... ....... ⎪
Any line to St. Paul.............................................;....... ⎬ Ex75
Great Northern Railway to Gretna....,............................. ⎪
Canadian Pacific Railway to Banff Hot Springs.................... ⎭
Return same route.

Fares same as route R T 129.

‡Route R T 131—

Grand Trunk Railway to North Bay ............................... ⎫
Canadian Pacific Railway to Banff Hot Springs ...... .......... ⎬4968R
Returning same route............................................... ⎭
   (Tickets good for six months from date of sale.)

Fares .—

| | | | |
|---|---|---|---|
| Detroit | $ 85.00 | Niagara Falls | $ 85.00 |
| Port Huron | 85.00 | Buffalo | 86.00 |
| London | 85.00 | Toronto | 85.00 |
| St. Thomas | 85.00 | Kingston | 90.00 |
| Hamilton | 85.00 | | |

# To Chicago and Return.

‡Route R T 132—

Grand Trunk Railway to Port Huron........................... ⎫
Chicago & Grand Trunk Railway to Chicago ................ ...... ⎬ 3 R
Returning same route............................ .............. ⎭

Fares :—

| | | | |
|---|---|---|---|
| London | $ 16.75 | Kingston | $ 30.00 |
| St. Thomas | 17.50 | Brockville | 30.00 |
| Hamilton | 20.90 | Ottawa | 31.00 |
| ¶Niagara Falls | 23.50 | Montreal | 33.00 |
| ¶Buffalo | 23.50 | Quebec | 38.00 |
| Toronto | 23.50 | Sherbrooke | 37.00 |

¶Good only for thirty days from Niagara Falls, Buffalo or Suspension Bridge.

‡Route R T 133—

Grand Trunk Railway to Detroit ............................. ........ ⎫4000R
Wabash Railroad to Chicago ................................... ⎭

Fares same as Route R T 132.

Route R T 134—

Grand Trunk Railway to Collingwood (or Wiarton)..... ...... ...T 76
*Great Northern Transit Co.'s Steamer to Sault Ste. Marie...............T 95
*Lake Michigan & Lake Superior Trans. Co.'s Steamer to Chicago ......T 96
Chicago & Grand Trunk Railway to Port Huron....................T 90
Grand Trunk Railway to starting point ........... ..............T 76

Fares :—

| | | | |
|---|---|---|---|
| †London | $25.00 | Kingston | $ 34.80 |
| †St. Thomas | 25.30 | Brockville | 36.90 |
| Hamilton | 26.50 | Ottawa | 39.20 |
| Niagara Falls | 28.85 | Montreal | 42.50 |
| Buffalo | 29.85 | Quebec | 47.50 |
| Toronto | 27.50 | Sherbrooke | 46.50 |

Marked † via Wiarton; not marked, via Collingwood.

Route R T 135—

Same as Route R T 134 to Chicago.
Wabash Railroad to Detroit ....................................T 91
Grand Trunk Railway to starting point ........................T 58

Fares same as Route R T 134.

*Meals and berths included,

## To Chicago and Return.—*Continued*.

Route R T 136—

|  | FORM. |
|---|---|
| Grand Trunk Railway to Sarnia, Goderich, or Kincardine | T 76 |
| *North-West Transportation Co.'s Steamer to Sault Ste. Marie | T 97 |
| *Lake Michigan & Lake Superior Trans. Co.'s Steamer to Chicago | T 96 |
| Chicago & Grand Trunk Railway to Port Huron | T 90 |
| Grand Trunk Railway to starting point | T 76 |

Fares :—

| London | $ 24.55 | Kingston | $ 34.80 |
|---|---|---|---|
| St. Thomas | 25.25 | Brockville | 36.90 |
| Hamilton | 26.50 | Ottawa | 39.20 |
| Niagara Falls | 28.85 | Montreal | 42.50 |
| Buffalo | 29.85 | Quebec | 47.50 |
| Toronto | 27.50 | Sherbrooke | 46.50 |

Route R T 137—

| Same as Route R T 136 to Chicago. | |
|---|---|
| Wabash Railroad to Detroit | T 91 |
| Grand Trunk Railway to starting point | T 58 |

Fares same as Route R T 136.

## To Duluth, Minn., and Return.

Route R T 138—

| Grand Trunk Railway to Sarnia | |
|---|---|
| *North-West Transportation Co.'s Steamer to Duluth | }568R |
| Returning same route | |

Fares :—

| London | $33.00 | Kingston | $40.30 |
|---|---|---|---|
| St. Thomas | 33.00 | Brockville | 42.40 |
| Hamilton | 33.00 | Ottawa | 44.70 |
| Niagara Falls | 35.25 | Montreal | 48.00 |
| Buffalo | 36.25 | Quebec | 53.00 |
| Toronto | 33.00 | Sherbrooke | 52.00 |

Route R T 139—

| Grand Trunk Railway to Port Huron | |
|---|---|
| *Lake Superior Transit Co.'s Steamer to Duluth | }773R |
| Returning same route | |

Fares :—

| London | $38.10 | Kingston | $46.30 |
|---|---|---|---|
| St. Thomas | 38.85 | Brockville | 48.40 |
| Hamilton | 39.00 | Ottawa | 50.70 |
| Niagara Falls | 41.25 | Montreal | 54.00 |
| Buffalo | 42.25 | Quebec | 59.00 |
| Toronto | 39.00 | Sherbrooke | 58.00 |

Route R T 140—

| Grand Trunk Railway to Sarnia, Goderich or Kincardine | T 76 |
|---|---|
| *North-West Transportation Co.'s Steamer to Duluth | T 97 |
| Transfer to St. Paul & Duluth Depot | T 80 |
| { St. Paul & Duluth Railroad to St. Paul | T 98 |
| { Or, Great Northern Railway to St. Paul | T 99 |
| Choice of six routes to Chicago as follows :— | |
|   Chicago & Northwestern Railway to Chicago via Elroy | T 93 |
|   Chicago, Milwaukee & St. Paul Railway to Chicago | T118 |
|   Chicago, St. Paul & Kansas City Railway to Chicago | T119 |
|   Wisconsin Central Line to Chicago | T 89 |
|   Albert Lea Route—M. & St. L., B. C. R. & N., C. R. I. & P. to Chicago | T 77 |
| { Chicago, Burlington & Northern Railroad to Oregon | T122 |
| { Chicago & Iowa Railroad to Aurora | T121 |
| { Chicago, Burlington & Quincy Railroad to Chicago | T120 |
| Transfer to Chicago & Grand Trunk Depot | T 80 |
| Chicago & Grand Trunk Railway to Port Huron | T 90 |
| Grand Trunk Railway to starting point | T 76 |

Fares :—

| London | $40.60 | Kingston | $50.85 |
|---|---|---|---|
| St. Thomas | 41.35 | Brockville | 52.95 |
| Hamilton | 42.55 | Ottawa | 55.25 |
| Niagara Falls | 44.90 | Montreal | 58.55 |
| Buffalo | 45.90 | Quebec | 63.55 |
| Toronto | 43.55 | Sherbrooke | 62.55 |

*Meals and berths included.

## To Duluth, Minn., and Return.—*Continued.*

Route R T 141—                                                                  FORM.
   Same as Route R T 140 to Duluth and return to Chicago.
     Transfer to Wabash Railroad Depot....................................... ...T 80
     Wabash Railroad to Detroit .............................................. .T 91
     Grand Trunk Railway to starting point ................................T 58
   Fares same as Route R T 140.

Route R T 142—
     Grand Trunk Railway to Port Huron........................................T 76
     *Lake Superior Transit Co.'s Steamer to Duluth ... .....................T 88
     Same as Route R T 140 to starting point............................ ....
   Fares same as Route R T 140.

Route R T 143—
   Same as Route R T 142 to Duluth and return to Chicago.
     Transfer to Wabash Railroad Depot ....................................T 80
     Wabash Railroad to Detroit .............................................T 91
     Grand Trunk Railway to starting point ..............................T 58
   Fares same as Route R T 140.

Route R T 144—
     Grand Trunk Railway to Sarnia, Goderich or Kincardine ..... .......T 76
     *North-West Transportation Co.'s Steamer to Duluth ....................T 97
     Transfer to Northern Pacific Railroad Depot..........................T 80
   { Northern Pacific Railroad to Ashland ...............................T100
   { Milwaukee, Lake Shore & Western Railway to Milwaukee ..............T 92
   ( Chicago & North-Western Railway to Chicago.........................T 93
                   OR
   { Northern Pacific Railroad to Ashland ..............................T100
   { Wisconsin Central Line to Chicago .................................T 89
                    OR
     Chicago & North-Western Railway to Chicago.........................T 93
     Transfer to Chicago & Grand Trunk Depot ...........................T 80
     Chicago & Grand Trunk Railway to Port Huron .......................T 90
     Grand Trunk Railway to starting point .............................T 76
   Fares same as Route R T 140.

Route R T 145—
     Grand Trunk Railway to Port Huron.....................................T 76
     *Lake Superior Transit Co.'s Steamer to Duluth ........................T 88
     Returning same as Route R T 144.
   Fares same as Route R T 140.

## To Mackinac Island or Sault Ste. Marie and Return.

‡Route R T 146—
   (Good only in July and August. Tickets must be limited to August 31st.)
   Grand Trunk Railway to Collingwood or Wiarton ..... } 4808R Via Collingwood,
   *Great Northern Transit Co.'s Str. to Mackinac Island.. }      or
   Returning same route ................................ } 4376R Via Wiarton.
   Fares :—

| | | | |
|---|---|---|---|
| †London | $ 16.00 | Kingston | $ 23.30 |
| †St. Thomas | 16.00 | Brockville | 25.40 |
| Hamilton | 16.00 | Ottawa | 27.70 |
| Niagara Falls | 18.25 | Montreal | 31.00 |
| Buffalo | 19.25 | Quebec | 36.00 |
| Toronto | 16.00 | Sherbrooke | 35.00 |

   Marked † via Wiarton; not marked via Collingwood.

## To Mackinac Island and Return.

‡Route R T 147—
   (Good only in July and August. Tickets must be limited to August 31st.)
   Grand Trunk Railway to Port Huron ...............................
   Detroit & Cleveland Steam Nav. Co. to Mackinac Island............. } 4412R
   Returning same route ............................................
   *Meals and berths included.

# To Mackinac Island and Return.—*Continued*.

Fares :—

| | | | |
|---|---|---|---|
| London | $ 10.10 | Kingston | $ 18.30 |
| St. Thomas | 10.85 | Brockville | 20.40 |
| Hamilton | 11.00 | Ottawa | 22.70 |
| Niagara Falls | 13.25 | Montreal | 26.00 |
| Buffalo | 14.25 | Quebec | 31.00 |
| Toronto | 11.00 | Sherbrooke | 30.00 |

**Route R T 148—**                                                         FORM.
Grand Trunk Railway to Detroit............................................T 58
Michigan Central Railroad to Mackinac City ........ ................T102
Mackinac Trans. Co.'s Steamer to Mackinac Island ....................T103
Returning same route.

Fares:—

| | | | |
|---|---|---|---|
| London | $17.05 | Kingston | $28.95 |
| St. Thomas | 17.15 | Brockville | 31.05 |
| Hamilton | 20.10 | Ottawa | 33.35 |
| Niagara Falls | 22.05 | Montreal | 36.65 |
| Buffalo | 22.05 | Quebec | 41.65 |
| Toronto | 21.65 | Sherbrooke | 40.65 |

**Route R T 149—**
R.W.
Grand Trunk Railway to Collingwood (or Wiarton) ............T 76
*Great Northern Transit Co.'s Steamer to Sault Ste. Marie.. .............T 95
Steamer to Mackinac City ................................................T 78
Michigan Central Railroad to Detroit..................................T102
Grand Trunk Railway to starting point...................................T 58

Fares:—

| | | | |
|---|---|---|---|
| †London | $19.55 | Kingston | $29.15 |
| †St. Thomas | 19.60 | Brockville | 31.25 |
| Hamilton | 21.10 | Ottawa | 33.55 |
| Niagara Falls | 23.35 | Montreal | 36.85 |
| Buffalo | 24.35 | Quebec | 41.85 |
| Toronto | 21.85 | Sherbrooke | 40.85 |

Marked † via Wiarton; not marked via Collingwood.

**Route R T 150—**
R.W.
Grand Trunk Railway to Port Huron ...............................T 76
Detroit & Cleveland S. N. Co. Steamer to Mackinac Island .............T101
Mackinac Trans. Co.'s Steamer to Mackinac City .....................T103
Michigan Central Railroad to Detroit..................................T102
Grand Trunk Railway to starting point..................................T 58

Fares :—

| | | | |
|---|---|---|---|
| London | $13.60 | Kingston | $23.65 |
| St. Thomas | 14.00 | Brockville | 25.75 |
| Hamilton | 15.60 | Ottawa | 28.05 |
| Niagara Falls | 17.95 | Montreal | 31.35 |
| Buffalo | 18.95 | Quebec | 36.35 |
| Toronto | 16.35 | Sherbrooke | 35.35 |

# To Marquette, Mich., and Return.

‡**Route R T 151—**
Grand Trunk Railway to Port Huron................................. .....⎰773R
*Lake Superior Transit Co.'s Steamer to Marquette.... ................⎱

Fares:--

| | | | |
|---|---|---|---|
| London | $24.10 | Kingston | $32.30 |
| St. Thomas | 24.85 | Brockville | 34.40 |
| Hamilton | 25.00 | Ottawa | 36.70 |
| Niagara Falls | 27.25 | Montreal | 40.00 |
| Buffalo | 28.25 | Quebec | 45.00 |
| Toronto | 25.00 | Sherbrooke | 44.00 |

**Route R T 152—**
Grand Trunk Railway to Collingwood (or Wiarton).....................T 76
*Great Northern Transit Co.'s Steamer to Sault Ste. Marie............ ....T 95
Duluth, South Shore & Atlantic Railway to Marquette ....... .........T104
Returning same route.

*Meals and berths included.

## To Marquette, Mich., and Return.—*Continued*.

Fares:—

| | | | |
|---|---|---|---|
| †London | $23.50 | Kingston | $30.80 |
| †St. Thomas | 23.50 | Brockville | 32.90 |
| Hamilton | 23.50 | Ottawa | 35.20 |
| Niagara Falls | 25.75 | Montreal | 38.50 |
| Buffalo | 26.75 | Quebec | 43.50 |
| Toronto | 23.50 | Sherbrooke | 42.50 |

Marked † via Wiarton; not marked via Collingwood.

Route R T 153—

FORM.

Grand Trunk Railway to Port Huron........................... T 76
Detroit & Cleveland S. N. Co.'s Steamer to St. Ignace........ T101
Duluth, South Shore & Atlantic Railway to Marquette.......... T104
Returning same route.

Fares:—

| | | | |
|---|---|---|---|
| London | $17.60 | Kingston | $25.80 |
| St. Thomas | 18.35 | Brockville | 27.90 |
| Hamilton | 18.50 | Ottawa | 30.20 |
| Niagara Falls | 20.75 | Montreal | 33.50 |
| Buffalo | 21.75 | Quebec | 38.50 |
| Toronto | 18.50 | Sherbrooke | 37.50 |

Route R T 154—

Grand Trunk Railway to Collingwood (or Wiarton)............. T 76
*Great Northern Transit Co.'s Steamer to Sault Ste. Marie........ T 95
*Lake Superior Transit Co.'s Steamer to Marquette............. T 88
*Lake Superior Transit Co.'s Steamer to Port Huron............ T 88
Grand Trunk Railway to starting point..................... T 76

Fares —

| | | | |
|---|---|---|---|
| †London | $25.55 | Kingston | $33.30 |
| †St. Thomas | 25.95 | Brockville | 35.40 |
| Hamilton | 26.00 | Ottawa | 37.70 |
| Niagara Falls | 28.25 | Montreal | 41.00 |
| Buffalo | 29.25 | Quebec | 46.00 |
| Toronto | 26.00 | Sherbrooke | 45.00 |

Marked † via Wiarton; not marked via Collingwood.

Route R T 155—

Grand Trunk Railway to Port Huron......................... T 76
*Lake Superior Transit Co.'s Steamer to Marquette........... T 88
Duluth, South Shore & Atlantic Railway to St. Ignace........ T104
Mackinac Transportation Co.'s Steamer to Mackinac City...... T103
Michigan Central Railroad to Detroit...................... T102
Grand Trunk Railway to starting point..................... T 58

Fares:—

| | | | |
|---|---|---|---|
| London | $25.10 | Kingston | $35.15 |
| St. Thomas | 25.55 | Brockville | 37.25 |
| Hamilton | 27.10 | Ottawa | 39.55 |
| Niagara Falls | 29.45 | Montreal | 42.85 |
| Buffalo | 30.45 | Quebec | 47.85 |
| Toronto | 27.85 | Sherbrooke | 46.85 |

## To Milwaukee, Wis., and Return.

‡Route R T 156—

Grand Trunk Railway to Port Huron........................... }
Chicago & Grand Trunk Railway to Durand ................... } 973R
Detroit, Grand Haven & Milwaukee Railway & St'r to Milwaukee..... }
Returning same route.

Fares:—

| | | | |
|---|---|---|---|
| London | $16.75 | Kingston | $30.00 |
| St. Thomas | 17.50 | Brockville | 30.00 |
| Hamilton | 20.90 | Ottawa | 31.00 |
| *Niagara Falls | 23.50 | Montreal | 33.00 |
| ¶Buffalo | 23.50 | Quebec | 38.00 |
| Toronto | 23.50 | Sherbrooke | 37.00 |

¶Good only for thirty days from Niagara Falls, Buffalo or Suspension Bridge.

*Meals and berths included.

# To Milwaukee, Wis., and Return.—*Continued.*

‡Route R T 157—                                                    FORM.
    Grand Trunk Railway to Detroit .......................................  
    Detroit, Grand Haven & Milwaukee Railway and Str. to Milwaukee } L.S.41R
    Returning same route ... ...................................  
Fares same as Route R T 156.

## To Minneapolis and Return.
### SEE ST PAUL.

## To Pacific Coast and Return.

(SAN FRANCISCO, LOS ANGELES, SAN DIEGO, COLTON, SAN JOSE, SAN BERNARDINO,
PORTLAND, SEATTLE, TACOMA, VANCOUVER AND VICTORIA.)

Tickets, good for six months, and carrying stop-over privileges, are on sale at
all principal Grand Trunk Offices. Passengers are offered a great variety of routes,
and side trips may be made taking in points of interest off the main line. Full
particulars as to fares, etc., furnished on application to any City or Station Ticket
Office of the Company.

## To Portage Lake (Houghton), and Return.

Route R T 158—
    Grand Trunk Railway to Port Huron..........................  
    *Lake Superior Transit Co.'s Steamer to Portage Lake ............ .... } 773R
    Returning same route ........................  
Fares :—

| | | | |
|---|---|---|---|
| London | $ 28.10 | Kingston | $ 36.30 |
| St. Thomas | 28.85 | Brockville | 38.40 |
| Hamilton | 29.00 | Ottawa | 40.70 |
| Niagara Falls | 31.25 | Montreal | 44.00 |
| Buffalo | 32.25 | Quebec | 49.00 |
| Toronto | 29.00 | Sherbrooke | 48.00 |

Route R T 159—
    Grand Trunk Railway to Collingwood (or Wiarton) ...................... T 76
    *Great Northern Transit Co.'s Steamer to Sault Ste. Marie...... ......... T 95
    Duluth, South Shore & Atlantic Railway to Houghton...................T104
    Returning same route
Fares :—

| | | | |
|---|---|---|---|
| †London | $ 28.25 | Kingston | $ 35.55 |
| †St. Thomas | 28.25 | Brockville | 37.65 |
| Hamilton | 28.25 | Ottawa | 39.95 |
| Niagara Falls | 30.50 | Montreal | 43.25 |
| Buffalo | 31.50 | Quebec | 48.25 |
| Toronto | 28.25 | Sherbrooke | 47 25 |

Marked † via Wiarton; not marked via Collingwood.

Route R T 160—
    Grand Trunk Railway to Port Huron.......................... T 76
    Detroit & Cleveland S. N. Co.'s Steamer to St. Ignace......... .. ......T101
    Duluth, South Shore & Atlantic Railway to Houghton.............. .T104
    Returning same route
Fares :—

| | | | |
|---|---|---|---|
| London | $ 22.35 | Kingston | $ 30.55 |
| St. Thomas | 23.10 | Brockville | 32.65 |
| Hamilton | 23.25 | Ottawa | 34.95 |
| Niagara Falls | 25.50 | Montreal | 38.25 |
| Buffalo | 26.50 | Quebec | 43.25 |
| Toronto | 23.25 | Sherbrooke | 42.25 |

Route R T 161—
    Grand Trunk Railway to Port Huron....................... T 76
    *Lake Superior Transit Co.'s Steamer to Portage Lake (Houghton)......T 88
    Duluth, South Shore & Atlantic Railway to St. Ignace...................T104
    Mackinac Trans. Co. to Mackinac City....... ...............T103
    Michigan Central Railroad to Detroit .............................T102
    Grand Trunk Railway to starting point ........................... T 58
    *Meals and berths included.

## To Portage Lake and Return.--*Continued.*

Fares :—

| | | | | |
|---|---|---|---|---|
| London | $ 29.85 | Kingston | $ 39.90 |
| St. Thomas | 30.30 | Brockville | 42.00 |
| Hamilton | 31.85 | Ottawa | 44.30 |
| Niagara Falls | 34.20 | Montreal | 47.60 |
| Buffalo | 35.20 | Quebec | 52.60 |
| Toronto | 32.60 | Sherbrooke | 51.60 |

Route R T 162—                                                    FORM.
　Grand Trunk Railway to Collingwood or Wiarton .... ............T 76
　*Great Northern Transit Co.'s Steamer to Sault Ste. Marie ...............T 95
　*Lake Superior Transit Co.'s Steamer to Portage Lake ...............T 88
　*Lake Superior Transit Co.'s Steamer to Port Huron...... ..........T 88
　Grand Trunk Railway to starting point.................................,..T 76

Fares :—

| | | | | |
|---|---|---|---|---|
| †London | $ 30.55 | Kingston | $ 38.30 |
| †St. Thomas | 30.95 | Brockville | 40.40 |
| Hamilton | 31.00 | Ottawa | 42.70 |
| Niagara Falls | 33.25 | Montreal | 46.00 |
| Buffalo | 34.25 | Quebec | 51.00 |
| Toronto | 31.00 | Sherbrooke | 50.00 |

Marked † via Wiarton; not marked via Collingwood.

## To Port Arthur, Ont., and Return.

‡Route R T 163—
　Grand Trunk Railway to Sarnia.............................................
　*North-West Transportation Co.'s Steamer to Port Arthur............. }568R
　Returning same route ...........................................

Fares :—

| | | | | |
|---|---|---|---|---|
| London | $ 30.00 | Kingston | $ 37.30 |
| St. Thomas | 30.00 | Brockville | 39.40 |
| Hamilton | 30.00 | Ottawa | 41.70 |
| Niagara Falls | 32.25 | Montreal | 45.00 |
| Buffalo | 33.25 | Quebec | 50.00 |
| Toronto | 30.00 | Sherbrooke | 49.00 |

‡Route R T 164—
　Grand Trunk Railway to Sarnia ........................................
　*North-West Transportation Co.'s Steamer to Port Arthur ......... }
　Canadian Pacific Railway to North Bay ............................  } 5066
　Grand Trunk Railway to starting point..........................

Fares same as Route R T 163.

‡Route R T 165—
　Grand Trunk Railway to Toronto .....................................
　Canadian Pacific Railway to Owen Sound....................... }
　*Canadian Pacific Steamship Line to Port Arthur ..................... } 4359 R
　Returning same route...............................................

Fares :—

| | | | | |
|---|---|---|---|---|
| Kingston | $ 37.30 | Montreal | $ 45.00 |
| Brockville | 39.40 | Quebec | 50.00 |
| Ottawa | 41.70 | Sherbrooke | 49.00 |

## To St. Paul or Minneapolis and Return.

‡Route R T 166—
　Grand Trunk Railway to Port Huron............................ }
　Chicago & Grand Trunk Railway to Chicago...................... }Ex74
　Choice of six routes to St. Paul or Minneapolis............ .......... )
　Returning same route.

Fares :—

| | | | | |
|---|---|---|---|---|
| London | $36.75 | Kingston | $50.00 |
| St. Thomas | 37.50 | Brockville | 50.00 |
| Hamilton | 40.90 | Ottawa | 51.00 |
| Niagara Falls | 43.50 | Montreal | 53.00 |
| Buffalo | 43.50 | Quebec | 58.00 |
| Toronto | 43.50 | Sherbrooke | 57.00 |

*Meals and berths included.

## To St. Paul and Return.—*Continued.*

‡Route R T 167—
Grand Trunk Railway to Detroit .......................
Wabash Railroad to Chicago....................... } Ex75
Choice of six routes to St. Paul or Minneapolis .... ... ...........
Returning same route.
Fares same as Route R T 166.

‡Route R T 168—
Grand Trunk Railway to Port Huron ......................
Chicago & Grand Trunk Railway to Durand......................
Detroit, Grand Haven & Milwaukee Railway and Str. to Milwaukee... } Ex72
Choice of three routes (C. & N. W. Ry., C. M. & St. P. Ry., and Wisconsin Central Line) to St. Paul or Minneapolis ...................
Returning same route.

Fares :—

| | | | |
|---|---|---|---|
| London | $34.75 | Kingston | $48.00 |
| St. Thomas | 35.50 | Brockville | 48.00 |
| Hamilton | 38.90 | Ottawa | 49.00 |
| Niagara Falls | 41.50 | Montreal | 51.00 |
| Buffalo | 41.50 | Quebec | 56.00 |
| Toronto | 41.50 | Sherbrooke | 55.00 |

Route R T 169—
Grand Trunk Railway to North Bay..................... T 76
Canadian Pacific Railway to Sault Ste. Marie..................... T105
Minneapolis, St. Paul & Sault Ste. Marie Ry. to St. Paul or Minneapolis T 77
Minneapolis, St. Paul & Sault Ste. Marie Ry. to Sault Ste. Marie........ T 77
Canadian Pacific S. S. Line to Owen Sound ..................... T 78
Canadian Pacific Railway to Toronto..................... T105
Grand Trunk Railway to starting point..................... T 76

Fares :—

| | | | |
|---|---|---|---|
| Toronto | $38.00 | Montreal | $53.00 |
| Kingston | 45.30 | Quebec | 58.00 |
| Brockville | 47.40 | Sherbrooke | 57.00 |
| Ottawa | 49.70 | | |

Route R T 170—
Grand Trunk Railway to Sarnia, Goderich or Kincardine..... ........ T 76
*North West Transportation Co.'s Steamer to Duluth........ .. ...... T 97
Transfer to Depot ..................... T 80
{ St. Paul & Duluth Railway to St. Paul..................... T 98
{ Or, Great Northern Railway to St. Paul..................... T 99
Returning same route.

Fares :—

| | | | |
|---|---|---|---|
| London | $40.00 | Kingston | $47.30 |
| St. Thomas | 40.00 | Brockville | 49.40 |
| Hamilton | 40.00 | Ottawa | 51.70 |
| Niagara Falls | 42.25 | Montreal | 55.00 |
| Buffalo | 43.25 | Quebec | 60.00 |
| Toronto | 40.00 | Sherbrooke | 59.00 |

Route R T 171—
Grand Trunk Railway to Detroit.....................
Detroit, Grand Haven & Milwaukee Railway and Str. to Milwaukee..... } Ex72
Choice of three routes (C. & N. W. Ry., C. M. & St. P. Ry., and Wisconsin Central Line) to St. Paul and Minneapolis ...................
Returning same route....
Fares same as Route R T 168.

## To Sault Ste. Marie and Return.

Route R T 172—
Grand Trunk Railway to Collingwood (or Wiarton)... { 4376R Via Wiarton.
*Great Northern Transit Co.'s St'r to Sault Ste. Marie.. { 4808R Via Collingwood.
Returning same route.

Fares :—

| | | | |
|---|---|---|---|
| †London | $16.00 | Kingston | $23.30 |
| †St. Thomas | 16.00 | Brockville | 25.40 |
| Hamilton | 16.00 | Ottawa | 27.70 |
| Niagara Falls | 18.25 | Montreal | 31.00 |
| Buffalo | 19.25 | Quebec | 36.00 |
| Toronto | 16.00 | Sherbrooke | 35.00 |

Marked † via Wiarton; not marked via Collingwood.
*Meals and berths included,

# To Sault Ste. Marie and Return.—*Continued*.

‡Route R T 173—

Grand Trunk Railway to Sarnia................................................  } FORM.
  *North-West Transportation Co.'s Steamer to Sault Ste. Marie ......... } 568R
Returning same route. ...................................................

Fares :—

| | | | |
|---|---|---|---|
| London .............. | $ 15.10 | Kingston............ | $23.30 |
| St. Thomas............ | 15.85 | Brockville .......... | 25.40 |
| Hamilton ............ | 16.00 | Ottawa ............ | 27.70 |
| Niagara Falls........ .. | 18.25 | Montreal........... | 31.00 |
| Buffalo .............. | 19.25 | Quebec............ | 36.00 |
| Toronto .............. | 16.00 | Sherbrooke ......... | 35.00 |

‡Route R T 174—

Grand Trunk Railway to Port Huron .............................. }
  *Lake Superior Transit Co.'s Steamer to Sault Ste. Marie .............. } 773R
Returning same route.... .................................

Fares :—

| | | | |
|---|---|---|---|
| London .............. | $ 17.10 | Kingston. ........... | $ 25.30 |
| St. Thomas............ | 17.85 | Brockville .......... | 27.40 |
| Hamilton ..... ... | 18.00 | Ottawa. ........... | 29.70 |
| Niagara Falls........ | 20.25 | Montreal........... | 33.00 |
| Buffalo'.............. | 21.25 | Quebec............ | 38.00 |
| Toronto .............. | 18.00 | Sherbrooke........ . | 37.00 |

‡Route R T 175—

Grand Trunk Railway to Toronto ............................. }
Canadian Pacific Railway to Owen Sound................... }
  *Canadian Pacific Steamship Line to Sault Ste. Marie.............. } 4359 R
Returning same route............................................ }

Fares :—

| | | | |
|---|---|---|---|
| Kingston............ | $ 23.30 | Montreal............ | $ 31.00 |
| Brockville ............ | 25.40 | Quebec ............. | 36.00 |
| Ottawa............... | 27.70 | Sherbrooke......... . | 35.00 |

Route R T 176—

R. W.   Grand Trunk Railway to Collingwood (or Wiarton).................... .T 76
  *Great Northern Transit Co.'s Steamer to Sault Ste. Marie...............T 95
  *North-West Trans. Co.'s Steamer to Sarnia...........................T 97
  Grand Trunk Railway to starting point...............................T 76

Fares :—

| | | | |
|---|---|---|---|
| †London ...... ......... | $ 17.55 | Kingston............ | $ 25.30 |
| †St. Thomas ............. | 17.95 | Brockville .......... | 27.40 |
| Hamilton............ | 18.00 | Ottawa............ | 29.70 |
| Niagara Falls ......... | 20.25 | Montreal........... | 33.00 |
| Buffalo ....... | 21.25 | Quebec ........... | 38.00 |
| Toronto .......... .... | 18.00 | Sherbrooke......... | 37.00 |

Marked † via Wiarton; not marked via Collingwood.

Route R T 177—

R. W.   Grand Trunk Railway to Collingwood (or Wiarton)...... .........T 76
  *Great Northern Transit Co.'s Steamer to Sault Ste. Marie ...............T 95
  Canadian Pacific Railway to North Bay..............................T105
  Grand Trunk Railway to starting point ..............................T 76

Fares :—

| | | | |
|---|---|---|---|
| †London .............. | $ 18.00 | Kingston............ | $ 25.30 |
| †St. Thomas............ | 18.00 | Brockville .......... | 27.40 |
| Hamilton ............ | 18.00 | Ottawa ............ | 29.70 |
| Niagara Falls........ | 20.25 | Montreal ......... | 33.00 |
| Buffalo ............. | 21.25 | Quebec ............ | 38.00 |
| Toronto .............. | 18.00 | Sherbrooke......... | 37.00 |

Marked † via Wiarton; not marked via Collingwood.

Route R T 178—

R. W.   Grand Trunk Railway to Sarnia, Goderich or Kincardine ..............T 76
  *North-West Transportation Co.'s Steamer to Sault Ste. Marie ..........T 97
  Returning same as Route R T 177.
Fares same as Route R T 177.

  *Meals and berths included.

# To Sault Ste. Marie and Return.—*Continued*.

Route R T 179—  
FORM.

    Grand Trunk Railway to Toronto........................................ ....T 76  
    Canadian Pacific Railway to Owen Sound ...............................T105  
    \*Canadian Pacific Steamship Line to Sault Ste. Marie ....................T 78  
    Canadian Pacific Railway to North Bay.................................T105  
    Grand Trunk Railway to starting point ..................... ........T 76

Fares :—

| | | | |
|---|---|---|---|
| Kingston | $ 25.30 | Montreal | $ 33.00 |
| Brockville | 27.40 | Quebec | 38.00 |
| Ottawa | 29.70 | Sherbrooke | 37.00 |

# To Winnipeg, Man., and Return.

:Route R T 180—  
    Grand Trunk Railway to Port Huron........  
    Chicago & Grand Trunk Railway to Chicago..........  
    Choice of six routes to St. Paul or Minneapolis ..................  
    Northern Pacific Railroad to Winnipeg..............................    Ex 74  
OR { Great Northern Railway to Gretna.............................  
    Canadian Pacific Railway to Winnipeg.......................  
    Returning same route.......................

Fares :—

| | | | |
|---|---|---|---|
| London | $ 59.25 | Kingston | $ 72.50 |
| St. Thomas | 60.00 | Brockville | 72.50 |
| Hamilton | 63.40 | Ottawa | 73.50 |
| Niagara Falls | 66.00 | Montreal | 75.50 |
| Buffalo | 66.00 | Quebec | 80.50 |
| Toronto | 66.00 | Sherbrooke | 79.50 |

:Route R T 181—  
    Grand Trunk Railway to Detroit ..........................  
    Wabash Railroad to Chicago ...........................  
    Choice of six routes to St. Paul or Minneapolis .....  
    Northern Pacific Railroad to Winnipeg ......................    Ex 75  
OR { Great Northern Railway to Gretna.............................  
    Canadian Pacific Railway to Winnipeg ...................  
    Returning same route.....................  
Fares same as Route R T 180.

Route R T 182—  
    Grand Trunk Railway to Port Huron........ .............  
    Chicago & Grand Trunk Railway to Durand ...................  
    Detroit, Grand Haven & Milwaukee Railway to Milwaukee.......  
    Choice of three routes to St. Paul or Minneapolis ..............    Ex 72  
    Northern Pacific Railroad to Winnipeg.............................  
OR { Great Northern Railway to Gretna.............................  
    Canadian Pacific Railway to Winnipeg...................  
    Returning same route....................

Fares :—

| | | | |
|---|---|---|---|
| London | $57.25 | Kingston | $70.50 |
| St. Thomas | 58.00 | Brockville | 70.50 |
| Hamilton | 61.40 | Ottawa | 71.50 |
| Niagara Falls | 64.00 | Montreal | 73.50 |
| Buffalo | 64.00 | Quebec | 78.50 |
| Toronto | 64.00 | Sherbrooke | 77.50 |

:Route R T 183—  
    Grand Trunk Railway to Detroit............................  
    Detroit, Grand Haven & Milwaukee Railway and Str. to Milwaukee ..  
    Choice of three routes to St. Paul or Minneapolis... ..................    Ex72  
    Northern Pacific Railroad to Winnipeg .........................  
OR { Great Northern Railway to Gretna.............................  
    Canadian Pacific Railway to Winnipeg.......................  
Fares same as Route R T 182.

:Route R T 184—  
    Grand Trunk Railway to Sarnia.............................. } 3137  
    \*North-West Transportation Co.'s Steamer to Port Arthur.............. } or  
    Canadian Pacific Railway to Winnipeg ............................. } 4447  
    Returning same route.

    \*Meals and berths included.

# To Winnipeg, Man., and Return.—*Continued.*

Fares :—

| | | | |
|---|---|---|---|
| London | $50.00 | Kingston | $58.00 |
| St. Thomas | 50.00 | Brockville | 58.00 |
| Hamilton | 50.00 | Ottawa | 58.70 |
| Niagara Falls | 50.00 | Montreal | 60.00 |
| Buffalo | 51.00 | Quebec | 65.00 |
| Toronto | 50.00 | Sherbrooke | 64.00 |

Tickets good for forty days from date of issue.

Route R T 185—                                            FORM

Grand Trunk Railway to Toronto .........................................  
Canadian Pacific Railway to Owen Sound...........................  
*Canadian Pacific S. S. Line to Port Arthur.........................  } 4446
Canadian Pacific Railway to Winnipeg................................  
Returning same route...........................................................

Fares :—

| | | | |
|---|---|---|---|
| Kingston | $58.00 | Montreal | $60.00 |
| Brockville | 58.00 | Quebec | 65.00 |
| Ottawa | 58.70 | Sherbrooke | 64.00 |

Tickets good for forty days from date of issue.

Route R T 186—

Grand Trunk Railway to Sarnia, Goderich or Kincardine ............. T 76  
*North-West Transportation Co.'s steamer to Duluth.................... T 97  
Transfer to Northern Pacific Depot .......................................... T 80  
Northern Pacific Railroad to Winnipeg..................................... T100  
Returning same route.

Fares :—

| | | | |
|---|---|---|---|
| London | $55.50 | Kingston | $62.80 |
| St. Thomas | 55.50 | Brockville | 64.90 |
| Hamilton | 55.50 | Ottawa | 67.20 |
| Niagara Falls | 57.75 | Montreal | 70.50 |
| Buffalo | 58.75 | Quebec | 75.50 |
| Toronto | 55.50 | Sh'rbroke | 74.50 |

Route R T 187—

Grand Trunk Railway to Sarnia, Goderich or Kincardine.............. T 76  
*North-West Transportation Co.'s Steamer to Duluth.................... T 97  
Transfer to Great Northern Depot........................................... T 80  
Great Northern Railway to Gretna.......................................... T 99  
Canadian Pacific Railway to Winnipeg .................................... T106  
Returning same route.

Fares same as route R T 186.

Route R T 188—

Grand Trunk Railway to Sarnia, Goderich or Kincardine.............. T 76  
*North-West Transportation Co.'s Steamer to Duluth.................... T 97  
Transfer to Northern Pacific Railroad Depot............................. T 80  
Northern Pacific Railroad to Winnipeg.................................... T100  
Northern Pacific Railroad to St. Paul...................................... T100  
Choice of six routes to Chicago as follows :—  
   Chicago & Northwestern Railway to Chicago, via Elroy............. T 93  
   Chicago, Milwaukee & St. Paul Railway to Chicago............... T118  
   Chicago, St. Paul & Kansas City Railway to Chicago....... T119  
   Wisconsin Central Line to Chicago....................................... T 89  
   Albert Lea Route—M. & St. L., B. C. R. & N., C. R. I. & P. to Chi'go. T 77  
   { Chicago, Burlington & Northern Railroad to Oregon............T122  
   { Chicago & Iowa Railroad to Aurora....................................T121  
   { Chicago, Burlington & Quincy Railroad to Chicago..............T120  
Transfer to Chicago & Grand Trunk Depot............................... T 80  
Chicago & Grand Trunk Railway to Port Huron......................... T 90  
Grand Trunk Railway to starting point...................................... T 76

Fares :—

| | | | |
|---|---|---|---|
| London | $59.55 | Kingston | $69.80 |
| St. Thomas | 60.25 | Brockville | 71.90 |
| Hamilton | 61.50 | Ottawa | 74.20 |
| Niagara Falls | 63.85 | Montreal | 77.50 |
| Buffalo | 64.85 | Quebec | 82.50 |
| Toronto | 62.50 | Sherbrooke | 81.50 |

*Meals and berths included.

## To Winnipeg, Man., and Return.—*Continued*.

Route R T 189—                                                         FORM.
    Grand Trunk Railway to Sarnia, Goderich or Kincardine ..............T 76
    *North-West Transportation Co.'s Steamer to Duluth....................T 97
    Transfer to Great Northern Railway Depot ..........................T 80
    Great Northern Railway to Gretna.....................................T 99
    Canadian Pacific Railway to Winnipeg ...........................T106
    Canadian Pacific Railway to Gretna....................................T106
    Great Northern Railway to St. Paul.........................T 99
    Returning same as Route R T 188.

Fares same as Route R T 188.

# Side-Trip Tickets.

    These tickets may be issued with any of the Tourist or Excursion Tickets in this book, which read to or through the point from which side-trip tickets start.

### Port Kent to Ausable Chasm and Return.
(In connection with tickets over D & H. C. or C. T. Co.)

Route S T 1—                                                          FORM.
    Keeseville, Ausable Chasm & Lake Champlain Railroad ..............T 86
    Returning same route ..............................................T 86
    Fare..... ....................................................$ .55

### Montreal to Ausable Chasm and Return.
‡Route S T 2—
    Grand Trunk Railway to Rouse's Point......................T 16
    Delaware & Hudson Railroad to Port Kent ..............T 21   OR
    Keeseville, Ausable Chasm & Lake Champlain R. R. to Ausable  4704 R
      Chasm..... .................................T 86
    Returning same route.
    Fare.................................................$5.75

### Portland or Danville Jct. to Bar Harbor and Return.
(In connection with tickets to Portland, Etc.)

‡Route S T 3—
    Maine Central Railroad to Mount Desert ......................
    Ferry to Bar Harbor ................................. X347
    Returning same route ...........................
    Fare .........................................$11.00

‡Route S T 4—
    Same as Route S T 3, but limited to continuous passage each way.......3340
    Fare.........................................$8.50

### Bethlehem Jct. to Bethlehem, N. H., and Return.
Route S T 5—
    Profile & Franconia Notch Railroad to Bethlehem...................T 26
    Returning same route................................T 26
    Fare .........................................$1.00

### Portland to Biddeford, Me., and Return.
Route S T 6—
    Boston & Maine Railroad to Biddeford.. .............T 31
    Returning same route................................T 31
    Fare .........................................$ .75

## Montreal to Bluff Point (Hotel Champlain) N. Y., and Return.

‡Route S T 7—

FORM.

Grand Trunk Railway to Rouse's Point....................T 16 } ON
Delaware & Hudson Railroad to Bluff Point...................T 21 {1573 R
Returning same route.
Fare................................................................$4.55

## Quebec to Cacouna and Return.

Route S T 8—

Intercolonial Railway or R. & O. N. Co.'s Steamer to Cacouna .........T110
Returning same route ................................T110
Fare..........................................................$4.00

## Quebec to Chicoutimi and Return.
(See Quebec to Ha! Ha! Bay and Return.)

## Montreal to Cornwall and Return.

‡Route S T 9—

Grand Trunk Railway to Cornwall .................................. } 2501
Grand Trunk Railway or R. & O. N. Co.'s Steamer to Montreal.........
Fare.........................................................$3.35

## Boston to Cottage City, Mass., and Return.

Route S T 10—

Old Colony Railroad to New Bedford..............................T 77
New Bedford, Martha's Vineyard & Nantucket S. B. Co. to Cottage City.T 78
Returning same route.
Fare ...........................................................$3.00

## Montreal to Elizabethtown and Return.
(ADIRONDACKS.)

Route S T 11—

Grand Trunk Railway to Rouse's Point.. ......................T 16 } ON
Delaware & Hudson Railroad to Westport ... .................T 21 }X352
Stage to Elizabethtown ......................................T 79 }
Returning same route.
Fare.......................................................$8.85

## Quebec to Ha! Ha! Bay or Chicoutimi and Return.

‡Route S T 12—

Intercolonial Ry. or R. & O. N. Co.'s Steamer to Rivière du Loup T110 } ON
Steamer to Ha! Ha! Bay or Chicoutimi ...... .............T 6 {X67
Returning same route.
Fare ........................................................$8.75

‡Route S T 13—

R. & O. N. Co.'s Steamer to Ha! Ha! Bay or Chicoutimi........T111 } ON
Returning same route.............................T111 } X379
Fare ........................................................$8.00

## Portland to Kennebunkport, Me., and Return.

Route S T 14—

Boston & Maine Railroad to Kennebunkport.........................T 31
Returning same route..............................................T 31
Fare .......................................................$1.90

## Montreal to Kingston and Return.

‡Route S T 15—

Grand Trunk Railway to Kingston.................................. } 2500
Grand Trunk Railway or R. & O. N. Co.'s Steamer to Montreal.........
Fare ......................................................$9.50

## Windsor (Walkerville), Ont., to Kingsville and Return.

Route S T 16—

Lake Erie, Essex & Detroit River Railway, Walkerville to Kingsville...T 77
Returning same route...............................................T 77
Fare ......................................................$1.50

## Montreal to Lachine and Return.

Route S T 17—
Grand Trunk Railway to Lachine................................
Steamer (shooting the Rapids) to Montreal.......................
Fare.........................................................$0.50

## Montreal to Lake Placid and Return.
(ADIRONDACKS.)

Route S T 18— FORM.
Grand Trunk Railway to Rouse's Point.........................T 16
Deleware & Hudson Railroad to Plattsburg.....................T 17
Chateaugay Railroad to Saranac Lake.........................T113
Stage to Lake Placid.........................................T 79
Returning same route.
Fare........................................................$13.00

Route S T 19—
Grand Trunk Railway to St. Johns.............................T 11
Central Vermont Railroad to Burlington.......................T 12
Champlain Transportation Co.'s Steamer to Plattsburg.........T 18
Chateaugay Railroad to Saranac Lake.........................T113
Stage to Lake Placid.........................................T 79
Returning same route.
Fare........................................................$13.00

## Quebec to Lake St. John, Que., and Return.

Route S T 20—
Quebec & Lake St. John Railway to Lake St. John..............T112
Returning same route........................................T112
Fare.........................................................$7.50

## Montreal to Massena Springs, N. Y., and Return.

‡Route S T 21—
Grand Trunk Railway to Massena Springs.....................T 32 } on
Returning same route.......................................T 32 } 2900
Fare.........................................................$4.50

## Quebec to Montmorency Falls and Return.

Route S T 22—
Quebec, Montmorency & Charlevoix Railway to Montmorency Falls...T 87
Returning same route.........................................T 87
Fare.........................................................$0.25

## Quebec to Murray Bay and Return.

‡Route S T 23—
Richelieu & Ontario Navigation Co.'s Steamer to Murray Bay..T111 } on
Returning same route.......................................T111 } X351
Fare.........................................................$4.00

## Toronto to Muskoka Lakes, Georgian Bay and Return.

‡Route S T 24—
Grand Trunk Railway to Gravenhurst...........................T 76
Muskoka & Georgian Bay Navigation Co.s Steamer to Rosseau.T114 on
Stage to Parry Sound.........................................T 79
Steamer to Midland..........................................T114 X349
Grand Trunk Railway to Toronto...............................T 76
Fare.........................................................$8.00

Route S T 25—
Reverse of route S T 24....................................X350

## Toronto to Muskoka Lakes and Return.

‡Route S T 26—
Grand Trunk Railway to Gravenhurst...........................T 76
Muskoka & Georgian Bay Nav. Co.'s St'r All Round Muskoka
Lakes and back to Gravenhurst .............................T114 } X382
Grand Trunk Railway to Toronto...............................T 76
Fare.........................................................$7.00

## Boston to Narragansett Pier, R. I., and Return.

Route S T 27—                                                              FORM.
    Old Colony Railroad to Providence.................................T 77
    New York, Providence & Boston Railroad to Kingston................T 76
    Narragansett Pier Railroad to Narragansett Pier.......................T 77
    Returning same route.
    Fare............. ...................................................$3.25

## Boston to Newport, R. I., and Return.

Route S T 28—
    Old Colony Railroad to Newport................... ...............T 77
    Returning same route ...........................................T 77
    Fare................................................ $2.50

## Toronto to Niagara Falls and Return.

Route S T 29—
    Steamer Empress of India to Port Dalhousie.......................T 4
    Grand Trunk Railway to Suspension Bridge (Niagara Falls)..........T 3
    New York Central & Hudson River Railroad to Niagara Falls, N. Y....T 2
    Or New York, Lake Erie & Western Railroad to Niagara Falls. N. Y....T 1
    Returning same route.
    Fare .....................................................$2.25

Route S T 30—
    Niagara Navigation Co.'s Steamer to Lewiston .....................T 10
    New York Central & Hudson River Railroad to Niagara Falls..........T 9
    Returning same route.
    Fare .....................................................$2.25

Route S T 31—
    Niagara Navigation Co.'s Steamer to Niagara......................T 59
    Michigan Central Railroad to Suspension Bridge or Niagara Falls....T102
    New York Central & Hudson River Railroad to Niagara Falls, N. Y....T 2
    Or New York, Lake Erie & Western Railroad to Niagara Falls, N. Y....T 1
    Returning same route.
    Fare......................................................$2.25

## Portland to Old Orchard Beach and Return.

Route S T 32—
    Boston & Maine Railroad to Old Orchard.. .... ................T 31
    Returning same route ...........................................T 31
    Fare ...................................................$ .50

## Montreal to Ottawa and Return.

‡Route S T 33—
    Grand Trunk Railway to Coteau Jct...........................T 32 ⎫ OR
    Canada Atlantic Railway to Ottawa...........................T116 ⎬ 2626
    Ottawa River Navigation Co.'s Steamer to Montreal..... .....T117 ⎭
    Fare.....................................................$5.00

‡Route S T 34—
    Grand Trunk Railway to Lachine............................ ...T 32 ⎫ OR
    Ottawa River Navigation Co.'s Steamer to Ottawa ..............T117 ⎬ 2627
    Canada Atlantic Railway to Coteau Jct........................T116 ⎬
    Grand Trunk Railway to Montreal .... ................ ......T 32 ⎭
    Fare.....................................................$5.00

## Plattsburg to Paul Smith's and Return.

### (ADIRONDACKS.)

(In connection with tickets via D. & H. Railroad or C. T. Co.)
Route S T 35—
    Chateaugay Railroad to Bloomingdale............................T113
    Stage to Paul Smith's..........................................T 79
    Returning same route.
    Fare....... .........................................$7.70

## Danville Jct. to Poland Springs and Return.

(In connection with tickets reading over G. T. Ry. to Portland, Etc.)
Route S T 36—
    Stage to Poland Springs . .. ...................................T 79
    Stage to Danville Jct ..........................................T 79
    Fare.................................. ...............$1.50

### Portland to Portsmouth, N. H., and Return.
(In connection with tickets via G. T. Ry. to Portland, etc.)

Route S T 37—

FORM.

Boston & Maine Railroad to Portsmouth.................................T 31
Boston & Maine Railroad to Portland......... ........ ...........T 31
Fare................................................................$3.10

### Montreal to Prescott and Return.

‡Route S T 38—
Grand Trunk Railway to Prescott ..............................T 32 ⎞ or
Grand Trunk Railway or R. & O. N. Co.'s Steamer to Montreal..T 56 ⎰ 2502
Fare................................................................$5.60

### Bethlehem Jct. to Profile House, N. H., and Return.

Route S T 39—
Profile & Franconia Notch Railroad to Profile House....................T 26
Profile & Franconia Notch Railroad to Bethlehem Jct. ......... ......T 26
Fare............. ...........................................$3.00

### Montreal to Quebec and Return.

‡Route S T 40—
Grand Trunk Railway or R. & O. N. Co.'s Steamer to Quebec............ ⎞ X 41
Grand Trunk Railway or R. & O. N. Co.'s Steamer to Montreal........ ⎰
Fare.....................................................$5.00

### Richmond to Quebec and Return.

Route S T 41—
Grand Trunk Railway to Levis... ...............................T 27
Ferry to Quebec .................................................T 37
Returning same route.
Fare................................................. .....$3.00

### Groveton to Quebec and Return.

Route S T 42—
Grand Trunk Railway to Levis..................................T 27
Ferry to Quebec .................................................T 37
Returning same route.
Fare.................................... .............$9.00

### Quebec to Ste. Anne de Beaupre and Return.
("LA BONNE ST. ANNE.")

Route S T 43—
Quebec, Montmorency & Charlevoix Railway to St. Anne de Beaupré...T 87
Quebec, Montmorency & Charlevoix Railway to Quebec ...............T 87
Fare................................................................$0.85

### Fabyans to Summit Mt. Washington and Return.

Route S T 44—
Concord & Montreal Railroad to Base of Mt. Washington...............T 25
Mount Washington Railway to Summit..................................T 41
Returning same route.
Fare ..............................................................$6.00

### Quebec to Tadousac and Return.
(SAGUENAY RIVER.)

‡Route S T 45—
Intercolonial Ry. or R. & O. N. Co.'s Str. to Riviere du Loup ....T110 ⎞ or
R. & O. N. Co.'s Steamer to Tadousac...................... .......T 6 ⎰ X 66
Returning same route............................................
Fare.............................................................$6.75

### Brockville to Westport and Return.
(RIDEAU LAKES. FISHING GROUNDS.)

Route S T 46—
Brockville, Westport & Sault Ste. Marie Railway to Westport...........T 77
Returning same route.
Fare.......................................... .............$3.00

**Portland to York Beach, Me., and Return.**

(In connection with tickets to Portland, etc., on Grand Trunk Railway.)

Route S T 47—                                                             FORM.
Boston & Maine Railroad to Portsmouth .................................. T 31 } or
York Harbor & Beach Railroad to York Beach.................T 77 }
Returning same route.......................................................... } X433
Fare...................................................................................$4.10

---

# EXCURSIONS

—FROM—

# Boston, Portland and Lewiston, Me.,

—TO THE—

## White Mountains, Rangeley Lakes, Quebec and Montreal.

(Agents at Portland and adjoining stations must be careful not to exceed the special round trip fares shown to Grand Trunk local stations, when selling to intermediate points.)

## To Andover, Me., and Return.

‡Route R T 191—                                                           FORM.
Grand Trunk Railway, Portland (or Lewiston, T 76) to Bryant's Pond ..T 74
Stage to Andover ............................................................T 79
Returning same route.
Fares :—
Boston (rail to Portland, T 50)......................................$10.50
Boston (steamer to Portland, T 81)..................................  8.85
*Boston (steamer to Portland, T 81) .................................  7.75
Portland............................................................  6.85
Lewiston ..........................................................  5.60

## To Aziscohos and Return.

‡Route R T 192—
Grand Trunk Railway, Portland (or Lewiston, T 76) to Bethel...T 74 }
Stage to Cambridge ..........................................T 79 }
Steamer to Magalloway .;....................................T 78 } or
Stage to Aziscohos Falls ....................................T 79 } X426
Returning same route........................................ }
Fares :—
Boston (rail to Portland, T 50) ......................................$17.00
Boston (steamer to Portland, T 81) ...................................16.00
Portland............................................................14.00
Lewiston ...........................................................13.25

## To Bemis and Return.

‡Route R T 193—
Grand Trunk Railway, Portland (or Lewiston, T 76) to Bryant's Pond...T 74
Stages to Andover and South Arm (two coupons) ....................T 79
Steamers to Upper Dam and Bemis (two coupons) ....................T 78
Returning same route.
Fares :—
Boston (rail to Portland, T 50) ..................................... $14.25
Boston (steamer to Portland, T 81) ...................................13.25
Portland............................................................12.00
Lewiston .........................................................11.00
*Tickets for entire journey limited to continuous passage in both directions.

## To Bemis and Return.--*Continued*.

‡Route R T 194—

FORM:

| | |
|---|---|
| Grand Trunk Railway, Portland (or Lewiston, T 76) to Bethel. ........ | T 74 |
| Stage to Cambridge.. ............................. | T 79 |
| Steamer to Sunday Cove............................ | T 78 |
| Stage to Middle Dam .............................. | T 79 |
| Steamers to Upper Dam, Bemis (two coupons) .......... | T 78 |

Returning same route.

Fares:—

| | |
|---|---|
| Boston (rail to Portland, T 50)....................... | $18.50 |
| Boston (steamer to Portland, T 81)..... ................. | 17.50 |
| Portland ........................................ | 16.00 |
| Lewiston ........................................ | 15.00 |

## To Berlin Falls, N. H., and Return

‡Route R T 195—

Grand Trunk Railway to Berlin Falls and return .................... 2900

Fare:—

Portland ................................................ $ 5.50

## To Bethel and Return.

Route R T 196—

| | |
|---|---|
| Boston & Maine Railroad to Portland................................ | T 50 |
| Grand Trunk Railway to Bethel............................ | T 74 |

Returning same route.

Fare:—

Boston ...................................... $ 7.75

Route R T 197—

| | | |
|---|---|---|
| Steamer to Portland.... | T 81 } | or |
| Grand Trunk Railway to Bethel.... .. .................. | T 74 } | 2744 |

Returning same route.

Fares:—

| | |
|---|---|
| Boston ...................................... | $ 6.50 |
| Boston (limited to continuous passage)...................... | 5.50 |

‡Route R T. 198—

Grand Trunk Railway to Bethel and return ..... ..... 2900

Fare:—

Portland.................................. $ 4.45

## To Bryant's Pond and Return.

Route R T 199—

| | |
|---|---|
| Boston & Maine Railroad to Portland......................... | T 50 |
| Grand Trunk Railway to Bryant's Pond.......... .. | T 74 |

Returning same route,

Fares:—

Boston................................................ $ 7.50

Route R T 200—

| | | |
|---|---|---|
| Steamer to Portland..... . ......... | T 81 } | or |
| Grand Trunk Railway to Bryant's Pond...... | T 74 } | 2747 |

Returning same route.

Fares:—

| | |
|---|---|
| Boston................................................ | $ 5.85 |
| Boston (limited to continuous passage)...................... | 5.00 |

‡Route R T 201—

Grand Trunk Railway to Bryant's Pond and return .. .............. 2900

Fare:—

Portland ................ ................ ........ $ 3.85

## To Byron (Houghton's) and Return.

Route R T 202—

| | |
|---|---|
| Grand Trunk Railway, Portland to Mechanic Falls... ................ | T 74 |
| Rumford Falls & Buckfield Railroad to Canton................. | T 82 |
| Stages to Mexico, Byron (two coupons)....................... | T 79 |

Returning same route.

Fares:—

| | |
|---|---|
| Boston (rail to Portland T 50) .......................... | $11.00 |
| Boston (steamer to Portland T 81).... ..................... | 10.00 |

# To Cambridge and Return.

### (LAKESIDE.)

‡Route R T 203—FORM.
    Grand Trunk Railway, Portland (or Lewiston T 76) to Bethel ..........T 74
    Stage to Cambridge (Lakeside)................................................T 79
    Returning same route.

    Fares :—
        Boston (rail to Portland T 50)..................................$12.00
        Boston (steamer to Portland T 81)............................ 11.00
        Portland............................................................ 9.00
        Lewiston.......................................................... 8.00

# To Canton and Return.

Route R T 204--
    Boston & Maine Railroad to Portland............................ .........⎫
    Grand Trunk Railway to Mechanic Falls.... ........ .... ......⎪ 2654
    Rumford Falls & Buckfield Railroad to Canton.....................⎬
    Returning same route ......................................⎭

    Fare :—
        Boston.............................................................$ 8.50

Route R T 205—
    Steamer to Portland ......... ........................⎫
    Grand Trunk Railway to Mechanic Falls...........................⎪ 2653
    Rumford Falls & Buckfield Railroad to Canton....................⎬
    Returning same route......⎭

    Fare :—
        Boston .............................................................$6.00

# To Colebrook and Return.

‡Route R T 206—
    Grand Trunk Railway, Portland (or Lewiston, T 76) to North Stratford .T 74
    Upper Coos Railroad to Colebrook ........................ ..............T 83
    Returning same route.

    Fares :—
        Boston (rail to Portland, T 50) .................................$12.10
        Boston (steamer to Portland, T 81) ........................... 11.10
        Portland............................................................ 9.10
        Lewiston .............. ........................................... 8.30

# To Connecticut Lake and Return.

‡Route R T 207—
    G. T. Ry., Portland (or Lewiston, T 76) to North Stratford ....T 74⎫
    Upper Coos Railroad to Beecher's Falls.......................T 83⎪ or
    Stage to Connecticut Lake...................................T 79⎬ X427
    Returning same route ................................⎭

    Fares :—
        Boston (rail to Portland, T 50) .................................$15.20
        Boston (steamer to Portland, T 81) ........................... 14.20
        Portland............................................................ 12.20
        Lewiston ...................................................... 11.40

# To Crawford House and Return.

‡Route R T 208—
    Boston & Maine Railroad to North Conway.....................T 30
    Maine Central Railroad to Crawford House, Fabyans .. ...... ....T 28
    Concord & Montreal Railroad to Base............................T 25
    Mount Washington Railway to Summit...........................T 41
    Milliken's Stage to Glen House.................................T 40
    Milliken's Stage to Gorham....................................T 79
    Grand Trunk Railway to Portland ..............................T 74
    Boston & Maine Railroad to Boston.........................T 50

    Fares :—
        Boston.............................................................$19.75
        Portland ......................................................... 19.75

# To Dixville Notch and Return.

‡Route R T 209—                                                    FORM.
    Grand Trunk Railway, Portland (or Lewiston, T 76,) to Bethel.........T 74
    Stage to Cambridge.......................................................T 79
    Steamer to Errol Dam ...................................................T 78
    Stage to Dixville Notch.................................................T 79
    Returning same route.
  Fares :—
    Boston (rail to Portland, T 50,).............................$15.00
    Boston (steamer to Portland, T 81,) ........................ 14.00
    Portland ...................................................... 13.50
    Lewiston...................................................... 12.50

‡Route R T 210—
    G. T. R., Portland (or Lewiston, T 76,) to North Stratford..............T 74
    Upper Coos Railroad to Colebrook .......................................T 83
R.W.   Stage to Dixville Notch .................................................T 79
    Stage to Errol Dam .....................................................T 79
    Steamer to Cambridge ..................................................T 78
    Stage to Bethel ........................................................T 79
    Grand Trunk Railway to Portland (or Lewiston, T 76) ..... .........T 74
  Fares:—
    Boston (rail to Portland, T 50).............................$15.00
    Boston (steamer to Portland, T 81) ........... .......... 14.00
    Portland ...................................................... 12.00
    Lewiston...................................................... 11.00

# To Errol, N. H., and Return.

### (UMBAGOG HOUSE.)

‡Route R T 211—
    Grand Trunk Railway, Portland (or Lewiston, T 76) to Berlin Falls.....T 74
    Stage to Errol..........................................................T 79
    Returning same route.
  Fares:—
    Boston (rail to Portland, T 50) ............................$11.50
    Baston (steamboat to Portland, T 81)........................ 10.50
    Portland....................................................... 8.50
    Lewiston....................................................... 7.50

# To Fabyan House and Return.

‡Route R T 212—
    Boston & Maine Railroad, Boston to Portland.........................T 50
R.W.   Grand Trunk Railway, Portland to Groveton Jct .....................T 74
    Concord & Montreal Railroad to Fabyans.............................T 25
    Maine Central Railroad to North Conway.............................T 28
    Boston and Maine Railroad to Boston................................T 30
  Fares:—
    Boston............................................$10.00
    Portland... ....................................... 10.00

‡Route R T 213—
    Boston & Maine Railroad, Boston to Portland ...... .......... ...T 50
    Grand Trunk Railway to Gorham....................................T 74
R.W.   Milliken's Stage to Glen House ...................................T 79
    Stage to Glen Station ............................................T 79
    Maine Central Railroad to Crawford House, Fabyans................T 28
    Concord & Montreal Railroad to Nashua.............................T 25
    Boston & Maine Railroad to Boston................................T 29
  Fares:—
    Boston....... ...................................$15.25
    Portland........ .... .... ....................... 15.25

‡Route R T 214—
    Boston & Maine Railroad, Boston to Portland .... ............. ...T 50
    Grand Trunk Railway to Gorham....................................T 74
    Milliken's Stage to Glen House...................................T 79
    Milliken's Stage to Summit.......................................T 39
    Mount Washington Railway to Base.......................T 41
    Concord & Montreal Railroad to Fabyans...........................T 25
    Concord & Montreal Railroad to Bethlehem Jct...... ..............T 25
    Profile & Franconia Notch Railroad to Profile House................T 26

## To Fabyan House and Return.—*Continued*.

|  | FORM. |
|---|---|
| Stage to North Woodstock | T 79 |
| Concord & Montreal Railroad to Nashua | T 25 |
| Boston & Maine Railroad to Boston | T 29 |
| Fares:— | |
| Boston | $23.90 |
| Portland | 23.90 |

‡Route R T 215—

|  |  |
|---|---|
| Boston & Maine Railroad to Nashua | T 29 |
| Concord & Montreal Railroad to North Woodstock | T 25 |
| Stage to Profile House | T 79 |
| Profile & Franconia Notch Railroad to Bethlehem Jct | T 26 |
| Concord & Montreal Railroad to Fabyans | T 25 |
| Concord & Montreal Railroad to Base | T 25 |
| Mount Washington Railway to Summit | T 41 |
| Milliken's Stage to Glen House | T 40 |
| Milliken's Stage to Gorham | T 79 |
| Grand Trunk Railway to Portland | T 74 |
| Boston & Maine Railroad to Boston | T 50 |
| Fares:— | |
| Boston | $21.90 |
| Portland | 21.90 |

## To Glen House and Return.

‡Route R T 216—

|  |  |
|---|---|
| Grand Trunk Railway, Portland (or Lewiston, T 76,) to Gorham | T 74 |
| Milliken's Stage to Glen House | T 79 |
| Returning same route. | |
| Fares:— | |
| Boston (rail to Portland, T 50) | $11.00 |
| Boston (steamer to Portland, T 81) | 10.00 |
| Portland | 8.00 |
| Portland (Saturday to Monday) | 5 00 |
| Lewiston | 7.50 |
| Lewiston (Saturday to Monday) | 5.00 |

‡Route R T 217—

|  |  |  |
|---|---|---|
| | Boston & Maine Railroad, Boston to Portland | T 50 |
| | Grand Trunk Railway to Gorham | T 74 |
| R.W. | Milliken's Stage to Glen House | T 79 |
| | Stage to Glen Station | T 79 |
| | Maine Central Railroad to North Conway | T 28 |
| | Boston & Maine Railroad to Boston | T 30 |
| | Fares:— | |
| | Boston | $13.50 |
| | Portland | 13.50 |

## To Gorham, N. H., and Return.

(ALPINE HOUSE.)

Route R T 218—

|  |  |
|---|---|
| Boston & Maine Railroad to Portland | T 50 |
| Grand Trunk Railway to Gorham | T 74 |
| Returning same route. | |
| Fare:— | |
| Boston | $8.00 |

Route R T 219—

|  |  |
|---|---|
| Steamer to Portland | T 81 |
| Grand Trunk Railway to Gorham | T 74 |
| Returning same route. | |
| Fares:— | |
| Boston | $7.00 |
| *Boston | 6.75 |

‡Route R T 220—

|  |  |
|---|---|
| Grand Trunk Railway, Portland to Gorham and Return | 2900 |
| Fare:— | |
| Portland | $5.00 |

*Tickets for entire journey limited to continuous passage in each direction.

# To Groveton, N. H., and Return.

Route R T 221—
R. W
    Boston & Maine Railroad, Boston to Nashua.... T 29 ⎫  FORM.
    Concord & Montreal Railroad to Groveton Jct................T 25 ⎬ or
    Grand Trunk Railway to Portland.....................T 74 ⎬ 3042
    Boston & Maine Railroad to Boston ......................T 50 ⎭
  Fares :—
    Boston............................................$11.20
    Portland ............................................ 11.20

Route R T 222—
    Grand Trunk Railway to Groveton.......................T 74
    Returning same route...............................T 74
  Fares :—
    Boston (rail to Portland, T 50) .....................$10.75
    Boston (steamer to Portland, T 81)................... 9.75

# To Indian Rock and Return.

‡Route R T 223—
    Grand Trunk Railway, Portland (or Lewiston, T 76) to Bryant's Pond..T 74
    Stage to Andover..................................T 79
    Stage to South Arm. ...............................T 79
    Steamer to Upper Dam .. .. .........................T 78
    Steamer to Indian Rock .............................T 78
    Returning same route.
  Fares :—
    Boston (rail to Portland, T 50). .....................$14.50
    Boston (steamer to Portland, T 81)................... 13.50
    Portland......................................... 11.50
    Lewiston......................................... 10.50

# To Island Pond and Return.

Route R T 224—
    Boston & Maine Railroad to Portland... ................T 50
    Grand Trunk Railway to Island Pond...................T 74
    Returning same route.
  Fare :—
    Boston............................................$11.40

Route R T 225—
    Steamer to Portland ...............................T 81
    Grand Trunk Railway to Island Pond...................T 74
    Returning same route.
  Fare.—
    Boston............................................$10.40

Route R T 226—
    Grand Trunk Railway to Island Pond and return......... 2900
  Fare :—
    Portland. ..........................................$8.50

# To Lancaster, N. H., and Return.

‡Route R T 227—
    Grand Trunk Ry., Portland (Lewiston, T 76) to Groveton Jct ........T 74
    Concord & Montreal Railroad to Lancaster...............T 25
    Returning same route.
  Fares :—
    Portland..........................................$9.00
    Lewiston and Auburn ............................... 7.40

# To Lewiston, Me., and Return.

‡Route R T 228—
    Grand Trunk Ry. to Lewiston and return ................ 2900
  Fare :—
    Portland (ticket limited to one month)................$1.60

# To Magalloway and Return.

Route R T 229—
    Boston & Maine Railroad to Portland...........................T 50     <sub></sub> FORM.
    Grand Trunk Railway to Bethel...... .....................T 74    OR
    Stage to Cambridge...............................................T 79
    Steamer to Magalloway................................ ........ .T 78   2966
    Return same route.
  Fare :—
    Boston .....................................................................$14.00

‡Route R T 230—
    Grand Trunk Railway, Portland (or Lewiston, T 76) to Bethel..........T 74
    Stage to Cambridge ..............................................T 79
    Steamer to Magalloway ..........................................T 78
    Returning same route
  Fare:—
    Boston (steamer to Portland, T 81).............................$13.00
    Portland..................................................... 11.00
    Lewiston..... .......... ................. 10.25

# To Mechanic Falls and Return.

Route R T 231—
    Boston & Maine Railroad to Portland....................................T 50
    Grand Trunk Railway to Mechanic Falls.................................T 74
    Returning same route.
  Fare ·—
    Boston.................................................................$6.55

Route R T 232—
    Steamer to Portland....... .....................·............T 81
    Grand Trunk Railway to Mechanic Falls................................T 74
    Returning same route.
  Fare:—
    *Boston.................................................................$3.75

# To Middle Dam and Return.

‡Route R T 233—
    Grand Trunk Ry., Portland (or Lewiston, T 76) to Bethel...............T 74
    Stage to Cambridge...............................................T 79
    Steamer to Sunday Cove..........................................T 78
    Stage to Middle Dam ........ ...................................T 79
    Returning same route.
  Fares :—
    †Boston (rail to Portland, T 50)................................$13.50
    Boston (steamer to Portland, T 81)............... ............ 12.50
    Portland ....................... ............................... 10.75
    Lewiston.................. ................................. 10.00

‡Route R T 234—
    Grand Trunk Railway, Portland (or Lewiston, T 76) to Bryant's Pond...T 74
    Stages to Andover, South Arm (two coupons) ........ ...........T 79
    Steamer to Middle Dam..........................................T 78
    Returning same route.
  Fares:—
    Boston (rail to Portland, T 50)................................$12.50
    Boston (steamer to Portland, T 81)............................ 11.50
    Portland...................................................... 9.50
    Lewiston...................................................... 8.50

Route R T 235—
    Grand Trunk Railway, Portland (or Lewiston, T 76) to Bethel..........T 74
    Stage to Cambridge.......................................... .. .......T 79
    Steamer to Sunday Cove .........................................T 78
    Stage to Middle Dam............................................T 79
    Steamer to South Arm..........................................T 78
    Stages to Andover, Bryant's Pond (two coupons).................T 79
    Grand Trunk Railway to Portland (or Lewiston, T 76)...................T 74

*Tickets for entire journey limited to continuous passage in each direction.
†Or form 3160 may be used from Boston.

## To Middle Dam and Return.—*Continued.*

Fares:—
    Boston (rail to Portland, T 50)............................$13.50
    Boston (steamer to Portland, T 81)..................... 12.50
    Portland.......... .......... ............... 10.75
    Lewiston............................................. 10.00

## To Montreal and Return.

**Route R T 236—**                                FORM.
    Boston & Maine Railroad to Portland...................................T 50
    Grand Trunk Railway to Montreal........................................T 74
    Grand Trunk Railway to St. Johns.......................................T 11
    Central Vermont Railroad to Windsor.....................................T 12
    Vermont Valley Railroad to Bellows Falls..............................T 13
    Cheshire Railroad to Fitchburg..........................................T 14
    Fitchburg Railroad to Boston............................................T 15
    Fare:—
        Boston..............................................................$16.00

**Route R T 237—**
    Same as Route R T 236 to Montreal.
    Grand Trunk Railway to Groveton Jct... .............................T 32
    Concord & Montreal Railroad to Nashua...............................T 25
    Boston & Maine Railroad to Boston.....................................T 29
    Fare:—
        Boston..............................................................$16.00

**Route R T 238—**
    Same as Route R T 236 to Montreal.
    Grand Trunk Railway to St. Johns......................................T 11
    Central Vermont Railroad to White River Jct............................T 84
    Boston & Maine Railroad to Concord....................................T 35
    Concord & Montreal Railroad to Nashua ...............................T 34
    Boston & Maine Railroad to Boston....... ..................T 29
    Fare:—
        Boston.............................. ....$16.00

**Route R T 239—**
    Boston & Maine Railroad to Portland ....................} 3146-going.
    Grand Trunk Railway to Montreal ......................... { 3147-returning.
    Returning same route.
    Fare:—
        Boston................................ ......$16.00

**Route R T 240—**
    Boston & Maine Railroad to Nashua ....................｜
    Concord & Montreal Railroad to Concord ..................｜
    Boston & Maine Railroad to White River Jct.. ........ ｜ 3184-going.
    Central Vermont Railroad to St. Johns.................... ⎰ 3185-returning.
    Grand Trunk Railway to Montreal...........................｜
    Returning same route.... .........｜
    Fare:—
        Boston................. ..........................$16.00

**Route R T 241—**
    Boston & Maine Railroad to Portland .... ..........................T 50
    Grand Trunk Railway to Levis...........................................T 74
    Ferry to Quebec .......................................................T 37
    Grand Trunk Railway or R. & O. N. Co.'s Steamer to Montreal.........T 36
    Returning same route.
    Fare:—
        Boston..............................................................$23.00

**Route R T 242—**
    Boston & Maine Railroad to Nashua.............................T 29
    Concord & Montreal Railroad to Wells River ......................T 25
    Boston & Maine Railroad to Sherbrooke .....................T 33
    Grand Trunk Railway to Montreal........................ ......T 32
    Returning same route.
    Fare:—
        Boston..............................................................$16.00

## To Montreal and Return.--*Continued.*

**Route R T 243—**
R.W.  Same as Route R T 242 to Montreal.  FORM.
Grand Trunk Railway to Portland......................................T 32
Boston & Maine Railroad to Boston..................................T 50
Fare:—
Boston.......................... ..........  ...........$16.00

**Route R T 244—**
R.W.  Same as Route R T 242 to Montreal.
Returning same as Route R T 238 ................. ...................
Fare:—
Boston...............................................................$16.00

**‡Route R T 245—**
Grand Trunk Railway, Portland to Montreal and return...............X204
Fare:—
Portland...............................................................$12.50

## To New Gloucester and Return.

**‡Route R T 246—**
Grand Trunk Railway, Portland to New Gloucester and Return....... 2900
Fare:—
Portland (ticket limited to one month).........................$1.25

## To North Stratford and Return.

**Route R T 247—**
Boston & Maine Railroad to Portland..........................T 50 ) or
Grand Trunk Railway to North Stratford ...... ...... ... ....T 74 } 2704
Returning same route.
Fare:—
Boston...............................................................$11.00

**Route R T 248—**
Steamer to Portland...........................................T 81 } or
Grand Trunk Railway to North Stratford.......................T 74 } 2706
Returning same route.
Fare:—
Boston...............................................................$10.00

**‡Route R T 249—**
Grand Trunk Railway to North Stratford and Return..... .............2900
Fare:—
Portland ...............................................................$8.00

## To Poland Springs and Return.

**Route R T 250—**
Boston & Maine Railroad to Portland ...............................)
Grand Trunk Railway to Danville Jct...............................} 2921
Stage to Poland Springs ..........................................)
Returning same route.
Fare:—
Boston...............................................................$6.00

**Route R T 251—**
Steamer to Portland...............................................)
Grand Trunk Railway to Danville Jct................................} 2922
Stage to Poland Springs...........................................)
Returning same route.
Fare:—
Boston...............................................................$5.00

## To Quebec and Return.

**Route R T 252—**
Boston & Maine Railroad to Nashua..... .............................T 29
Concord & Montreal Railroad to Wells River..........................T 25
R.W.  Boston & Maine Railroad to Sherbrooke............................T 33
Grand Trunk Railway to Levis......................................T 27
Ferry to Quebec...................................................T 37
Ferry to Levis ...................................................T 37
Grand Trunk Railway to Portland...................................T 27
Boston & Maine Railroad to Boston.................................T 50
Fare:—
Boston............................................... ..........$18.00

# To Quebec and Return.—*Continued.*

Route R T 253— FORM.
 Boston & Maine Railroad to Portland ...................................T 50
 Grand Trunk Railway to Levis...........................................T 74
 Ferry to Quebec ... .........  ...........................................T 37
 Ferry to Levis ...........................................................T 37
 Grand Trunk Railway to Groveton Jct.....................................T 27
 Concord & Montreal Railroad to Nashua...................................T 25
 Boston & Maine Railroad to Boston.......................................T 29
 Fare :—
  Boston...........................................................$18.00

Route R T 254—
 Boston & Maine Railroad to Portland.................. ...................T 50
 Grand Trunk Railway to Levis.........  ................................T 74
 Ferry to Quebec ...................................... .................T 37
 Returning same route.
 Fare :—
  Boston...........................................................$18.00

‡Route R T 255
 Grand Trunk Railway, Portland to Quebec and return............ ..... 2900
 Fare :—
  Portland................... ....................$14.20

## To Rangeley Outlet and Return.

‡Route R T 256—
 Grand Trunk Railway, Portland (or Lewiston, T 76) to Bryant's Pond...T 74
 Stages to Andover, South Arm (two coupons)... .......................T 79
 Steamers to Upper Dam, Indian Rock, Rangeley Outlet (three coupons.T 78
 Stage to Phillips........................................................T 79
 Sandy River Railroad to Farmington......................................T 85
 Maine Central Railroad to Portland (or Lewiston, T 28) ... ........... T 52
 Fare:—
  Boston (rail to Portland, T 50)............................. $15.50
  Boston (steamer to Portland, T 81).............................. 14.50
  Portland ....................................................... 12.50
  Lewiston........................................................ 11.50

## To Shelburne, N. H., and Return.

Route R T 257—
 Boston & Maine Railroad, Boston to Portland .................... .......T 50
 Grand Trunk Railway to Shelburne.................................... ...T 74
 Returning same route.
 Fare :—
  Boston............................................................ $8.00

Route R T 258—
 Steamer to Portland.....................................................T 81
 Grand Trunk Railway to Shelburne.......................................T 74
 Fare :—
  Boston ........................................................$6.50
  *Boston ....................................................... 5.75

‡Route R T 259—
 Grand Trunk Railway to Shelburne and Return ..................... 2900
 Fare :—
  Portland ...... ..................... .................$5.00

## To South Arm and Return.

‡Route R T 260 –
 Grand Trunk Railway, Portland (or Lewiston, T 76) to Bryant's Pond...T 74
 Stages to Andover, South Arm (two coupons) ...........................T 79
 Returning same route.
 Fares :—
  Boston (rail to Portland, T 50)..................................$12.50
  Boston (steamer to Portland, T 81)........................... 11.50
  Portland ....................................................... 9.35
  Lewiston........... .............................................. 8.10

 *Tickets for entire journey limited to continuous passage in each direction.

# To South Paris and Return.

Route R T 261— FORM.
    Boston & Maine Railroad to Portland.................................. T 50
    Grand Trunk Railway to South Paris........... ............ .....T 74
    Returning same route.
    Fare:—
      Boston ..................................................................$7.00

Route R T 262—
    Steamer to Portland .................................................T 81
    Grand Trunk Railway to South Paris ...... ...................T 74
    Returning same route.
    Fares:—
      Boston ..................................................................$5.10
      *Boston ................ .....................................................4.25

‡Route R T 263—
    Grand Trunk Railway to South Paris and Return..................... 2900
    Fare:—
      Portland (ticket limited to one month)........... ...... .. .....$3.10

# To Upper Dam and Return.

‡Route R T 264—
    Grand Trunk Railway, Portland (or Lewiston, T 76) to Bryant's Pond...T 74
    Stages to Andover, South Arm (two coupons).................. ...........T 79
    Steamers to Middle Dam, Upper Dam (two coupons)... ...... ......T 78
    Returning same route.
    Fares:—
      †Boston (rail to Portland, T 50).................................$13.50
      Boston (steamer to Portland, T 81) ............................ 12.50
      Portland ...................................................... 10.50
      Lewiston......... ............................................. 9.75

‡Route R T 265—
    Grand Trunk Railway, Portland (or Lewiston, T 76) to North Stratford.T 74
    Upper Coos Railroad to Colebrook ....................................T 83
    Stage to Dixville Notch ..............................................T 79
R.W.  Stage to Errol Dam....................................................T 79
    Steamer to Sunday Cove...............................................T 78
    Stage to Middle Dam..................................................T 79
    Steamer to Upper Dam.................................................T 78
    Steamer to South Arm.................................................T 78
    Stages to Andover, Bryant's Pond (two coupons)........... .........T 79
    Grand Trunk Railway to Portland (or Lewiston, T 76)..................T 74
    Fares:—
      Boston (rail to Portland, T 50). ...................... .. ..........$17.50
      Boston (steamer to Portland, T 81)........... .. ............ 16.50
      Portland.....:........................................................ 14.50
      Lewiston........ .................................................. 13.50

‡Route R T 266—
    Grand Trunk Railway, Portland (or Lewiston, T 76) to Bethel .........T 74
    Stage to Cambridge........ .... .......... ......................T 79
    Steamer to Sunday Cove...............................................T 78
    Stage to Middle Dam .................................................T 79
    Steamer to Upper Dam ................................................T 78
    Returning same route.
    Fares:—
      Boston (rail to Portland, T 50)........ ........................$15.50
      Boston (steamer to Portland, T 81)............................ 14.50
      Portland.............................................................. 12.50
      Lewiston......... . ............................................ 11.75

‡Route R T 267—
    Grand Trunk Railway, Portland (or Lewiston, T 76) to Bryant's Pond..T 74
    Stages to Andover, South Arm (two coupons)... .......................T 79
    Steamer to Upper Dam, Middle Dam (two coupons) .. .. ..............T 78
    Stage to Sunday Cove ...................................... .. ...............T 79
    Steamer to Cambridge ................................................T 78
    Stage to Bethel .....................................................T 79
    Grand Trunk Railway to Portland (or Lewiston, T 76)................ .T 74

*Tickets for entire journey to be limited to continuous passage in each direction.
†Form 2984 may be used from Boston.

## To Upper Dam and Return.—*Continued.*

Fares :—
 Boston (rail to Portland, T 50).............................. .....$14.75
 Boston (steamer to Portland, T 81) ........................... 13.75
 Portland.......................... ......................... ......... 11.75
 Lewiston............. ................... . .................. 10.75

## To Yarmouth, Me., and Return.

‡Route R T 268—
 Grand Trunk Railway, Portland to Yarmouth and Return............ 2900
 Fare :—
 Portland (ticket limited to one month)......................$ .65

---

# STEAMBOAT CONNECTIONS.

## ——1890——

**BLACK DIAMOND LINE STEAMERS** for Charlottetown, Sydney and St. John's, Newfoundland, commencing Saturday, May 10, leave Montreal every week or ten days during season, as advertised from time to time.

**BAIE CHALEUR STEAMER** leaves Dalhousie Wednesdays and Saturdays at 4.00 A. M. Returning, arrives at Dalhousie Monday and Thursday evenings.

**CANADIAN PACIFIC STEAMERS** leave Owen Sound for Port Arthur, Wednesdays and Saturdays at 3.30 P. M.; returning, leave Port Arthur Saturdays and Tuesdays. Leave Owen Sound for Sault Ste. Marie Tuesdays and Fridays at 10.30 P. M.; returning, leave Sault Ste. Marie 5.00 A. M. Fridays and Mondays.

**DESORONTO NAVIGATION CO'S STEAMERS** leave Gananoque for Clayton, etc., at 7 00 A. M. and 3.45 P. M. daily except Sunday.

**DETROIT & CLEVELAND STEAM NAVIGATION CO'S STEAMERS** for Lake Huron ports, leave Detroit 10.00 P. M. Mondays and Saturdays, and Port Huron 6.30 A. M. Tuesdays and Sundays ; also leave Detroit 9.00 A. M. and Port Huron 4.00 P. M. Wednesdays and Fridays. Leave Detroit for Cleveland 11.00 P. M. daily, Sundays included, during June, July, August and September.

**EMPRESS OF INDIA STEAMER** leaves Port Dalhousie at 10.25 A. M. and 7.05 P. M. on arrival of trains from Buffalo, Niagara Falls and Suspension Bridge. Returning, leaves Toronto at 7.30 A. M. and 3.40 P. M.

**GREAT NORTHERN TRANSIT CO'S STEAMERS** leave Collingwood Mondays and Thursdays at 8.00 A. M. for Parry Sound, Byng Inlet and French River. Returning on Wednesday and Saturday evenings. Also leaves Collingwood on Mondays, Thursdays and Saturdays at 1.00 P. M. for Sault Ste. Marie.

**HUDSON RIVER DAY LINE STEAMERS** leave Albany daily (except Sunday) at 8.30 A. M., arriving at New York at 6.00 P. M. Returning, leave New York at 8.40 A. M., arriving at Albany at 6.10 P. M. Last trips of the season about Oct. 15th.

**INTERNATIONAL LINE STEAMERS** leave Portland for St. John Mondays, Wednesdays and Fridays at 5.00 P. M. Leave St. John for Portland Mondays, Wednesdays and Fridays at 7.25 A. M. Also, leave Annapolis Mondays, Thursdays and Saturdays for St. Johns.

**LAKE CHAMPLAIN STEAMERS** leave Plattsburg on week days at 7.00 A. M., Burlington 8.40 A. M., arriving at Fort Ticonderoga at 12.25 P. M. Leave Fort Ticonderoga at 1.30 P. M., Burlington 5.00 P. M., arriving at Plattsburg at 7.00 P. M.

**LAKE GEORGE STEAMERS** leave Caldwell on week days at 9.40 A. M., arriving at Baldwin at 12.50 P. M. Returning, leave Baldwin at 1 P. M., arriving at Caldwell at 4.25 P. M.

**LAKE SUPERIOR TRANSIT CO'S STEAMERS** leave Port Huron Sundays, Tuesdays, Fridays and Saturdays at 7.00 A. M., June 1st to Sep. 15th. Before and after above dates, four sailings each week during navigation.

**MUSKOKA & GEORGIAN BAY NAV. CO'S STEAMERS** leave Muskoka Wharf on week days for points on Lakes Muskoka, Rosseau and Joseph, on arrival of mail train. Leave Midland and Penetang on week days for Parry Sound on arrival of mail trains.

**NIAGARA NAV. CO'S STEAMERS** leave Lewiston on arrival of trains from Buffalo and Niagara Falls, at 8.00 A. M., 10.30 A. M., and 5.30 P. M. Returning, leave Toronto at 7.00 A. M., 2.00 P. M., and 4.45 P. M., daily except Sunday.

**NORTHWEST TRANSPORTATION CO'S STEAMERS** leave Sarnia Tuesday and Friday at 9.00 P M. calling at Goderich and Kincardine.

**OTTAWA RIVER NAV. CO'S STEAMERS** leave Lachine daily, except Sunday, on arrival of train leaving the Grank Trunk R'y Station, Montreal, at 8.05 A. M. Also leave Lachine, on arrival of Grand Trunk R'y train, leaving Montreal at 5.05 P. M., running the Lachine Rapids and under Victoria Bridge.

**PEOPLE'S LINE STEAMERS** leave Albany at 8.00 P. M. daily, except Sunday, for New York. Returning, leave New York at 6.00 P. M. daily except Sunday.

**QUEBEC S. S. LINE STEAMER** leaves Quebec every second Tuesday, commencing with May 13th, until the end of October.

**RICHELIEU & ONTARIO NAVIGATION CO. STEAMERS** leave Toronto at 2.00 P. M., from June 2d till Sept. 16th daily (except Sundays, and tri-weekly Mondays, Wednesdays and Fridays, Sept. 17th to 29th, inclusive) calling daily (except Mondays) at Kingston at 4.30 A. M., Clayton 6.00 A. M., Round Island 6.15 A. M., Thousand Islands Park 7.45 A. M., Alexandria Bay 7.15 A. M., Prescott 9.30 A. M., shooting the Rapids of the St. Lawrence, arriving at Montreal at 6.30 P. M.

Leave Montreal daily (except Sundays) at 7.00 P. M., arriving at Quebec 6.30 A. M. Returning, leave Quebec 5.00 P. M., arriving at Montreal at 6.30 A. M.

Leave Quebec from June 24th to Sept. 13th, Tuesday, Wednesday, Friday, and Saturday at 7 30 A. M., for the Saguenay River, Ha! Ha! Bay, Chicoutimi and intermediate landings. Returning, arrive at Quebec the second day after departure. Before June 24th and after Sept. 13th, leave Quebec Tuesdays and Fridays only.

**STEAMER FILGATE**, take 8.05 A. M. train Montreal to Lachine, connecting with steamer and running Lachine Rapids, arriving at Montreal 9.30 A. M.

# SOUND STEAMER LINES.

**FALL RIVER LINE STEAMBOAT EXPRESS** leaves Boston at 6.00 P. M. and 7.00 P. M. week days, and 7.00 P. M. Sundays, connecting at Fall River with steamers for New York, where steamers are due at 7.00 A. M. Returning, steamers leave New York at 5.30 P. M. and 6.15 P. M. week days and 5.30 P. M. Sundays.

**STONINGTON LINE STEAMBOAT EXPRESS** leaves Boston daily (Sundays excepted) at 6.30 P. M., steamer arriving at New York at 6.00 A. M. Returning, leaves New York at 5.00 P. M. from new Pier 36, N. R.

**NORWICH LINE STEAMBOAT EXPRESS** leaves Boston at 6.35 P. M. week days, steamer arriving at New York at 7.00 A. M. Returning, leaves New York at 5.30 P. M.

**PROVIDENCE LINE STEAMBOAT EXPRESS** leaves Boston on week days at 6.00 P. M., arriving at New York at 7 A. M. Returning, leave New York at 5.30 P. M. from Pier 29, N. R.

**For rail and stage connections see Time Table folders of the Grand Trunk Railway, forms A. and B.**

# LIST OF

## Summer ◉ Boarding ◉ Houses

### AND

## HOTELS.

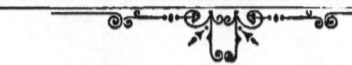

# LIST OF HOTELS AND SUMMER BOARDING HOUSES ON OR NEAR THE LINE OF THE GRAND TRUNK RAILWAY.

| Ry. Station and P. O. Address. | Hotels or Boarding Houses. | Landlords or Proprietors. | Accommodates. | Price per Day. | Price p'r Week. |
|---|---|---|---|---|---|
| Belceil Station, Que | Hotel | P. A. Loiseau | 35 | $1.00 | $5.50 |
| " " | Boarding House | E. Bernard | 25 | 1.00 | 5.50 |
| " " | Boarding House | J. P. Prefontaine | 20 | 1.00 | 5.50 |
| Belceil Village, Belceil Stat'n, Que. | Hotel | A. Noisinse | 30 | 1.00 | 5.50 |
| Berlin Falls, N. H. | Wilson House | C. C. Knapp & Son | 50 | 1.50 | 5.00 to 7.00 |
| " " | Berlin House | H. F. Marston | 100 | 1.50 to 2.00 | 5.00 to 8.00 |
| " " | Boarding House | J. I. Tucker | 20 | 1.25 | 5.00 |
| " " | Boarding House | D. Spaulding | 20 | | 5.00 |
| Bethel, Me | Bethel House | W. F. Lovejoy & Son | 100 | 2.00 | 7.00 to 12.00 |
| " | Elms House | Mrs. T. B. Gorrish | 40 | 1.50 | 6.00 to 10.00 |
| " | Lock Mountain House | Miss P. H. Lock | 40 | 1.50 | 5.00 to 7.00 |
| " | Spring Grove House | Mrs. A. W. Valentine | 25 | 1.25 | 5.00 to 6.00 |
| " | Cottage | S. B. Twitchell | 35 | 1.25 | 6.00 to 8.00 |
| Bryant's Pond, Me | Glen Mountain House | A. Dudly | 50 | 1.50 | 6.00 to 8.00 |
| " " | Lake Side Cottage | O. F. Bowker | 15 | 1.00 | 6.00 |
| Gilead, Me | Hotel | C. Gammon | 15 | 1.00 | 3.50 |
| Gorham, N. H | Boarding House | Mrs. D. C. Sary | 20 | 1.00 | 5.00 |
| " | Glen House | C. R. Milliken | 400 | 4.50 | 25.00 |
| " | Alpine House | G. D. Stratton | 150 | 2.50 | 15.00 |
| " | Willis Cottage | Q. Evans | 30 | 1.50 to 2.00 | 8.00 to 10.00 |
| " | St. Charles Cottage | Charles Philbrooke | 55 | 1.50 to 2.50 | 7.00 to 10.00 |
| " | Elm Cottage | Mr. Spofard | 20 | 1.50 to 2.00 | 7.00 to 9.00 |
| " | Randolph Hill House | H. G. Snow & Co | 75 | 2.00 to 2.50 | 7.00 to 10.00 |
| " | Ravine House | L. M. Watson | 75 | 2.00 to 2.50 | 7.00 to 10.00 |
| " | Lary House | Miss A. Lary | 75 | 1.50 to 2.00 | 7.00 to 10.00 |
| Groveton, N. H | Eagle Hotel | E. M. Tibbetts | 30 | 1.50 | 4.00 to 10.00 |
| " | Melcher House | Tibbetts & McNally | 30 | 1.50 to 2.00 | 4.00 to 10.00 |
| " | Union House | P. L. Stark | 30 | 1.00 | 4.00 to 6.00 |
| " | Boarding House | Mrs. Richardson | 10 | | 4.00 to 6.00 |
| Island Pond, Vt | Stewart House | C. M. Dyer | 100 | 2.00 | 7.00 to 12.00 |
| " | Esser House | O. T. Davis | 100 | 1.00 | 3.50 to 5.00 |
| Lennoxville, Que | Cottage House | C. McDougall | 100 | 1.50 | 6.00 |
| " | Ramsey's Hotel | G. R. Ramsey | 25 | 1.00 | 3.50 |
| " | Boarding House | Mrs. Balfour | 10 | 1.00 | 4.00 |
| Massena Spr'gs. N. Y., Hatfield, N. Y. | Scott's House | Scott Grimsby | 250 | 2.50 | 10.00 to 14.00 |
| " " Massena " | Hatfield Hotel | Hatfield Bro's | 150 | 2.00 | 6.00 |
| " " Massena " | White's Hotel | S. F. Danforth | 40 | 2.00 | 6.00 |
| " " " | Allen House | H. W. Bardsley | 60 | 2.00 | 10.00 |
| " " Hatfield, " | Bentley House | J. S. Bentley | 40 | 2.50 | |
| " " Hatfield, " | Harrogate House | Shedden & Stearns | 40 | 2.50 | 7.00 to 10.00 |

| | | | | | |
|---|---|---|---|---|---|
| Massena Spr'gs, N.Y., Hatfield, N.Y. | Wheeler House | Mrs. Wheeler | 25 | 2.00 | 7.00 |
| " " | Boarding House | E. M. Smith | 25 | 1.50 | 7.00 to 10.00 |
| " " | Boarding House | Mrs. F. Smith | 20 | 1.00 | 6.00 |
| Norway, Me. | Elm House | Mr. Whitmarsh | 20 | 1.00 | 5.00 |
| " | Beals Hotel | H. E. Hincks | 80 | 2.00 | |
| Portland, Me. | Falmouth House | J. K. Martin | 400 | 3.00 to 4.00 | 7.00 to 10.00 |
| " | Preble House | M. S. Gibson | 200 | 3.00 to 3.50 | 20.00 to 30.00 |
| " | United States Hotel | Foss & O'Connor | 150 | 2.00 to 2.50 | 14.00 to 30.00 |
| " | City Hotel | E. Sweat | 100 | 1.50 to 2.00 | 14.00 to 30.00 |
| " | Merchants' Exchange | G. Watson | 100 | 2.00 to 2.50 | 8.00 to 12.00 |
| " | Perry Hotel | J. J. Perry | 40 | 1.50 | 6.00 to 12.00 |
| " | Atlantic House | Geo. Vibber | 50 | 1.50 | 6.00 to 7.00 |
| " | Eagle House | A. E. Pratt | 51 | 1.50 | 5.00 to 7.00 |
| Richmond, Que. | St. Jacobs Hotel | J. S. Snow | 50 | 1.50 | 5.00 to 7.00 |
| " | St. Lawrence Hotel | T. Barrett | 50 | 1.00 | 12.00 |
| " | Phoenix Hotel | T. Lane | 50 | 1.25 | 10.00 |
| " | American House | G. Hall | 50 | 1.00 | 10.00 |
| " | Globe Hotel | J. Speer | 50 | 1.00 | 10.00 |
| Rouse's Point, N.Y. | Windsor Hotel | C. F. Beck | 70 | 2.50 to 3.00 | 10.00 to 14.00 |
| " | Massachusetts Hotel | J. Cogan | 36 | 2.00 | 5.00 to 7.00 |
| " | Holland Hotel | A. E. Bennett | 35 | 2.00 | 5.00 to 7.00 |
| " | Frontier Hotel | R. H. McKinnie | 14 | 1.75 | 4.00 |
| " | Montgomery Hotel | A. Couteri | 30 | 2.00 to 3.00 | 7.00 to 10.00 |
| " | | A. W. Leach | | | 5.00 to 8.00 |
| St. Hilaire, Que. | Iroquois House Hotel | Mrs. C. Lewis | 250 | | 4.00 |
| " | | B. F. Campbell, Manager | | 2.50 | 10.00 to 11.00 |
| " | Commercial Hotel | A. Bernard | 10 | 1.00 | 6.00 |
| " | Richelieu Hotel | Jos. Auclaire | 25 | 1.00 | 6.00 |
| Shelburne, N. H. | Boarding House | Louis Dery | 5 | 1.00 | 5.00 to 6.00 |
| " | Winthrop House | C. C. Hibbard | 40 | 1.00 | 6.00 to 7.00 |
| " | Shelburne Spring House | S. J. Morse | 50 | 1.00 | 5.00 to 7.00 |
| " | Philbrook House | A. E. Philbrook | 60 | 1.00 to 1.50 | 7.00 to 10.00 |
| " | Gates' Cottage | S. A. Gates | 40 | 1.00 to 1.50 | 5.00 to 10.00 |
| Sherbrooke, Que. | Hotel | Clark & Ingram | 80 | 2.00 | 5.00 to 7.00 |
| " | Hotel | Magher & Co. | 75 | 1.50 | 6.00 to 10.00 |
| " | Hotel | Cole & Richardson | 150 | 1.50 | 6.00 to 10.00 |
| " | Hotel | Camerand & Dupont | 75 | 1.50 | 4.50 to 6.00 |
| " | | J. Gauthier | 75 | 1.50 | 4.50 to 6.00 |
| South Paris, Me., Paris Hill, P. O. | Andrews House | W. M. Shaw | 20 | 1.00 | 5.00 |
| West Milan, N. H. | Ammonoosuc House | J. J. Barrett | 10 | 1.00 | 4.50 |
| " | Mountain View House | C. N. Blanchard | 13 | 1.50 | 6.00 |
| West Paris, Me. | Maple House | O. E. Tucker | 25 | 2.00 | 7.00 |
| Yarmouth, Me. | Royal River House | O. E. Lowell | 40 | 2.00 | |
| " | Boarding House | F. Drinkwater | 30 | | |
| " | Boarding House | J. M. Bucknam | 10 | | Special terms can be made |

# HOTELS AND SUMMER BOARDING HOUSES SITUATED WITHIN EASY DISTANCE OF THE GRAND TRUNK RAILWAY.

| Dist. from Station (G.T. Ry.) | Hotels or Boarding Houses. | Landlords or Proprietors and Postoffice Address. | Accommo-dates. | Price per Day. | Price per Week. | Remarks. |
|---|---|---|---|---|---|---|
| 16 | Boarding House | J. H. Chandler....Dummer, N. H | 40 | $1.25 | $5.00 to 7.00 | Daily conveyance and steamer from Lake Side daily. Berlin Falls, N. H., nearest G. T. Ry. station. |
| 30 | Umbagog House | G. T. Stratton......Errol, N. H | 50 | 2.00 | 5.00 to 7.00 | |
| 65 | Rustic House or Camp Caribou | J. Danforth.......Camp Caribou | 50 | | 7.00 to 12.00 | |
| 52 | Camp Caribou | J.S.Danforth Parmachene Lake, Me | 50 | 2.00 to 5.00 | 7.00 to 12.00 | Stage leaves Bethel daily; steamer from Lake Side daily. Bethel Me., nearest Grand Trunk Railway station. |
| 27 | Lake Side | A. L. T. Co......Lake Side, N. H | 40 | 2.00 to 5.00 | 7.0 to 12.00 | |
| 37 | Brown Farm | B. M. Co., Wentworth's Loca'n,N.H | 20 | 1.50 | 7.00 | |
| 39 | Anglers' Retreat | A. L. T. Co.....Middle Dam, Me | 30 | 2.00 | 10.00 | |
| 22 | Andover House | A. W. & E. P. Thomas Andover, Me | 50 | 2.00 | 7.00 to 10.00 | Stage from Bryant's Pond, Me., the nearest G. T. Ry. station. |
| 22 | Cushman House | C. E. Cushman.....Andover, Me | 50 | 2.00 | 7.00 to 10.00 | |
| 22 | French Hotel | J. A. French......Andover, Me | 50 | 2.00 | 7.00 to 10.00 | |
| 46 | Upper Dam Camp | Union Water Power Co....Upper Dam, Me | 50 | 2.00 | 7.00 to 10.00 | |
| 8 | Hubbard | W. Hubbard......Paris Hill, Me | 25 | 1.00 | 5.00 | Stage from South Paris, Me., the nearest G. T. Ry. station. |
| 3 | Mansion House | H. Ricker & Son..... | 100 | 3.00 | 10.00 to 18.00 | Conveyance from Danville Jc., Me., the nearest G. T. Ry. station. |
| 3 | Poland Springs House | ..Poland Springs, Me | 400 | 4.00 | 15.00 to 25.00 | |
| ..... | The Algonquin | Chas. V. Carter.. St. Andrews, N. B | 1400 | 3.50 to 5.00 | 17.50 to 26.00 | |

| Distance from Upper Coos and H. Rys. Station. | Hotels or Boarding Houses. | Landlords or Proprietors and Postoffice Address. | Accommo-dates. | Price per Day. | Price per Week. | Remarks. |
|---|---|---|---|---|---|---|
| ¾ | Monadnock House | T. D. Rowan......Colebrook, N. H. | 100 | $2.00 | $7.00 to 14.00 | |
| ½ | Private House | Mrs. W. S. Phillips, " | 12 | | 7.00 | |
| 4 | Farm House | S. B. Whittemore, " | 6 | | 6.00 | |
| 2 | Farm House | D. Fletcher, " | 6 | | 6.00 | North Stratford, N. H., nearest G. T. R'y station, connecting there with the Upper Coos and Hereford Rys. |
| 8 | Farm House | T. Noyes, " | 6 | | 6.00 | |
| ¾ | Private House | G. A. Gleason, " | 6 | | 7.00 | |
| 7 | Farm House | G. Marshall, " | 6 | | 6.00 | |
| ½ | Private House | J. W. Cooper, " | 6 | | 7.00 | |
| ½ | Private House | H. Bedel, " | 10 | | 7.00 | |
| 10 | Camp | M. B. Noyes, Diamond Point, N.H | 30 | | 7.00 | |
| 10 | Hotel | Geo. Parsons, Dixville Notch, N.H | 50 | 2.00 | 7.00 | |
| ¾ | Hotel | D. Heath, West Stewartstown, N.H | 50 | 2.00 | 7.00 | |
| ¾ | Farm House | D. Heath, West Stewartstown, N.H | 10 | | 7.00 | |
| 15 | Hotel | O.G.Bumford,Con'cticutLake,N.H | 50 | 2.00 | 7.00 | |

# IN THE PORTLAND (Me.) DISTRICT.

| House | Proprietor / Location | No. | $3.00 to 4.00 | Weekly | Distance / Notes |
|---|---|---|---|---|---|
| Ottawa House | M. S. Gibson & Co......Cushing Island, Me | 400 | $3.00 to 4.00 | 14.00 to 30 00 | 3 miles from Portland* by steamer. |
| Cape Cottage | B. C. Gibson...Cape Elizabeth, Me | 75 | 3.00 | 10.00 to 25 00 | 2 miles from Portland on B. & M. R. R. |
| Ocean House | C. Daeser " | 75 | 3.00 | 10.50 to 14 00 | " |
| Boarding House | M. Starling,Falmouth Foreside, Me | 80 | 1.50 | | |
| " | Mrs. A. Norton, " | 12 | " | 7.00 | |
| " | J. Thompson, " | 8 | " | 7.00 | |
| " | E. H. Ramsdell, " | 20 | " | 7.00 | |
| " | E. Gilmonton, " | 12 | " | 6.00 | |
| " | L. D. Wells, " | 15 | " | 7.00 | |
| " | Dr. C. P. Kenney, " | 10 | " | 10.00 | 6 miles from Portland* on shore of Casco Bay. |
| " | J. Winning, " | 6 | " | 15.00 | |
| " | F. Thompson, " | 4 | " | 6.00 | |
| " | Miss L. Sturdwant, " | 12 | " | 7.00 | |
| " | Mrs. W. Blanchard, " | 20 | " | " | |
| " | D. Hamilton, " | 12 | " | " | |
| " | Mr. Milliken, " | 16 | " | " | |
| Summer Side House | J. E. Jenks......Little Chebeaque Island, Me | 30 | 2.00 | 7.00 to 10.00 | |
| The Waldo | Horace S. Crowell, " | 150 | 3.00 | 10.00 to 15.00 | 3 miles by steamer from Portland.* |
| Avenue House | M. C. Sterling....Peak's Island, Me | 50 | 2.00 | 10.00 | |
| Bay View | Capt. J. Sterling, " | 100 | 2.00 | 10.00 | |
| Bethel House | Mrs. A. McDonald, " | 30 | 1.50 | 7.00 | |
| Oak Cottage | R. T. Skellings, " | 20 | 1.50 | 8.00 | |
| Central Cottage | S. Skellings, " | 20 | 1.50 | 8.00 | |
| Central House | S. S. York, " | 20 | 1.50 | 8.00 | |
| Chapman House | Mrs. Chapman. " | 75 | 2.00 | 10.00 | |
| Hyland Cottage | W J Gardiner, " | 20 | 1.50 | 8.00 to 10.00 | 2½ miles from Portland, * in Casco Bay. |
| Innis House | Mrs. S. Innis, " | 20 | 1.50 | 8.00 | |
| Oak Cottage | H. Skillings, " | 20 | 1.50 | 8.00 to 10.00 | |
| Oceanic House | R. F. Sterling, " | 60 | 2.00 | 10.00 | |
| Peak Island House | E. A. Sawyer, " | 80 | 2.00 | 10.00 | |
| Summer Retreat | Mrs. Torrington, " | 60 | 2.00 | 8.00 | |
| Toronto Cottage | A. V. Ackley, " | 20 | 1.50 | 8.00 | |
| Union House | E. A. Jones, " | 65 | 2.00 | 10.00 | |
| Valley View House | W. S. Trefether, " | 50 | 2.00 | 10.00 | |
| Hope Island House | J. B. Osgood....Hope Island, Me | 25 | 1.50 to 2.00 | 7.00 to 9.00 | In Portland Harbor. |
| Casco Bay House | C. E. Cushing....Long Island, Me | 65 | 1.50 to 2.00 | 7.00 to 9.00 | |
| Dirigo House | J. Perry, " | 80 | 1.50 to 2.00 | 8.00 to 10.00 | 4 miles from Portland,* by steamer. |
| Granite Spring House | E. Ponce, " | 100 | 1.50 to 3.00 | 10.00 to 20.00 | |
| Meredith House | Mrs. R. Hooper....Pine Point Beach, Me | 25 | 1.50 to 2.00 | 8.00 to 10.00 | |
| Pine Point House | M. F. Milliken " | 25 | 1.50 | 7.00 | 9 miles from Portland,* on B.&M.R.R. |
| Sportsman's House | T. W. Rellsburn " | 18 | 2 00 | 10.50 | *A station on the G. T. Ry. |

# IN THE MUSKOKA AND NIPISSING DISTRICT.

| Dist. from G. T. Ry. Station. | Hotels or Boarding Houses. | Landlords or Proprietors and Postoffice Address. | Accommodates. | Price per Day. | Price per Week. | Remarks. |
|---|---|---|---|---|---|---|
| 40 | Boarding House | J. Croswell....Ahmic Harbor, Ont | 25 | $1.00 to 1.25 | $6.00 to 8.00 | By Boat from Burk's Falls, nearest G. T. R'y Stat'n |
| | Queen's Hotel | Jno. Higgins....Bracebridge, Ont | 50 | 1.00 to 1.50 | 6.00 to 8.00 | |
| | British Lion | Jno. Leishman, " | 40 | 1.00 to 1.50 | 6.00 to 8.00 | |
| | Burk House Hotel | D. F. Burk....Burk's Falls, Ont | 100 | 1.50 to 2.00 | 7.00 to 10.00 | |
| | Clifton House Hotel | D. McMinn, " | 40 | 1.00 | 3.50 | |
| | Cataract House | S. Adams, " | 50 | 1.00 | 3.50 | |
| 16 | Jelly's Hotel | J. Jelley....Baysville, Ont | 20 | 1.00 | 5.00 | |
| 16 | Forest House | W. Higgins, " | 20 | 1.00 | 5.00 | Bracebridge nearest G. T. R'y station. |
| 16 | Norfolk House | M. Howard, " | 20 | 1.00 | 5.00 | |
| 20 | Boarding House | W. Cowan, ....Cecebe, Ont | 20 | 1.00 | 7.00 | |
| 20 | Boarding House | O. Taylor, " | 20 | | 7.00 | By Boat from Burk's Falls, Ont, nearest G. T. R'y station. |
| 60 | Hotel | W. Taylor, ....McKellar, Ont | 25 | 1.00 to 1.25 | 6.00 to 8.00 | |
| 25 | Peignton House | J. F. Pain....Clevelands, Ont | 75 | 1.00 | 6.00 | By Boat from Muskoka Wharf. |
| 31 | Colebridge House | S. A. Cole....Colebridge, Ont | 25 | | | Baysville to Colebridge by steamer |
| 31 | McKay House | A. McKay, " | 12 | | | Bracebridge nearest G. T. R'y station. |
| | Dominion Hotel | P. Conway....Huntsville, Ont | 40 | 1.00 | 6.00 | |
| | Queen's Hotel | R. Gilchrist, " | 25 | 1.00 | 6.00 | |
| | Nipissing Hotel | T. Birch, " | 25 | 1.00 | 6.00 | |
| 12 | Tourist House | E. J. Gouldie....Dwight, Ont. | | | | |
| 12 | Boarding House | J. McCutcheon, " | | | | By Boat and Stage. Huntsville, Ont, nearest G. T. R'y station. |
| 10 | Boarding House | J. Frazer, ....Huntsville, Ont | 25 | 1.00 | 7.00 to 8.00 | |
| 25 | Kyle House | J. Kyle....Magnetawan, Ont | 50 | 1.00 to 1.25 | 6.00 to 8.00 | By Boat from Burk's Falls, nearest G. T. R'y stat'n |
| | Windsor Hotel | D. B. Lafranier....Gravenhurst, Ont | 50 | 1.00 to 1.50 | 6.00 to 8.00 | |
| | Albion Hotel | F. Wesley, " | 35 | 1.00 to 1.50 | 6.00 to 8.00 | |
| | Caledonian Hotel | J. Sharp, " | 50 | 1.00 to 1.50 | 6.00 to 8.00 | |
| | Grand Central Hotel | J. Boyd, " | 50 | 1.00 to 1.50 | | |
| | Bala House | T. Currie....Bala, Ont | 50 | 1.25 | 7.00 | |
| | Clifton House | J. Board, " | 50 | 1.25 | 7.00 | |
| 14 | Beaumaris Hotel | E. Prowse....Beaumaris, Ont | 150 | 1.50 | 8.00 to 10.00 | Steamer from Station to Hotel, Muskoka Wharf, Ont, nearest G. T. R'y station. |
| 25 | Boarding House | C. J. Minett....Clevelands, Ont | 75 | 1.00 | 5.00 | |
| 35 | Boarding House | M. Collins....Clover Port, Ont | 20 | 1.00 | 5.00 | |
| 35 | Craigielea House | J. C. Walls....Craigielea, Ont | 25 | 1.00 | 5.00 | |
| 23 | Ferndale House | R. G. Penson ....Ferndale, Ont | 50 | 1.25 | 7.00 | |
| | Robinson Bay House | T. M. Robinson..Gravenhurst, Ont | 20 | 1.50 | 6.00 | |
| 32 | Morinus House | P. & L. Marcotte..Juddhaven, Ont | 20 | 1.00 | 5.00 to 6.00 | |

| | Hotel | Proprietor & Location | Capacity | Per Day | Per Week | |
|---|---|---|---|---|---|---|
| 16 | Milford Bay House | R. Stroud....... Milford Bay, Ont | 50 | 1.25 | 7.00 | |
| 16 | Strawberry Bank House | T. W. Wroe, " | 30 | 1.00 | 5.00 | |
| 16 | Wingberry House | W. Mortimer, Mortimer's Point, Ont | 40 | 1.00 | 6.00 | |
| 21 | Boarding House | J. M. Tobin .... Oakland P'k, Ont | 30 | 1.00 | 5.00 | |
| 60 | Boarding Hotel | Belvidere Hotel Co........Parry Sound, Ont | 150 | 1.00 to 1.50 | 6.00 to 8.00 | |
| 60 | Seguin House | Mrs. McKinley, " | 40 | 1.00 to 1.50 | 6.00 to 8.00 | |
| 60 | Thomson House | W. F. Thomson, " | 100 | 1.00 to 1.50 | 6.00 to 8.00 | |
| 18 | Lake View House | J. Hutton........Point Kay, Ont | 30 | 1.25 | 7.00 | |
| 22 | Vanderburg House | C.W.Vanderburg, Port Carling,Ont | 40 | 1.00 | 5.00 to 6.00 | |
| 22 | Inter-Laken Hotel | R. A. Arksey, " | 40 | 1.25 | 7.00 | |
| 22 | Stratton House | J. Fraser, " | 50 | 1.25 | 7.00 | |
| 45 | Hotel | H. Fraser & Sons.......Port Cockburn, Ont | 150 | 1.50 | 10.00 | |
| 25 | Prospect House | E. Cox.......Port Sandfield, Ont | 150 | 1.25 | 8.00 | |
| 40 | Hotel | J. Monteith........Rosseau, Ont | 150 | 1.25 | 8.00 | |
| 40 | Hotel Maplehurst | J. P. Brown, " | 75 | 2.00 | 10.00 to 12.00 | |
| 49 | Stanley House | W. B. Maclean, Stanley House, Ont | 50 | 1.25 | 8.00 | |
| 50 | Craig Ross Lea Hotel | W. T. Thomson ... Star Lake, Ont | 50 | 1.00 to 1.50 | 6.00 to 8.00 | |
| 25 | Windermere Hotel | T. Aiken ........ Windermere, Ont | 150 | 1.00 | 5.00 to 6.00 | |
| 25 | Fife House | D. Fife, Jr., " | 75 | 1.00 | 5.00 to 6.00 | Steamer from Station to Hotel. Muskoka Wharf, Ont., nearest G. T. R'y station. |

# INDEX.

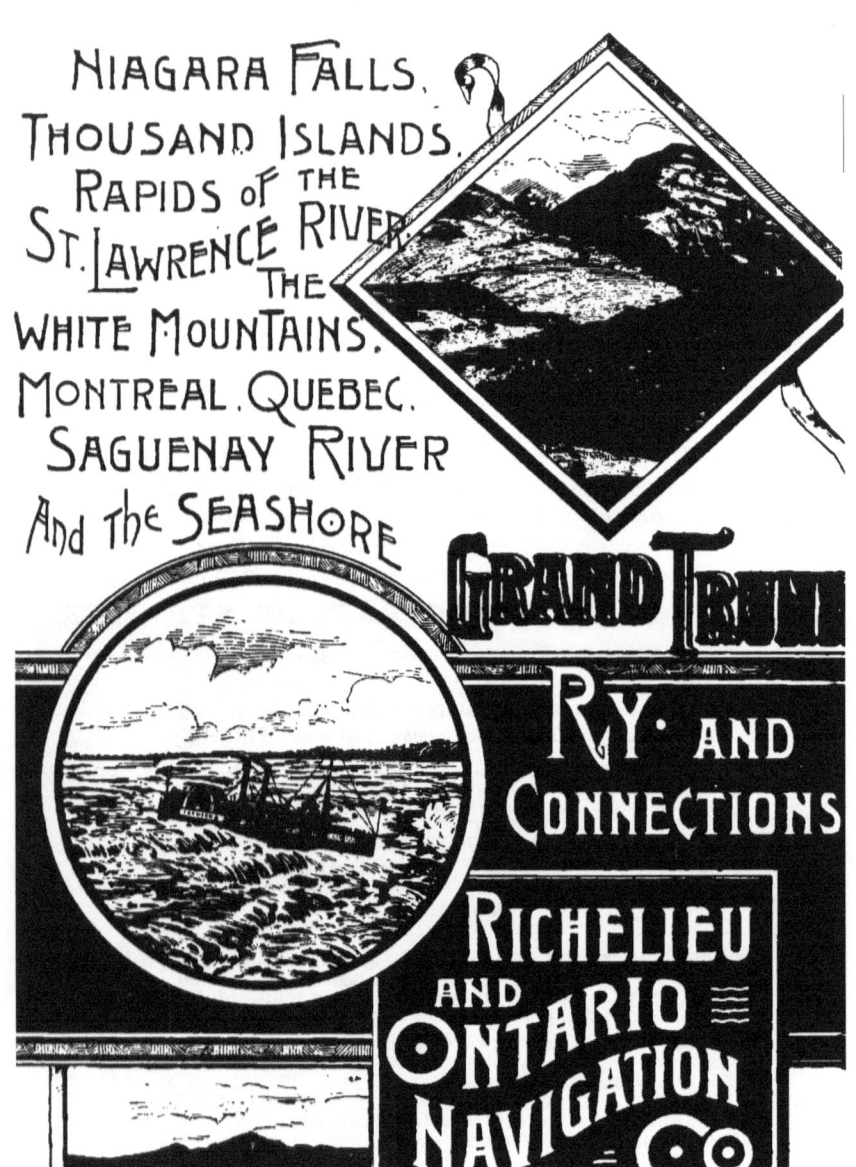

NIAGARA FALLS,
THOUSAND ISLANDS,
RAPIDS OF THE
ST. LAWRENCE RIVER,
THE
WHITE MOUNTAINS,
MONTREAL, QUEBEC,
SAGUENAY RIVER
AND THE SEASHORE

GRAND TRU
RY · AND
CONNECTIONS

RICHELIEU
AND
ONTARIO
NAVIGATION
CO

www.ingramcontent.com/pod-product-compliance
Lightning Source LLC
Chambersburg PA
CBHW031114020726
47495CB00007B/2192